# BOOKS BY KATHRYN

## By God's Authority
"...if snowflakes can climb..."

## By God's Authority, the sequel
"...by faith, dreams can come true..."

## The Sentinel

# *The* Sentinel

## A NOVEL

## Kathryn

WESTBOW
PRESS
A DIVISION OF THOMAS NELSON
& ZONDERVAN

'The Sentinel' is a work of fiction. Any resemblance to actual persons, living or dead, events or locales is entirely coincidental. Names, places, and incidents are purely the product of the imagination of the author.

WestBow Press books may be ordered through booksellers or by contacting:

WestBow Press
A Division of Thomas Nelson & Zondervan
1663 Liberty Drive
Bloomington, IN 47403
www.westbowpress.com
1 (866) 928-1240

ISBN: 978-1-4908-6095-4 (sc)
ISBN: 978-1-4908-6096-1 (hc)
ISBN: 978-1-4908-6097-8 (e)

Library of Congress Control Number: 2014920935

Printed in the United States of America.

WestBow Press rev. date: 12/09/2014

For my sons, Kelly and Keith, U.S. Navy proud,
who have provided me with laughter, memories
and a family I never imagined was possible.

Sometimes, one doesn't have to look very
far to recognize a problem.

Sometimes, one's senses are triggered by a thought, a
spoken word, a glance, a photo, a touch, even a scent.

Sometimes, intellectually, instead of being a sentinel,
one should choose to ignore all of the above.

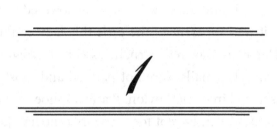

# 1

oday was the last day of their current employment. It would be their last day of flying for Premier Airlines, their home away from home. This flight would take them to Boston and by night fall, they would return to Denver. Waiting to board, wistfully yet excited, staring off into space, they both wondered what their new line of work would bring into their lives. Kassie, a laid back blond with blue eyes, and Jacki, a spontaneous brunette with eyes the color of pitch, were about to embark in a career with a different set of rules. Their retirement from Premier would propel them into a new profession for which they both had been studying over the last five years.

"This is just not true!" It came from the lady seated across from them in the terminal. "She was murdered! Sure as anything."

"Whoa," whispered Jacki, under her breath. Kassie came back to her senses after being in a daze, contemplating what she had just heard. "Did you hear that?" Kassie nodded affirmatively.

"Ma'am? Are you alright?" Kassie was compassionate if she was nothing else. She knew the lady must be feeling troubled. "Is there something I can say to help you?" Kassie moved across the aisle and sat beside her. Sitting in an airport lounge was normally very boring.

As stewardess's they had had to wait in plenty of them, as most flights were not on time.

The lady, around fifty, was an attractive woman, with long weathered gray hair and dark eyes. After she lowered the paper she was reading, it was apparent to the girls this lady could've used a make-over. Her attire was well worn, in a shade of brown that didn't suit her coloring. Her nails were not painted and most noticeable was the run she had in her left nylon. Platform shoes did nothing to enhance her legs, either. Except for the words she had just uttered, she could've been anyone's mother, grandmother, aunt or sister. However, her words were forceful and full of anxiety, leading Kassie to believe there was much more to her than how she appeared at the moment.

"I'm sorry if I upset you girls. I didn't mean to be overheard. But it's true, you know. I just don't believe she died in this... this...a skiing accident. I just don't! I never will!" Kassie glanced at the photo on the front page of the newspaper. An attractive woman, very young and beautiful, long light colored hair with opaque eyes, stared at her from the pages of the Sentinel Star. "She was so beautiful, it just isn't right, you know!" She folded the newspaper, deliberately, on her lap, placing it in her handbag. Reaching over her shoulder to retrieve the cane, one that had seen better days hanging over the back of her seat, she stood up.

"You're distraught. Anyone can see that. You're sure there isn't anything I can do to help you?"

"Just be careful who you marry." With that said she picked up her handbag and using her cane, walked off rather briskly for someone who had to rely on a stick with duct tape.

Kassie felt badly for the lady, but she wasn't sure exactly why. She glanced at Jacki, who just gave a shrug as though it was an everyday occurrence. Over the loudspeaker, their flight to Boston was announced.

As flight attendants, both women were at the top of their game, both in salary and prestige. Had it not been for their lucrative salaries and static schedule, neither would've have been able to attend Nursing school. Incredibly, they not only graduated in the top one percent of their class but both were hired by Mercy Regional Hospital. 'Mercy,' as it was called, was the surgical center of the Rockies, located on the far eastern side of Denver, overlooking the foothills and beyond to the magnificent Rocky Mountains. As they began their routine in flight, Kassie wondered aloud.

"I didn't ask where she was going, or if she had a flight to catch, or if she was waiting to meet someone!"

"*What are you talking about?*" It was Jacki, with incredulity.

"The lady, the lady! I didn't ask for her name or what she did for a living. It may have taken her mind off the article in the paper."

"I *do not believe* that you're still obsessing over a lady you just met, someone you'll never see again or that you even care!" Jacki started to roll the cart of drinks toward the aisle in first class. "If I were you, I'd just forget about it. She was an old biddy that thought the stars told her the girl in the photo was murdered. There! You have it. Now drop it!"

Kassie was by no means convinced she was just another 'biddy,' whatever that meant. With Jacki, one never knew. However, she had her own work to do. There would be time to think about it later.

On their approach prior to landing back in Denver, one of the other flight attendant's suggested either Kassie or Jacki should make the parting comments. Jacki hastily volunteered. Attempting to discourage her from the inevitable, Kassie knew it would be to no avail.

"Ladies and gentlemen. This is Christmas Eve and we've just secured a spot on the runway in Denver, so join the party! We hear they have lights on the slopes, so if you're feeling lucky, go skiing. The stores are open until midnight; don't get run over when it's time to go home. If the people you're staying with are relatives and they've already locked their doors for night, don't call us. We'll be asleep! Wherever you dine, the cuisine will undoubtedly be more satisfying than our tasty 'airline meals,' but they won't be free! Please remember, your luggage is our luggage if you leave it behind! For those with children who missed their earlier flight, we apologize that you missed Santa. He'll be back next year or so I've been told. Our Captain says 'Adios,' and we flight attendants 'thank you' for putting up with us on this flight. Our shift ended three hours ago! We're glad you chose to fly with Premier Airlines and hope you choose Premier the next time you fly. We sincerely enjoy your company; it's great for our job security. Merry Christmas…and watch your step as you disembark. It's icy out there! Thank you and have a great time in the Mile High city." She finished long before the passengers stopped laughing. Turning to Kassie, she continued. "Good thing this is our last flight. Termination is an ugly word." Kassie shook her head in disbelief.

# 2

etting comfortable in their new positions at Mercy was not as simple as it sounded. Both Kassie and Jacki had to get accustomed to being awake every day during daylight hours. Even though their shifts varied they took the same route to work every day. Their uniforms varied in color and fit; instead of heels their shoes bore heavy padded soles. "Sketchers wore well and didn't embarrass the dress code.

Familiar as they were to routine, they went to work at the same place, same floor with the same people, nursing the same ill people they'd seen the day before, and the day before that. Ironically, both had decided having been a flight attendant probably prepared them better to do an outstanding job as a nurse more than any other previous profession they could've had. The public in any situation, in the air or on the ground, could try a person's faith to the point where to throw their hands in the air and holler *"I'm tired of being politically correct!"* would have been a relief. But working in the airline industry they learned to clean up after little babies, swab the deck after those who'd had too much to drink, furnish a second upchuck bag to the lady who didn't want to soil her suit and listen to the traveling salesman who felt it was his duty to complain about the food and that his beer was not cold *enough*; just to name a few situations of which there were many. Particularly frustrating was trying to settle their passengers down when the plane hit turbulence; like children getting their first haircut or sitting in the dentist's chair and seeing a needle disappear in their mouth. It was always the unexpected that curled their hair! Already accustomed and conditioned to people from all walks of life, it didn't take long before both women excelled in their nursing positions. They persevered.

Money had never been a problem for either of them. Kassie was raised on a horse and cattle ranch in Wyoming, where hard work included everything from shoveling manure in the horse barn to helping her mother wash dishes for a crew of eight employed ranch hands. From the time she first climbed on a horse, she couldn't remember a time when she wanted for a thing her parents couldn't provide. If they refused to purchase a little 'item I want' for her, she saved her allowance and purchased it herself.

Kassie was raised to respect people regardless of origin or influence. It didn't make any difference to her if it was her family, their family's pastor, a hired man on the ranch or the passengers and crews who flew the skies. In addition to being conversant with each, she treated everyone with the same respect that she wanted in return.

She never considered the hundreds of head of cattle that her father raised to be any part that belonged to her. It was always 'my father's cattle' and 'my mother's horses.' Except for Spinster.

Spinster was a black Arabian mare who for some unknown reason never had a foal. To Kassie, that didn't matter. Kassie and Spinster were inseparable; they were best friends. Spinster was the colt she had raised by herself after receiving it from her parents on her twelfth birthday.

While her father and his hired men worked with the cattle, her mother supervised the household staff and played with the three prize horses she had raised from birth. All were Arabians in varying shades of chestnut brown to black. Registered stallions, they were pampered and ridden by her mother. Well trained, and exquisitely built, they were used for stud.

Upon graduating from high school, she chose not to attend college. Even though her parents appeared offended by her choice, it was never an ambition of Kassies' to get more schooling. Working at one of the local banks, she lived at home and saved her money. It didn't take long before she knew she wanted more out of life than a staid position at a bank. She wanted to travel. Knowingly aware to do it cheaply, she decided to become a flight attendant. Her parents weren't too thrilled with her choice; she was of age and ultimately, didn't try to change her mind.

Jacki, on the other hand, came from a household of enormous wealth and status. Raised by her parents, whose father never seemed to work and a stay-at-home mother, she was brought up in an area considered by many to be the wealthiest community in the United States: Key Largo, Florida. She was totally spoiled with 'things,' knowing she had more than any other child her own age; she determined at an early age to 'accomplish' something other than accumulating 'stuff.' She was the apple of her father's eye and a totally destructive force to her mother's aspirations for her. From the date of her thirteenth birthday until she turned seventeen, Jacki was an incorrigible, manipulative and disrespectful girl, to her parents, grandparents and especially her friends. She attended private school, wearing a dreaded uniform every day. A beautiful girl, tall, with beautiful brunette hair and dark brown eyes, her physical attributes were *not* the most memorable to those around her; her mouth was.

The day she graduated from high school, she left home. Her father saw to it she always had money in her pocket for living expenses and her extravagant Lamborghini always had fuel. She attended the University of Memphis for two years before she submitted her application to become a flight attendant. It wasn't until she worked with the public on cross country flights that she realized some of what she had missed growing up. She came to love people, their differences, their idiosyncrasies, the sharing of their very modest, relatively speaking, lives.

At twenty-two, she began to feel normal, like all the little girls she had known in grade school. She gave up her weekly pedicure. The clothes that she had purchased from Neiman Marcus and Saks Fifth Avenue got turned into a wardrobe of jeans and sweaters purchased at the local Mart. After being accepted to nursing school, she sold her Lamborghini and bought a used Ford Escort. Her parents thought it was a dreadful investment. Since Jacki was now paying for her own fuel…and clothes…she felt it was her decision to make. And then, she met Kassie.

# 3

"**H**ey! I'm over here." Lincoln almost didn't recognize him; if it hadn't been for his sun bleached hair and his rock solid frame, he may well have overlooked him.

"Good to see you, Link."

"Hey! Let's go get your bags." Lincoln started for the baggage pickup.

"I didn't bring anything with me as I'm only staying a day or two. Perhaps I didn't make that clear to you."

"Got a job you gotta' go back to? That sucks!"

"Something like that. Janine know who's coming?"

"Like you asked, I didn't tell her. It'll be a big surprise. Since I've been out of the Navy, you're the first buddy that has come for a visit."

"Really. Glad I have that distinction. Let's take a drive up Lake Shore Drive. I'd like to see if anything has changed since I've been in Chicago."

"Janine has a great meal planned for us. Sunday's are special, you know. After church, we usually watch a game or two on TV and then have a really nice dinner, 'bout five. I think getting married is just about the best thing that I did since I've been back. What about you? Married?"

"Nah. Too busy."

"Too busy! What have you been up to since you separated from the Navy?"

"Counting the days until I could afford to visit my old buddies."

"Sure wish you would've stuck around until we completed the last horrendous week. You'd have enjoyed our deployments." The silence didn't seem to bother Lincoln as he drove well over the speed limit. After a few moments, he asked, "Where have you been working?"

"Around. I don't stay in one place too long." The planetarium was on the right side as they sped down the Shore drive. "Hey, let's pull in here and look at the stars…if the place is open. I've only done that once before but it was cool."

"Sure, that won't take long. But just for a minute, okay? Janine's waiting."

"Sure." Lincoln drove into the parking lot which was bare of all vehicles. It was a star-studded evening with no cloud cover. He turned the key in his vehicle to off. For an instant there was an eerie silence.

Lincoln never knew what hit him; he was in eternity before he could utter another word. His wife would learn later that a cartridge had entered his skull above his right ear. That piece of knowledge came from the detective working the homicide. An airport parking stub was found in his car. She also learned that no one saw her husband at the airport, at least not by any of the personnel the police questioned. Several flights arrived within minutes of each other; even more departed within the same time frame. Foot traffic being heavy, no one remembered seeing two well built but not especially handsome guys in the terminal.

It was his first mark. It would not be his last. He was proud of himself for accomplishing it with plenty of time to hail a taxi and make his plane reservation later that evening.

"What kind of couch do you think we should get?" It was Jacki.
"We have a couch."

"We've had that couch for how many years? Let me guess. Seven years. Oh, excuse me. Ten years! As long we have known each other."

"So, it's still perfectly fine. Besides, it has just become comfortable. You have to break these things in, make them your own." Kassie was always deliberately frugal, something that came natural to her. But there were times when it was just easier to give in to Jacki's desires. After a little thought, she said, "So when do you want to go look?"

"Tomorrow. We're both off work so we have all day."

They came home owning a leather white couch, two lazy-boy arm chairs, in linen white-on-white, and three huge throw pillows. Two were red plaid and the third was pale yellow. Both were decorated beautifully with cording and ribbon and ironically, they complimented each other. Kassie had to admit that in spite of the cost she was as excited as Jacki in giving their apartment a face lift. For them it was a cash sale. And why not? They both were doing well.

"Before they deliver the new furniture, let's polish the wood floors. They really need it." Kassie had been taught by her mother

11

how to make their wood floors on the ranch shine. She saw no reason why she couldn't accomplish the same thing in their apartment.

"And what part of this chore is going to be mine?" asked Jacki.

"It'll be fun. It'll give the apartment a whole new look and smell."

"Smell?"

"Yes. Next I'm sure you'll want to change the window dressing to white sheers, of which I highly approve. It was just painted before we moved in so let's clean the windows and replace the screen in your bedroom."

"What's with this 'we' business? You're beginning to make this a full time project, honey. I do have to still make time to date!"

"Good grief! You and your boyfriends. You'll have time, trust me. I hope I live to see the day when you run out of boyfriends!"

The makeover projects began. They both worked full time as registered nurses, and Jacki still had plenty of time to date. Kassie could've cared less. Her hobbies kept her busy. Since they each had their own bedroom, Kassie decided that she would decorate hers in white with red accessories for accent color. Jacki decided yellow would dominate in hers.

Their apartment was on second floor, overlooking a greenway. The windows across the front of the living and dining rooms faced the foothills, now covered in snow. Their location was just far enough east for them to feast their eyes on the magnificent Rocky Mountains. It was by all standards a very nice location.

Both women were meticulous concerning housekeeping and their personal effects. Their uniforms were always clean and pressed, never wearing one two days in a row. Dishes were never allowed to accumulate in the sink. Any other duties were divided between them. They'd always worked congenially together from the time they first roomed together.

While fixing dinner, Jacki informed Kassie that she going out on a date. "After we do dishes, I need to clean up quickly. Important guy, you know."

"No, I didn't know. Who is this one or do I already know him?"

"Yyyyaaaa. You've probably met. He's the blond physician always making rounds on third. Dr. Reynolds," Jacki responded, nonchalantly.

"Oh, my gosh. I don't even want to know how you got a date with him."

"He thinks I'm charming! I had to agree, although I didn't say that."

"Is this one going to be Mr. Right?" Kassie could've cared less, but since Jacki didn't answer, Kassie had doubts it would be.

Kassie was accustomed to staying at home when she wasn't working. Their apartment was a beautiful sanctuary of peace and quiet, especially now that the furniture was updated and the Bose music system was in place. The sheer wispy white curtains on the clean floor-to-ceiling west windows allowed the sun to flow into the living and dining areas, showing off their cleaned and polished wood floors. There were French doors between the kitchen and dining room, off which led into the living room. They also had French doors opening from the living room to a hallway from where the two bedrooms and bathrooms were located. One bathroom was a Jack and Jill setup; the other was for guests only.

Neither set of parents had come to visit them in their new digs but neither of the women gave it much thought. They'd been on their own for nearly ten years; their parents were entrenched in their own lives as were the girls in theirs.

Oil painting occupied Kassie some of her free time. Several of her works were already hanging on their walls. With their apartment located on the southwest portion of the building, there was nothing to impede the sun from filling every corner of their domain. The fireplace was located on the east wall of the living room which made a comfortable setting to enjoy the seasonal changes in Denver. By November, a glowing fireplace would only enhance the coziness of their apartment.

They were definitely opposites, Kassie and Jacki, and yet, they always made their friendship work. They had their communal space and each had their own private area. Each bedroom had enough space to have a sitting area; that's where Kassie set up her easel and became absorbed in whatever she was painting at the time.

After a couple hours of enjoying the freedom to create, she decided to retire, not once contemplating whether she should stay up and wait for Jacki to return. Her clean uniform hung on the bedroom door, her makeup removed, what little she wore, and with her alarm set, she crawled into bed. Tomorrow promised to be another exciting and fulfilling day.

When Jacki returned from her date, it was close to midnight. Too bad Kassie was sound asleep; she'd have to wait until morning to tell her the 'blond heartthrob' that she looked forward to dating wasn't long on manners. Somehow, she knew that Kassie would understand. Although, he was a physician with money; if nothing else, Jacki deduced he could always afford a good meal at Red Lobster or a weekend in the mountains. Just because she became a normal American female didn't mean she had to give some of the sweeter things in life!

# 5

It wasn't until she saw the lady walking with a cane on the street below in the parking lot of the hospital that she remembered the lady she met at the airport. Today, the lady walked stiffly as though she were walking against a brisk wind. Built smaller than the woman at the airport, Kassie couldn't help but wonder what had happened after she left them sitting there, thinking. She thought about the photo of the girl in the paper; such a loss and all because of a skiing accident. Why would an older lady think that it was murder? Who was she? Did she know the girl? Where did the girl live? Where did the lady with the cane live? Why did she need a cane? All were questions that she could've asked but didn't.

Upon throwing away her Dixie cup, she returned to work. Her break was over. Breaks were something they didn't get that often.

Kassie worked the surgical floor, third floor of Mercy, where some of the patients stayed anywhere from two days to ten, where some of the patients cried out for pain medication and some didn't, depending on their pain threshold. Currently most surgery was being done on an outpatient basis, so the patients that arrived on third incommunicado had some serious trauma issues.

"Kassie, Mr. Edwards needs his ostomy bag changed. He just called the desk: he's already had a bowel movement." The colonoscopy performed on Mr. Edwards was a surgical procedure in which his stoma was formed by drawing the healthy end of his large bowel through a hole to the outside of his abdominal wall and stitched into place. After his stoma appliance, an enclosed bag, was attached to the opening, it became an alternative means for him to excrete his feces. Depending on how well he healed, it could be a permanent situation or it could be reversed. Either way, at the moment, a full stoma appliance was grossly uncomfortable for the patient.

Kassie, despite the foul odor that usually accompanied a full ostomy bag change, had empathy for the individuals that had had a large portion of their bowel removed. As such a patient healed from the surgical procedure, the acceptance of the outside fecal bag was often welcomed, as the alternative would in many cases have involved death. Mr. Edwards was such a patient. In contrast to so many others, he was a kind gentleman, soft spoken, 62 and now free of his cancer. When Kassie had finished changing the bag, she placed the covers over him gently.

"Thank you, nurse. You're so gentle. I really appreciate that. You know, my daughter is a nurse but she works in OR. The operating room. *Sorry*. She really loves it. For myself, I could never watch someone be cut open. I'm a white collar worker in a bank, well, you know...I couldn't watch."

"Does your daughter live close?"

"Colorado Springs. When she comes to visit I'll introduce you to her, if you're working."

"I believe I would enjoy meeting her. Try to relax now." Kassie adjusted the IV tubing that delivered solution to the patient along with the piggyback solution containing pain medication, allowing the medication to surge into his veins whenever he pushed the button. As she left, she turned out the light, closing the door quietly.

The more she thought about it, the more excited she got. It would take more schooling, more determination and an adjustment to her schedule, but she felt she was up to it. It was in Kassie's nature to be the best that she could be. Both she and Jacki had worked for nearly a year at Mercy. It was time to move on.

"Jacki, I'm going back to school." Kassie had made up her mind.

"What for?" Jacki was polishing her toenails. Her fingernails, already painted a bright red, were flawless. "What occupation are we going to embark on now?"

"I don't know about you, but I want to become a surgical nurse."

"Too much schooling! When are you going to start enjoying life, get out and date, party, you know, live!"

"What would you have me do? Ask an intern for a date? I don't think so. I still believe that if a man is a gentleman at all, he'll ask the lady."

"That's so old fashioned! Ugh! Good luck with that." Jacki had long decided that if she wanted to date someone, it was not beneath her dignity to ask the man out for coffee, a drink or movie. It was one of the great distinctions between the two women. Nothing they ever argued over, it was just a fact.

"So, when do you think you'll start looking into it? If I know you, you've already started. How is it that I'm always the last to know?"

"Why don't you join me?" Kassie fiddled with her knitting, at least what she could learn out of a book. "You were an exceptional flight attendant, you're a great nurse, so why not continue to learn and join…"

"*Not!* I'm almost thirty-three and I'm looking to settle down. The right man just hasn't found me yet."

"Is that all you think about? Men! Show me one like my father and you'll have my attention! Until then…well…"

"Well what? How old are you? Two measly years younger than I am! Hey, girl, you're not getting any younger either. Unless you don't want to have a family?"

"*Yes. I do*. But…the man I marry will put his Christianity first. Like my mother always said. 'There's enough problems in this world there need not be any faith problems between you and the man you intend to spend the rest of your life loving,' which means that I want to marry a Christian man, tall, dark and handsome. Well educated and respectful to everyone, someone who wants to make a lifelong commitment to his marriage." Kassie paused and then continued, after she caught a glimpse of Jacki's thoughts by the look on her face. "Oh, he must be well built, not spindly nor humpbacked, have beautiful eyes…and be rich!"

"Oh, stop it! You are so pathetic! They don't make those guys anymore." She felt truly sorry for her roommate. "You are going to wind up being an old, educated woman…a spinster…with a lot of money. I like the money part, but I sure don't want to grow old alone."

Kassie listened while Jacki continued to berate her for not dating. Kassie didn't want to be alone forever, either, even though she never really felt alone. Maybe that wasn't conducive to her situation, but for now, there wasn't a man alive that she'd rather spend time with in place of her independence and doing her own things.

Kassie hadn't forgotten the difficulties that presented themselves, working and attending school at the same time. She preferred to ignore it. Or was she just getting old? It seemed that the days on third floor were getting longer. If boredom was her problem, then she needed to do something different with her life. Yes. She had already decided to go back to school.

"I'm going to Boyd Lake with Dr. Reynolds this weekend. Probably Sunday. It's supposed to be cold; so much better to snuggle."

"I distinctly remember you saying that Dr. Reynolds wasn't your type. Or did I just dream that little conversation? Besides……"

"No. But I changed my mind."

"There's three inches of snow on the ground. Are you kidding me? Or are you going ice skating somewhere? If all you want to do is walk in the snow, you can do it here in Central Park!" It was the middle of November: snow came early. The foothills were covered and in the mountains, the snow had built up a huge base for skiing. However, any snow on the Front Range in Colorado could disappear in a couple days.

Kassie couldn't believe the activities Jacki did half the time. It had been like that from the moment they met. Always searching for Mr. Right! Most of the pursuits Jacki indulged in didn't seem to bring her any measure of true happiness. She was always edgy and unsettled; always waiting for the next party. It wasn't Kassie's problem; she had learned to live with Jacki's up's and down's. Eventually, she hoped Jacki would learn that all good things come to those who are patient...and kind.

"We talked about skating in Fort Collins but just walking….. walking with *the most handsome surgeon* that everyone drools over... come on. It doesn't get any better than that." Jacki could hardly wait until the weekend was over so she could talk about the event at Mercy. The nursing staff on fourth floor knew as much about Jacki's dates as she did herself. "Are you planning anything...different?"

Kassie established in mere moments from Jacki's statement about her upcoming date with Dr. Reynolds that it was the most lucrative way for her to get away from the apartment, work and life, in general. It was also the easiest way in the world to make the rest of the female staff at Mercy jealous!

Kassie would've never considered Dr. Reynolds a handsome man. With a goatee and hair that curled around his ears, she found him to be 'hairy' and unkempt. She couldn't handle the reality the generation of younger nurses thought. 'He's so cute!'

"And to think when you first met….." Kassie mumbled under her breath.

"I heard that! Foolish me!"

"Whatever. I'll probably go to church and then to the library. And if I'm lucky, I'll take a nap in the afternoon. By the way, did you remember to buy some milk and chocolate chips?"

"Milk is in the refrigerator and the chips are on the counter."

# 6

The library was nearly empty. Kassie considered that to be a good thing. No distractions. If she could keep her eyes open she might get some studying done.

"Would you mind if I sat with you? I'll try not to disturb you but I would feel more comfortable being close to someone in this cold, spacious room." His name was Brad Phillips. Dr. Brad Phillips. Kassie had seen him making rounds on third floor. It was apparent to her every nurse with whom he spoke nearly fainted after each encounter. She wondered why! Kassie was not immune when watching him at work. If ever there was a man of her dreams, physically, Brad Phillips, with his trim, black hair, his starched, unwrinkled white coat, his tall physique and his manner of speaking, would fill her prescription. Kassie had decided Brad Phillips was not her type; he was too polished to look in her direction. Each day, Brad Phillips made his rounds, filled out his paperwork and left the floor. He was warm and engaging; even Kassie could see that. She did wonder what he might be like away from work; although that probably didn't happen very often since he was a serious surgical resident. But! The thought did play havoc with her mind.

Now here he was, speaking to her. His eyes were dark, probably black; still, they were filled with kindness and mirth. He was certainly unlike any boss or pilot or any other man she had ever known, except for her father. She couldn't help but wonder if he was black Irish. To her complete surprise, she was not the least intimidated by his presence. She felt tranquil with his approach, no sweaty armpits, no itchy scalp, no feeling of dominance, just a sweet presence. Brad Phillips carried himself in such a way that said "I know who and what I am' without a trace of arrogance.

"Not a problem." His question required an answer and Kassie wasn't sure if stating the obvious was sufficient. Her eyes returned to her notes as he sat down and began his own studies. She'd already been at her studies a couple hours; her eyelids were getting heavy. A few minutes later, Brad Phillips woke her from her slumber.

"Pardon me, could you direct me to the bathroom?"

"Around the corner on your left," she whispered.

"Thank you," Brad said as he got up to leave.

He's a resident! Dr. Brad Phillips. He doesn't know where the bathrooms are in the library? There was something very troubling about the question. Had he never been to the hospital library before? Where did he do his studying? Did he have to study or was this the first time he cracked his books? How she wished she never had to study. But, she reasoned, that was what school was all about, study and apply. When he returned, Kassie would have to ask him about his study habits.

"Where do you normally study?" she whispered.

"At my apartment, mostly. Sometimes on the bus, sometimes never!" He smiled.

"Must be nice."

"Do you come here often…to study?" His voice was so mellow, she thought; a pleasant, deep baritone.

"Not really." Kassie found it so easy…this little discussion they were having. She was beginning to understand why the nurses he spoke to felt so at ease with him.

"Where do *you* study?" he asked.

"At home."

"And where might that be? Do you live in Denver?"

"My apartment." At least Kassie was staying awake, but this conversation wasn't going anywhere.

"Do you always answer in two words or less?" Perceptive, he was. She had to laugh to herself. Here she sat with the most virile of men and he'd already figured out conversation at this moment was not high on her list of things to do. She decided he was owed more than perfunctory answers.

"Please forgive me. I haven't meant to be rude. It's just that I'm studying to become a nurse in OR. And since I desire the position, I think I ought to step out and up and do really well."

"And you said your name was…."

"I didn't." She paused.

"There you go again!"

A slow smile enlightened her face. "People call me Kassie."

"And I'm Brad. Glad to meet you. So, you are a registered nurse. How long have you been practicing?"

"Almost a year. I've been working third floor and….."

"I know." It was a softly spoken statement, barely audible, but Kassie caught it.

"…and I enjoy helping those patients who are really hurting, suffering, not that those who have medical problems don't suffer. So many surgical patients have never seen the inside of a hospital until one day they're faced with surgery. I really enjoy trying to make them comfortable and try to listen to what they have to say." Brad sat and listened. Kassie knew what she was saying was being absorbed in its entirety by the man sitting across and down from her at the table. After several minutes, Brad broke the silence, again.

"Let's get a cup of coffee and then I'll see you home."

"Okay. Maybe that's what I need to wake up." She laughed. Agreeing to have coffee with Dr. Brad Phillips was the easiest, most relaxed decision she'd ever made. It was effortless, spontaneous, like a breath of spring air.

Over coffee in the library cafeteria and walking to her apartment, they touched on many things. Neither had ever been married. Both had parents that were still living and together. Neither one had siblings, but both secretly wished that they would've had at least one. At least that's the impression Kassie had. Snow crunched beneath their boots. Below freezing, Kassie was glad her apartment was only three blocks straight west of the hospital.

"Where do you live, if I may ask?"

"Actually, at Mercy." His laugh was the infectious kind, straight from the gut. No pretense, no ambiguity. Knowing that wasn't his real home, he continued. "I...live...two blocks south of here and two flights up. I'm in a warmer climate!" Laughing together kept the cold from seeping into their bones. As they approached her apartment building, she said,

"You'd best get home. I'd invite you in but...."

"I quite understand and I applaud..."

"...I really don't know you...very well." They stood for a moment in the icy air before Kassie turned to enter her building.

"I'll see you tomorrow...maybe? At work?" Brad hesitated in spite of the cold. Leaving Kassie standing at the doorway to her apartment building was the last thing he wanted to do.

"Perhaps." Kassie was just this side of shivering.

"There you go again. One word answers." Before he turned to leave, he continued. "I've enjoyed our little chat. A lot. Good night, Kassie."

"Good night, Dr. Phillips."

After she was out of sight, he started for his own apartment. He was as sure about Kassie as he was about everything else he did with his life. Her humble spirit, her soft melodic voice, and the very excuse she gave him for not inviting him into her apartment...yes, he knew. This woman was unlike the other women he had known. This woman knew what she wanted...and she was willing to work for it. This 'lady,' he thought to himself, was friendly but cautious, intelligent but humble, waiting for the right man to come into her life, someone to share her beliefs, her joys and her serenity. She would settle for nothing else. He had already admired her from afar. Now he would have to be patient because if he became too presumptuous, he knew he would drive her away. At this moment it was the last thing he wanted to contemplate. Yes. So far, Kassie had definitely been all that Brad thought she might be. Her body language was unmistakable. 'Leave me alone unless you want to be a part of my world.' Just before he entered his apartment building, he said aloud the words that were forming in his mind.

"I do believe I love you, Miss Kassie. Oh, yeh!" The lady coming out of the building glanced his way: knowing that he was a bachelor she smiled at the words she had heard. Always alone, always serious, to know that he was now happy also brought his neighbor a sense of satisfaction.

"Amen and amen." She turned and continued on her way. Brad didn't hear a word she said.

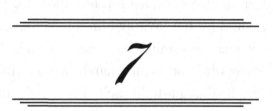

U pon hearing the news, Jacki decided she couldn't wait until evening at home to tell Kassie. Hustling down the stairs, from fourth to third floor, she found Kassie at the nurse's station.

"I've got the 25th through the 1st of January off. I can't wait. I'm so excited!" Jacki got excited about a lot of happenings.

"I can tell!" Kassie kept typing.

"Kass, has your vacation been approved?" Kassie explained to Jacki that she had from the 27th of December through the 4th of January off and yes, she was also happy about it.

"Yes. Mine was approved!" Kassie smiled and winked at Jacki.

"I'll explain when we get home, but this vacation will be the best ever." Jacki turned to leave. Every year was the same. Kassie began to wonder if Jacki would grow up by her *next* birthday.

"Hello, Kass." It was Brad making his surgical rounds. After looking toward the voice, Jacki nearly fainted. "Did it feel good to get inside last night?" Jacki couldn't believe her ears or her sight when she saw this gentleman speaking to Kassie on a first name basis. When did all this happen and who was he?

"Yes. It did. Thanks for asking, Dr. Phillips." Always maintain decorum at work. She gave him a polite but sweet smile.

"Did your Christmas plans work out?" Brad picked up Mr. Edmonds chart.

"They did. I'll be off for a few days. Maybe I can get in some relaxation time."

As he turned to leave the station, he said, "I'm happy for you." Then he left as quietly as he had appeared. Jacki, meanwhile, stood there with her mouth half open.

*"Who...was...that?"*

"I'll tell you later. Don't have the time now." Jacki shook her head as if who she just saw was a mirage. She tiptoed to the stairwell in anticipation of hearing about the man, obviously a surgeon, with the deep baritone voice.

That evening, Jacki arrived home about the time Kassie had finished baking lasagna. Jacki had been Christmas shopping and once her pre-wrapped presents were put under their five foot undecorated tree she filled her plate with lasagna and tossed salad. Kassie had poured a small glass of red wine for each of them. The fireplace was glowing and the apartment was luxuriously toasty. Dinner was the icing to the beginning of a wonderful evening. As they settled down to eat, Jacki asked,

"So. Tell me how you met Dr. Brad Phillips? Oh, yes, I inquired and they, you know, the break room bunch, confirmed beyond a shadow of a doubt that it was *the Dr. Brad Phillips*."

"You first. Didn't you have something you wanted to tell me that couldn't wait….?"

"Ah…that was before I saw you with Dr. Phillips. Honestly, how did you become such intimate friends?"

"Intimate? I wouldn't call our casual acquaintance 'intimate'." Kassie had second thoughts about what she had just said. That Brad and she had spent a few precious moments together away from work was a fact that Kassie hid from Jacki and the world; she reaffirmed their relationship to herself. And precious they were. Kassie had to smile. Until now.

"The two of you are very, *very* comfortable in each other's company. Anyone can see that. I'm just wondering when all this 'intimacy' had a chance to grow."

"Jacki. Dr. Phillips and I are very busy studying. He's my friend. We met on third floor...actually, a little after that...in the library. All we've done is have coffee and walk home together. Both of us are kind'a wrapped up in our professions. Besides, Dr. Phillips doesn't have any money to spend on dating. He'll have a couple large loans to pay off when...."

"Kassie! Honestly! When do you ever think of yourself? Besides, he'd be a real good catch. A surgeon!" She paused and took a deep breath. "By the way, I'm spending a few days in the mountains with Howard, skiing at Breck. When we get back, I'll be flying south to spend a few days with my parents."

In Colorado, 'Breck' was short for Breckenridge, considered to be one of the best skiing locations in the world, especially during the holiday seasons when Breckenridge was packed with people, activities and a festive atmosphere...and lots of snow.

"Another weekend with Dr. Howard Harriman. Good old Harry! Alas, alone, just the two of you out on some cold mountain, skiing. I'd rather be riding Spinster, *alone*. By the way, just out of curiosity, does Dr. Reynolds every say anything to you when you oblige Dr. Howard Harriman with your time?"

"Not yet! Hey! Are you going to visit your family or do you have other plans?" Jacki thought it was a shame though they were roommates, their schedules didn't allow their paths to cross much anymore. They viewed life from different perspectives and yet...

"I purchased tickets online yesterday, just getting under the wire! I skipped 'stand by.' My parents really wanted me to come home this year. Being an only child can be a drag, sometimes...you should know a little bit about that." She was still for a moment. "They're not getting any younger." Kassie loved her parents but at a distance. Her whole adult life seemed to revolve around her identity, whether she could be successful on her own. The last thing she wanted was for her parents to feel as though they had to take care of her. As a youngster she was showered with love and security from her parents as well as the ranch hands. Their unconditional love was perhaps the greatest gift they could've given her. But! Going back to the ranch to live wasn't in her immediate plans.

Jacki, on the other hand, also being an only child, didn't deem it necessary to travel to see her parents. Her obligation to them stopped as soon as she was on her own. Seeing them every few years, she felt that she was doing them a favor. Her life, so far removed from what she knew as a child, was richer and by far more beneficial to her present liking. She was happy to be one of them, her peers. Having strived 'to be normal' like her friends brought her to a worthy place and it felt marvelous. How long had it been since she'd been home? Well! This year was as good as any.

After dishes were finished, Kassie retired to her room to study and Jacki reached for her cell. As she was dialing, Kassie hollered,

"Hey! Isn't this the longest you've had one beau?"

# 9

The Christmas season always came too soon. There were presents to buy, cookies to make, decorating to do, although both had already accomplished that task. Jacki had finished her gift buying before they had the tree decorated. Kassie's gift to her parents would be a painting, quite large, spotlighting the ranch in the background with Spinster and her mothers' three Arabians, front and center. She had no earthly idea just how she'd get it to Montana by plane but she was aware people had carried larger and bulkier things than just a painting.

On one hand, Kassie was looking forward to going home; her former home. She had to remind herself. After ten plus years, she still thought of the ranch as 'home.' The other hand didn't want to leave because of Brad. Brad said he was going to spend both holidays working and getting some rest. He knew his parents wouldn't mind; he'd been on his own for so long. Besides, he knew his parents were in good health since he'd just been home for a weekend prior to meeting Kassie. Also, his vehicle was an old '92 Chevy pickup that was on its last legs and he didn't want to push it too hard. It appeared to Kassie his excuses were convenient, but why? Why would he want to stay in his apartment, really, if he had three days leave? Maybe he couldn't afford a gift for them? For sure, he didn't have any extra money. Maybe that was it. Whatever the *real* reason, Kassie was pretty convinced that neither would she ask and neither would he volunteer the information? The last thing Kassie wanted to do is to put Brad in a position where he would feel compelled to lie in order not to share whatever his innermost thoughts may have been.

Brad met her as she exited the hospital. Their companionship was just that, easy, friendly and respectful. They always appeared to look forward to being together, to discuss the day's events or to laugh over something a patient said to them. Their conversations were such that if anyone had overheard them no one's name or reputation would be defamed. The only the time the future came up was when Kassie discussed moving into the surgical unit or when Brad was exploring where he would like to set up practice, if indeed that's what he would do.

Brad really wanted to be in partnership with another surgeon. He was forty-two; he'd been through a lot in his life. His intelligence and intuition told him not to hurry. His faith and prayer told him that all good things come with time. God's timetable, not his.

"What do you want for Christmas?" Kassie had no idea what his answer would be.

"A new truck!" He watched Kassie's expression. "How about that for a gift? Or do you think I should be satisfied with a pair of slippers?"

Kassie laughed. A new truck. Well, that severely limited what she could get him for Christmas. "How about some cookies?"

"That'll do. Lots of chocolate, pecans…that's pronounced '*pee-cans*,' candied cherries, peanut butter…they're my favorite…you know the usual goodies."

"I'll see what I can do. Perhaps you'd like to come over to my place and hangout. We could order in pizza?" Kassie made it sound more like a question than an invite.

"When?" The swift comeback surprised Kassie, and her face revealed it. "I thought you'd never ask!"

"Well! Jacki is spending a couple days with a friend of hers, but she'll be back before she leaves on the 25th. Do you want to come over this evening?" Kassie was almost afraid what his answer might be. What if he said no! What could she say in return? And if he said yes, what then? She tried to remember what shape their apartment was in. At the moment, she couldn't think of a thing except.....what?

"That's the best idea you've had for a long time. So I'm taking advantage of the opportunity." Brad could see Kassie blush and he immediately tried to put her at ease. "I'd like to shower and change clothes first. How about seven?"

"Great! **Great!** I mean great, I'll see you then." As he broke off from their walk to go to his apartment, she watched as Dr. Brad Phillips crossed the snow packed street, with an assuredness and agility that spoke volumes about his character. Not once did she worry about spending time alone with him in her apartment. In fact, she was looking forward to the evening. She wouldn't be alone; she'd be with her new best friend.

As she flipped the switch to ignite the fireplace, the phone rang. Her first thought was that something had come up and Brad couldn't make it. It was the first time she felt pangs of regret at the thought of not being able to spend an evening with him.

"It's Jacki. I should've listened to you. This was a big, *big* mistake to go to Julia's house. I should have gone straight to Florida!"

"Why are you whispering? Are you alright?" Kassie was concerned.

"I'm fine. I've done a lot of things in my life that I may live to regret but this is one time I put my foot down. If one of the guys decides to return to Denver tonight, I'll catch a ride home."

"Jacki, what is going on? Who is at this party? Have you been hurt...skiing?"

"I can't talk now. I'll explain when I get back. I just wanted you to know that I won't be gone for three nights. Not if I can help it!" Whispering, she continued. "Please keep your cell with you, in case I call."

$$10$$

"Your apartment is very comfortable…like…tasteful and cozy. It's you, in every corner." He paused for a moment. They sat opposite each other in the lounge chairs on either side of the fireplace, eating pizza. Kassie had retrieved a Pepsi for each of them along with some extra napkins. "Tell me more about yourself…and your family that I don't already know?"

"My family is great. My father is an ex-Navy Seal and my mother used to be an elementary teacher, until they had me. Father always said it was the best decision he ever made when he left the Navy and married mother.

"Mother was raised on the ranch. When her parents were fatally killed in an auto accident, the ranch became my mother's. The hired hands stayed with her to help with the cattle and after a couple good years she was able to buy an Arabian stallion, something she had always wanted." She paused, thinking how hard it must have been for her mother to be alone. "It gave mother a chance to raise and breed Arabians."

"Did your parents know each other before your father became a Navy Seal?"

"They had gone to school together but never dated. Father came from a broken home…in many ways. Lots of alcohol and lots of debts. He has two brothers, Pat and Mike. Mother had a brother who ran away from home when he was fifteen. They never knew what happened to him until one day he showed up at the ranch…I was only seven at the time so I really don't remember much about him. But no one ever spoke of him after that…Henry…that I ever heard."

"It sounds to me…." Brad extended a knowing smile. Kassie read his mind!

"No! My father told me many times that he tried to use every excuse in the book not to marry my mother. He knew the townspeople would talk about the poor boy who married the girl with money! But she waited for him to see himself for what he could become, for what he had already attained in his life. I mean…come on. He became a Navy Seal. That takes courage and a lot of guts."

Brad listened to her every word, while he looked at the flames, the embers from the artificial logs in the fireplace casting shadows that enveloped both of them. Yes, it took stamina and guts to be a Seal; it also took an indomitable spirit. For a moment, Brad wasn't in the room. His mind had taken a detour to somewhere far away. A different place. A different time. He caught himself and was ashamed for having taken a moment to reflect.

"I'm sorry. How long was your father a Seal?"

"I'm not sure. Several years though. They didn't get married until they were both thirty-four. I remember that because mother thought she might be an old maid before my father would realize that he was going to be her husband." Kassie smiled as she was talking about her parents. They were so good to her; she had come to appreciate them so much more now that she was older…if that was possible. "Have you ever ridden a horse?"

"Where did that come from?" Brad had to chuckle.

"Well. I was wondering. If your Chevy could make the trip to Estes, then we could go riding horseback tomorrow. You said you were off until the night shift."

"Did I say that I could ride a horse? As a matter of fact…."

"Good. I'll pay for the horses…and the gas. It will be my gift to you."

'My gift to you.' The offer was so typical of Kassie, thought Brad. There were takers in this world and there were givers. Kassie was definitely the latter. She was a delightful change. So many of the women he'd known were so into themselves that they couldn't see him. The impression Brad had of the other women he had dated only saw a 'Dr.' in front of his name. Brad was slowly recognizing that Kassie was one in perhaps a million, that his love and trust would not be wasted. It scared him. He knew, the longer he let the thought linger in his conscious brain, the more difficult it would be to let it go. To let her go! Brad knew he would have to do something about that but he also didn't want to lose this friend he had made. He didn't know one end of a horse from the other, but he would go horseback riding. To be close to Kassie. To please her by accepting the gift of her time. To contemplate what life might be like to be in her company for an extended period of time. *Like for the rest of my life.*

"Tomorrow it is, then. About what time should we leave?" He set his Pepsi aside. "You know, we should have a nice breakfast together before we exercise. If I came by about nine, would that be too early?"

"That would be fine. It'll give us plenty of time to drive up, window shop and ride. I think I'll call early in the morning just to make sure my favorite stable will be open, say around noon?"

"By the way, I've never been on a horse. Anything I should know about boarding a horse before we continue making these *out-land-ish* plans?" He had to chuckle to himself and when he grinned, his dimples came into view, thus causing Kassie to sheepishly blush.

"You'll do fine, mate." Kassie removed their plates and drinks. When she turned around from the kitchen sink, Brad was standing in front of her. It startled her! She had never been close to a man before without having been somewhat attached to them through a dating relationship. Her previous long term 'boyfriends' had always managed to become overbearing; some became manipulative. At that point, Kassie would always end the relationship.

"It's getting late. If you'll allow me…" Brad smiled. Kassie didn't let him finish. Instantly nervous, she turned away.

"Of course. I'll get your coat and scarf." He followed her to the front door. After he had put on his coat, tucking his scarf tightly inside, he turned toward her.

"Kassie, thanks for having me over. I hope you had as good a time as I have." With a bit of merriment in his eyes, he continued. "It's been a long time since I've enjoyed an evening with a lady…and a fireplace that didn't smell up the place!" Kassie blushed. She brushed his sleeve as though there were wrinkles that needed smoothing out. Their eyes met as she looked up at him.

"Me, too. I mean, *that the fireplace didn't smoke.* Actually…I mean…sharing an evening with a gentleman. Thank you for coming over." Before she finished speaking, he gently placed his hands on her arms, bent and kissed her softly on her left cheek. Not saying a word, he opened the door, turned, smiled and left. Kassie closed the door behind him, gently.

Two more hours and it would be midnight. Where had the time gone? What had just happened to her this evening? Kassie crawled into bed and instead of reading, which was her usual habit, turned out the light. The moonlight flooded her room with a soft luminescence as she laid thinking about a man who had been her friend for just a few weeks. Was his soft kiss that of one friend to another? Why was her heart pounding? She took a breath and exhaled slowly. That didn't help either. She had waited twenty-nine years for this feeling. BUT! She would give Brad a long rope. If he continued to be a gentleman and worthy of her love, she would know soon enough. If he tried some stupid stunt as some of her other 'boyfriends' had, Kassie would simply add another male to her list of incorrigible men. She had to give herself time and give Brad the benefit of any doubts for the time being.

After breakfast at LaBlanche, a nook of a restaurant two blocks east of Mercy, a relatively warm and sunny day found Brad and Kassie driving to Estes. It was while they were in the pickup she chose to give a Christmas present to Brad.

"What's this?" It was a small box about the size of a package of cigarettes. Brad didn't smoke or drink, but Kassie had yet to learn if he didn't do those things because he didn't have the money or because he didn't believe in them. From her past experiences with men, their bad habits didn't show up until later in their relationships. She was tired of going down that road. So when Brad looked at the carefully wrapped box, Kassie watched for his reaction. "I can't accept this! I didn't get you anything. Besides," as he looked at the box, "I've never smoked." He looked dismayed. Brad started to hand it back to her but Kassie gently pushed his hand back and waited. She smiled.

"You won't be disappointed, I promise. It's something you've wanted for a long time." At the next rest stop, Brad pulled over on the side of the road. Highway 34 was heavily traveled this time of year. Plus, in select spots the highway was not only snow packed but icy. He left the truck running.

"Okay. If it pleases you."

"Oh, it will!" Kassie laughed. Brad caught the insinuation.

"Is something going to jump out at me? Or will I just burn my fingers?"

"Just open it. You'll love it!" At least Kassie hoped he'd love the irony of it.

"A red Ford dually! How thoughtful of you! Miniature of course!" He laughed at the sight of it. This was a woman who actually listened to what he was saying. And yes, he needed a new truck, but not on his salary. Not yet. Brad placed it back in the box.

"Oh no, you don't! Here. It's magnetic. It goes right here." She took the miniature vehicle and placed on his dashboard. "You can always dream. One day, hopefully, you'll be able to afford a real one, just like this one." Kassie was tickled that he was a little taken back by the miniature toy. Brad didn't mock her for it, nor did he seem displeased.

"You shouldn't have," he said as he pulled back onto the highway. From now on, he decided, he would be extra careful what he said or mumbled under his breath. Kassie listened well. He wouldn't want to divulge anything he didn't want her to know.

Riding horses was second nature to Kassie. She couldn't remember a time when she didn't know how to ride. However, as she watched Brad lead his horse outside the stable, she began to wonder if this was going to be as simple as she first thought. After she mounted her horse, she spoke.

"Take the lead rope, put your foot in the stirrup and hoist yourself up. It might feel clumsy at first but that's only natural. The horse is trained not to move so relax and enjoy."

"Easy for you to say." Brad did as he was told until the horse started walking. "Whoa!" He dropped the lead rope and grabbed the reins. "Now what? How do I get the rope off?"

"I'll get it." She moved her quarter horse over to the head of Brad's horse and reached for the lead rope, at which time she dislodged the buckle and let it drop to the ground. "There. Ready? Just hang on. This will be great fun." Kassie took the lead.

The trail allowed for only one horse; they were prohibited from riding side by side. Occasionally, Kassie turned to see if Brad was still maintaining his composure of self assuredness. He was always so confident, she thought. Although he was hesitant about the experience of this little horseback ride, he was doing fine. When they reached the highest point on the trail, Kassie stopped and dismounted. The view from the top of the mountain was spectacular. The muted rays of the sun glistened off the rooftops of the homes. Immediately below them was the Stanley House, a huge structure built as a hotel in the early 1900's. It was there that Hollywood filmed a horror movie that

Kassie would probably never see. There was nothing she liked about hearing or seeing people act ugly toward each other. Ironically, the Stanley House often held weddings and receptions as well.

"How do you feel? You're doing great!"

"I don't think I'll ever walk the same again. My butt is numb and my legs are shaking."

"Just lean forward and throw your right leg over the saddle and dismount. You'll be fine."

The dismount was not glamorous. His legs wouldn't hold him as he slumped to the ground.

"Brad! Are you alright? You must have used too much pressure in your stirrups to hold yourself upright. Your muscles are new to this exercise. Don't worry. You'll be fine. Come on. Hang onto my arm and we'll rest awhile and enjoy the view."

"Wow! This is beautiful! I never took the opportunity to see this before. The ride up here was great but this. This view is spectacular!" Brad put his arm around her shoulders. Even though he was totally conscious of her body next to his, he felt totally at ease in her presence. He hoped she felt the same. They stood silent for awhile, neither feeling as though they needed to speak. It was bitterly cold but they were dressed for it. The breath of the horses seemed to hang in the air. The silence of the place was deafening. Neither moved.

Kassie was beginning to shake. She doubted it was from the cold. She was five foot nine and yet she felt so small standing next to him. His six foot four frame seemed to dwarf her and his arm…well…..she snuggled closer. Upon deciding she could wait here forever, he moved.

"Let's go back before you and I both freeze. There's a breeze kicking up. I don't want you to catch a cold."

"Okay." Better they leave, she thought, than for her to say something that she might regret.

The ride down was uneventful, each silent, making conversation with their individual thoughts. Brad felt so close to her. Well, he was, physically. But on this little excursion, Brad felt something other than just a close friendship. Had he let it happen? Kassie was a tall, good looking woman, a kind person with a glowing career. Who was he to barge in on her and place himself in her dreams? But he just did and Kassie didn't have a whole lot to say about it. From the first day he saw her on third floor, it was all but over. He knew then he wanted to meet her, get to know her, find out if she held the same values he did. She was intelligent, smart, yet humble. He wanted to learn if her ambition would stand in the way of a good marriage. There, he said it. Now, he was shivering. It wasn't from the cold!

Kassie wanted to be held by him forever. What was happening to her? Thinking back to all her other beau's, she had never felt compelled to be so honest, to be so open. Brad made it easy. She felt she could trust him; wasn't that what love was all about? There. It was out in the open. She thought the word: love. Now she worried it was too soon to even contemplate the term. They'd had a friendship for such a short time. It was too soon. The last thing that crossed her mind before they dismounted back at the stable was that if she said anything, or asked anything that might upset him, she may lose him. Deciding to keep her relationship with Brad humorous and light, she would wait for him to tell her about his family, his upbringing, his friends and his previous life. She compelled herself to be patient.

"That wasn't as bad as it could've been. I actually stayed on! I rode a horse! But I'm pretty sure I need a shower."

"Of course. We both smell of horse and hide! A shower right now would be great!" The handler took the reins of both horses as Brad and Kassie retreated to the pickup. Once outside the fence, Kassie picked up some snow, made a snowball as quickly as she could and playfully threw it at Brad. He ducked...and laughed. Two seconds later, they were having a snowball fight. It was when Kassie bent over and caught one of Brad's snowballs on her forehead that it all came to a screeching halt. Kassie slumped on the snow, waiting for her head to clear.

"Are you alright? Kassie?" Instead of trying to pick her up, Brad sat next to her in the snow, wrapping his arms about her, placing her head into his left shoulder. He removed what little snow was left on her head.

"I'm sorry. You'll be alright. You'll be fine. Just rest your head on my shoulder." Why did this have to happen today? They were just playing, continuing to have a grand outing. His thoughts went back to earlier days in his life when he found himself holding someone, trying to push back a less than happy outcome. "Say something, Kassie?"

"I'll be fine. It just caught me off guard. Your snowballs are *hard!*" She laughed.

"Yours weren't *soft* either. Besides", he said cautiously, "you started the fight. So are we even?" They both laughed at the incongruity of their situation. Neither of them wanted to make the other uneasy but here they found themselves in the snow, holding on to each other. Wondering.

"We're even."

"Here." Brad stood up. "Let me help you." He raised Kassie by her shoulders and began to brush some of the snow off her jacket. Again, they started toward the pickup. "We've got time for a latte. Does that sound good?"

"That sounds delicious." What was even more delicious to Kassie was the fact that she was with Brad, knowing that he had held her, knowing that he was sorry for something that could've happened to anyone. Indeed, she had started the fight and while it lasted it was immensely exhilarating.

Back in Denver at her apartment, Brad walked her to the entrance of her building. It was getting late and both wanted a shower.

"Thank you for the beautiful Ford, Kassie. I had a great time. I just need to learn how to walk again!" Kassie turned to look at him and burst out laughing.

"My pleasure. I have a chiropractor that will place my head back on its stem and I'll have him send you the bill!" She laughed while he looked off into space. "Your legs will feel better after you take a hot shower...and you'll be able to walk. Riding takes a lot out of your legs, but you did great. Thanks for a wonderful time." Kassie didn't want him to leave.

"The bill! *Your bill!* If I can't walk tomorrow, you'll be doing surgery. Now we're talking bills!" Brad held her gently while they laughed. It had been a wonderful day.

"I better go." Reluctantly, he walked toward the truck, stopped and stood looking back at her. He returned, stepping lightly, careful not to slip on any ice. Taking her face in his cold hands, he kissed her lightly on the mouth. "I...I better go."

The apartment felt empty. There was no music, no movement, no aroma of food cooking and no fireplace burning. Kassie had come back to a cold, impersonal apartment more times than she cared to remember. Many times it was a hotel room where the only thing she did was brush her teeth, sleep and shower. Then it was on to another plane, another city.

After hanging up her coat and shedding her cold weather sweaters, putting on her slippers, she slumped into the lounge chair by the fireplace. Her life of travel as a flight attendant was incredibly fortuitous in preparing her to be a nurse. But did she want to work as a nurse the rest of her life or was there more she wanted? Unequivocally, she wanted a husband, children, and a house she could help make into a home. Her dream had always been that. But there was more she wanted. Her special man must be someone who lived by faith, walked in faith and practiced his faith. She had watched as too many of her acquaintances had married men because they were handsome or tall or made a good wage. They even had the audacity to call it love. Love of what? Fellow flight attendants fell in love with guys they met on a plane; only to find out they were married. For those few attendants who legitimately married, the reasons for their breakups were obvious to those looking. Their kind of 'love' was convenient and superficial. Kassie wanted none of that.

Brad had never mentioned his family or the life he'd had without Kassie bringing it up first. He never mentioned going to any particular church; he did attend chapel services at the hospital. The more she thought about those things the more she realized what she didn't know about Brad was a whole lot more involved than that which she knew. Best not to fall too hard for this guy…this one in a million. She wasn't about to get hurt again.

Before starting work the following morning, she stopped at the chapel, a place where she could find the peace she needed to see herself through a worthwhile God given day. After all, she was free to work, laugh, move around, eat anytime and live her life without impediments. Not so for her patients! If Kassie brought nothing else to her profession, she wanted to be a spark of hope to those who couldn't do the things she occasionally took for granted.

The chapel itself was rather small, holding about fifty people at the most; it was warm and dimly lit. The altar was plain; the wall behind was void of decoration except for a simple gold cross. Different denominational services were held in the chapel throughout every Sunday, but it stayed open twenty-four seven. For those ambulatory patients on third floor who desired to attend on services on Sunday, Kassie tried to accommodate their wishes.

"Good morning, Kassie."

"Good morning, Dr." Dr. Stephen Selway was a relatively new surgeon at Mercy having replaced the Assistant Chief of Surgery, who left to become a partner in a private practice. Kassie was a bit taken back by his presence, not knowing his background. She found it curious but refreshing to find him entering the chapel on a weekday. So many medical personal were atheists; to find any surgeon entering the chapel any particular morning was invigorating.

She heard Jacki return in the early hours of the 25th. Since Kassie had to report for work early, she'd have to wait until tomorrow evening to hear Jackie's story.

"What happened?" Jacki looked as though she hadn't slept for a week; the bags under eyes were black and puffy. Kassie figured Jacki had pretty much slept the whole day. There'd been plenty of those on cross-continental flights.

"I'm so sorry for disturbing you, making you worry. You won't believe what I witnessed. When did I become so stupid? I always thought I was pretty well educated, independent, informed and resourceful but after the last day or two...."

"Would you just fill your plate and tell me what happened?"

"I was the only single there! Some broad told me Dr. Howard Harriman was married; he was too drunk to give me any kind of answer. When I asked him about it he just laughed. His friends were doing drugs!...Jeez!...I was shocked! I thought I'd left all that behind when I left the airline industry!"

"Jacki! Are you positive? That's quite an accusation!"

"Let me say that I didn't see him do lines of white powder but he got totally wasted. I insisted on sleeping on the couch and he got totally bent out of shape!" She began to eat but kept on talking with her mouth full. "It seems the good doctor has told different stories to different people. Couldn't get a straight answer from anyone. If ever… can't say that…I wish I could meet someone other than a physician or surgeon."

"Jacki. Were the women that you were with, are they nurses?"

"Some were. I really don't care. It's so good to be home." She continued to eat as though she was famished.

"Get some rest. Come to think of it, your vacation doesn't really start until…today! How'd you get two days off prior…"

"Cindy. She pulled double shifts for two days so that I could go. I shouldn't have gone. Having a bad time is one thing. Now I owe her two days relief. Next time I decide to do this sort of thing again, Kassie…" Jacki shifted her body on the couch to a more comfortable position. "I probably shouldn't get too comfortable…you do anything while I was gone?"

"Couple of errands. Bought a couple gifts. Kicked around, went to work."

"Hummm."

"Come on, Jacki, let's get you into bed before you fall asleep."

"I just don't understand how people can justify doing drugs…or drink…that much. Kass. Glad I got that out of my system when…hey, you're a good influence on me."

Grabbing her hands and pulling, Kassie extracted Jacki from her prone position and gave her support as she walked to her bedroom. After helping her remove her outer clothing, Jacki flopped into bed, asleep again before her head hit the pillow.

Later that morning, with her bags all packed, Jacki poked her head into Kassie's bedroom, said goodbye, and left to catch her plane. Kassie mumbled something into her blankets.

"Give your parents a hug for me. Merry Christmas."

Kassie didn't get up until noon. What little house cleaning she had to do before she too went on vacation didn't take much time. Everything she was going to take to her parents was basically packed. She had two shifts left before she could leave. That was uppermost in her mind. She had to leave! For some unexplainable reason she decided she'd rather have spent the holidays with Brad. Knowing him for so short of time, she found it hard to accept that she had grown so close to this gentleman in her life. And yet…Brad had become the one entity she looked forward to seeing every day.

Kassie was pleased they'd spent Christmas Eve day together. A warm fire, some leftover lasagna. What more could she ask for? Neither she nor Brad wanted to spend money; each other's company was sufficient.

On the evening of the 26th, as Kassie came out of the bathroom at Mercy, she saw Brad and Stephen Selway leave the chapel. Brad had never mentioned that he went to the chapel. It was a pleasant surprise, one that Kassie welcomed. Stephen Selway, on the other hand, was a different matter. His body language didn't lend itself to being the kind of man that would attend church, go to a chapel or pray. Yet, here he was again. It was the second time Kassie had seen him at the chapel. Brad caught Kassie's eye.

"I won't be able to come over this evening. Got an appointment I don't want to miss." Kassie was disappointed.

"Will I see you before I leave?"

"What time do you leave?"

"Eleven in the morning which means I'll have to be at DIA (Denver International Airport) by nine."

"I wish I could take you to the airport. I wish I could be going with you." Being somewhat playful, he continued. "I wish you weren't going. It'll be pretty lonely around here." Kassie was a bit shaken. It was exactly how she felt but had been reluctant to say so.

"Is it okay if I call you?"

"Sure. I'll look forward hearing from you. Be careful what you tell your parents about me!" Kassie stepped back, giving Brad a look of disbelief.

"Who said I'd tell them anything about you?" She laughed. Brad smiled.

"Just thought I'd mention it." Brad moved close to her and leaning over he kissed her on her right cheek. "When you arrive at your parents, may you be filled with surprises? Have a great time. I'll be with you in spirit. Are you going to the chapel?"

"Yes. I have much for which I'm thankful. I'll see you when I get back, okay?"

"I'll be here."

Kassie felt she was leaving a good part of herself behind, knowing that for the nine days she'd be gone, she'd be thinking more about Brad than enjoying her time away. It wasn't going to be fair to her parents. She'd have Spinster to ride and old friends to see. It would've have been more satisfying doing those things with Brad, she thought. Oh well, they could continue their relationship when she got back.

After attending chapel services, she went home to finish securing the wrapping on the painting. She wondered what kind of meeting was so important for him to attend they couldn't be together this particular evening. That was life. It's always the unexpected that helps your faith to grow. Besides, she found herself trusting Brad implicitly. She would go home to her roots, think about Brad and how he might fit in with her family. As close as she was to her parents, across many miles, she wanted to know the man she chose could love her family as much as she did. Was that too much to ask? Of anyone? Kassie didn't think so. She wasn't sure how badly she'd miss him. It wouldn't take long to find out.

Brad hadn't spoken but a few sentences about his parents, except to say that he was paying for his education, lock, stock and barrel. Kassie assumed that his parents contributed nothing as he never mentioned calling them or having heard from them. Brad was hesitant to speak when she asked if he was going to visit his parents over the holidays. He was always straightforward, confident and responsible in making decisions where the two of them were concerned. He was in the process of becoming a fine surgeon with opportunities ahead of him, choices he would have to make as to where he would practice. And yet, Kassie detected a bit of hesitancy on his part to speak of Harmon and Janette Phillips. Surely they would be proud of their son and what he had become and the brilliant future before him. And yet.....Kassie still wondered.

# *12*

r. Stephen Selway. Noted surgeon, single, reclusive, wealthy, somewhat good-looking who appeared to have the weight of the world on his shoulders when he walked. He was of medium build, close to six feet tall with hair the color of honey. His most predominant feature was his eyes. A soft blue, with a ring of hazel around the edges, it appeared that his eyes were fathomless, so one could never measure their depth. Like a Boulder opal. She had seen similar eyes in the people she had met in Russia when she and Jacki had occasion to fly to Moscow.

Kassie was convinced that his credentials were impeccable as everyone who worked with him in surgery was impressed with his efficiency and expertise. Since Kassie had yet to work with him, her personal knowledge of his work was unknown.

He drove to work in a black Porsche, with gold trim. He dressed as though he belonged in such a vehicle. Before changing into scrubs, which he wore on third floor, he came to work in a suit and matching vest, impeccably pressed, as though he never sat down while wearing it. His shirts were starched white, straight from the cleaners. Diamonds, the size of grapes, substituted as cuff links. His shoes were not just polished; they appeared to have several coats of acrylic so any foreign matter touching their surface would be whisked away immediately. Most people would characterize him as being 'dashing."

It appeared that he had but one fault: his demeanor. Dr. Stephen Selway was not a happy man. He had been raised by agnostic parents who, if they thought there was a true God, never subjected him to any Biblical teachings or church. As he got older he began to question his own existence. The fact they never mentioned God's name in his presence left a vacancy in his mind...and heart...he desperately needed to fill. Presently, his mind seemed cluttered with circumstances outside of Mercy. His body language spoke the truth to anyone who was willing to look. Everyone was curious to know what was annoying him but no one was brave enough to inquire.

He came to Mercy from Indianapolis where he had been Chief of Surgery. The scuttlebutt seemed to indicate he was happy not being Chief anymore: too much pressure. Pressure in the workplace always made people seem dour and unsmiling. Dr. Selway certainly wasn't the first surgeon or professional to show the strains of responsibility on their face. Mercy considered him to be a valued employee. Solemn face or not, it was definitely his superb work ethic and knowledge that the administration wanted on their staff.

The fact he attended worship in the chapel was an attribute those who worked with him came to admire. Dr. Selway knew the physical aspects of the human body were not just thrown together or evolved. They were designed and constructed in a way which allowed man to be fully capable of working, playing and resting. As many times as he'd done surgery, he knew without a doubt men and women were created by an intelligent, all-knowing entity, a being that appeared evasive to the good surgeon. It was for that reason alone that he sought guidance and enlightenment.

Perhaps he was searching for something that was as elusive to him as knowing what made a heart ache or feel remorse. During his schooling, being taught by professors who were either agnostic or atheist, the subject of a soul never came up. When he was procedurally doing what he was taught, he wondered, in his naiveté, why he never found a soul? Everyone was supposed to have a soul! What happened to the soul when a person died? To those questions he didn't have any answers. Whenever Dr. Stephen Selway entered a church or chapel he hoped to find that for which he was searching. It was at that juncture that he hoped to find peace for his troubled heart and mind.

# *13*

Upon arriving in Cheyenne, Kassie found her father waiting for her at the luggage pickup. To see her father in good health was itself a wonderful Christmas present.

"Your mother is busy cooking and baking. She's invited some of your friends over for the evening. You know how she is!"

"And you're not! Come on, Dad. I've never known you to turn away anyone from a good home cooked meal. And that includes the wranglers. And the neighbors!"

"I suppose. How many suitcases?"

"Only one...I carried my backpack."

Once in the car, they both relaxed. It would be a long drive home. They took the I-25 corridor north through Chugwater, Douglas to Casper, where they stopped for gas and ate lunch at a local café.

"How's Spinster doing? She's so old already. I thought I might take her out..."

"Spinster died about a month ago. I didn't want to tell you. We were afraid you would just fret over it. Mother picked out a yearling for you. One of her Arabians sired the colt. He's a real beauty." Kassie felt an emptiness that comes from losing a close friend. She knew Spinster was getting on in years; she held out hope that she would ride her again.

"What did you do with her?"

"Buried her. With the tractor. I dug a hole and we fork lifted her to her resting place. Even marked her grave!" He smiled. "You weren't the only one that loved Spinster."

"No. I suppose not."

When they finished eating, they again took I-25 through Edgerton and Gunbarrel. About 18 miles north of Gunbarrel, they turned left onto a gravel road. Fifteen miles later, Kassie saw the entrance to the ranch. 'Colbert Cattle Ranch' was engraved across the top of the arch. It was a familiar and welcoming sight. Kassie always became anxious once they reached the ranch. She couldn't wait to get on the back of her horse and go riding into the mountains.

Her mother met them at the front door.

"Oh, it's so wonderful to have you home. You look so good! And dinner is about ready. A couple of your friends wanted to see you so your father asked them to join us tonight for dinner. I suppose he's already told you."

The two men that her father invited were still single and very much available. Kassie saw them each time she came home. What she had wanted to tell them each time, she refrained from doing so. In her heart, she had no intention of marrying a 'home town' boy. Unlike her mother, she wanted to marry someone exciting, different and someone she didn't know from birth!

The two men that were coming to dinner were the sons of neighboring ranches. Derek, along with his family, ranched several quarters of land to the east of I-25 whereas Todd ran his father's ranch equivalent in size to the hundreds of acres her father had. Todd's ranch land bordered the Colbert ranch on the north with only a fence between them. Both of their ranches were healthy monetarily, running large herds of beef cattle.

At dinner, Kassie's mother did much of the talking. Derek and Todd said very little. Their only real interests were their respective

ranches and politics. Never one to disrespect her parents, she kept
her opinions to herself. But with these two bachelor's, it wasn't easy.

"You were awfully quiet this evening. Something bothering you?"

"Mother. I pray that you and father are not planning on having
me come back to the ranch and marry one of those two. If I were you,
I'd not hold my breath!"

"Well. They're nice men. And you'd be close."

"Mother, please."

"Well. They haven't had any children out of wedlock..nor have
they spent any time in jail…and they're really responsible…"

"Mother. Some other time. Maybe." After the table was cleaned
and the dishes neatly stacked in the dishwasher, Kassie asked her
mother for a favor.

"Can I ride one of your Arabs tomorrow? It won't be like riding
Spinster but it will do."

"Sure you can. Did your father tell you about the yearling we have
for you? We were anxiously waiting for you to come home to meet
him. He's beautiful, a colt sired by one of my Arabs."

"I will, later." Kassie could tell that the years they had spent apart
had left them with different priorities. They knew precious little
about Nursing and although she knew a lot about the ranch and how
it worked, her parents were only interested in the here and now. Even
their personalities had changed. Kassie had become an independent
lady, making a living away from the ranch. Her parents had settled
into a laidback lifestyle that involved horses, cattle, ranch hands and
neighbors. It was a highlight for them to go to town for groceries!

It wasn't that Kassie didn't love the ranch. She did, immensely. Her
problem was two-fold. The nearest hospital was thirty-five minutes
away and she had no intention of living on the ranch by herself. Deep
in her soul, she knew there must be an answer to her dilemma. She

wasn't getting any younger. That someone like Brad could ranch and still have his own profession was a dream she allowed herself to have. The whole idea was really far-fetched, even for Kassie. Better to drop the dream and just live her life.

The yearling was everything her parents had said he was and even more. Black as the ace of spades, he was the picture of perfection. From his perfectly caved forehead, to his pointed ears, to his elevated tail, he pranced around the corral knowing he was gorgeous. Her mother had named him Vanity from the day he was born. He certainly acted up to his name. At the same time, he was a sweetheart. When Kassie entered the corral, Vanity came prancing over as though he expected her to give him a carrot or an apple. He sniffed her hands, raised and lowered his head rapidly, as if to say, "Where are my goodies?"

Wherever Kassie walked, Vanity followed. Before she traveled back to Denver, they would become inseparable.

New Year's Eve came quickly, sooner than it should have, Kassie thought. She had no idea if Brad would be available when she called. Her parents hadn't bothered to ask her if she was seeing someone or if her plans to become a surgical nurse had changed. Ironically, Kassie didn't share with her parents the fact she was interested in a certain surgeon. It would have prompted too many questions.

Not having spoken to him for three days seemed like forever at the moment. In her room she tried to look at her study notes but the atmosphere was not conducive to the activity. The something that was missing, of course, was Brad Phillips.

When they parted, she was quite aware that he hadn't asked if he could call her. Perhaps, she thought, she was feeling more for him than he was for her. She forced that thought from her mind; it was buried in that cesspool of conflicting thought along with all the other negative memories she had ever encountered. Negative thoughts such that had they materialized, she would've never become the lady that she was. And a 'lady' she tried to be. The concept had been told to her by her father and she saw it lived through her mother. Yet. Surely a lady can call a gentleman friend without bringing too much pressure to bear on their relationship. The fact remained that even a telephone call to Brad seemed to be too presumptuous. However...

Brad's cell rang several times. No answer. Not surprising. Holidays seemed to bring out the depressed, accident prone drunkards and die hard partiers. The emergency rooms would be filled with problems: people complaining about the wait, people without hospital insurance, people needing surgery. Depression and death went hand in hand around the holidays. Situations of every kind were time consuming and tiring. Perhaps Brad wasn't in a position to pick up his cell phone. Kassie decided to try later.

14

ew Years Day found her in the paddock saddling one of the Arabs.
"May I ride with you?" asked Laurie, as she walked in the barn. Kassie had just finished putting the saddle on Cadence.

"Of course. I'll help you saddle...." Kassie tied off the reins to Cadence.

"No. I can do it. Do it every day. But I don't have someone to ride with everyday. It'll be nice." Laurie saddled Murray, a sculptured bronze horse with four white socks. "Let's ride up to the forks. Not much snow up there this year. Might see some of the cattle."

Wherever they rode would've been fine with Kassie. Her mother was always quiet when they rode together. Conversation was always delayed in favor of just enjoying the beauty around them. It didn't take long before Laurie pointed to a spot they had always called the 'forks.' Once there, they dismounted and tied off the horses. Brushing the snow off a flat rock, they sat down and surveyed the valley below. A few stray cattle were poking around looking for a few blades of grass. At this time of year, her father and the ranch hands always brought hay out for them to eat. If the winters were bad and the snow deep, the cattle were rounded up and kept close to the barns on the ranch.

"You've decided to go into the OR. Quite a change from the third floor, wouldn't you say? I thought you liked it there."

"I did. But, being a surgical nurse is more of a challenge. The more I learned on the surgical wing, the more I wanted to know. Besides….." Kassie's mind floated away, thinking of Brad. She wondered what he was doing at the moment. She wished he could've been here beside her.

"You were saying…."

"Oh, nothing. Just thinking about school and work." Kassie decided to change the subject. "It's so peaceful out here. No traffic, no people, no pollution, just silence. I wish I could take some of it back with me."

"Well! You'll just have to come home more often." It was cold and getting colder. Laurie mounted up, followed by Kassie. "Have you ever thought about coming back…to stay?"

Kassie heard her mother's question but decided to ignore it. How could she ever get her mother to understand that her life was so far removed from theirs? She didn't want to go anywhere without Brad. Of that she was sure. It took these few days away from him to know the 'something' that had been missing in her life was now filled with admiration and respect for a gentleman named Brad. Had she been asked, she would've never voiced that someone like Brad could be interested in her. Kassie would've never made the first move toward him, or even spoken to him.

As they neared the ranch, Kassie felt a sense of loneliness that she'd never experienced before. She'd eat dinner with her extended family, try calling Brad again, play cards with a couple of ranch hands or watch TV and retire to bed. She'd have to be satisfied with her dreams.

"I'd like to make a telephone call, mother. I'll be upstairs if you need me." Kassie dialed Brad's cell phone. No answer. She tried calling Jacki. No answer.

It wasn't in Kassie's nature to fret about things or situations over which she had no control. The feeling of being alone, even though in the presence of her family, was almost overwhelming. As she looked around her room, she saw the things that were so important to her growing up. Photos with Spinster, trophies she had won at the State Fair, the curtains her grandmother had made for her, the quilt at the end of her bed made from scraps of her old clothes…all these belonged to her childhood. At the moment, none of them brought any sense of fulfillment. She was alone in her thoughts. Now she couldn't reach either Brad or Jacki. The fourth of January couldn't come soon enough.

"Dinner's ready." It was her mother.

# 15

B rad had wanted to spend their last evening together before Kassie went on vacation. However, he couldn't begin to quantify the negative results that may have occurred had he decided to 'blow off' his meeting. Though all prospects were in the preliminary stages, the interviews being held by teleconference that evening were too important to miss. With several major hospitals looking for a surgeon and Brad at the end of his residency, it was vital that he acknowledge to himself what he would be willing to accept, keeping in mind what they were willing to offer. He went into the meeting expecting nothing extraordinary so that if a lucrative and prized position opened up for him, he would be pleasantly surprised.

When the conference call was over, it was already too late to call Kassie. He would wait until she got back or until she called him. He had learned to be patient from the day his father had told him that as his son he would have to make something out of himself, that nothing was going to be handed to him. He was just a young boy when he first heard the words "Become somebody. Make your own mark in this world. Make a difference!" His father, Harmon Phillips, had done just that.

Harmon Phillips had graduated with a degree in economics. After working several years for a major international banking firm, he had saved enough money to purchase oil leases from those willing to sell them. He lived sparsely: a small apartment, a minimum of furniture, enough food to survive and drove an old miniature compact that got thirty-two miles to a gallon. At thirty four, he sold enough oil leases to the Baker Brothers Oil and Drilling Company, money from which he bought shares in the gold market; it enabled him to 'retire' from another day of work in his life. He could've lived off the royalties and dividends that were generated by his good fortune.

That was not his plan, however. Harmon Phillips went to work as an investment counselor in the bond market. His good fortune continued. When he was forty years old he met a lady whose beauty was beyond compare to anyone he'd ever met. Her name was Janette Moore, and she was heir to the Moore Trucking Company out of Dallas. Smitten with her good looks, he indulged his ambitious nature long enough to ask her father for her hand. Only after her father had determined that Harmon Phillips could give her a life to which she was accustomed, did he answer, affirmatively. With all the wealth he had accumulated up to this time in his life, nothing compared to the riches he received from the love of this very fine woman. Beautiful, cultured and knowledgeable in the pragmatic side of business, she wasn't only the love of his life; she also became his indispensable and trustworthy business partner. By the time Brad was born, the two of them had amassed a fortune such that there was nothing out of their reach. Needless to say, Mr. Angus Moore was ecstatic. He was also enthralled with his grandson, Brad.

It was Brad's maternal grandfather that helped set him on a track of reaching his full potential. Since Brad felt intimidated by his father, it was Angus 'pa-pa' Moore that instilled in him the will to succeed in anything he decided to accomplish. It was 'pa-pa' Moore that opened Brad's eyes to the art of learning by reading, not just for school but about everyday life: how different people lived, the places they worked, their priorities, their struggles and their shortcomings.

Brad learned at an early age through reading he could accomplish anything he wanted to do in life, given time and a lot of hard work. Because of 'pa-pa,' he also learned to appreciate the sacrifices his father had made to become the man he was.

'Pa-pa' Moore taught him the value of having a good 'woman' for a wife, one with the virtues of honesty, integrity and high moral character. But above all, 'pa-pa' taught him the value of a lady who believed in Christ. He reiterated that with Christian values, all the principles of an upright woman would be present. His 'pa-pa' provided his wisdom to Brad in the only way a grandfather can: with love. A deeply seated love that encouraged Brad to have the courage and tenacity to live his life, prayerfully, as a Christian, in whatever he chose to do, in His will. It would ultimately become the most precious fulfillment he could achieve in his life. As a young man, he knew the choices he would eventually make would determine the consequences that would follow him through his life. 'Pa-pa' made that very clear.

"With the way the world is headed, a righteous man doesn't have a chance at anything exemplary if he doesn't have a good woman as a helpmate." 'Pa-pa' Moore's words held a special place in Brad's thoughts and life. Though his parents were essential in helping him prepare for a world that didn't include their wealth, it was 'pa-pa' Moore's encouragement and humility that allowed Brad Phillips to accomplish all that he had attained thus far.

Brad had been patiently waiting to find the right woman to be his helpmate. Having taken his grandfather's advice he, too, believed in the one and only Christ that ever lived, the same Christ who was crucified and resurrected to live again. Brad firmly believed that he was alive this very day because of what Christ wanted him to accomplish. There were certainly enough times he could've lost his life, never to realize what it could've been. Through his faith Brad had come to the realization that the accumulation of 'stuff' was like a chain around his neck; it had to go wherever he went. Brad felt the need to aspire to that which many men of his age never discussed: the art of giving. He knew the value of satisfaction he received when he gave unselfishly. Close to becoming the surgeon he wanted to be, he had found Kassie. Timing on God's timetable, he knew, was perfect.

Aside from working, and the pressures it brought, the thought of having Kassie by his side was overwhelming. He wondered should they get married, if she would be willing to relocate to a hospital and a community he chose in which to practice. Would she be willing to live sparsely while he opened his own practice? Would she continually want to work as a surgical nurse? Did she want a family and still work? What were her *real* goals? Could she be satisfied to be a stay at home mother? She was definitely an independent woman with wants and needs of her own. What would her parents think? Kassie was an only child. Did they expect her to take over the ranch? So many questions to be answered and…it was giving Brad a headache. He decided as soon as she got back from Wyoming, he'd share his innermost thoughts and dreams with her and pray what he heard in return would solidify his longings and his future.

His reality, Brad decided, would be his faith, family and work. In that order! Any affluence he attained would be which he had aspired to and not any monies, if any, he would receive from his family. It was a stipulation he would fulfill by not immediately telling Kassie about his family's wealth. Not at this point in their relationship. He certainly didn't deny his parents the wealth they had accumulated. It wasn't as if they just sat on it! Their philanthropy was to be admired, had they chose to tell anyone about it. They didn't and Brad knew that they were happier for keeping silent about their personal projects. They enjoyed the good fortune of truly loving each other and any material possessions they had were just that: tangible stuff. It was accumulated through years of diligent work but they also knew that through no fault of their own, it could be lost so quickly.

# 16

The morning of the 4th, Jacki was waiting at the airport when Kassie's plane landed. Collecting her suitcase, they walked to the car. Jacki's vehicle was an outdated Pinto that had seen better days. But it ran and was good on gas mileage.

"Did you have a good time over New Years?" Kassie asked of Jacki.

"My parents opened their house to everyone they knew. It was a madhouse! Kids screaming and hollering, dirty diapers and broken toys, old folks who had a hard time getting around, those who used their walkers or chairs on wheels, more food thrown away than was eaten; the place was a mess. It took me two days just to recover! Got back just in time to wash and iron my clothes and make my shift the next morning."

"Did you *enjoy* your time with your parents?" Kassie decided to ask the question a different way.

"I did, but their life is so different than mine. It's getting harder to relate, for them as well as for me. Oh, I love them dearly and they understand, and they love me too. It's....it's just that they've become so...materialistic. Sometimes....I think....they throw such huge parties for recognition, for the social aspect of their relationships. Their life appears to be so...so empty. Perhaps they were always that way. But, that's not me. *Not anymore.*" Jacki grew quiet. Then. "Maybe it's me that's changed. I'm more aware of what I've become...different...than what it was like for me growing up." Despite their differences Jacki had no idea what she would do if something ever happened to them. "But I must tell you everything I've done since I got back."

Kassie couldn't put it into words. It appeared to her as though Jacki *actually* began to recognize the difference between her dreams and her reality. Now, her reality was more important to her. Yes, Miss Jacki was finally growing up, thought Kassie. It was wonderful to witness.

"Yes, please do. Where did you leave your cell that you didn't return my call? I called twice."

"By the time I crawled in bed, after unpacking, I misplaced it. I didn't have a phone to answer! Anyway! My battery died! I fell into bed, exhausted. Next thing I remember I was waking up to the alarm. New Years was over. It was time to go to work." She paused. "At the hospital, there was a note left in my mail slot on fourth. Dr. Selway wanted to invite me out for dinner. I gave him a call and I accepted!"

"No way, Jacki. I didn't think he had the qualifications that you... prefer."

"He's not as handsome, I admit, as I would *prefer.* However, he treated me to a nice dinner at the new Theatre in the Round restaurant. It was actually quite lovely." She checked her rear view mirror after turning on the left hand signal. "At least he didn't smoke a joint or ask me to participate in something illegal!"

"So, do you think you'll see him again?" Kassie was a little more than curious. There weren't many men that Jacki dated more than once. "What about Dr. Harriman?"

Jacki waved her hand as if to say 'Who cares?' Her mind at present was filled with thoughts of Stephen Selway. "I'm seriously thinking about it. I could do a lot worse, you know. Harriman is alright. He just hasn't called."

"Oh, I'm sure." Kassie was beginning to wonder if Jacki, at some point, really wanted to settle down or just liked the newness of every new man she dated. So much for growing up! "I had a fairly good time. Spinster died. My father buried him. He and mother gave me a new yearling colt. He's so beautiful and full of life. He's an Arab... called him Vanity...he knows he's gorgeous.

"I'll probably spend more long weekends at the ranch. My parents are in their sixties. When I think about their ages...well, mother and I rode into the foothills several times. It was so beautiful and serene. They have a lot of snow. And...I rode one of mother's Arab stallions. *What a treat*! Just like sitting in a rocking chair. You'll have to join me at the ranch, if we can ever finagle a weekend off together."

"As long as I never have to ride a horse!"

"You'd love it. You're a natural. Think positively! It wouldn't be the first new thing you've ever tried." They laughed at the incongruity of the thought.

It was January and it was freezing. Though they were both bundled up, the frigid air somehow seeped through their clothing. By the time they arrived at Kassie's apartment, neither one was speaking. Upon entering the apartment, Brad and Kassie exhaled the last vestiges of cold that penetrated their lungs.

"I'll make us some hot chocolate. Throw the backpacks on the chair. And please, turn on the fireplace and the blower."

"Sounds like a plan." Brad was only too happy to do both.

Sipping their chocolate and trying to study, both of them were well aware of the others' presence. They were totally comfortable with each other, neither expecting anything but each other's company. Being together after work had become fairly routine especially when Kassie's schedule coordinated with that of Brad's.

This particular evening Jacki had to work late; it was a good thing. With Jacki around, the three of them sometimes played cards until Brad went home. It was after one of those evenings that Jacki told Kassie that Brad was a whole lot more than just a tall, handsome and intelligent surgeon. Kassie knew only too well what Jacki was trying to say.

"Men are always attracted to me and of course, I take advantage of their resources." Jacki laughed, knowing she spent more nights eating out than she spent eating at home. "But Brad is different. There's a quiet, almost serene strength that he radiates. It's quite intoxicating! I'm surprised you haven't mentioned it!" Jacki waited for Kassie to respond. "I'm quite surprised that he prefers your company over mine. After all, I'm also available." Kassie heard Jacki loud and clear.

"Are you saying that you're a catch he shouldn't pass up? How long have you felt this way? Is that what you thought all those years we flew together? Or is it just Brad?" Kassie confirmed to Jacki what she already knew about her companion. "Brad is nice to everyone but I suspect he has a set of standards that far exceeds yours or mine. I just happen to be the one girl he wants to hang out with." For as long as she could remember, it was the only occasion where she felt intimidated by something said. It's so unlike me, she thought.

"Why, Kass, *I finally have your attention.* Don't be intimidated! I'm just saying. He is so all around gorgeous that you'd think he would already be married or at least, dating some socialite, with money. Know what I mean?" Jacki was at a loss of words to clarify exactly what she was feeling. She wanted to tell Kassie that she was fortunate a guy with such a brilliant future was truly interested in her and in her alone. What some women wouldn't do for a guy like Brad! Jacki had long decided therein lay the real reason Brad was seeing Kassie. Dating, actually, but never really going anywhere or spending any money. Brad wanted to spend his precious free time with a lady that was herself very discriminating in the men she would date. A woman every man wanted to date didn't appeal to him. Brad was looking for a special woman…and Jacki knew that Kassie could very well be that lady.

Kassie was blond; she had survived about every cruel joke there was, especially from the airline crews. But she always accepted them with grace and style. She knew who she was deep inside where it really counted. That set her apart; she wasn't a classless, unbelieving, unattached bimbo looking for the first available man to ask for her hand in marriage. Kassie was willing to wait. Her mother had told her when she was just a little girl 'the man you marry will seek you out before you know he even exists.' Jacki was very cognizant that the gentleman Kassie Colbert would agree to marry someday would indeed be a very fortunate man.

"All I'm saying is...I wish I could be more grounded...more appealing, if you will...to someone like Brad. Like, for instance, Stephen Selway. By the way, did I tell you that we're going to the Boulder Dinner Theatre this coming weekend?"

"You just did! It seems that you're being wined and dined by this guy on a regular basis. Anything serious?"

"Nah. But he sure knows how to treat a lady." Jacki took in a deep breath. "Did I just call myself *a lady*?"

"Yup! It sounded wonderful."

Time passed. Jacki was enjoying the company of Dr. Stephen Selway and Kassie was nearing the end of her advanced training. The four of them got together a couple times at their apartment, drinking tea and playing cards. Jacki had even started to attend services in the chapel with Dr. Selway; he was a very persuasive man.

Kassie, however, had the unsettling feeling that Brad was somewhat uncomfortable in Stephen Selway's company. There wasn't any particular moment or action on Brad's part that prompted her to think negatively about Dr. Selway. At least not directly. Or was it that Brad was more reticent to speak in Dr. Selway's presence? Since they were both surgeons, perhaps Brad was just giving Stephen Selway the respect he deserved due to his age and experience. Kassie, however, couldn't rid herself of the intuitive burden that somehow Brad knew something about Stephen Selway he wasn't willing to share with anyone, even her.

# 18

"**W**ould you believe it? Dr. Harriman has asked me to attend a formal dinner at Dr. Selway's home this coming Saturday. I told him I'd think about it." Jacki was troubled.

"Hey, I thought you'd never date Harriman again. Besides, why didn't you tell him…as if he didn't know…that you've been seeing Stephen?"

"I did. Kass, I did. And…I said it in a very nice way. My first thought…at Stephen's home…my word…what would Stephen think? Why hasn't Stephen asked me to his own home for dinner?" Jacki was troubled, and rightly so.

"So…..how are you going to find out why…why Stephen didn't ask you?"

"I'm not! I've got until tomorrow to answer Dr. Harriman. Maybe Stephen will say something to me before…."

"I'm glad I'm not in your shoes right now." Kassie put the last of the dishes away and was about to turn on the TV when Jacki's cell phone started to vibrate. "You want me to get that?" Jacki was just about to close the bathroom door.

"Please. Whoever it is…I'll be right out."

"Hello."

"Hi, Kass. How are you?" It was Dr. Selway.

"I'm great. And yourself?"

"Fine. I'm glad you answered the phone. I'm giving a dinner party this Saturday and I was hoping you'd be my guest?" Flustered, Kassie juggled the phone after trying to put it closer to her ear. It hit the floor and slid toward the kitchen. She was speechless! When Jacki came out of the bathroom, she saw a Kassie she'd never seen before...flustered and blushing.

"What's wrong, Kass?"

"Ahhhh.......the phone. I think it's for you!" Kassie was in a state of disbelief. "Here.....I'll get it. It must've slipped out of my hand. It's over there....." Kassie forced her body to become mobile and tried to retrieve the cell phone so she could disconnect it.

"That's okay. I've got it. Who is it?" Not waiting for Kassie to answer her she said, "Hello." There was a click on the other end of the phone. "That's funny. Whoever it was just hung up. If it's important they'll call back." Jacki flung the phone on the couch. "Did you recognize the voice?"

"No! No, I didn't!" Kassie walked deliberately to her bedroom. "I'm going to read for awhile." Upon entering her room Kassie quietly closed the door. Almost silently, barely a whisper, she lamented. "I just told a *deliberate* lie! To my best friend!" Sitting on her bed, she eyed her own cell phone resting on her pillow. For whatever reason, she had left it in her bedroom when she got home. She picked it up. Almost afraid to see if anyone had called her, she looked at her messages. There were two: Dr. Selway and Brad. The messages were short and to the point.

"Sorry I missed you. Perhaps I can reach you on Jacki's phone." Dr. Selway.

From Brad, it was even shorter. "Kassie, when you can, give me a call. Please."

Kassie didn't pick up the latest novel she'd been sporadically reading; she couldn't concentrate. What was going on? Why was

Dr. Selway inviting her to his dinner party? What about Jacki? Why wasn't he inviting her? What was she going to tell Jacki? She wasn't about to lie again. As she lay looking up at the ceiling, a cold chill ran through her body. Her immediate thought was how Dr. Selway could be such a deceitful man to invite her instead of the woman he had been dating. What just happened? It was beyond her comprehension to think Dr. Selway thought for a minute she would accept a date with him...or with any man other than Brad. What was he thinking? Whatever it was, it wasn't healthy. Kassie was sure before this little episode got ironed flat someone was going to get hurt.

It seemed she'd been in her bedroom for hours when she heard the doorbell ring. The next thing she knew Jacki was knocking on her bedroom door telling her Brad wanted to see her.

"He seems so distraught. I'll tell him you'll be right out." Jacki left the door ajar while Kassie took a brush to her hair. After giving herself a 'once over' in the long mirror that hung on her wall, she joined Brad in the living room. Even to Kassie, Brad looked a bit apprehensive. He walked up to her and taking her hands in his, said,

"Can we talk?" Then, as if he remembered his manners, said, "I'm sorry to come over without asking but we need...." The sound of his voice was barely audible.

"Sure. I'll get my sweater and shoes. Give me a minute?" She retreated to her bedroom, picked up her cell phone, grabbed a heavy sweater, flipped off her slippers and met Brad by the door.

"You guys going out in this cold weather?" Jacki barely tolerated frigid temperatures.

"Not for long. Just a short walk. Get some fresh air, you know. Healthy, that sort of thing." Brad was nervous. Kassie put on her boots, while Brad grabbed her coat. Throwing a scarf around her neck, she slipped into her coat as Brad appeared anxious for them to leave.

Once outside of the apartment building, Kassie asked, without hesitation, already knowing the answer, "Brad, is there something wrong?"

"Did you know that Stephen Selway had been married? Did Jacki ever mention anything to you about it?"

"No, she didn't. That doesn't surprise me. I mean the fact he'd been married. If she knows! When did he get a divorce?"

"He didn't. His wife died." Brad was upset. "Did he call you today?"

"Yes. As a matter of fact," she answered, as she reached for her cell phone, "he called this evening. You can hear his message." Brad listened to the line or two that Stephen Selway left on Kassie's phone. When he handed the phone back to Kassie, she continued. "He called and talked to me on Jacki's phone. Actually Jacki was busy and I answered the phone for her. He invited me to attend his dinner party as his guest? I was so shocked, I dropped the phone. What if she had picked up the phone instead of me?"

"Did you give him any kind of an answer?"

"Didn't have the chance. I said I dropped…"

"He didn't call back?"

"Not that I'm aware of. In fact, Jacki picked up the phone from the floor and when she said 'Hello' he hung up. I went to my room. I almost called you but I didn't know what to say. Evidently he thinks I date around like Jacki." Kassie wanted to say more but didn't. She wanted to tell Brad that she wouldn't think of seeing anyone else except him. This wasn't exactly the right time. The silence between them as their boots crunched the snow was deafening.

Brad wondered if he should ask her…tell her…even suggest to her what he was thinking. Today had been a turning point. Stephen had insinuated to him when they were scrubbing for surgery he thought Kassie was the kind of woman he wanted to be around more often. Brad didn't respond to him; he just knew he had to talk to Kassie before he lost her. He decided to verbalize his feelings for her. Not saying anything concrete concerning his feelings was beginning to eat on his insides. He stopped walking. Kassie took a few more steps before she realized he was just standing behind her, saying nothing, but looking concerned.

"Kass." How do I say this, he wondered. He'd never said anything like it before in his life. But then, he had never before felt like he did tonight either. "Kass." He stepped up to her and took her in his arms. "I really...I wouldn't want to...I'm not sure how to say this...."

"That you love me?" Kassie whispered. He leaned back and looked at her as though he was seeing her for the first time. Taking her face in his hands, he leaned down and kissed her, gently, as if she might break.

"Yes, Kass, I love you. I didn't realize until just now how very much I also *need* you. I don't want to control your life or your feelings but I really don't want you to be dating anyone......"

"Sssshhhhhhhh. I have no desire to date anyone else. Ever. From the moment you spoke to me at the library, I knew. I've waited a long time for the right kind of gentleman to find me and now that he has...," she smiled... "well, you must know that I love you, too. So very much, isn't it obvious?"

"I guess I was waiting for you to make some move or some gesture that would let me know what you felt but.....I should've known better. You're not like any other woman I've ever met."

"I'm glad you decided to say it first." They arms encircled each other as they started to walk back to the apartment.

The phone call from Selway was still a very present troubling problem. What to do?

"What should I tell Jacki? Or should I even tell her at all?"

"It depends on your relationship with her. I assume you trust her." Brad wasn't too sure he'd trust Jacki.

"Well, Dr. Harriman asked her to attend the same party so he must know what Stephen was up to, wouldn't you think?"

"Kass, how much does Jacki really know about Dr. Selway? I mean, they've had a couple dates and he seems to be decent enough, but there's something that bothers me about him. Even when we're playing cards...."

"I knew it! I just knew it! You're always so quiet when we're around him." Kassie was glad she hadn't raised the issue before.

"I know. Maybe underneath it all, I don't trust him. At least where it concerns his lady friends! Anyway, let's not think about him right now. I just want you to know that......I've waited all my life for someone like you. I don't want to lose you."

"You won't lose me, Brad." Just love me, Kassie thought. "Hold me?" They kissed again.

"I wish I could stay...or celebrate....but gotta' go. Let me know what you decide about Jacki. Okay?"

"Okay."

They approached Kassie's apartment in silence, Brad's arm around her shoulders. Both of them were lost in a contentment neither of them could verbalize, a serenity neither of them wanted to lose.

# 19

Kassie said nothing to Jacki, but two days later Jacki brought the subject up herself.

"I told Harriman I would go with him. We had lunch together and…I'm not sure what's going on but I have to wonder who Selway is bringing to his own party."

"Maybe he won't bring anyone." Kassie thought it might be the brightest thing he could do for everyone involved. "Besides, he'll be too busy entertaining. I'm surprised you're still willing to go?"

"Harriman's a nice guy. It's just that I've been dating Selway…and I'm sure those guys talk. I've heard where they talk about everything from their marriages to children to how many women they've had on the side…all during surgery. I've never been in surgery so I really don't know that to be true. Hey! You'll be in surgery soon. You can fill me in on all the juicy details on these guys."

Kassie was slated to enter OR as a Surgical nurse on the first of June. She had one exam to take; one more interview to pass. She could hardly wait.

"Jacki! There's a code under which all of us operate. You walk into work, you're the professional. You leave work and you forget you were ever there. You ought to know that! Besides, I'm not sure how it will work out if Brad decides to stay on at Mercy for awhile. I know he's been offered some lucrative positions elsewhere but he seems reluctant to make a move, just yet."

"*Maybe* he's waiting for you." Sarcasm was one of Jacki's attributes. Kassie wasn't about to discuss how she and Brad felt about each other. They had deliberately decided to keep their close relationship private as long as humanly possible. Otherwise, conflicts could arise since they both worked at the same hospital. It was bad enough tongues would wag over the slightest hint of gossip. They wanted nothing to interfere with the thoughts and plans beginning to take shape in their own lives.

Brad and Kassie had duty on the day of Selway's dinner party. Kassie had her hands full working with Mr. Edwards and Mr. Carter, both of whom needed dressing changes. Both also wanted to spend some time in the chapel. Since one of the floor nurses, Sissy, had called in sick, Kassie was also responsible for Mrs. Hathaway, who needed an ostomy bag change and Mr. Longren, who needed his leg dressing changed and someone to complain to about the inadequacies of the nursing staff at Mercy. After chapel services, and getting Mr. Edwards and Mr. Carter back into their beds, trying to make them comfortable, she went out to the nurses' station and collapsed in a chair.

"I really don't know how Sissy puts up with Mr. Longren. He is totally unhappy." The head nurse, who was charting at the time, smiled but didn't look up.

"If he were the only patient to complain, but alas…..and *he likes you!*" Kassie doubted very much that Mr. Longren actually liked her but she accepted the compliment. Turning her chair around, she saw Brad walk up to the counter. After reaching for the charts, he looked at Kassie as if to say with a slight twist of his head 'follow me.' Together they walked toward Mr. Reynold's room.

"Kass, you won't believe this," Brad whispered, "but Selway *insists* that we attend his dinner tonight. Are you okay with that?"

"Why? I was under the impression we weren't…what do you think?"

"I think he's putting the screws to me! Pardon me, for being so blunt. If I don't go he may well consider writing me up for being insubordinate."

"*He can't do that!*" she whispered. "You haven't done anything wrong!"

"Ah. That's the rub. He said his dinner invitation was an 'order' and I was to bring you as well. As long as I'm in surgery with him and he remains my superior, I don't have a choice. I just know that when I'm on my own, he *will not* be the example I follow." She discreetly touched his arm as they entered the room of the jovial Mr. Edwards.

Kassie pulled up MapQuest and put in Selway's address. His home was located in the exclusive Worthington Heights subdivision, approximately twelve miles from Kassie's apartment. After calling Brad, she showered. Jacki sat by the fireplace putting on nail polish.

After dressing, Kassie presented herself in the living room in a black evening dress that gracefully touched the floor. The sheer sleeves blended into the full coverage of her sequined top which was attached at the waist to several layers of black flowing crepe. Her earrings were the only other adornment she wore. With her long blond hair piled in ringlets on her head and her red lipstick, she was an image she hoped would stay with Brad a long time.

"Wow! *Look at you*! When did you buy that dress?" It was Jacki, waving her hands in the air to dry her nails.

"When you weren't looking!" Kassie laughed.

"Puts my dress to shame! You know, the old red flame, with the see through back. Guess I'll have to go shopping."

"You always look beautiful in anything you wear. Me! Well, I try."

"You! My roommate! You did alright by yourself. Gosh, you look gorgeous! Ouch! That pains me to say that, you know."

"Don't overdo it. You'll hurt yourself! *But!* I'm glad you like it."

At exactly six thirty there was a knock at the door.

"Kass, stand over by the fireplace. Hurry! I'll get the door!" Kassie did as she was told, thinking Jacki was too theatrical in her dealings with men. "Brad. Come on in. Let me have your coat."

"We ought to get going. I don't want to be late." Late was a word Brad didn't acknowledge existed!

"Oh, of course not. Harriman is picking me up in fifteen minutes. Come in."

As Brad rounded the corner coming out of the kitchen, he saw Kassie. If ever a man was shocked by what he saw, it was Brad Phillips.

"Hi." Barely audible, Kassie started to walk toward him. Brad just stood silent, not moving, not thinking, and not believing the beautiful creature approaching him. Illusions are dangerous; they lie. But the woman who stood in front of him, reaching up, touching his face with her soft hands and giving him a whisper of a kiss was no illusion. For Brad, reality was the stabilizing factor that drove him, keeping him grounded. For a moment he hesitated even touching her waist with his hands for fear she might break. It was a moment etched in his mind forever. In addition to being the woman that he admired for the virtues he'd already witnessed, Kassie was real, despite resembling a fragile doll. In every way, she was the reality Brad wanted in his life more than anything else he had ever desired.

"You..are...beautiful." Softly spoken, as only Brad, this virile, tall, black Irishman could say it. He couldn't bring himself to move.

"Shall we go." Kassie took his hand and moved toward the door. Jacki stood by the fireplace and heaved a sigh of satisfaction. If only, she thought, if only she could meet a man the likes of Brad Phillips who looked at her the way Brad looked at Kassie. Someday. If only.

Dr. Selway's house was an old Tudor style brick and window layout, with a three car garage. A two-story, the floors were polished wood, old and worn, with fourteen foot ceilings and a spiral wood staircase that would rival the most elaborate since Scarlett O'Hara strutted on hers. The area rugs were magnificent in style and color with shades of red being the predominant hue. It crossed Kassie's mind that as a surgeon, Dr. Selway had done quite well for himself. She couldn't help but wonder why he had such a huge elaborate home and lived by himself.

Ironically, Brad was thinking the same thing. Instead of all this luxury, he could've bought a smaller house and invested some of his money in much needed philanthropic measures. Somehow, Brad didn't think Dr. Selway thought about such things.

Being offered a glass of wine, Brad and Kassie walked over to the grand piano, covered with photographs perfectly placed on the closed lid. She could see Dr. Selway pictured in a couple, usually with a signature on each; people she didn't recognize but knew they must've meant something to the surgeon. One photo looked like it may well have been a family photo taken in the fully manicured backyard of some home. As she looked at it, she wondered if Dr. Selway's wife had been one in the group.

"There you are! I was waiting for you and Jacki to get here. I would like the two of you to sit beside me as we eat." Dr. Selway put his arm around Kassie's waist and moved her toward the dining room. Brad bristled at the movement. Jacki and Dr. Harriman saw the gesture also. Whatever relaxation there was planned for this dinner party, it evaporated when the tension in the room became thick as molasses.

The dinner guests numbered twenty-one, with Dr. Selway being the only attendee without a date. Most were physicians and their wives and all seemed to be extremely pleasant. With Jacki on one side and Kassie on the other, Dr. Selway was thoroughly enjoying himself.

"How late do want to stay?" Brad asked Kassie. Dinner was over; they were on their second glass of wine.

"Whenever you say. I'm not at all comfortable being here and without you, I'd be miserable."

"Okay." Brad walked casually over to Dr. Selway as Kassie stood by the piano. "I want to thank you for the wonderful dinner. It was a pleasure sharing an evening with all our cohorts in such a comfortable setting. Thank you again."

"Are you leaving? Surely not! Perhaps I can get you another drink. Josh? Would you get Dr. Phillips another glass of wine. Chardonnay, is it?"

"No, please. We must be going." Brad turned his head, nodding negatively at Josh, the young man that waited on them at dinner. Barely perceptible, Josh nodded, affirmatively. As Brad turned to leave, he saw Kassie holding a photo that she found at the piano. Coming up behind her, he spoke quietly.

"I'll walk with you when you pay your respects to the host…if you wish." Brad was concerned. Not about Kassie but about what Dr. Selway would do next. Kassie replaced the photo and turned to Brad, smiling.

"Thank you but that won't be necessary." She walked up to Dr. Selway, put out her hand and said, "Thank you for the wonderful dinner. I enjoyed it." As she turned to leave, he grabbed her by the waist and tried to kiss her. Her hand found the surface of his face in such a way that it stung her fingers and surprised him. The look he gave her was one of contempt. But Kassie was ready. Looking him in the eye, she said, sweetly, softly,

"You may admire the merchandise, but never assume you can touch it!"

The guests who saw the somewhat violent action on Kassie's part acted as though they never saw a thing, which for Kassie was just the way it should have been. She decided, should it happen again, she'd have to slap him with more force.

Retrieving their coats, Josh showed them to the door. After getting Kassie settled in his old pickup, and before he started the engine, he looked at the woman seated to his right. Kassie was no pushover. Brad now understood that if a problem arose that would cause either one of them any embarrassment or distress, his 'lady' would know how to handle it in her own unique way. The strength of character she possessed, he thought, was delightful, deliberate and extraordinary.

"That was some put down. Brilliant! Did you hurt your hand?"

"Of course not!"

"Come here." And with that, he kissed her passionately.

"Everyone left soon after you did. I'll bet his guests were gone before nine! What a chunk of human debris! I can't believe it was the same man I'd been dating! Oh, did I see the light!"

"Jacki. If he wouldn't have tried to…touch me, I would probably still think he was an okay date. But Jacki, you can do so much better. Don't settle for a man with roving eyes and fingers. You know very well, if he does it once in front of you, he's done it before with someone else and he'll do it again."

Before they retired to their individual bedrooms for the night, there was one more thing that Kassie wanted to add. "You know. My mother taught me a lot about men. The one thing that sticks in my mind above others is this; I can hear her saying it even today. 'Once a married man has strayed, his mind and heart have already been compromised.' Perhaps I'm assuming too much, and yes, I know he's divorced. I'm sure it's true for women as well although the driving force behind them may be different."

"I know. I know. Perhaps having a date with Dr. Harriman wasn't such a bad idea after all. I mean, he's not handsome or tall or extraordinary in any way, but even he was shocked to see Selway act like he did. He treated me to a soda after we left. It was kinda sweet, actually."

Kassie smiled. She wanted Jacki to find someone worthy of her as a woman, someone to love and care for her, respect her for who and what she was, instead of being treated as an ornament or house pet. Perhaps with time, Kassie thought, Jacki would realize there was more value in waiting for the right man to find her than in trying out the latest and best when it came to suitors. Kassie could only hope.

# 20

"After my oral exam next Thursday, I'm taking off a few days. Mother's been working with Vanity. Besides, I feel the urge to ride."

"Does Brad know yet?"

"As a matter of fact, he does. He's all for it. He thinks I need a vacation. *I think he needs one*; he's always got his nose in a book. Plus, he's short on money."

"What did Brad do for a living before he went to med school?" Jacki was curious but until Kassie had brought up his finances, she'd never thought to ask.

"Different things. He got some money upon the death of a relative and…as he said, he sold all his worldly goods. He'll still have a big debt when he finally leaves Mercy. Which brings up another point. He's said he got a nice offer from both John Hopkins and M. D. Anderson. I get the feeling he hasn't got his mind set on either. Regardless of what I think, he'll be the one to make the decision, although, M. D. Anderson is *so* on the cutting edge of technology. Houston might be a nice place to live."

"It's hot! It's humid! It's sticky! Ugh! You sure won't need moisturizing cream in Houston! It's worse than Florida, and Florida without a breeze is ghastly!"

"Well, I'm not concerned about it. The most important thing to me is that Brad is comfortable and happy wherever he decides to practice. I remember my mother telling me that there are three things you never take away from your man: his faith, his work and his hunting privileges."

"Brad hunts?"

"I don't think he would know one end of a rifle from the other. Like my father and Jake taught me, he could teach Brad in a hot Houston minute. Which reminds me! I'll have to ask if mother filled out the paperwork for me so I can acquire an out of state hunting license. Might be fun to take Brad deer hunting."

"Good luck with that one." Jacki put her magazine on the table and meandered to the kitchen. "Let's have pizza tonight. We've got a couple in the refrigerator. I'll fix'm. Won't take long." Kassie kept knitting. Besides painting, her mother had interested her in knitting while she was young. She had started with simple things such as scarves; she was now starting a sweater.

After pizza was done, she decided to take a last look at her studies before retiring to bed. Her cell phone surprised her.

"Hello."

"Hi, love. It's Brad. I'm already missing you and it's not even next week. What were the days you were going to be gone?"

"Hi. Oh, you won't miss me. You'll be too busy. I wish you could come with me."

"Soon, very soon. You can teach me how to ride those horses you talk about and love so much. Hey, would you like to go out for a chocolate, somewhere cozy, like the Sugarloaf Café?" Kassie had to laugh.

"It's less expensive at my house! But sure."

"I'm so glad you asked. I'll be right over. Jacki home?"

"She is right now but she's going out with Dr. Harriman in a little bit. I'll put the water on. See ya."

"Sounds good."

# 21

On the plane, Kassie relaxed. She wondered how they graded on orals because after the staff complimented her, she was informed her schedule in OR would begin when she returned from Wyoming, which was considerably earlier than June. The duties would be posted when she returned to work.

Sleeping was not an option; she was too excited about her new upcoming responsibilities. She could hardly wait to tell her parents in person about her new role. The confidence she had in herself would tell them everything they wanted to know.

Arriving in the afternoon, she looked forward to having an early evening horseback ride. Anxious to see Vanity, she wasted no time in going to the barns. Jake, one of her father's wranglers, saw her entering the stable.

"Hey! You're back. How's our 'angel' doin'?"

"Angel, eh? My goodness, Jake, good to see you again, too. You have a saddle handy I can use?"

"You bet! Yours in fact. Here, I'll help ya." While Jake grabbed the saddle, Kassie walked to Vanity's stall. As she led him into the galley, he pranced as though he was walking on hot coals, his tail in a high arc and his head tucked in front of his muscular arched neck.

He was a sight to behold. A fine specimen of an Arabian stallion, Kassie thought.

"Mother said he rides like a rocking chair. Have you ridden him yet?"

"Yup…and yup! He's a real beauty! Good temperament, too. Doesn't get overly excited about anything. A word of warning though; he responds quickly. Best be prepared." Kassie nodded she understood.

Vanity comprehended every word she said. He loved the caresses that Kassie lavished on him, rubbing his head, scratching behind his ears and telling him she loved him from the first time she laid eyes on him. She asked him not to be too frisky their first time out; after they knew each other a bit more, they'd be more comfortable with each other. She also told Vanity that, although he was one of God's magnificent creatures, he could never replace Spinster. They both seemed to understand the bonding that would transpire with their first ride together must be captured and held during the long absences when she wasn't around. Somehow, Vanity heard and understood it all.

Kassie took him slowly at first into the foothills, around boulders, into ravines and across dry beds. A rabbit scampered ahead of him; Vanity responded with a nod of his head and a snort. She took him higher and higher, until they reached the pinnacle of the overlook she and Spinster had visited so many times. Together, it seemed they could not only oversee the ranch but the whole world from their perch.

Kassie dismounted, and walked to a small ledge where she sat down. The snow was beginning to melt; the sun felt warm on her face. The movement in the short grass caught her attention before she heard the rattle. Rattlers on the ranch were not commonly seen but everyone on the ranch knew of their precarious existence. Vanity reacted faster than she did. Letting go of the reins, she started to stand up. Vanity reared once, then twice, coming down on the snake with an executionary blow. Acting as though he had done what was expected of him, Vanity stood still, snorting once or twice. The look in his eyes said it all. 'I'm ready to go when you're ready.' He didn't move until Kassie was safely in the saddle. Neck reigning informed him which way to go.

The following day she asked Jake if he and the other hands had applied for hunting licenses for the coming fall.

"We did. All of us. There's a lot of deer and antelope runnin' in the ravines this spring. Your father applied too. How about you?"

"I may have to resort to buying it over-the-counter, if there's any available. I'm not sure what the price is for an out-of-state hunter."

"There always is!" Jake was the wrangler that had taught Kassie how to handle a firearm. After she knew how to hit a target of pop cans and apples, her father taught her the finer points of handling a pistol and the immense responsibility that accompanied such an art. She learned quickly how to gage distances, how to adjust to a moving target and how to compensate for weather conditions.

Although grounded in her strong and fundamental Christian beliefs, her quiet and reserved disposition never suggested to anyone outside of her family and the wranglers at the ranch her engaging love affair with firearms. Her respect for such a weapon was monumental. As a result, she had learned to be extremely accurate, efficient and prudent with the knowledge in which she had been entrusted.

"Well. Sounds like you'll be coming back to the ranch more often. That's a good thing, Kassie. We've missed ya'."

"Yep! I've missed the ranch, too."

"Your parents will be glad to hear that!"

The following two days, she spent much of her time with Vanity. On Sunday morning, after church, she asked an old high school classmate if she'd like to come over and ride him. Kassie was informed her classmate was four months pregnant with her third child. Riding

Vanity was not a good idea at the moment. It also reminded Kassie she wasn't getting any younger.

Late Sunday afternoon, her father took her to the airport to catch the plane back to Denver. She had missed Brad; now she would miss Vanity. Soon, she hoped Brad could spend time with her on the ranch, to explore with her the features that she loved about the outdoors, about her parents and about riding horseback in the backcountry. She could only pray he would come to love it as much she did.

# 22

"Commander. You wanted to see me."

Standing behind his desk, he was an imposing figure. Lean, tall and tan, his demeanor would've never indicated that SEAL Team 4 was originally under his command. To the last member in every SEAL Team unit, everyone knew who he was. Affable when he wanted to be, demanding when it was necessary and poignant when it was called for, he had the respect of those men who had trained and worked with him in the SEAL arena.

"Yes. Grab a chair." As he sat down behind a clear and uncluttered desk, he smiled. "I guess trying to talk you out of retiring from the Navy fell on deaf ears." The one sheet of paper that graced his desk was being handed over to the visitor. "Going to med school has become a priority for you. From you I would expect no less."

"Thank you, Sir."

The commander sat back in his chair, relaxed. "You know that there have been a couple changes...modifications...to your retirement? Relax. Between you and me, this is off the record."

"What do you have in mind, Sir?"

Thinking...the commander chose his words deliberately. The man sitting in front of him was exceptional, not just as a Navy SEAL, but as a human being. A man of integrity and moral astuteness, one who cared about his demeanor as well as his soul, he was chosen by the commander for what amounted to a special circumstance.

"As you know, this will be a *different* kind of assignment, one that will take place in the private sector of your life in your retirement but it will also help you financially to reach your goal of becoming a surgeon." He paused, rolling the pen with his hand on the desk. "Interested?"

How could he not be interested? The commander had stated that the assignment would benefit him financially. Evidently going to med school wouldn't interfere with whatever he'd be asked to do. Questions came to mind that needed to be answered. But first.....

"Do I have a choice...off the record, of course?"

"Choices always exist when you're retired military. But you're a Navy Seal. So I would have to say no."

"Perhaps you could start from the beginning, namely, what the assignment entails. If I have any questions after you finish....."

"Let's hope you don't. First of all you will be paid monthly. A stipend but worth your while. Your background and training has prepared you with the discipline you'll need to complete this mission. The bottom line: a SEAL is missing!"

# 23

From what Kassie could glean from Jacki, Dr. Howard Harriman had become quite the gentleman. Although he was just another surgeon on staff at Mercy, he was noticed by the physician's and nursing staff's as being pleasant to work with, patient and friendly, rather reticent but always prompt. Jacki would see him at lunch or, if she was lucky, once her shift was over. When they would date, it was always a movie or dinner at a reasonably priced restaurant. They took in a couple local plays and had attended a Broncos football game or two.

He and Jacki were the same age. Neither had been married; so much of their conversation dealt with the past experiences each had had before they met. Jacki, having traveled the world, appeared to be more interesting to Dr. Harriman than Dr. Harriman's schooling and work was to Jacki.

Dr. Howard Harriman was the second of eight children, with parents who were alcoholics. Both were teachers in public schools, where the compensation to both was adequate due to their accumulated tenure. The Harriman's oldest child married at eighteen and had no desire to get more schooling. Since Howard wanted to go into medicine, it was assumed once he got his education, he would repay his parents by helping his siblings get their education. With the meager financial help that his parents could give him, with their monies being divided between their families' needs, alcohol and Howard, it wasn't enough by any means to escape from borrowing monies to see him through school, internship and residency. At thirty-five, Dr. Harriman had a bucket load of debt to repay. According to Jacki, his budget was sorely lacking when it came to extras.

However, it appeared to Kassie, Dr. Harriman treated Jacki as a lady should be treated and if for no other reason, she respected him for the pleasure. She also reckoned if by some small chance they were to get married, their future looked brighter together than his present situation, alone.

When Jacki came home the evening Kassie returned from another short trip to Wyoming and announced that she and 'Howie' were engaged, it prompted Kassie to make a statement.

"He gave you an engagement ring! Perhaps a cigar band?"

"Even better. It's plastic. Came in a cereal box!" They both laughed. "The truth is, we're engaged, without a ring. But it doesn't bother me."

"Bothers you?"

"Yaaaa. Like, what are they going to say at work?"

"Jacki. You of all people. Since when what people said at work ever bother you? I can't believe you even said that?" But Kassie knew what she meant. Everyone they knew at Mercy was aware of Jacki and her dream, of marrying the perfect man, if ever such a man existed. She had made it very clear the man she married would have to be exemplary in every way; included was his ability to secure a handsome income. Jacki was essentially saying by being engaged to Dr. Harriman, she had somehow lowered her standards and was afraid the staff may well point it out to her. Jacki didn't look at things as other folks did; everything was weighed against the background of her youth. Most of the people she worked around wouldn't take the time or effort to busy themselves with her lack of a ring!

Kassie didn't look at men in the same way Jacki did. She never had. Jacki was looking for someone to take care of her and all her 'wants.' Kassie wanted a friend, a companion to share her life with, to raise a family, to enjoy all the riches that came from a marriage based on faith. Jacki was raised to love the tangible things in life; although she had left the trappings of her childhood behind, it was still part of her DNA. Kassie was impressed by the intangible; faith, hope and love.

"Dr. Harriman, or 'Howie' as you put it, is a fine man as far as I can tell. Everything you've told me about him makes him ideally suited for a woman like you; boisterous, vivacious, extraverted......"

"Okay, already. So I'll have to eat craw for a while. At this point, I'm happy Dr. Harriman knows he loves me."

"And...."

"I think in time I may love him, too."

"And..."

"He doesn't drink...much...anymore...and he doesn't do drugs!"

Kassie didn't know how to respond to Jacki's statement. She wondered if Jacki even knew what love entailed. She wished there was a formula she could point to that would enable Jacki to see beyond the physical, beyond the surface qualities of a human being. She could hope before Jacki married anyone, she would look deep enough to find the spiritual realm of his personality; in what did he believe? Did he live by faith? Did he love his work? Did he know the true meaning of *love*? Would he put his wife first...or second, only to God? The answers to these questions were immensely important to Kassie. What people had to say about any relationships carried on by others had no relevance in her life. At least, that's what she thought! It was just gossip anyway.

"I'm happy for you, Jacki. Relax and enjoy your time together. If it is meant to be, it will be." She started for her bedroom. "While I was at home, mother and I went through some recent photos. It was fun." Instead of continuing into her bedroom, she returned to the living room and curled up on the couch. "Mother made so many scrapbooks for me. I never realized how many photos she'd taken or that I had won so many ribbons. She put them all together. She did an impressive job."

"Did you bring any back with you?" Jacki was sitting in the chair by the fireplace.

"No. I didn't." Kassie started to fiddle with her hair, making ringlets that wouldn't stay in place. "You know, Selway sure had a lot of photos on his piano. Did you see them?"

"Sorry, dear. I was busy watching 'sleezy Selway' bother the ladies. There wasn't a woman there he didn't...."

"I wonder if he's a photographer of sorts or if he just has a lot of family photos. There sure were a bunch of them. A lot of older people. Some were taken in someone's beautiful back yard as far as I could tell. They were interesting, to say the least."

"Did you hear anything I said before you interrupted me? Why are you obsessing over some photos you saw at Selway's house?"

"I'm not obsessing, Jacki. It's just that....he doesn't strike me as the kind of guy who would take a lot of photos, or have all those photos placed on his piano." Kassie couldn't explain it but she had a feeling it just wasn't normal. Not for a guy like 'sleezy Selway,' as Jacki so eloquently put it. Again, Kassie got up and started toward her bedroom. "I'm glad mother saved all those old memories. Good night, Jacki. I'll have a clearer head tomorrow."

# 24

Working beside Selway, Harriman and Brad Phillips in surgery was a dream Kassie learned to appreciate. Donned in their blues, face masks, gloves and whatever paraphernalia they deemed necessary to wear and at the pace at which things happened in surgery, it was a waste of time to speculate how her day would unfold in the pressure cooker of any given surgical suite.

Each surgeon, Kassie learned, had their own way of accepting the tools of their trade when at the operating table. A scalpel, for instance. Dr. Harriman wanted the handle *slapped* in his hand, the blade facing to his right. Dr. Phillips wanted it *placed* in his hand, allowing the pressure of the handle to be maneuvered as he saw fit. Dr. Selway expected his surgical nurse to *anticipate his need* for a scalpel or any other surgical instrument he may need. Demanding a lot of his attending nurse was a given. The perfection he required, however, was not always met.

Lately, some of the nursing staff in the surgical suites disliked the 'modis operandi' of Dr. Selway. When procedures didn't go smoothly for him, he became short-tempered. He expected the nurses to read his mind! He was the surgeon, not them! Nervous anticipation ran high when Selway was scheduled in surgery.

Needless to say, each surgeon had their favorite nurse with whom they liked to work. Perhaps it was familiarity with each other that put them at ease. Certainly, each surgeon could expect a certain degree of professionalism and expertise from his attending nurse. The main reason, though, was if a surgeon became upset about what he could do or couldn't do for the survival of a patient on the table, he absolutely needed to know that he could unload his frustration on his attending nurse, without her crying or reporting him to their superiors. It was an unwritten pact which existed between them. Hear no evil, see no evil, repeat no evil.

Surgery was not always a cure for the amount of different and difficult maladies accompanying the patient. In addition, surgeons were given the courtesy of opportunity to say no to a procedure they didn't think would benefit the longevity or quality of life for a patient. However, since surgery was their livelihood, after consulting with the medical physician in charge of each case, surgeries were accomplished sooner rather than later, especially when a patient requested it. Hysterectomies were a good example. What bothered the surgeon more than the patient was in spite of the willingness of the patient to have the procedure performed, there was always the possibility of unseen surgical complications.

It was no surprise to anyone that malpractice insurance premiums were extremely costly for any physician or surgeon. Patients could sue for damages over a sponge being left in the abdomen as well as a bruise left in the cleft of an arm from a needle insertion that left a permanent mark. People were unpredictable; it was the unknown factors that surgeons dealt with everyday. As a result, baldness was rampant among the male surgical species.

Brad and Kassie had discussed the likelihood of working together before she got to surgery. Between them they decided professionally it was wiser not to team up with each other. However, there are always exceptions. The day Brad's attendant nurse called in ill she agreed to step in to help. As a team, it went well. Both of them appreciated the other's abilities.

Everyone in the surgical unit was ready when the patient was rolled in and placed on the cold steel table in the center of the suite. The patient, a woman about sixty, with gray hair and blue eyes, looked terrified. Kassie read the stats on the chart and found she was scheduled for a cyst removal on her left leg. Replacing the chart and checking to see that a black X had been put on her left leg, on the area of the existing cyst, she saw Brad enter the unit.

"How are you feeling, Mrs. Bradley? Have you had surgery before?" Kassie reached for her wrist and checked the arm band. "You are Mrs. Hazel Bradley?"

"No. Yes. I mean, I mean I'm Hazel Bradley. I don't know what to expect." Kassie could see the tension in the eyes of Mrs. Bradley as she lay, stiff and unmoving, waiting to see what transpired next.

"Mrs. Bradley. Are you allergic to any medication?" It was Brad asking as he approached the table.

"Just sulfa," she answered. The nurse standing to his right nodded that Mrs. Bradley had responded correctly.

"Mrs. Bradley. We're going to remove the cyst from your left leg today so you can walk better, without pain. Would you like that?" Kassie didn't wait for an answer. She lifted the sheet covering Mrs. Bradley's left leg and looking at Brad, pointed to the spot marked with an X. "Mrs. Bradley, the man above your head is going to place a mask on your face that will deliver oxygen to you while you're sleeping. Just breath normally; it may be cold at first."

The anesthesiologist prepared the predetermined amount of Sodium Pentothal and allowed it to flow into the IV line already placed in Mrs. Bradley's right arm. "Starting with ten, I want you to count backwards out loud for me. Will you do that for me? You can start now." Kassie smiled at her patient.

"Ten.....nine.....eight............." Mrs. Bradley was silent. Kassie looked at her face again and found it a bit disturbing. From somewhere in the past, Kassie remembered the lady at the airport. The resemblance between the two women was uncanny. Of course, it wasn't her! But they looked so much *alike*!

During the whole procedure, she handed the instruments to Brad, as if she was on auto-pilot, never missing his hand, always handing him the instrument he had requested. But on her mind was the lady at the airport. She wondered if she would ever see her again.

# 25

In Colorado, if you waited long enough, you could see snow falling in the morning, windy and cold, and by noon, the sun would be peeking out from behind the clouds. By evening, the temperature would be above freezing and the snow, melted. Not so in the mountains. In fact, it was said if there was still snow in the crevasse on the east side of Mt. Meeker on the Fourth of July, there would be enough water for the farmers on the Front Range for the whole year.

Skiing was definitely more than a hobby; it was a lifelong pursuit for those who enjoyed it. The same went for hunting, fishing, backpacking and every other outdoor sport you could name. And of course, Denver was home to the Denver Broncos, the Avalanche, the Rockies, the Nuggets and the Rapids. If ever there was a sports town, Denver had to be it.

Colorado also had its own sand dunes, along with the Black Canyon, Ouray Canyon and Grand Canyon, to name a few. In addition, it was one of four states where one of their corners converged: Colorado, Arizona, New Mexico and Utah. It wasn't the cheapest place to live but it was by far, the most diversified. It was also home to the Air Force Academy and the Wilson Shooting Range.

The Wilson Shooting Range was located in the sand hills northeast of Denver some seventeen miles from DIA. Denver was steadily growing but housing developments had yet to encircle Mercy. When Denver International Airport was built, it appeared to sit in the middle of a desert, miles and miles away from mankind. At present, the drive to DIA included housing and businesses that were an ever reaching extension of the city. Occasionally, while Brad was working, Kassie took the shuttle bus out to the range. It was there that she practiced shooting her .38 semi-automatic.

When she graduated from High school, it was her choice to go into law enforcement. Her gentle but persuasive father convinced her she should wait a year or two and then decide. He knew she was an excellent shot with a rifle, and even better at plinking with a handgun. Following all the rules she had been taught, it was her quiet, reserved and unrivaled patience her father knew would serve her well in whatever she attempted to accomplish. But law enforcement? Her parents weren't keen on the idea. Kassie never mentioned joining the Navy and, in several ways her father couldn't bring himself to voice, he was glad. He wanted the best for his only child. She was young; she had the rest of her life to decide.

While in Wyoming she always took time to target practice, most of the time accompanied by Jake. Sometimes her father would ride along and watch. Until they got into the foothills where backdrops were more prevalent, they enjoyed the ride.

The Wilson range was marked in 50, 100 and 500 yard increments with paper targets at which to aim. After spending an hour plinking and retrieving a box full of empty cartridges, she decided she'd had enough. Her accuracy was proficient; the feel of the handgun in her hand, comfortable. Aside from anything else she considered a hobby, target practice with a revolver or rifle was the most challenging… and satisfying. More so than knitting but not as relaxing as painting!

Catching the shuttle bus, she stopped at the shopping mall within blocks of her apartment. Better to do some window shopping before she went back to the apartment in case Jacki asked what she'd done all day. At least she wouldn't have to lie!

No one outside of her immediate family was aware Kassie knew how to shoot much less owned a .38 revolver. Of all the time she had spent working and living with Jacki, Jacki never became aware of her part time diversion. Brad didn't know either. As far as Kassie was concerned, it would remain confidential. For the present.

# 26

Kassie was sitting by the fireplace, knitting, when Jacki returned to their apartment after work. Dinner in the form of a hot casserole was waiting for her. Jacki looked worse than yesterday's dirty laundry. Kassie waited until she had changed clothes, filled her plate and had made herself comfortable on the couch.

"Anything new and interesting?" asked Kassie.

"Not really. Howie did mention he didn't appreciate how Selway conducted himself with the staff. And no, I'm not sure what happened that it came up." Jacki seemed content to just sit and eat.

"You know, today I remembered some of the crazy stuff that happened when we were flying. Funny how those memories pop up and come flooding back when you least expect them. Like the exasperating time we had getting the worms away from the little boy who was sure they would die if he packed them in his suitcase." Kassie laughed lightheartedly. "I'll never hear another shriek from a woman...ever... like the lady sitting next to him! Oh, well." She paused to remember. "Or the lady who carried a satchel full of snowballs, taking them to her grandson in Fort Worth. 'He's never seen snow!' Water dripping everywhere coming out of the overhead bin. *What a mess!*" Kassie couldn't help herself; laughing out loud was good for the soul. "We had some good times. Oh, how we used to complain; the passengers, the food, the grind, the sleepless nights. Did you ever think that some of our complaints would be the same in nursing?"

"It pays better!" Jacki was always conscious of the bottom line.

"Hey. Remember the trouble we had with the couple who had first class seats and some elderly gentleman and his grandson had taken their seats? Wow! Wonder if we'll ever find the wrong patient in a bed that belongs to someone else. Stranger things have happened."

"That was the same flight that I gave the first of my many little departing speeches before disembarking at the gate. Remember?"

"I'll never forget it! I thought we'd all get fired."

Jacki remembered as though she had voiced it that morning. "Ladies and Gentleman, passengers of Premier Airlines, flight 313, out of New York, New York. We're so glad you chose to fly Premier instead of World Aero Wide Airlines. Their acronym of WAWA doesn't appeal to us either. It was a bumpy ride for which we apologize. However, the wings remained intact and the commodes didn't back up. Several passengers found it difficult to keep their food down so please don't slip and fall on the slobber. Premier is a relatively new airline and as flight attendants, we work only three days a week. Due to Obamacare, insurance is extremely expensive so please don't hurt yourself on the way out. We apologize for our meals not filling you up or putting you to sleep but at least our linens were clean! As you enter the terminal there will be no one to help you with your questions or to take your complaints; all airlines are cutting back on personnel. We apologize for that. However, we're just as glad to be on the ground as you are. We've enjoyed having you along for the ride; you're our job security. Be sure to collect your entire luggage; what you leave behind is ours. From all of us at Premier Airlines to all of you, be careful out there and feel free to fly with us again. Very soon.

Good night." Laughter between the two women always came easily. "I wonder if they miss us!"

Even though the TV was on neither of them watched the screen. Jacki all but fell asleep and Kassie was working on making a hat for a chemo patient who was as bald as a baby's behind, without diaper rash. Following the knitting directions on the first one she made, the following ones would take less time.

In having Jacki recall her parting comments, Kassie remembered the couple who had such a difficult time with the fact that someone had taken *their* seats. Kassie felt that the solution would be rather simple since seat assignments could be rearranged.

"May I see your boarding passes, please?" The gentleman fished them out of his pocket, handed them to Kassie and proceeded to scowl. Glancing at the gentleman's tickets Kassie turned to the grandfather and his grandson, who was about 10 and said, "Your seat numbers are in coach; this is first class. I'm so sorry for the mix-up. If you'll follow me, I'll show you to your assigned seats." To the couple standing in the aisle holding up the boarding of passengers, she said, "Please be seated." Turning again to the grandfather, she continued. "I apologize for your inconvenience. Your seat numbers in coach correspond to the same seat numbers in first class. It was just an oversight." Before returning the boarding passes to the gentleman who was genuinely disgusted at being the center of attention, she saw that their destination was Zurich. That's all she noticed for at that moment, the passenger reached out and grabbed the passes, sticking them into his satchel. "I apologize for this interruption. Please, make yourselves comfortable. Now," as she turned to the boy and smiled, "please follow me."

As she put away her knitting, she wondered why that particular moment in time came back to her in such clarity.

# 27

It wasn't an ordinary dream; one of happiness and joy. Filled with apprehension, she awoke bathed in perspiration. Her skimpy nightshirt was soaked. She reeked of 'sweat.' Her hair was wet and her head was pounding. She'd had headaches before but this was something else. She rolled over, swung her legs over the side of the bed and nearly collapsed. The pain in her temples was excruciating; her eyes felt like they were hemorrhaging. Each ear felt as though it was plugged with wax such that she wanted to pick it out with the head of a bobby pin. Someone had taken a bat to her head; she was sure of it.

She could barely read the clock and since the alarm hadn't gone off, she realized there was still time to call in sick. However, it was something she'd seldom done before. In all her years of working, sick days were an anomaly to her. She decided to take a couple Acetaminophens, lie back down and give herself ten minutes to see if the pain would subside. But twenty minutes later didn't make any difference. She called the hospital.

"It'll be okay, Kass. Only two surgeries today and they're covered. Selway and Phillips are doing the honors. Is there anything I can do for you, perhaps a chocolate latte or a cold beer? Knowing you, it's not from a hangover so go back to bed and we'll see you tomorrow. Love you." Cindy was a dear friend and a very accomplished OR nurse. Kassie was happy it was she who answered the phone.

She waited until the drumbeat in her temples subsided to a level where she could turn on the radio. Even the soft music of 101.1 FM was too loud. She felt the need for food and thought perhaps it would help but after eating a bowl of Krispies and raspberries, the headache was still present.

Pushing the bowl aside, she laid her head on the cool table. Closing her eyes just enhanced the pain; with no outside stimulation she had only the pain to deal with and it wasn't going away.

The maze of photographs presented themselves again. Hanging on the wall they were placed side by side. No color, just black and white. People's faces were screaming, threatening, sneering; they looked miserable. Every few seconds one photograph would appear to pop out at her, an enlargement she couldn't ignore. The music playing in the background was too loud. A woman's voice from somewhere behind her was trying to explain the meaning of having all these people come to life. Several of them jumped out of their photographs and began dancing. The scene changed to a swimming pool where a party was escalating. Noise was everywhere. Children were screaming, climbing all over the chairs, racing on the lawn.

When Kassie turned to look for an escape, all the photographs were bare. All the people had come to life. She became frantic and scared. There was no place she could hide. Apprehensive and alone, a lady came up to her, smiled and returned to the photograph. A lady, in her fifties, with unruly hair. She carried a cane.

Kassie woke up with a start and a yell. She was sweating; the table was wet where her face had been. Her head was boiling hot and her eyes couldn't focus. The few seconds she'd fallen asleep seemed like an eternity. The radio still playing was entirely too loud.

Going to the medicine cabinet, she 'borrowed' a Percocet from Jacki's stash and after swallowing it, prayed that whatever brought this headache would 'take a leave of absence' and let her head return to normal. Grabbing a washcloth and wetting it with cold water, she returned to bed. The coolness of the washcloth on her forehead didn't help but it didn't make her headache any worse. Within seconds she turned the cloth over and placed it over her eyes.

Kassie rarely had dreams that she could remember after a few minutes of being awake. And she'd never had the same dream twice. With that thought, she was glad that this dream was past.

She hated the idea of having an unexpected day off, spending it in bed, with a headache that came out of nowhere. There were things that she wanted to do on the days when she was free of her responsibilities at work; numerous things, such as painting, knitting, target practice, reading, and as of late, scrapbooking.

When she returned from visiting her parents she had invested in a small 8 X 8 album in which she wanted to place photos of Vanity, from when he was first born until now or until she ran out of pages. The paper and tape she bought would suffice for such a small scrapbook but while working on it, she began to wonder if she shouldn't have bought a larger album. After all, horses lived ten, twelve, even twenty years. For now, she would be satisfied just to make a scrapbook approaching the perfection as those her mother had made.

Now, if her head would return to normal! The Percocet worked its wonders. Eventually, Kassie fell asleep.

# 28

It promised to be a long spring, with some enduring snow on the ground. Her nasal passages were being overworked. Her allergies would last as long as there were the fragrances of blossoms in the air; a box of Kleenix was always present.

Both Kassie and Brad had spring fever. Kassie had been to Wyoming a couple extended weekends. Now, she wanted to have Brad come with her. Brad decided to stay on staff at Mercy until the end of the year. It was time for him to meet her parents.

"When did you sign up….?" asked Kassie.

"Actually, I didn't. But I discussed it with Guiterrez. He affirmed the crazies on the slopes were about over so whenever I wanted to take a break for a few days, I should let him know."

Dr. Juan Guiterrez was Brad's immediate supervisor. A skilled surgeon himself, he was a kind and generous man who saw his passion for surgery as a gift granted to him by God. He and his family were faithful and practicing Catholics and Brad always felt at ease working with him. Their respect for each other was enormous and satisfying to both.

"That was very nice of him. When do you want to take the time… what would you like to do?" While Kassie furiously blew her nose for the umpteenth time, Brad gave her a look knowing he already knew what Kassie wanted him to say. Despite all her wonderful attributes, Brad thought she was too serious at times. Even though he, too, was the serious type, Brad was also a type A personality. Give him something to be serious about and he would make a decision.

"Let's see. Why don't we take a train ride from Denver to Grand Junction? The beauty of the passes this time of year would allow us to see all those hiding places that were hidden when the trees were all filled out. Or…we could explore the Black Canyon. Of course, they don't run the train at the bottom anymore; we'd have to take a boat ride. I know! Let's go white water rafting! The water will be too high soon….."

"Brad! I'd rather go bungee jumping off the back side of Sports Authority Mile High Stadium! If I'm going to die, I want a crowd!" Brad sat there wondering, just for second, if she was serious. Nah! She couldn't be! He picked up the pillow that was lying between them, and playfully threw it at her. She ducked!

"I'd really like to go horseback riding, at the ranch, your parent's ranch, in Wyoming."

"Okay." Kassie was stunned but delighted and rather than push the subject, she let the statement hang in the air.

"Why, I thought you'd never ask!" Taking the time to move closer to Kassie, he couldn't think of a better time to give her the attention she deserved; to show the love he felt so deeply for her. "If it's okay with you, let's plan it for next week. I don't have any surgeries scheduled for Thursday and Friday and I'm not on call for the weekend that I'm aware of but I'll check with Guiterrez. How about you?"

"I'm not scheduled for next weekend. Maybe I could get Cindy to cover for me for a couple days. Rhonda always like overtime so maybe she'd work her off days for me, too. I'll check in the morning when I go in."

"Do you think your parents will mind such a short notice?"

"Are you kidding? They want to meet you as much as I want you to meet them." After a moment of thought, she continued. "You're the only friend I'll have taken home with me."

"The only one?" Brad smiled, mischieviously. "Only one?"

"Well, you know. The only one....."

"The only one......?"

"The only gentleman I've ever loved. Except my father."

"I like the sound of that. The only one I've loved. Kassie, I've never taken a girl home to my parents either. Loved or just liked. Does that surprise you?"

"No, Brad, it doesn't. Look how long it took you to love me?" If only Kassie could've seen his heart. Love wasn't something that came easy for Brad although he had experienced it before in very different circumstances with an entirely different objective. And someday, he would share it with her. But not now. It wasn't the right time.

With their plans solidified, the weekend couldn't come quick enough. Guiterrez was conducive to the whole idea and Cindy and Rhonda worked out their schedules, with the help from their supervisor, to allow Kassie the time off.

Selway was upset. Kassie had been scheduled to be his attending nurse for several surgeries during the time she would be off. Selway could be downright ugly when he didn't get his own way. After all, he was a surgeon and at least to his patients, didn't they consider him to be next to God? Of course, he wasn't the only one to feel that way. However, most surgeons knew they pulled their pants on one leg at a time just like every other man. Except for their schooling and training they could've been doing the work of any individual far away from the surgical suite; that is, if they were properly schooled and trained in a particular field of endeavor.

Dr. Selway thought he was special thereby making him one obnoxious and belligerent human being to be around. He considered himself above everyone *common* thereby distancing himself from all but his closest associates. He wasn't aware of the trait in himself; it was just easier to find fault with everyone else.

# 29

Turning onto the gravel portion of the road that led to the ranch, Kassie asked, "Are you as nervous as I am?"

"Nah. They're gonna love me." He laughed. "Are you?"

"Kinda. As much as I dislike admitting it, I know they're gonna' love you as I do! I hope you and my father have something to talk about. He's been a Seal and you've….well, you've been in school. I don't know what surgeons and Seals or ranchers have in common but men….they've always got things they can discuss."

"Don't you worry about it? Your father and I will get along just fine. I've been waiting a long time to meet them. It'll help me figure out what makes you tick!"

"Brad Phillips! If you don't know by now….."

"I think I do. Relax."

"Are you going to ride with me in the morning?"

"Will I have a choice?"

"Nope!"

"Thought so."

They rode horseback the next morning and the next. Brad considered it a privilege to be welcomed so openly by Kassie's parents.

Even though Mark Colbert was a reticent gentleman, talking with Brad came very natural to him. At the dinner table, in the evening by the fireplace, at breakfast at 6 AM in the morning, pitching manure or feeding the cattle, the two men appeared to be inseparable during Brad's visit. Since Brad was sleeping in the living room on a hide-a-bed, he was aware when Mark was ready to work in the morning; Brad was a willing accomplice.

"Your father really likes Brad. I do too. You know, I thought your father was the most handsome man I'd ever met but I have to admit that Brad is a handsome gentleman. Offered to help me put dishes in the dishwasher last night! That doesn't really surprise me, though. I'd always wanted you to find someone that fit in the family, you know, that we could learn to love as much as we love you, the kind of man your father is….."

"Mother, you're rambling!"

"Am I? I hadn't noticed."

Kassie watched Mark and Brad straddle the corral fence, watching Vanity prance around. She was elated that the two of them enjoyed each other's company. She was almost positive anything her father had to say about the ranch would enlighten Brad considerably. Better to learn from her father than from her.

"I know you've waited a long time to find Mr. Right. Do you think Brad is that someone? Does he believe…is he a Christian?"

"He has this overpowering amount of faith, more than I ever expected. It's almost as though….."

"Perhaps he has been tried in situations he has yet to share with you. You've been patient this long. What does a little longer hurt? You said he hasn't been married! Know anything about his past that upsets you?"

"No, not really. Monetarily, he's had to struggle making ends meet in getting to this point in his career but he never really talks about it.

And…he rarely mentions his parents. That's another reason why I'm glad to see him get along with father."

"Well," Laurie said, as she hugged Kassie, "I think you've made a wise choice. I'm glad you brought him home."

In addition to spending time together, sitting on the upper rail of the corral fence, the two men talked and walked.…and fed the cattle and talked…while Kassie and her mother prepared the meals. Between music playing on the radio and bringing up Brad's parents, Kassie's mind moved to a totally different subject.

"Mother. Have you ever had dreams that seem so real they scare you after you wake up? I mean, like, do they ever come true?"

"I don't dream that often. Plus, I never remember them later. In fact, I can't remember the last time I dreamt about anything. Don't tell me you're having dreams about work!"

"It's never about work. It's about photographs, a lot of them. They pop out at me as though they want my attention. They're usually family photos of people I know nothing about. It's scary! I must've had at least a dozen by now." Kassie doubted there were that many; the fierceness of their existence earned the enhancement of the occasions.

"They never vary! Are they of different people?" Laurie was interested.

"There's this one that's always present. Funny thing, I think I may have seen it before. I thought I'd look through some of the scrapbooks again and see if I can find it. The background is full of trees so it must've been taken somewhere other than here on the ranch."

"Kassie, we've a lot of trees! Or haven't you noticed?"

"I know. But these were different. I don't know how to explain it but I wish I'd get a good look at the photo before it disappears in my dream."

"Maybe it'll come to you when you least expect it. Like good fortune! Or an answer to a prayer! They always come right on time."

Kassie believed her mother because her mother was a believer in all things good. Rarely did she voice a complaint. If Laurie did say something off color, she always couched it with a giggle or laugh. It wasn't part of her nature to find fault.

After dinner, and the table cleared of dishes, the four of them sat watching television, each serenely tucked in their own reverie.

# 30

The two of them were driving to town, not so much to get the supplies that Laurie wanted as to be able to talk to one another. Brad had a secret from Kassie that he wanted to share with Mark; Brad instinctively knew Mark would be the only one to understand.

"Mark, there's something I need to tell you," said Brad. Mark was silent as Brad shifted on his seat. "I've been a US Navy SEAL as well." Brad didn't know exactly what to expect; he couldn't believe he'd just uttered the words. Mark was silent for what seemed an indeterminate amount of time. When he spoke, his words weighed heavily.

"Once a Navy SEAL, always a Navy SEAL. It's a mindset that you have; it can't be erased. Take it from one who knows. Kassie must've told you that I was a SEAL also?"

"Yes, she did. For which I'm grateful. Since I separated from the Navy, I've not discussed my career with anyone. It's been difficult at times. Remembering." They both fell silent. *"Kassie doesn't know."* It was barely a whisper. As difficult as it was to discuss his career as a SEAL…even Brad didn't understand exactly why he had chosen to never discuss his days with his SEAL Team. But for the present he preferred that Kassie not know. "It's just that I have been given so much…to serve my country was a privilege. I love the United States!

After being deployed to Iraq, Iran, Afghanistan and Korea…..these people have so little. So many have nothing!"

"I know." Mark didn't think he should say much; it appeared as though Brad had a lot of memories to unload.

"Some of the situations we were in…as well trained as we were… it's a miracle that any of us survived." Brad was quiet, thinking, remembering. "One of my buddies caught a slug under his left arm; he kept on fighting. When we got back to the chopper…it was Iraq… he looked at me and mouthed, "You're my only friend. Thank you." The noise blocked any kind of verbal transmission. After giving me a shove toward the chopper, he turned around and opened fire. He must've killed ten Iraqi's coming at us. I grabbed his uniform…and held onto him as the chopper lifted off. "You're the family I never had. Say a prayer for me." He kept talking but I couldn't hear all he said. His eyes closed; I held a dead buddy back to the base. It was tough, you know. Doesn't matter how much training you've had or the hardships you must go through to get a final seal of approval…I never allowed myself to think that one of us wouldn't return home."

"I lost my buddy, also. I remember his death almost every day and thank God that it wasn't me. Selfish, I suppose, but true."

"The tours that followed just weren't the same. I was exhausted from seeing poverty, destitute people being slaughtered by their own government. And for what? A little piece of property? A title that will go to someone else the moment they die! What is there about power that makes some men think they'll live forever?"

"Brad. In raising Kassie, I've tried to instill in her the ability to connect with people less fortunate than she, people she may meet only once in her lifetime. It's one thing to know it; it's another to live it. Having been a SEAL has made me a more compassionate human being and obviously, the same happened to you."

"When it came time to re-enlist, I separated from the Navy. In looking back, I know that I've become a surgeon in order to give back somehow, to help others. Being a SEAL…I still think of myself as a SEAL…it's what we were trained to do, for our country, against all enemies. It's a great feeling to give…..to give back."

As they pulled up to the grocery store, Mark turned off the ignition and with a smile, said, "Great to have you on board."

# 31

On Saturday evening, the four of them visited until after midnight, sharing stories, laughing, each finding a comfortable place for themselves as a family. Nothing was brought up about the conversation between Mark and Brad; the two women wouldn't have known how to respond.

"We're going to church in the morning, Brad. Would you like to join us?"

"I would. What time?"

"Same time as chapel services," Kassie added. "We usually go to the nine-thirty service."

There's was a small church, with a congregation of about two hundred. The Colbert family was well known and well liked. So, everyone had to meet and shake hands with Kassie Colbert's 'friend.'

"Brad, you say. Nice that you could join us."

"When are you coming *home* to live?"

"Are you going to *live* on the ranch?"

"Such a good looking fellow you are!" Mrs. Nesbitt blushed!

"Are you getting hitched soon?" Kassie knew Mr. Remke would ask.

"A surgeon, eh? My wife has a bum knee….."

"We have a hospital in Cheyenne."

"Always looking for a 'cut and patch' man!" Mr. Hanson was never without a John Deere hat. He was a cowboy, right down to his bow-legged frame.

"Nice to have a young man *join* the church."

"A good Christian man belongs in church on Sunday. Welcome."

"Yep! We're in need of some new blood."

"Ya' use ta' the col'? It gets mighty col' up here." Mr. Rudel hollered. "Can ya' fix my ears? Deaf, ya' know!"

"How nice of you to visit. Can you *stay*?"

"Will you drive to work? It's a long way into town...." Kassie wondered if Mrs. Cradle, who at eighty years old was still as spry as a chicken, thought Brad would 'fly' to work.

"Mark could use a strong man at the ranch. Another hand never hurts."

"You sure clean up good. Wish my boy would!"

"Come back, ya' hear?"

About an hour later, the four of them were driving to the ranch. Kassie explained that the people in town and around their ranch were a little inquisitive, but they meant well. Brad smiled broadly knowing although the people he knew growing up were nothing like the people he had just met, he determined these friends of the Colbert family were kind, gentle and family-oriented citizens who loved the Lord and loved life. Brad felt a contentment that he'd never known before. The people he had just met accepted him for what he was, a gentleman with a profession, a man they could talk to, someone they'd like as a neighbor.

Sunday afternoon, Brad and Kassie took a ride into the mountains. The air was crisp, the sun was out. The ground cover glistened with diamonds; the rhythmic sound of the horses' hooves made music in the crusted snow. It was the perfect day to be free. When they returned in the evening, Brad made an unselfish suggestion, one that aligned with his character.

"In the morning, would you like to take another ride in the mountains before we leave? Perhaps your parents would like to go with you." For having parents who, at times, were so self-absorbed and *busy*, Brad wanted Kassie to spend as much time as she wanted with her loving, unpretentious parents.

That evening, as Brad reclined on the hide-a-bed, his thoughts turned to family. He was more than pleasantly surprised with the level of comfort he felt in Kassie's home. It was the kind of home he dreamed of having for the family he wanted some day. No concealed motives, no hidden agendas, no false pretenses. He remembered the camaraderie he had experienced with his family of SEAL's; at that point, it was the closest communion he'd had with anyone in his life, except for 'pa-pa." He wondered how his parents would react when they met the Colbert's. The couples were so different. It was a disturbing thought, although interesting.

Brad's father told him to make something of himself. Well, he did, he thought. College, the Navy, becoming a Navy SEAL and med school. In the beginning Brad excelled because of his father. Now, he was excelling in spite of him. His parents weren't evil, although they never attended church, except for social functions. They were just terribly misguided individuals who didn't know what to do with all their money except spend it on all things philanthropic; which in itself could be considered an acquired virtue.

Perhaps he was being too judgmental; he loved his parents and they loved him in their own way. They had plenty of time, money and interest to contribute to lives less fortunate. But 'donations' also contributed to their wealth! It was still giving but in a way that allowed Brad to rethink their motivation. At some point in his life, he had decided to give of himself, unselfishly, without remorse. To be generous to those less fortunate. It was a seed planted in him by his 'pa-pa.

The following morning the three of them returned around the time Brad finished making breakfast.

"Hope you guys like crispy bacon, burnt toast and rubbery eggs? Everything is warm though."

"It'll do," Mark said with a twinkle in his eye.

"How thoughtful of you, Brad. It was a little frosty this morning. It's wonderful to come in and be warm with a hot meal waiting." Jake and two of the other wranglers were at the table, ready to eat. Brad smiled to himself. This had to be living at its best.

"Come back soon. We'll brand some calves." Mark wasn't good at saying goodbye; they simply shook hands. Kassie gave her father a hug; she hugged her mother, as well.

"Do come back soon, Brad." Laurie held him tightly as she said goodbye. "You've been such a joy." Brad felt himself oddly moved by her sincere sentiments. He stepped away, placing his hand softly on the small of Kassie's back.

"You know we will!" He placed a kiss on Kassie's forehead. "Thank you for sharing your home with me. It was my pleasure meeting you."

Mark winked at Brad, letting Brad know that he was now considered family. "See you later."

The sun was warm, the sky was blue and the truck ran smoothly. It was going to be a good day.

# 32

"**D**id you discuss it with your mother?"

"No, I didn't. I want it to be a secret for awhile. There's plenty of time for her to prepare a wedding when we can afford it."

"What kind of wedding would you prefer? Large, small, in between? Elope? Probably not. I would never do that to your parents. You're their only child; it wouldn't be the correct thing to do."

"Oh, Brad, you're right. It would break their heart." After giving it a moment's thought she said, "Preferably, I would like a small, intimate wedding, solemn, at church and all, but lots of fun."

"Then it's settled." Brad had only one thing to add. "I love you, Kassie Colbert."

Kassie remembered the ride that she and Brad took on Saturday morning. Crisp and cold, it was. The breath from the horses hung in the air as did that of Brad and Kassie. They rode to the top of Beacon Mountain where in days past, someone had seen fit to place several logs around a fire pit that was as old as the ranch itself. After dismounting, they walked to the east side where a precipice dropped a couple hundred feet. Below them stood several whitetail deer, drinking water from a stream originating from somewhere on the rock face. As tranquil as Kassie could remember, Brad put his arm around her waist. She loved this land, with its diversity and beauty. Every time she rode to this spot she saw something different, something new, always moments in time she'd never forget.

She wondered what Brad was thinking. It didn't take long for her to find out.

"Kassie, would you marry me?" She turned to face him and answered.

"I thought you'd never ask." Brad faced her and they embraced a long time. Then, she pushed him away. "BUT! You must do this right because I never intend to do this again!" Instinctively, Brad got the hint. He took her hand, led her to one of the logs and with his hands on her shoulders, forcing her to sit while he got down on his knees.

"Kassie. Your father and mother already know what I'm about to say, but I know they won't bring it up if you don't." Her mouth dropped open. "If only you knew how much they love you. Anyway, your father and I had several conversations and it was during one of those talks that I asked him for his permission to marry you." Kassie smiled. Without saying so out loud, she should've known Brad would do the right thing. "SO! I pray I show my love for you as much as they do. With that said, will you marry me, be my wife, my helpmate, my friend, my lover?"

"Yes, yes," and then, into the mountain air she shouted, "**Yes**, Brad Phillips, I would be honored to be your wife." The echo came back loud and clear. He took her hands, smiled and began to rise.

"Can I get up now?" They both laughed like school children, free and easy. "My knees are freezing!"

# 33

She didn't tell Jacki either. She knew that it would be all over the hospital before second shift began. Kassie was comfortable with her decision. From the moment she met Brad, from the moment he spoke, she knew Brad was special. She loved the very essence of him, his heart, his gentleness, his kindness, his faith…and everything else people saw when they met him, which, according to some, were his height, strength, good looks and smile, with dimples so deep they could've held a day's worth of rain. Kassie knew there was much more to the man; not to be put on a pedestal, but to appreciate.

"We're invited to the Selway mansion for dinner this coming Saturday. By the way, did you open your mail?"

"Yes."

"Did you and Brad get an invitation? It's supposed to be more elaborate than the last shindig he threw."

"No."

"Oh!"

"So!" Kassie didn't care if she ever went back to the Selway house.

"Maybe Brad got the invitation?"

"Maybe."

"You don't sound as though….I can't say as I blame you. But surely…"

"No!"

"Well, we're going. If for no other reason, it's a night out with free food and drinks!"

Kassie was reading the Sentinel, trying to digest what she read. Combining what was written together with what she knew was happening at the hospital, it just didn't make sense.

"Did you read the latest bulletin at the hospital?"

"Yeh! I did. Something, eh? Now they want us to report……."

"Jacki. Did anyone ever approach you about…..about applying to be head nurse on fourth?"

"No. They wouldn't do that. They know I'm somewhat of a scatterbrain. Not really! You know that, but let them think what they like." Jacki gave it a second thought. "Why? Are you applying for that position… in surgery? Good grief! You haven't been there that long!"

"Someone did. That was my statement as well. 'Haven't been here long enough.' Besides, I don't know that I'd want the job."

"Me, either. I have plenty of hours to work, thank you very much!" As Kassie read the paper, Jacki continued ironing. When she came back from hanging some clothes, she said, "Besides, you'd make a terrible boss; no double breaks, no substitutions on the schedule, no switching shifts without two weeks notification, comfortable shoes and spotless uniforms, no smoking, no chewing gum……."

"Alright. *Alright.* I get the idea."

"You're Miss Conservative, at work and at home. Remember, the girls coming out of nurses training today never worked at anything else other than their present job; they complain when their feet hurt!" Kassie knew she'd be strict, stricter than the present supervisor. She was definitely a conservative at heart. She was raised to believe you give an honest day's work for an honest day's pay. No freeloading!

Thinking, it prompted Kassie to ask some questions that otherwise didn't occupy too much of her time.

"I wonder how many face lifts one must have to remain a member of Congress? How many illicit affiliations must a person have to be elected to Congress? How many lies do you have to tell in order for people to accept an untruth? Here, on the front page, another Senator has been caught lying about his involvement in kickbacks to government contractors and he's on the finance committee! And, of course, he's denying it."

"Whoa! What set you off?"

"This newspaper. It's full of malicious gossip and innuendos." Kassie threw the paper aside and picked up her knitting. "Why is it so difficult for members of Congress to answer a question with a simple answer of yes or no?" Kassie expounded. "Do you believe in abortion? No! Do you believe in letting freeloaders remain on Medicaid? No! Do you believe in stealing other people's money? No! How about maintaining a mistress while your wife…"

"Good grief, Kass! Slow down." Jacki interrupted.

"I'm serious. Dead serious. The morals and laws that pertain to us don't make a dent in their behavior. Why do you think they have to spend hours talking, speaking, mumbling…being evasive… …to justify whatever it is their doing?"

"I don't know except…because sometimes they aren't simple questions, Kass." It was Jacki's turn to be totally serious. "Ask me if I love Howie? I couldn't answer that with a simple yes or no!"

"You belong in Congress!"

# 34

Kassie woke up in a cold sweat. Again, her nightgown was soaked and with good reason.

Dreams are usually forgotten upon one's waking up. Kassie didn't forget! She couldn't! The Thursday night, before Selway's party, her dream was more real than it had ever been before. The photo's! They drove her crazy! The people came out of the photo's...whose photo's?... and danced in the living room...whose living room?... laughing and joking, having a great time, while Kassie watched the whole menagerie from her place on the ceiling. Before she left, the people were all back in their frames...sitting on piano...whose piano?

She had to decide whether to tell Jacki about her latest dream. She didn't want to burden Brad with it. There wasn't anything anyone could do to help her except, perhaps, a physician who'd only prescribe some sleeping agent; she wanted none of that! Sleeping agents presented problems of their own.

Selway had a piano with photo's sitting on it; several of them. But in her dream the piano was insignificant. But the photos...it was photo's like those that continued to come alive. If she mentioned it to Jacki, how could she word it? She'd think about it and decide later.

"My, my, don't we look spiffy! New dress?"

"You like it? Got it while you were in Wyoming. It's not exactly my shade of blue but I *love* the design." Jacki turned in a circle to allow Kassie to make her personal assessment.

"Jacki, it's beautiful. The color is fine. Is Howie going to wear a matching blue shirt?"

"Kass! How naive! It's a black tie event. White starched shirt, tux and bow tie and no white socks! Got it!"

"Jacs, just teasing!" Although, Kassie did wonder if Dr. Harriman owned a black tuxedo and bow tie or if he had to rent one. "I can see it all now. You'll have a sit down dinner, have a few drinks and wind up by the piano looking at photo's. By the way, have you ever seen a photo of Selway's deceased wife?"

"Nope. Have you?"

"Can't say that I have. Aren't you the least bit interested in what she looked like? I wonder if Howie….?"

"I'll check out the piano on Saturday. Maybe Howie knows what she looks like." While Jacki was changing into jeans, the doorbell rang. "Oh, my." Gracefully coming out of the bedroom, she grabbed her wrap off the back of the lounge chair, walked briskly to the door and waved goodnight to Kassie without turning around.

Later that evening, after Howie and Jacki had left to see a movie, Brad showed up at their apartment about eight-thirty. In his hand he held a package. After kissing Kassie and removing his jacket, he handed it to her.

"Gotcha a little something. Hope you like it." They walked to their favorite comfort zone in front of the fireplace where Kassie opened the package. Inside, tucked neatly between tissues, was a long velvet box, in blue. Looking at Brad, she carefully removed it, feeling the weight of it. Too heavy for what she surmised it might be, she carefully undid the safety latch. Upon opening the lid, she saw a remarkable sight. The bracelet, although she didn't know for sure, appeared to be made up of diamonds and emeralds that glittered in the light from the fireplace.

"Happy birthday, Kass." The statement was said so softly and genuine that Kassie was left speechless.

"How did you know...it was my birthday?"

"Your father told me. When I asked him, he said you were born on the coldest day in May they'd ever experienced on the ranch. Seems the furnace went out overnight. Your father claimed it was the cold that prompted your mother's contractions. Anyway, I thought it might be appropriate for your special day since I haven't given you an actual engagement ring. I only hope you wear it. Precious stones need to be worn to be beautiful."

"It's beautiful, Brad. Thank you." Kassie was overwhelmed for a moment. "But how can you afford….."

"I knew you'd ask, Miss Conservative. Let's just say it was in the family." Now Kassie became emotional. Never had she been so deeply moved by such a gift; freely given, with love. If it had truly been in his family, obviously the bracelet was a very personal and cherished heirloom. Having just received it, Kassie knew that she had just become a part of his family. "I can vouch for the stones. They truly are diamonds and emeralds. Quite old, actually. Whatever happens between us, they belong to you. And prayerfully, we'll both get to enjoy them together."

Kassie remembered how she felt when her parents had given her Spinster. Her horse was a living, breathing thing she could touch and feel. Exhilaration was what she felt; her parents trusted her to take care of a living being. But this bracelet, although in her book it was just 'stuff,' meant a lot to Brad and since he chose to give it her she would always remain mindful of his generosity and trust.

"Let me help you put it on. It's got a double safety latch."

"I noticed." Kassie was so humbled by the gift and the tenderness of the moment in which it was given. "Are you sure….?"

"I have never been so sure of anything......*anything* in my life. I plan on spending the rest of my life with you. I would only ask that in spite of who or what I am, or where I came from, that you will always love me."

"Well! When you put it that way!" Kassie leaned over and kissed him. Having Brad in her life gave her the promise of fulfillment that was yet to come. Their paths had crossed and Kassie had made a choice, knowing that any other path she may have taken wouldn't have been the one based on faith.

# 35

Since Kassie and Brad decided against going to Selway's, Kassie worked overtime for her friend, Caitlyn, in ER.

Going to work on third shift was tough when the weather was nice, much less on an evening when it was brisk. Colorado was known to have deadly blizzards in spring, with February and March being heavy snowfall months. It was almost June but there were few spring flowers poking their heads toward the sun!

As she walked along the avenue, the cool breeze slapping her face, it caused her to have the 'sniffles.' Traffic was almost at a standstill for a Saturday. If the residents and homeowners weren't working or eating, they were already in bed anticipating the next day off. Dutifully, she stopped at the crosswalk, looked both ways and was about to move, when she heard footsteps behind her. When she turned to look, there was no one there. She waited. No more steps. She crossed the median and continued toward the hospital. One more street to cross! One more block. She'd be able to warm up once inside the hospital.

Again, she heard steps. Paranoia was not her strong suit but she was beginning to know what it felt like. Again, she waited, afraid to turn around. For being so close to the hospital, there was absolutely no visible moving traffic. Already half past ten, she could run to the nearest apartment, push the talk button, holler 'stalker' and scare someone into their afterlife! However, if she ran across the street, perhaps she could turn to see who was behind her, and spare some unknown household a night of terror. She reached inside her pocket, grabbed her bottle of pepper spray and continued to walk.

Inside the hospital she sighed, not just because it was warm but because she knew she had been followed. She didn't have to see anyone to confirm her suspicions. Instincts should be followed, she thought.

Jacki was still in bed when Kassie returned to the apartment Sunday morning. After work, she and Brad had attended chapel services and decided to have lunch together in the cafeteria.

Going directly to her room so as not to awaken Jacki, she dropped her clothes by her bed. It had been a busy night with two skiing accidents and the third, the victim of a drunk driver. Unfortunately, one of the skiers died due to a traumatic head injury. It was just one of many reasons Kassie never went skiing. As far as she was concerned, they could've closed the slopes already since only the defiant skiers stayed until the snow turned to mud!

She sat with the boy's parents, trying to console the mother. What can you say…or do…for those who lose their nineteen year old only son who was the joy of their lives and who was determined to follow in his father's footsteps? Their son, who thought his destiny was to become an attorney, someone to represent the less fortunate, was now deceased; with him were buried all the dreams he'd had during his short life. Kassie wondered what his prayer life had been.

She remembered the lady she had met at the airport. Her anger, Kassie knew, was for a different reason. Just the same, both mothers' were grief stricken. There wasn't enough medicine in the world they could've been given to heal the hole in their hearts.

Kassie hadn't fallen asleep yet when Jacki came into her room.

"You awake?"

"I am now."

"Good. You will never guess what happened last night!"

Glancing at the clock, Kassie said, "It's one in the afternoon. I thought I'd try to catch up on my rest…since I work early shift in the morning."

"I'm sorry. But you have to hear…"

"Let me guess. You had one too many drinks, you tripped, fell and Selway came to the rescue. Howie was busy eating the pastries……"

"No! No! No! Kassie, the photo's! His wife was beautiful; a huge photo of her sits on the piano. Oh, by the way. Sorry! Happy birthday. I know I'm late…..what day is it again, the thirtieth?"

"Are you sure?"

"Yes, I'm sure! Happy birthday! I'll fix you something to eat or have you had breakfast? Scrambled eggs sound good?"

"I mean the photo of Mrs. Selway!" Kassie righted herself in bed. "What size photo was it? Were the other photos still there?"

"The former Mrs. Selway, or so I was informed! Actually, it's fairly large, even without the frame. Probably eleven by fourteen. I don't know. Forgot my tape." Then, she added, "Yes, there were others."

"He must've put it there recently," Kassie mumbled to herself. Recalling her dreams, the photos were always rather small, only enlarging when one would fly in her face. Why was she trying to connect the photos at Dr. Selway's with her dreams? She had viewed plenty of framed photos in art galleries, photo shops, hobby stores and the like. Somehow, the images in her dreams were different.

"What did you say? Stop mumbling! I'll talk to you later. Go to sleep. I'll wake you when Brad calls." Jacki jumped in the shower.

Kassie slept fitfully for two hours and after waking for a third time, she decided to get up and get dressed. It was enough rest, she figured; there were no dreams.

# 36

After a late lunch, she and Brad hung out at the apartment. It appeared that Jacki was still recovering from the night before; distracted but sociable. All three were content and settled in for the evening. Jacki, being Jacki, began to expound on her Saturday dinner date.

"There were only four couples that attended, including Selway and this buxom blonde. Can't remember what her name was but she was different; didn't say a word all evening. She smiled a lot! In fact, she looked somewhat like his now dearly departed wife, although she wasn't as pretty. But then, all blondes look alike."

"I beg your pardon! They may *look* alike but I can assure they are not!" Brad looked at Kassie as if to say, 'It's just Jacki talking. Relax.'

"Brad, I didn't mean Kassie. I apologize. So crass of me to make such a blanket statement!"

"Don't you think you should apologize to me? Instead of Brad?" Kassie pretended to look offended. But then she had a better idea. "Don't worry about it, Jacs. Your turn is coming."

"Anyway. The dinner was exceptional and the dessert was to die for. After dinner, we all retired to the living room. Selway plunked himself down between me and another gal. Believe me when I tell you both Howie and I, after a few drinks of wine, were happy to leave.

Selway slobbered all over the other gal while his date sat mute on the other side of the room. When he made a pass at me, Howie about fell out of his chair getting to me. I was off the divan with my coat on before I could say 'ouch.'"

"Did Stephen say anything when you looked at the photos?" It was Brad.

"Not really. Unless, of course, you count the fact he told me she was his 'deceased ex-wife, poor soul.' He was very disingenuous. I was glad when we left. Howie was disgusted at Selway's behavior. Like he said, he attends...."

"So he can put up with him at work and not be badgered." Brad almost felt the same way.

"Something like that. Anyway, the food was good....."

Kassie wondered about the photo of Stephen Selway's ex-wife. Why would someone call their deceased wife an 'ex-wife?' Why did he put her photo on display? What was his motive for doing so? And why did he continue to live in such a big house by himself? There were so many questions she had. Better to think of something else.

# 37

She had gone to the library to get another novel by John Grisham called 'The Brethren.' Walking out, she stopped to pick up a newspaper. Standing outside the library, thinking she had plenty of time, she walked back into the building and looked for a vacated computer, somewhat secluded. Putting aside the book and newspaper, she used her library card to log on. Googling 'newspapers,' she found the Denver Clarion. One of the Clarion's most noteworthy attributes was it always carried the homes for sale and those which sold. She scrolled back two years, went to the houses for sale section and started watching for the house on Beacon Avenue in Worthington Heights.

It didn't take long. The house, located at 333 Beacon Avenue in Worthington Heights, was listed in February of the previous year. The listing price was almost three million. Kassie wondered how Dr. Selway could afford such a price! The next month, according to the Clarion, the listing had been removed. She scrolled back to the February listing. Again, she scrolled forward. The house on Beacon Avenue supposedly was never sold. She knew, that for reasons of privacy, certain sales were never reported. Curious as to the lineage of the home, she backed out of the Denver Clarion and in the search bar wrote, *333 Beacon Avenue, Worthington Heights*. Since it was one of the older more stately houses built in the area, Kassie thought it would be interesting to explore its history.

It had been built and originally owned by the Statler family. The Statler's were not only 'old money' wealthy but were known for their philanthropy. The house had passed from the original owners to their son, Rodney Statler and his family. The grandson, Aubrey Statler, lived in the house by himself until he married late in life. Upon getting married to a wealthy socialite, the two of them refurbished the house to its original charm and beauty.

They had one daughter whom they named Carolyn Alain Statler, after her mother. Carolyn was raised to be a lady in every sense of the word. Well educated, inheriting an estate of her own, she married a local attorney. Upon the death of her parents, she and her husband, Roger Stiles, sold their home and returned to 333 Beacon Avenue, which was a part of Carolyn's estate.

Two years after the move, Carolyn was left a widow. Roger Stiles had died in the hospital after taking a nasty fall during one of his black ski runs. After having had surgery, his death was attributed to a blood clot in the brain. Originally from Indiana, it was there that he was laid to rest.

The article ended. No other names were given, no other circumstances acknowledged. Not a word was mentioned as to the wealth that must have passed to Carolyn.

Kassie googled *Carolyn Statler*. Since Carolyn and her husband, Roger, never had any children, she could've remained unmarried and had a fulfilling life, Kassie thought. However, she was only twenty-six when she was widowed. Her life, although filled with her social friends and her beloved projects, was just getting started. She had much to offer society. She had been blessed with altruistic parents, a good education and wealth that if used appropriately could accomplish great things.

The passage was personal. Kassie wondered if Carolyn herself had written it or perhaps some journalist composed it based on gossip. The article left Kassie with so many unanswered questions. Did she marry again? If so, what was the name of Carolyn's second husband? What possessed her to put the house up for sale in the first place? Why was there no record of the sale at 333 Beacon Avenue? Was there any connection between Carolyn Statler and Dr. Selway? Annoying Kassie most was how did Dr. Stephen Selway come to own a house that *disappeared* from the newspaper, listed at such an exorbitant price?

The house that Selway inhabited was once owned by a 'Carolyn.' It presented Kassie with another dilemma. What if? What if that Carolyn was the same Carolyn who became his wife?

# 38

Work was work; it kept her mind occupied. The questions concerning Dr. Selway were never far away. Maybe he, too, was wealthy but was more secretive about his good fortune. Maybe he didn't want his patients to know where he lived. Surely he had loved his 'deceased wife!' But his wife was dead! He was alone. For all practical purposes, Kassie pondered, it must be the life he presently wants.

Again, the article in the Clarion came to mind. What happened to Carolyn Alain Statler?

The more Kassie deliberated the list of her never ending questions, the more she wanted to know about the 'sleazy Stephen Selway' and his now ' deceased ex-wife.'

"What is that noise?" Jacki asked, as Kassie messed with the popcorn bag. "Looking for a toy?"

"No!"

"Just wondering."

The evenings the two of them shared popcorn in front of the fireplace would be replaced with daily walks and other outdoor activities. June was beginning to look like summer had arrived. Their apartment backed up to open space, thereby creating a haven of trees, bushes, grasses and a manicured lawn. Squirrels and rabbits, along with the myriad amount of birds were a delight, especially in the early mornings.

"Are you planning on going to the ranch?"

"I'm not sure. I think I'd like to do something really different. I'll have to see what Brad's schedule looks like, see what he wants to do."

"Speaking of Brad! Where do you suppose he got the money for that bracelet of yours?" Jacki was curious. Kassie decided it wasn't anyone's business how he got it or where.

"Maybe he's making payments! Or maybe, he inherited it! Surely, you don't expect me to ask him?"

"I suppose not! I wish Howie didn't have so many debts. He wants to pay them off before he buys another thing, he said. Wish he would get me a ring!"

"If your heart is in the right place you can be patient for a ring, Jacki. His priorities appear to be in order so….."

"How can you be so logical *all the time*? Just once, I wish you'd do something crazy. Life is so short…..honestly! And what really gets me…you're usually right!"

Kassie almost laughed out loud. Catching herself, she couldn't help but wonder what Jacki would've thought had she known what Kassie had done earlier in the day. Having gone to the library would remain her secret alone. Not for a moment did she believe Brad or Jacki would understand why she was so inquisitive about the house on 333 Beacon Avenue. Realistically, she didn't understand it herself!

# 39

The next morning, as Brad began making rounds, Cindy accompanied him. Brad was aware of the friendship that existed between her and Kassie. Cindy, however, was in awe of Brad, which was something Kassie couldn't get her head around. This particular morning, Cindy wanted Brad's opinion on a matter that was becoming a problem for her.

"I'm not sure how to say this so I'll just blurt it out. Dr. Phillips, Dr. Selway keeps asking me for a date. I've tried to make it very clear to him that I'm not interested but he doesn't quit asking. Any suggestions?" She looked at him as he smiled.

"Why don't you accept *one* date and make him as miserable as you can. For instance, suggest you go out to dinner. Order soup. Slurp it! Blow your nose without leaving the table. Shovel your food using both hands! Accidently knock over his water glass! Suck your coffee out of....."

"Stop! Stop! I get the idea. Maybe that'll work...but now...I have to go back to work." But she couldn't stop laughing.

"Mr. Mantoux, I heard you were misbehaving again." Mr. Mantoux had had surgery two days prior and was now awake and causing quite a stir on third floor.

"When can I get out of here, Doc? I can't seem to find my wife!"

"Looks like you found plenty of other women! You and I both know what you really want is another drink, sooner rather than later."

"That's not so. I'm a dirty old man and I miss my woman." He paused. "You think I'll still be able to…you know…"

"That doesn't give you permission to fondle the nurses! Besides, you don't want to tear the mesh that's holding your hernia together, especially in the crotch area." He laid Mr. Mantoux's chart on the bed. "Look, I'm expecting you to behave yourself and conduct yourself as a gentleman while you're in the hospital. Don't worry about whether your plumbing is going to work. You'll be just fine. You have to heal first." Picking up the chart, Brad said, as he was leaving Mr. Mantoux's room, "Behave!"

"Humpf!"

Cindy was at her station speaking to two other nurses when Brad finished rounds. He motioned for Cindy to step closer.

"I was thinking. If you go to the theatre, make sure you get a drink and some popcorn. Accidently spill the drink on Dr. Selway's precious pressed trousers and spit the shucks from the popcorn on the floor." Brad didn't crack a smile but Cindy laughed. "Of course, there are more drastic things you could do, but try those first. Good luck." Brad placed his pen back in his uniform pocket, smiled and left.

Cindy would have to share with Kassie what Brad had explained to her. Kassie would die laughing, she knew. She wondered if Kassie knew how fortunate she was in having Brad as a close friend; she was a lucky girl.

# 40

When the cell phone rang it took Kassie by surprise.

"Dr. Selway was in my face again!"

"You have got to be kidding!"

"**I'm not kidding**! On his rounds today, again he asked me out for dinner." Like a fly on sticky paper, Dr. Selway was determined to have a date with Cindy. "Of course, so much more can go wrong on a dinner date. Perhaps I'll wear nylons with runs in them…"

"You could always wear a much too long white slip under a black skirt. That reminds me! I remember a lady on the flight to Rome when she asked where she could go pee? When she exited the bathroom, she had a long train of toilet tissue stuck to the bottom of your shoe. I thought I would totally lose it! She tried to be so prim and nonchalant, returning to her seat. Try that on Dr. Selway! Maybe, if you're lucky, he'll begin to think you're a hopeless klutz and he'll find someone else to pester."

"I should be so lucky. I know if I turn him down…he'll pester me until I can't tolerate it anymore. I suppose I could mention it to Dr. Guiterrez. Maybe he could put a bug…."

"*I wouldn't do that*, Cindy, not just yet. Go ahead and accept his date. As I've heard it said 'it's free food and an evening out.' Let's see what happens on your first dinner date." Then she added. "Be careful...and let me know how things go."

Kassie was as puzzled as Cindy as to why Dr. Selway kept bugging her about accepting a date. His arrogance probably wouldn't let him take 'no' for an answer. By any stretch of the imagination, Kassie didn't think he was any great 'catch.' Although, she knew women who'd latch onto any man in pressed pants with a fly!

Cindy carried out Brad and Kassie's plans perfectly. Or so she thought. She and Dr. Selway dined at the Red Lobster restaurant. Immediately, after being seated, she blew her nose into the cloth napkin. She refolded it and placed it by her plate. Selway raised his hand and promptly asked the waiter for a clean napkin.

"This is much too fine a restaurant to give a lady a soiled napkin." The waiter looked astonished.

"Thank you, Dr. Selway. That was very delicate of you." Cindy almost choked.

"Stephen. Call me Stephen." While he smiled at her, Cindy thought of a hundred words that fit him better. As always, he was immaculately dressed; bow tie and black shiny shoes, with cuff links the size of horse shoes. Cindy, on the other hand, kept pulling up her black skirt, discreetly, so as to let the white slip show. In doing so, she *accidently* snagged her nylons. All she had to do now was wait for their dinner to arrive.

At work the next day, Kassie and Cindy met at lunch in the hospital cafeteria.

"You won't believe what happened last night. I was so embarrassed!"

"Wait a minute. Brad told me that if you followed his suggestions, Stephen would be the one embarrassed!"

"Let me try saying it another way! His coffee landed on *my* dress; I am now the proud owner of a dress that is incapable of being cleaned! Plus, the creep ate with his mouth open! Did you ever see anyone eat crab so fast that butter ran out the sides of his mouth, onto his chin?"

"What?"

"Oh, that's not all! As we were getting into the car, he was telling me about some lady who had breast implants, which prompted me to say something my brain didn't process before the words came out. I asked him what I could do about all my cellulite which sure didn't look good when I wore a bathing suit and before I could finish, he said that he would have to see it before he knew if surgery was necessary. He reached over and started to...you know... what was left of my beautiful....." Cindy took a breath.

"Why did you say such a thing? What did you do when he tried to...?"

"I thanked him for dinner and sternly, asked him to take me home. I was so humiliated, I slapped him. Can you *imagine*? Can he sue me for something like that?"

"Any witnesses?"

"Are you kidding?"

"Probably not. What time did you get home?"

"Not soon enough!" Cindy was quiet as they both munched on their sandwiches. Kassie was beginning to wonder if Cindy was a real prude and lacked any backbone or if Dr. Selway really was a *sleaze*. Maybe it was something in between which caused Kassie to immediately elucidate verbally.

"Are you going to continue seeing him?"

"Not if I can help it!"

"Cindy! Say no! Continue to say 'no' to him. You're the only one who can extract yourself from this ridiculous man. What a sleaze!"

"That's not exactly what I'd call him. I know I tried to do despicable things to embarrass him.....and I took Brad's advice..... but I think he's an overgrown pervert!"

"In addition to being a highly skilled surgeon, who owns a drop dead gorgeous house, who dresses in only the finest and drives....."

"Funny you should mention his house. He wanted to take me to his house after dinner and I refused. He said he was disappointed, that it was really a very nice 'home' at one time, but with only him living there….."

"Really!" Again Kassie remembered her very discreet research project. When they had both gone back to work, Kassie couldn't help but weigh the thought of Cindy having just *one more date* with Selway. Maybe Cindy could find out more about his 'deceased ex-wife,' which wouldn't ease Kassie's mind but would explain some of the behavior of a certain Dr. Stephen Selway.

# 41

While they ate their pizza for third time that week, Brad and Kassie discussed what happened with Cindy and Selway.

"Maybe I was out of line to tell her those things; however, if any girl would've done that to me on a date, well, it would've been the last time! Do you suppose she'll go out with him again?"

"Only if she gets paid!"

"Wow! That doesn't sound like Cindy!"

"That didn't come out the way I meant it!" Kassie was sorry she had said such an outright lie. "Cindy's okay, you know. Just wish Stephen would leave her alone. And why doesn't he leave her alone? Have you ever wondered? I sure have."

"All he's ever said to me was that he had had a refreshing date, whenever he's had a date, whatever that means. I know Cindy wouldn't…..."

"No, she wouldn't. I'm glad you understand her as much as I do. She's really a very sweet and kind-hearted girl." Kassie was beginning to surmise that Brad would rather be discussing something else. In the back of her mind, though, she secretively, somehow, had to convince Cindy to go on *one more date* with the man. She'd have to convince Cindy to get a cell photo of the ex-wife, or maybe…if that didn't work, then she and Brad would have to attend the next Selway dinner.

Kassie didn't have to wait long. Cindy told her about their next date before the weekend arrived. Selway was going to take her to Breck for skiing, not that she knew how to ski. However, Cindy had always wanted to learn so in her mind, a date with Selway to the ski slopes was just fine.

Before Cindy left, Kassie asked her if she could discreetly take a snapshot with her cell phone of the ex-wife photo on the piano, should the occasion arise, if or when they returned to his house. Kassie emphatically explained that she was interested beyond belief to know what his ex-wife looked like and that a photo would alleviate her curiosity. Without any further explanation, Cindy agreed.

Apprehensively, it appeared Kassie was waiting for something to happen; she had no clue as to what or why. Her work was fulfilling, her relationship with Brad was delightful but serious and her roommate was in a relationship of her own but.....the dreams. Why couldn't she figure out why the dreams kept returning? Perhaps it was the reason why she wanted to know what the deceased Mrs. Selway looked like. But why would there be a connection? The piano, of course. In her dreams a piano was always present. She began to wonder if she'd already seen a photo of the expired ex-Mrs. Selway and wasn't aware of it. Again, she reminded herself that patience was not her best attribute!

When Kassie returned to work on Monday morning, she sought Cindy out. They met for lunch again. She didn't want to appear hasty in asking the obvious.

"How was the skiing lesson? How many times did you fall and clunk your head? Don't tell me you never fell!"

"Oh, I fell but not enough to hurt myself. It was a good time, actually. Oh, by the way, I have something to show you." From inside her uniform pocket she pulled out her cell phone. After pulling up the screen, she added, "Have you ever seen someone so beautiful?"

Had someone hollered 'fire,' Kassie Colbert would've burned to death. She froze in her seat! Oh yes, the woman in the photo was beautiful. And, she thought, she looked like the kind of woman Selway would want on his arm. But more than that, she was a woman that Kassie had seen before. As she sat there, staring at Cindy's phone, shivers ran down her spine. Where had she seen this woman? Not in her dreams! She would've remembered that. She had to remember!

"Are you alright? I mean, I know she's pretty, BUT, not that stunning!" Cindy was correct but it didn't help Kassie's dilemma. She knew she had to collect her thoughts before Cindy asked her a question she wouldn't dare to answer.

"Yah. Yah. I'm...I'm just looking...she is beautiful, though, isn't she."

"Yup! Too bad she's dead! She looks like she'd have been a real darlin'." For Cindy, she simply had stated facts.

Dead! Kassie had to remind herself again. Yes, she's dead. Selway's 'deceased ex-wife.' How could she forget?

"Did you ask for her name.....I mean.....did Selway volunteer her name? Like, what do you think her name might be?" Kassie was beginning to sweat. What did she think she was doing, asking Cindy such a question? She certainly didn't want Cindy to start asking questions of her!

"Carolyn. That's her name." Kassie swallowed hard, so hard it hurt her gullet.

"Really!" she squeaked. What could she say? "Nice name." Kassie tried to discreetly swallow some water; it had a hard time going down.

"Yeh. Too bad she's dead." Cindy finished her sandwich. Before pulling the cell phone back, she said, "Seen enough?" Kassie nodded affirmatively. "Good." Cindy put the phone on 'silent' and both of them proceeded to pick up their trash.

As they rode back on the elevator, Cindy offhandedly added to their previous conversation.

"Stephen tried to make it appear she wasn't all that special. She'd been married before. It was Stephen's first marriage so…I didn't know men would view their wife in such a manner. Actually, I thought it was rather crude of him to utter those words to me." Kassie couldn't find her voice. Something about what Cindy had just said began to resonate in her brain. Carolyn. Married before. Disrespectful. Crude didn't come close to what Kassie was thinking.

# 42

The days were getting longer and with the melt from up high in the Rockies, purple crocus were poking their heads up toward the sun. Kassie and Brad had just returned from spending another three day weekend at the ranch. Kassie couldn't keep it to herself any longer since she knew her parents already knew; they discussed some of the details of what they thought their wedding would look like. Her parents were happy for them and easy to please. What really mattered was the absolute fact the four of them truly enjoyed being with each other.

During their visit, Kassie kept thinking about a certain 'Carolyn.' She couldn't know for sure if the 'Carolyn' she'd read about was the same Carolyn that had married Stephen Selway. It would be quite a coincidence if it was but she had no way of knowing until she could do more snooping.

Cindy had picked up on his disdainful manner when she had the conversation with Stephen concerning his ex-wife. Did Cindy suspect anything more? Kassie doubted she did. Why should she? Kassie didn't want Cindy to know what she had done or what she was about to do. Without being able to verbalize her curiosity, as much as she feared what she might learn, she wasn't comfortable sharing any of it with any one she knew. Not even Brad.

Cindy, Jacki and Kassie usually met for their lunches in the OR break room. Monday's were always busy; patients had either scheduled surgery for the beginning of the week or they got sick over the weekend, came into the emergency room, were admitted and waited until their physician returned from his weekend.

"How was your weekend?" It was Cindy.

"It was great! The outdoors is still quiet and peaceful in Wyoming."

"What did you do Jacki?" Again, it was Cindy.

"A whole lot of nothing." Jacki smiled. "We have a new male nurse on the floor. Kinda cute I'd say. He came from someplace in Ohio. Seems like a nice guy, though! Name's Samuel. But he prefers Sam." Cindy stopped drinking her soda.

"Oh! That reminds me. Stephen said Carolyn's first husband was named Roger. Roger S. something. Let me think. Roger Smith… Roger Stills…Roger Stiles! Stiles was his last name. Sorry I forgot to mention it. Must've slipped my mind."

Everything Cindy said verified what she had found. Kassie knew the name Roger Stiles. For certain now, she knew the Carolyn who owned the house was indeed Selway's ex-wife.

"Hey, I'll have to make it a point to meet him!" Jacki knew no shame.

"Jacki, you're engaged to Howard! What is wrong with you?"

"Tell me something, Kass! Do you ever look at other men?"

"Loving Brad as I do, no. As a matter of fact, I'm not so inclined since the man that I love is more gracious, more virile, more faithful, more supremely confident…"

"Got the point! However! Men look at other women all their waking lives. Give me one good reason why women shouldn't take a peek or two when some good eye-candy comes along? Huh!"

"They also say that you should pick your fights. This is one skirmish I choose not to have. See you guys later." Kassie disposed of her trash, washed her hands with soap and left the break room.

Someone answered with, "Whatever."

# 43

It was a Saturday. The evening shift. Since both Brad and Jacki were working, she decided to fill in for Cindy. Kassie knew it would be busy because there was less staff and more admissions on Saturday and Sunday. Weekends and holidays always seemed to enhance people's physical and mental problems.

It was around eight when the relatives of Sir Charles Van Den Burgh called and asked if Sir Charles was ready to leave the hospital. He would live with them in Denver until his body was healed enough so he could travel back to England. He suffered from diverticulitis and had had a portion of his gut removed to remove the pain and discomfort of the disease, but also to allow him to eat solid food. Complications after colonoscopy surgery had set in; he was transferred to fourth floor, where his gastroenterologist could look after him.

Sir Charles was a jolly soul, always as pleasant as a patient could be under the circumstances. Since he was beginning to feel better he wanted to leave the hospital. Kassie couldn't blame him. Most patients healed better at home.

When they called, Kassie checked his chart. A prescription had been left for him. It was written for Percodan. She noticed on the cover of his chart there were no allergies. Two sheets of release forms needed to be signed, as well. The narcotic prescription told Kassie to look inside the chart. Since her regular duties occurred in the OR and being unfamiliar with any of the patients on fourth she felt she had to check Sir Charles' paperwork against what his chart said.

What she found, aside from needing to send instructions on how to take care of his stoma and some extra dressings home with him, was the statement pertaining to Percodan. He claimed it made him 'sick to his stomach,' which in Kassie's mind was entirely enough information to change the Percodan to a pain killer he could tolerate. In addition to oxycodone, it also contained aspirin, contraindicated in someone with a stoma. He would need something for pain since he wasn't entirely healed and especially when he traveled home by air.

'Sick to your stomach' wasn't classified as an allergy but it would be a considered an adverse reaction. Percodan contained aspirin. Aspirin was classified as a non-steroidal anti-inflammatory medication which taken without food could cause severe irritation in the gastrointestinal tract, especially the stomach. Aspirin, along with all other NSAID's, especially Ibuprofen and Naproxen, could cause ulceration of the GI mucosa. In most patients NSAID's were tolerated; they worked proficiently in reducing pain for long periods of time, and could be taken without any side effects. The first generation of NSAID's were now being sold over the counter. They could be purchased and taken without the patient ever reading the warnings on the bottle. Unaware that prolonged usage could get them into trouble, many individuals suffered from side effects and adverse reactions which, if left untreated, could result in gastric ulcerations of the esophagus, stomach and intestinal lining. Thus, whenever prescribed, it was vital that every medical professional should be aware whether their patient's had ever taken NSAID's. Having just survived intestinal surgery, it was imperative that Sir Charles Van Den Burgh should not have his body subjected to aspirin.

In the chart it was noted that Mr. Van Den Burgh had been taught how to clean his open wound, how to empty his colonoscopy bag and replace it, when necessary. Other instructions included what to watch for in case of infection at the site and the foods that were compatible with an external stoma.

Also noted, Kassie found, Mr. Van Den Burgh was to make an appointment with his gastroenterologist in England as soon as he returned home.

Her first phone call was to the relatives of Sir Charles explaining there were a couple details needing to be clarified before he could leave. She would notify them with a telephone call as soon as she could reach his medical physician. Her second call was to Dr. David Krueger.

Trying to reach Dr. Krueger turned out to be quite a problem. In Sir Charles chart, Kassie couldn't find a contact telephone listing for after hours. So she contacted the switchboard. The switchboard operator said the only number she had was unlisted. 'No calls after five PM.'

"That's unacceptable! One of his patients is scheduled to go home but there's a problem with his release orders."

"Kassie, if I give you his number, he'll have my head on a platter in the morning. You know how he is!"

"No, I don't. I haven't had to deal with him one on one. I understand your dilemma. However, there is a problem with his patient that needs to be addressed, sooner rather than later."

"Kassie, I don't know about this. If I give you the number, don't call me back and tell me 'I told you so.' He's not going to tolerate your interrupting his evening at all. I've heard that he screams and hollers at the slightest infraction of his personal time. But here it is."

After taking down the number, Kassie made the call.

"Hello?"

"Dr. Krueger, this is Kassie from fourth floor at Mercy. Thank you for taking my call. I hate to bother you at home but I have a problem with your patient Sir Charles Van Den Burgh. I understand you are the specialist he has been seeing. He is scheduled to go home with relatives this evening. But the prescription you wrote for him is Percodan and it appears he is unable to take it. Plus, it isn't dated. Is there something else you could give him and I'll have a resident write it for him?" There was a long pause on the other end of the phone. Finally, he spoke.

"Is that all you called me for?"

Kassie was shocked...and disgusted. Controlled substance prescriptions were required by law to have certain items written and recorded on the face of the prescription. The current date, the physicians DEA number, the physician's signature, the patient's name and address, the name of the medication, providing the patient wasn't allergic to the drug, the strength of the medication, the appropriate directions on how to take the medication and the total amount of medication to be dispensed by a Registered Pharmacist. On a CLASS II medication there were automatically no refills but many physicians would mark the refill space with a zero anyway.

"I beg your pardon, doctor!"

"I *said*,… is that all you called me for?"

"Yes, it is, sir. I know it's a weekend but perhaps….."

"I'm going to say this to you once, Miss…..what did you say your name was?"

She wanted to say, 'I didn't.' But that would've been a lie. "Kassie." Why stop there, she thought. "From fourth floor, the medical wing."

"I'm not to be bothered in the evenings, after hours, or on weekends. Especially weekends! Is that clear?"

Kassie was stunned! What could she say that could...or would... alter his view toward his lack of professionalism? Patients, whether at home or in the hospital, became ill or had accidents every day of the week and anytime during the twenty-four hours in the day. Patients didn't choose to be patients at the physician's convenience! Although, with all the regulations that medical personnel faced and the fierce restrictions put on their time, perspective patients had a much longer wait time to even see a physician, much less be treated appropriately.

Kassie deliberated as to how she should word it; it could mean the end of her career at Mercy. Whatever the result, someone had to explain to Dr. David Krueger, by doing the best he could for his patients was his responsibility as a professional.

"Dr. Krueger. Most hospitalized patients require help 24/7. If you didn't want to be called in the evenings and on weekends, perhaps you should have chosen a different profession!"

Dead silence ensued on the other end of the line. Kassie wouldn't be deterred. She'd have a resident write a different prescription, send Sir Charles Van Den Burgh home with his relatives and tomorrow, if necessary, she'd look for another job.

# 44

She wasn't fired nor did she suffer any repercussions from her conversation with Dr. David Krueger. A week later she had to call him again on a different patient but with a similar problem. When he learned it was Kassie to whom he was speaking, Dr. David Krueger was a pleasant, professional and accommodating physician who actually thanked her for the call. Kassie didn't have to wonder why or how Dr. Kreuger could make such a quick turnaround. She figured he had complained loudly, in an arrogant manner to the Chief of Staff, probably wanting Kassie, the nurse who had the audacity to speak to him like she did, fired or reprimanded, to which the Chief probably said something to the effect that whoever the nurse was, she had a point. Dr. Krueger also got the point! *Listen to the lady!* The Chief of Staff himself had probably wanted to say as much to the esteemed physician as what Kassie had said; someone else had simply taken care of the problem for him.

"Why do you want a car? Mine isn't good enough for you?"

"Jacki. Sometimes I need to go into the city, like Cherry Creek, and you're busy driving your own....."

"Okay. When do you want to go looking? Do you even know what kind of car you want?" Jacki knew it would be an unanswered question. Knowing Kassie, she was positive Kassie already had a car in mind; she just needed a ride to get there.

Upon arriving at Joaquin's Automotive, Inc. she asked to see the Hyundai Elantra that she had previously inquired about concerning availability, price, existing mileage, year, gas mileage and color. The color was important to Kassie; gray, silver and white were out. Red was her color of choice. Maybe blue.

"You must be the gal who called on my lunch break. Nice to meet ya." Salesmen were normally a very congenial type, always ready to help, always ready to make a sale. "Let's take a look at the 2006 Elantra I discussed with you. It's a sweet little vehicle. Get's almost 40 miles per gallon…"

"I believe you said it gets 28 in the city."

"But it gets more MPG in the country. Anyway, let's take a look."

Jacki couldn't believe Kassie was so picky on a second hand vehicle. Kassie pointed out the tires looked rather used and perhaps they could put new tires on it before she bought it. She could live with the amount of little scratches on the hood, although she wondered how they got there. She also wanted to know the profession of the previous owner. Was it a housewife or a salesman? Not that one would've taken any better care of it than the other but she had her suspicions. As it turned out, a couple in their 60's had owned it; each scratch mark was named after one of their grandchildren, according to the salesman.

"Are you going to buy it, or are we just looking?" Jacki was growing impatient, as always, since it wasn't something she was purchasing. Had Jacki been buying a new car, never a used one, *again*, she would've asked the price, specified a color, demanded all the bells and whistles, and sent the bill to her parents. Maybe not! She had divorced herself from her parents monetarily so she could pursue her own dreams without interference.

When Kassie said she would take it, providing they could settle on a price, which the salesman uttered almost solemnly as the same amount that he had quoted to her on the phone, Jacki decided to leave.

Driving the car off the lot, Kassie realized, since she had her own transportation, she could shop, travel, and move around as she pleased. First, she'd find a local church to attend, thus making friends with those who shared the same Christian beliefs she had. Groceries and postage stamps were now within easy reach. No more transit bus rides! In fact, one of the most important reasons for having her own transportation was simply the fact she could go to city records and research all the questions she had concerning a certain, expired Mrs. Carolyn Selway.

# 45

"You bought a car! Lucky you. I'm happy for you. But what do I get you for next Christmas?" If anyone could be happy for someone they loved, it would be Brad, she thought. "I need to find a local church to attend; the chapel is for my friendly patients. It's their special place." Her plans also included going to the library downtown and to the Denver Clarion. The bottom line for her was a fact: she wasn't using Jacki's provision of her vehicle, wasting fuel and adding miles. Liberating as it was, a vehicle also gave her a sense of independence she'd never had before.

Brad knew only too well having a vehicle, regardless of the shape it was in, was a means of freedom. That Kassie now had that pleasure satisfied him a great deal. Things were looking up for both of them. He was a fully fledged permanent member of the staff at Mercy. He had entertained the thought for so long that when it happened, it became an afterthought. His life was full. Having waited so long for a lady he would want as his wife filled him with a peace even he couldn't understand. As much time as they spent together in their downtime, it never seemed to be enough. When apart from Kassie, he was only half the man he wanted to be.

His real family had been the SEALs. They drilled together, slept and ate together, worked and played together as one unit. Their life was not their own; the life of every other member of their team was just as important as their own. They struggled together training, watching each other's back. It would be all worth it; at least that's what he kept telling himself. His SEAL team would, could survive anything. That's when he got to know Karl.

Karl was the most humble of the men in his unit, always drilling as though he was the teacher who had to set the example. There wasn't an arrogant bone in his body. It was he who saw in Brad something more than a disguised, flamboyant past who had parents with money. Brad learned from him how to be a man of quiet dignity, always thoughtful of others and always thankful, even if it meant running an extra ten miles because one of them had to use the head and was late to the beach!

It was Karl who taught him how to treat a lady. It was Karl who shared with Brad his faith in Christ and how important He had become in his life. Brad renewed his faith with energy he had forgotten he had; he would never be alone in the field again. Besides Karl and the rest of the SEAL unit, Brad always had Him. His deep sense of peace was something he didn't understand; he'd never had it before. There was nothing left he had to prove to himself. Whatever the mission, wherever it took them, Brad somehow knew they would return. Until the day they returned to the States, and Karl wasn't with them.

# 46

Stephen Selway had invited the surgeons and their significant others to another dinner party; it was apparent that Selway's middle name was 'party.' He had invited Cindy and she accepted. Rather than cause a fuss, believing that Selway wasn't good enough for Cindy, Brad, Kassie, Jacki and Howie decided to attend anyway. Secretly, Kassie was delighted. Since she hadn't learned anything more at the library than she knew before, she looked forward to spending a little time at 333 Beacon Avenue. Selway had advised them to wear something casual since the weather would allow them to feast on the veranda.

Summer had definitely arrived; the evening was mild. No snow, no rain and no mosquito's, since their subdivision had already sprayed for the pesky critters! As each couple arrived, walking through the living room to the back, they could see that the veranda had a roof of some sort covering it. In one of the corners sat a bustling, free standing fireplace that was crackling and spitting on some rather damp wood. The area was warm and very cozy for the attendees all of whom seemed to be enjoying the atmosphere and the elegantly dressed tables. A red rose with ferns in a rather exquisite vase occupied the center of each table. The plates were of the Lenox variety with silverware polished to high sheen. There were five tables; four for the guests and the other topped with liquid refreshments. Paper lanterns hung above each table; no other light was necessary.

As Kassie was led by Brad, his hand barely touching the small of her back, to the veranda, he whispered, "Leave it to Stephen to have an elaborate outside *informal* barbecue!"

Dinner consisted of scalloped potatoes with dill, fried tomatoes, a frosted walnut salad and all the lobster they could eat. No one was left wanting for more. It truly was a dinner of magnificent proportions. Selway himself was very pleased everyone enjoyed it, except for the two chairs that were left empty. The Chief of Surgery declined to attend; his wife had fallen ill!

Cindy remarked to Kassie she felt so fortunate to be dating a fellow like Selway. Since Cindy had shared with Kassie the knowledge that Selway was really *behaving himself* and treating her very *kindly,* Kassie realized Selway, despite his earlier goofs, could possibly be a refined gentleman. She didn't have the heart to tell her she suspected Selway viewed Cindy as a 'fill in' until the real woman he wanted came along. As least, according to Brad and Howie, that's how Selway viewed their relationship.

"Please excuse me." Kassie left the table and started for the bathroom. When finished, she walked over to the piano. As sure as she was of herself, the large photo of Carolyn Selway gave her a chill she couldn't comprehend. Carolyn was indeed a beautiful woman; a warm smile, perfect teeth, long, perfectly coiffured blonde hair wearing a high neck laced trimmed red dress with a single strand of pearls, earrings to match. The portrait was so alive Kassie had to remind herself the girl in the photo was no longer living. She wouldn't be able to walk to the veranda and see Carolyn sitting next to Selway, knowing she would've been the life of the party. In fact, she had a hard time taking her eyes off the image. That is, until she noticed the same face in a much smaller photo.

Kassie looked closely at a group of people she had seen in her dreams. It startled her! Looking at the individuals in the small frame, she noticed a woman with a cane. That cane! Kassie thought she recognized the face of the woman caring a cane across her arm.

"Is there something you're looking for? Perhaps I can explain." Kassie straightened her posture and turned to face Selway. Emotionally pricked with a needle, she wondered if Selway could see her armpits suddenly get wet or hear her knees knocking. The frog in her throat made her voice sound as though it was coming from a tomb.

"No, not really. Well. Yes. I was admiring your wife's photo." As Selway moved to her side, she hoped he didn't catch the fact she already knew the large photo contained a photo of his deceased ex-wife.

"Oh, I thought you were looking at this one." He gingerly picked up the small photo and looked at it wistfully. "This particular one was taken when Carolyn's mother turned sixty. We all had a great time that day. Lots of our neighbors came over. Everyone loves her mother." Present tense! Sixty! The article in the Clarion said she was dead; that is, if the Carolyn in the photo was the same one who inherited the house. How could that be! Kassie realized whatever she said next had to be formed carefully.

"The background is beautiful, with the evergreens and all."

"Yes. It was taken at her mother's home. It seems like such a long time ago."

"Has it been long since you celebrated…her birthday?" Watch it, Kassie. You're getting too nosy!

"Two years ago. Not long, actually. Time passes so quickly. We celebrated just before Carolyn died." He placed the photo back on the piano, as if to say it was time to go back to the party. But Kassie had to ask one more question. Depending on what Selway said or did, she would live with the consequences.

"What is her name, Carolyn's mother's name?" Without hesitation, he answered.

"Caroline. She spells her name differently. C-a-r-o-l-i-n-e. Lovely woman." Moving toward the veranda, he continued. "Let's go back to the veranda, shall we?" That sounded great. Kassie needed some air!

# 47

In going back to the library, she didn't know exactly what she was going to look for or what, if anything, she would find, but the temptation to be in a solitary place where she could do internet searches was mighty appealing.

The Denver Clarion spoke of Carolyn Alain, spelled C-a-r-o-l-y-n, as having been the owner of the house. When looking up Caroline Alain Statler, the search bar went directly to Carolyn Alain. Kassie tried finding Carolyn Alain Selway and Caroline Alain Statler. To no avail, there wasn't a thing she learned that she didn't already know. Except. Why did Selway spell his mother-in-laws first name? It was bothersome, to say the least. She had searched the records for a Carolyn Statler? Did he suspect that she already knew the correct spelling of his wife's name? But why? How could he possibly know what she knew? Was he aware Kassie had searched for the history of the house at 333 Beacon? Frustrated, she drove home. Tomorrow, she'd check out the names at the Courthouse. Not that she would find anything different; it would simply assuage her curiosity and eliminate another source.

For whatever reason, Kassie had forgotten to take her cell phone with her. When she got back from the library, there was a message from Cindy. 'Could you work for me this coming Saturday? It's important.' Without giving it much thought, she responded to Cindy in the affirmative and put the hours on her schedule.

Brad was filling in for Dr. Creason in the ER on Saturday, which meant that should they get a lunch break at all, they could possibly spend the time together over sandwich and a Pepsi.

# 48

It was definitely a never-to-be-forgotten day in Colorado. Only those who lived on the Front Range could attest to the fact that getting up in the morning, watching the sunrise, whiffing the fragrant fresh air could make you feel alive like no other place on earth. So it was with Kassie. Today wouldn't be any different.

When the weather was pleasant, and for Kassie every day was exquisite, it reminded her of her beloved Wyoming. There were less people to contend with and much more open space than what her present circumstances afforded her. As hard as it sometimes appeared in Wyoming, going to get groceries or traveling into town to go shopping, driving miles and miles with only a few cows or horses along side of the highway, gave her a feeling of emancipation, liberation and freedom. The drive she took gave her time to mediate on the Lord and thank him for all her blessings. By the time she'd finish praying, she would've have reached Sheridan or Cheyenne; depending on how long she wanted to drive it would be time to find that perfect dress or scarf or boots…and groceries.

She sorely missed her home state. The older she got, the feeling of being separated from her family, and the ranch hands she grew up with, the familiarity of the land and the privilege of being able to ride the horses she adored, the absence of all that was so familiar, weighed heavily on her.

Kassie had traveled the world. Although Colorado came close to being ideal, there was no place on earth like her beloved Wyoming. It was where her heart resided and in doing so, even having Brad close, it called to her every time she pictured it in her mind.

This day, however, she was going to the range. Jacki was still asleep; she'd pulled a night shift. After making herself something to eat, she found herself in her bedroom, looking in the bottom drawer of her dresser under some of her sweaters. It was there she kept her firearm, wrapped in a leather sheath that could've easily passed for a brown sweater.

The manager of the range had taken quite a shine to Kassie from the first time she came to practice. Kassie kept the relationship friendly but distant.

"Where'd you learn how to shoot like that?" She was loading her revolver.

"Back home."

"And where might that be?"

"Wyoming."

"Wow! I'd love to hunt Wyoming. Do you hunt?"

"Not lately." She was getting ready to fire again.

"You live in Denver?" He hesitated. He already knew she didn't wear a wedding band. "What do you do?"

"Yes…Nursing."

"Do you always answer someone in two words or less?"

"That's me." Brad had asked her the same thing. Must be something in the water.

He was a pleasant chap. However, he was of no interest to Kassie. Besides, he was becoming a little too nosey. An hour later, after cleaning her revolver, placing it on the front seat, with the cylinder open, the chamber empty, she started the car.

She was about to turn onto the highway when a blue Ford pickup, that had been stopped at the red light, turned and passed Kassie, going to the range. She looked over to her left and saw the driver. She was surprised to say the least.

"*Samuel!*" She whispered under her breath. What is Samuel doing at the range? She wondered if he had noticed her. She didn't think so but the thought hung in her mind like a load of wet clothing. Samuel drove as if he was in a hurry, a faster speed than what he maneuvered at work. If he had seen her, the days of her practicing her aim might become common knowledge around the hospital.

When she got home, she heard Jacki stirring in her bedroom. Kassie quickly deposited the revolver back in her bottom dresser drawer and proceeded to change clothes. Despite her confusion seeing Samuel, it had been a fulfilling morning.

"Hey. About time you got up. You realize you've missed the best part of the day."

"Oh, yeh? And what part is that?" Jacki yawned.

"The part where you get up and make me breakfast!"

"Since when?"

"Since yesterday. Your turn." Kassie, in her need for nourishment, prepared breakfast for Jacki. In Jacki's state of depleted awareness, Kassie could've been eating burnt toast and rubber eggs!

As they sat and ate French toast, with lots of butter and syrup, with hot black coffee as a chaser, Jacki casually mentioned that Howie wanted to know if she and Brad would like to go rafting. They'd already asked Selway and Cindy and they thought it was a great idea. Kassie thought about it, wondering if it was too early in the season to hit the waters of the Arkansas River. The runoff would surely be churning the river water.

"I'll ask Brad."

"Howie already did. Brad wants to go."

"Why did you bother asking me then?"

"Watch out, Kass! You're beginning to sound like me!"

"What I meant was..."

"I know what you meant! You're always the one saying we should be considerate of others feelings. So! I was trying to be considerate toward you. I believe that's something you've been pounding in my head ever since we met."

"So I still have a choice to make. How considerate of you. I really mean it. Maybe you're learning."

"So you're up for it?"

"I didn't say that."

"Well?"

"I'll discuss it with Brad and let you know."

"Oh, I have a feeling I know where this is going!"

"Don't jump to conclusions." Kassie took her dishes to the kitchen and after rinsing them, placed them in the automatic to be washed later. Jacki followed her and did the same with hers.

"Well?"

"Jacki!" Jacki threw her arms in the air, feeling thwarted. "I will let you know." Kassie almost opened her mouth to say she'd seen Samuel earlier; anything to change the subject. She caught herself! And well she did. The last thing Kassie wanted to discuss with Jacki this day was what she was doing at a shooting range.

# 49

As it turned out, Samuel was an exceptional nurse. According to him, he had worked under some of the brightest surgical teams in the country. As he explained it, once he had graduated from John Hopkins, he had moved to Denver and worked at Children's Hospital. After two years, he moved back east and was employed at the Radiation Laboratory in Indianapolis; his work involved cancer patients, mostly children. By the time he moved to Texas, Houston already had need of a surgical nurse. It was in the OR he realized his full potential as a nurse, or so he said.

After three years of work, watching and waiting for an opening in Denver, he was finally hired by Mercy. The move was something he had wanted for a long time.

When not working on third, he substituted on the medical floor. He enjoyed his work and the pay that came with it. Although he didn't move as speedily as his counterparts wished, his excellence in working with the patients made him more than worthy.

When the girls decided to eat their lunch on fourth, Cindy invited Samuel to join them.

"So what up with name 'Samuel'?" Cindy was curious, at a distance.

"My mother wanted something different in a name."

"I heard that you lived in Denver before. Need I ask what brought you back?"

"I did live here for a spell." He hesitated before speaking again. "I guess you could say I missed the mountains."

The girls listened as they inhaled their sandwich in the med room on fourth. OR and ER along with third flour were extremely busy. After each took a swig of Pepsi, they returned to work. No half hour break today!

# 50

The resident in ER took one look at the little girl, softly crying, lying on the stretcher, carried by the two patrolmen that had ridden with her in the back of the ambulance. After a cursory exam, he exploded. Turning toward a nurse, he spoke.

"Help me get this child to OR. Call the floor and see if Dr. Selway or Dr. Guiterrez is available to do surgery. Now!" To the little girl, he said, "Don't worry. We're going to help you. Go ahead and cry. It's okay. I'll be listening." As the RN, along with the help of the police, moved the girl to a gurney, he spoke to the officers. "How long after you got the call did you bring her here to the hospital? Her wounds are fresh and raw. Perhaps one of you could fill me in as we walk."

Taking the elevator, the patrolman gave the resident the only information he had to offer. "We got a call from her neighbor. Said someone was screaming in the house next door. Could we come immediately, as though she knew what was going on? My partner and I were in the vicinity so we booked it over there. This little girl was on the floor in the house, screaming. Blood was on the carpet where she had thrashed! I think it was the mother standing in the doorway to the kitchen, crying, but we didn't waste any time. We put the child on a stretcher and here we are."

"We should have release papers signed before she goes to surgery. I'll leave it up to you gentlemen to bring those papers to me, signed, before she," nodding to the girl, "hits the recovery room. Understand? Now go! We'll take it from here."

It took very little time before third floor at Mercy knew that they'd be receiving a patient from OR that had been severely brutalized and beaten. In addition to being a child, she was alone. Her left arm had been broken, the skin torn and bleeding. Her face had scratches and was bloodied. What caused the surgeons outrage and grief were the antique scars and blotches of bloodied lashes she had on her back. Nothing the surgeons could've added would've prepared the personnel on third for what they saw when she arrived.

Her name was Della and she answered all questions with a moan. Her eyes darted from nurse to nurse, not knowing what to expect. After being briefed by Dr. Selway, the staff tried to make her as comfortable as possible. Speaking to her or asking questions in a soft, warm manner was as necessary to Della as it was to the staff. How could anyone do such damage to a little girl of about ten to be found in such a state?

When it was time to give her an injection for pain, Cindy carefully removed her gown to reveal a small but hefty arm. She also saw the scars on Della's right upper arm where she had been beaten. Almost without looking, Cindy gave her the shot, swabbed it again with alcohol, pulled down her sleeve and left the room. Cindy was about to get very ill.

# 51

ella, in spite of her injuries and the pain that accompanied them, was about as sweet as a little girl could be. Annette, the RN from the Emergency Room, wasn't the type of woman that Della would feel comfortable around. Although Jacki tried; she didn't make it through the first hour! She was too calloused and curt for a serious little girl with serious problems. Cindy, on the other hand, was the nurse Della enveloped. Somehow Della knew she and Cindy had something in common. They were both no nonsense women, regardless of the difference in their age. It had everything to do with what Cindy had lived and what she now saw Della was living.

It took all the stamina that Cindy could muster to attend to Della's needs. *Don't tell!* How many times had she heard those words as a child? So Cindy didn't tell, until the abuse got so bad that she tried to tell her mother, if for no other reason than to survive. *Don't tell!* It was as though her mother didn't want to hear anything Cindy had to say. There was an unspoken warning from her father to her mother, an intimidating look at his wife, using the same words: *Don't tell!*

Cindy knew the extended chances of Della returning to the hospital for further treatment for abuse were enormously high. Somehow, someway, Cindy had to alert the authorities what she suspected was going on in Della's household. What about HIPPA? If she were to go that route, it would have to be an entirely anonymous call. She knew she had to do it. No one was around to do it for her when she was Della's age; she suffered in silence. *Don't tell!* If only her mother would've listened to her!

"I've got another pain shot with me. The arm or the hip?" Cindy said with a smile in her voice.

"I never get them in my arm. My backside is a little sore, though." Della sounded down.

"Pretty soon, when you're healed enough…"

"I don't want to go home." A simple statement, said so softly had Cindy not been paying attention to Della's moods, she would've missed it. Tears welled up in Della's eyes. Turning her face away from Cindy, she repeated the same words. "I don't want to go home." It was barely a whisper.

A knife wielded into Cindy's heart couldn't have been more painful than the words she had just heard. This little girl, barely ten years old, was scared to death to tell anyone of what she had already lived. Watching Della, seeing the tears flow down her face, she remembered the wretchedness of her own pathetic life, the life she endured until she escaped her own prison-like conditions at home.

Cindy swabbed the area with alcohol, gave her the shot, swabbed again with alcohol, replaced the sheet that covered the little ingénue, while the child cried silently. Cindy was about to leave when a well of emotion inside of her took over. She leaned above the bed and gave Della a kiss on the side of her face. Then, taking her hand and holding it gently, she said what she should've kept to herself.

"This is not your fault! I won't let anyone do this to you anymore. Over my dead body!" Placing her little discolored hand beneath the sheet, she turned to leave. When the door closed, Cindy sobbed openly, unashamed, afraid of what might yet come.

# 52

ntitled to be notified, Cindy would spend Friday in court. Purposefully, she had asked Kassie to work for her the next day, not knowing what to expect from this latest encounter with the law. Even though she felt guilty, it wasn't because of something she had done. Rather, someone was in prison because of what they had done to her. Presently they were up for parole.

Cindy was raised in a family of differing opinions. Her mother was a quiet, unassuming woman who had three children; two boys and a girl. They were her life. It was she who saw to it each of her children was given a proper education, competed in extracurricular activities and taken to church on Sunday. Respect for others and good manners were high on the list of those ethical principals which she wished to pass on to her little crumb crunchers…rug rats…curtain climbers.

As far as Cindy was concerned, her mother was perfect, with one exception. Mrs. Rawlings didn't admit to having a clue as to what went on behind Cindy's closed bedroom door. Many were the times when Cindy tried to explain to her mother what was happening to her was not normal. As Cindy got older, into her high school years, Mrs. Rawlings avoided having any conversation with Cindy concerning her comings and goings, her ability to stay cooped up in her room or the reason why her father refused to put a lock on her door, from the inside. Whatever the reasons, her mother appeared oblivious to her daughter's concerns.

Her father had his opinions as well. He always showed the utmost respect for his wife and his children, *in public*. He was always present with them in church and in the community functions which they attended. His loyalty toward others and in his work was exemplary. The schooling his children received was important to him as well.

As a postal worker he never took a day off, never thought of calling in sick, and always taught his children how important it was to have a good job, to be loyal to their employer, preferably after they graduated from college. The discipline of his sons was always done with a softly spoken word or the taking away of a toy or wagon or computer for a day. He never spoke to them using curse words or threatened them with capital punishment.

However, he had a secret; his one perverted opinion. In front of the children's mother or in public, he gave his daughter the respect, love and admiration to which she was entitled. It was only in the middle of the night that he made Cindy cognizant of the fact should she choose to tell anyone...*ANYONE*...what happened between her and the man she called her father she alone would be held responsible for his death by his own hand.

Every night he came to her room, he made Cindy promise their liaisons would never be heard nor see the light of day. 'I am preparing you for the day you marry for everything between you and your husband should stay private.' The older she became, the less she believed him; she abhorred this self-righteous male who invoked his 'fatherly' privileges upon his only daughter.

When Cindy saw him enter the courtroom, in orange and in shackles, she knew should her father be paroled, she would again live in a state of fear. All the counseling in the world couldn't erase the memories of what her own father had done to her. Years of therapeutic counseling couldn't help her forgive the mother who chose to ignore her claims. It wasn't until she became a Christian that she found peace. Because of Christ and His love for her, she felt compelled to forgive her mother as Christ had forgiven her.

She had to hear for herself what decision the judge would make regarding his request for a parole. When she saw him walking into court, smiling like a Cheshire cat, the memories of all that had transpired between them had her living the nightmare all over again. A permanent restraining order against her father was no small item in the eyes of the law; if necessary, she would update hers.

His request for a parole was denied; he wasn't a happy man. Cindy was armed with the conviction should he be released, he would find some way to punish her for charging him with rape. The beatings she got when she wouldn't comply with her father's demands took a toll of a different kind. *Courage is fear that has said its prayers.* She took solace in knowing each day made her stronger, less fearful of the man who called himself her father. She prayed the day would come when he would admit to the courts what he had done; not to justify her claims but for him to recognize his sin.

Her prayer, the one she always repeated every night in bed, involved asking God to forgive her for feeling such hatred and animosity toward her father. *Time heals.* Someday, she thought, I'll be able to forgive him as only a child of God can do.

# 53

"Whew! What a day." It was Brad, who looked as dragged out as he sounded. Kassie was busy preparing a homemade recipe of brussel sprouts and mushrooms to be served with toasted garlic French bread. She and Brad had made a meal of it once before. As he relaxed on the couch, he continued. "Of all things, we had to unplug a guy today. He was in a lot of pain. It was to be expected, of course." Kassie put the casserole in the oven, set the temperature and the clock. After washing her hands, she sat next to Brad.

"You unplugged someone today? What did he swallow?"

Brad was instantly sorry for having brought it up. Kassie had already decided that the case was as innocuous as it was routine.

"He used a soft drink bottle instead of his partner. I'm sorry I brought it up." He leaned over, putting his head on her shoulder.

"I'm sorry for asking. I can't imagine…honestly?" Kassie wondered, although not out loud, what a surgeon would say to a patient who would do such a thing. Indignation didn't come close! Perhaps pity!

"We also had a little girl come to third floor today that had a broken arm and was severely beaten." Kassie waited to see if Brad would comment. When he didn't, she continued. "What is our world coming to? Parents beating their children, men preferring men, women with free access to the morning after pill, young children being given drugs to act as babysitters, infidelity running rampant, all of this even among some hospital personnel! I thought I was worldly enough to know some things but...I have serious doubts. People can be so hurtful toward others. Why? What is there to gain? By the way, did you see in the paper the article about the US sending artillery to South America? Somewhere in Mexico. The US ambassador was killed, along with several others. US Navy SEALs were killed; they were off duty but they went to help in spite of being told to 'stand down.' Why weren't these people protected? Have we become so numb to adversity that we don't protect our own?" Kassie was about out of breath. "Sometimes I wonder...what it is about power that makes individuals so narcissistic, so self absorbed, so conceited as to throw away lives that are contrary to their existence?"

"Whoa! Again, where did all that come from? You really are interested in politics!"

"No. I'm interested in what's fair...what's correct...what's truthful. He was a diplomat from *my country*! I expect our government to protect him! Besides, that brings up another question. When the United States sends artillery to another country, doesn't the US have a designated liaison to broker the deal?"

"What made you think of that? I mean...it probably involved the President of our country."

"No. Not necessarily. What if the ambassador was involved? What if someone didn't want that little piece of news to get around? What if...?"

"Kass! I know you do a lot of thinking without ever verbalizing it. I know you're well read. I know you go to the library every chance you get. But little lady, stop this train of thought! You'll only become more upset. There are some things that neither you nor I will ever solve." Kassie looked frustrated and Brad wasn't sure of what to say next. Giving it some thought, he continued. "No one can be sure of what happened unless they were involved. I know this for a fact. I'm not saying you are wrong. It's just that…"

"What? How do you know that for a fact? You've never been ambassador or a broker or put in harm's way without protection! How could you possibly know?" Kassie was perturbed but not irreverently so. After seeing Brad's frustration with her, she immediately felt she stepped across some invisible line, a line he didn't want to cross. "Brad, I apologize. It's just that…"

"Hey. Enough already. Come here." Kassie snuggled closer to him, putting her head on his shoulder. Without a doubt, Brad knew he had said too much. What was it? 'I know this for a fact.' He had almost led her into a question that he didn't want her to ask. She'd come close enough to the kind of interrogation and debriefing that he only wanted to forget. Yes, he knew a lot of facts about his government that if Kassie knew even a portion of them, she would pursue the printed word until she found the answers. If that were possible! It was a commendable trait; because of it she made an extremely thorough nurse. But for now, Brad simply didn't want to discuss his past and all it entailed. He had put it behind him upon leaving the Navy. That's where he intended for it to stay.

During those frustrating and perilous days he'd learned more than he cared to remember about the futility of life. The loss of his friend due to enemy fire, watching as children dug through garbage to find some morsel to eat, the ever present mosquitoes, rats and snakes with people living in tin and dung shacks that people called home. If you only knew, he thought. Someday. Someday, Kassie, I'll tell you all about it, but not today. Not yet.

# 54

The river was high and running fast. Although she'd been rafting before, the Arkansas could be a troublesome trek for someone who was not experienced in rafting. After paying their fees, they were led to a shed where they were told to climb into wet suits. Jacki and Kassie removed their shirts, shorts and shoes. Their swimming suits, which they had already been wearing, were left on.

Getting into a wet suit wasn't the easiest thing they'd ever done. The suit was supposed to fit like a second skin. Kassie noticed that Cindy was having difficulty with hers.

"Need some help?" Kassie asked as she moved over to Cindy's corner. "Here. I think you should remove your shirt."

"No. It'll be alright. The suit is just a little snug." With her back turned toward Kassie, she struggled to pull on the suit. Kassie could see she'd kept her shirt on; perhaps she thought the water would be too cold. As she approached, Cindy alarmed her with what she said.

"Just go away. I can do this. Just leave me alone!"

"That's alright. Let me help you." As Kassie tried to stuff Cindy's shirt down in the back, she became frustrated. There was too much bulk; it was bunched up on one side. She decided to lift the shirt to straighten it before she'd try again. It was then she saw some scars on Cindy's back. For a moment she just stared at them. Not knowing exactly what caused them she decided to refrain from asking what had happened. Carefully, she eased the shirt down and gingerly tucked it into Cindy's suit. Once they got Cindy zipped up, she turned around.

"Thank you for helping. It's really tight." She bent over, grabbing her shoes and socks and put them in a locker. "You ready? I'm not sure I'm going to enjoy this but I'll give it a try. How about you?"

Kassie was still visualizing the scared skin, with its black smudges and distorted flesh. What had happened? She wanted to ask so badly. But. This wasn't the time. Perhaps later.

"I'm not sure I'm going to enjoy this trek today anymore than you, but like you, I'll brave the cold water." Kassie laughed, nervously. Cindy glanced at Kassie as if there was something she wanted to share. But she, too, laughed, all the way to the dock.

"Look over there. Kass!"

"Where?"

"Three rafts over, to your right. In the red swim suit."

Though she clearly saw Samuel as he climbed into a raft, she began to wonder how he miraculously happened to go rafting on the same day the six of them were there.

"Oh my! Maybe Jacki mentioned something about us going. Did you say anything?" Kassie would question Jacki later.

"Of course not! Why do you think I feel…exposed?" She looked away, grabbed Kassie's arm and said, "Don't look at him! Maybe he doesn't know we're here."

That evening, as Kassie and Jacki were vacuuming and dusting their apartment, she wanted to ask Jacki if she had seen the scars on Cindy's back. Something in the back of her mind kept her from expressing it. Not that she didn't trust Jacki to keep from repeating it. The only thing Jacki *never* kept to herself was her encounters with men. But Kassie had answered her own doubts. What she saw on Cindy was her secret; she could wait until Cindy wanted to discuss them. Then she remembered that Cindy always wore a sleeved whatever, be it a sweater, blouse, housecoat…she'd never seen Cindy bare her arms. The more Kassie thought about it, the more she realized Cindy bore a concealed past that was more painful than what she cared to think about at the moment.

Rafting had been an adventure that was exhilarating and dangerous. Even though Jacki had been thrown out, she held onto the line she'd been given, and was hauled back to safety in the raft. They'd decided it was something they'd all probably do again, when the water wasn't so high.

As she lay in bed, trying to fall asleep, she thought of Samuel. First the shooting range and then today, at the dock. Why was Cindy upset at seeing him? She was definitely disturbed by him being there. But why? Crazy scenarios were floating through her mind. Maybe he had said something to Cindy she preferred to forget. Maybe it was Cindy's shyness that had her troubled when she saw him. Whatever it was, she'd think about it later. Tomorrow was another day. Surely it could wait.

# 55

Cindy lived quite comfortably in her one bedroom apartment. She didn't have many furnishings; she didn't need them. There were a couple photos of her on her bedroom dresser; one of her amongst vivid flowers in her grandmother's perennial flower garden, the other was Cindy with her grandmother sitting on the porch of her grandmother's home.

As she stood looking at the photos, the memories of that summer returned to her. She knew why she was at her grandmothers. Her grandmother listened to her. Her name was Helen. Grandma Helen. She was the one person in her world who listened to Cindy without placing blame.

Grandma Helen lived about a mile from Cindy. It was just a nice walk most of the time. But there were times when Cindy ran the whole mile. After she'd caught her breath, her grandmother would get some warm water and a soft towel and wipe her fresh wounds. After applying a soothing ointment, she'd sit beside Cindy and stroke her hair.

Helen had wanted to confront Cindy's father in the worst way about the way he was treating her. She knew that it wouldn't do any good. Cindy's father, Gilbert, was her son; her husband had beat Gilbert in the same way. She was too scared to do anything about it then; she was terrified to say anything now. Cindy was her granddaughter; how could she have known he would repeat his father's behavior on his daughter?

The best that Grandma Helen could do for her was to listen to Cindy and to be there when she needed help. Grandma Helen knew it wasn't nearly enough. As soon as she could, Cindy would leave her home just as her father, Gilbert, had done. Guilt-ridden as she was, Grandma Helen was glad Gilbert had left at sixteen. He needed to heal. But, Gilbert couldn't change his behavior. Not without help. Gil was doing to his daughter what had been done to him. A history of violence was repeating itself.

# 56

I t was a beautiful Colorado summer that spoke multitudes about the State. For Kassie, it became harder to spend her days working inside when in her reverie all she could think about was the feeling of having the wind flow against her face, her hair billowing out like the hair of Vanity's mane; the presence of strength under her as Vanity traversed the hillsides, showing no fear of speed or terrain, the two of them moving as one. The freedoms she had at the ranch existed for her nowhere else on earth.

Her desire of returning to her roots was never very far from her innermost thoughts. She loved the work she was doing. Perhaps more than she should. Although, more than she cared to admit, Wyoming and family tugged at her heart. The older she got the yearning for wide open spaces, emancipation from city life, became more seductive. But Kassie wanted more. How difficult would it be to be married, living on a ranch and working as a nurse an hour's drive from home? It wouldn't have to be her parent's place. She could be happy having a small place, large enough to have a couple horses.

Surgery never seemed to have a light day. Most of them were scheduled; the predictable became routine. Her sympathetic heart was always being compromised with what was called a necessary invasion as opposed to an optional invasion of the human body. Cancerous lesions, heart valve replacement, broken bones were considered necessary. Breast implants, face lifts and tummy tucks were optional! They were calls Kassie didn't have to make. She just wanted to be there to perform her duties and help the patients understand all would go well.

Some surgical procedures, however, didn't go well. Once in a great while an individual didn't wake up in the recovery room, with its smell of antiseptic and sound of pain. Those patients were relieved of the subsequent days of healing and the persistent pain that sometimes followed. Of course, on the way to the morgue they were oblivious to what they were missing; the family was left behind to take care of all the details of notification and burial.

Kassie didn't dwell on the negative nearly as often as she dwelt on the positive aspects of her job. It was just that death was so final, as least on this earth, she thought. When someone died under anesthesia, those patients weren't given a chance to say 'I love you' or 'I'm sorry' one last time. It was at times like these that she desired to have a full life, living it to its fullest, never forgetting to treat people as if it would be the last time she would speak with them. Kassie saw people from the inside out; what they wore, how they looked and where they lived spoke nothing to her. She looked deep into a person's eyes, looking beyond the superficial, to find out what the person was really like. It had always been like that, even when she was a child and especially as a flight attendant. As far as she was concerned, the exterior persona of any individual could hide a multitude of sins.

Cindy. The quiet, somewhat timid, young lady who had a heart of gold with a mind to match. At the moment, her heart ached for Cindy. Whatever her past held, it seemed to Kassie, she bore by herself. Scars are permanent, indelible, both on the mind and on the body. The memories could be shared, if one allowed it. Something in Cindy's life would have to occur, a trigger of sorts, in order for her to have the security and presence of mind to share what she had lived.

She felt so fortunate. Basically her life was even keel with the other young women she knew. Kassie had been blessed with great parents, a wonderful home, warm friends and two lucrative careers. There wasn't a thing she needed that she didn't have; many of her wants came with time. To top it off, she had met a man that more than fulfilled her dreams.

So much for her thoughts on this miserable rainy day. When she was able to stay indoors baking cookies, she enjoyed the rain. The world seemed a better place when nature was revived with moisture. Clean and unencumbered.

Now, if only she lived in Wyoming.

# 57

"Great day for plinking!" As he unpacked his rifle, inserting three cartridges, he continued. "You expect many shooters today? By the way, my name's Larry."

"Jeff here. Glad to meet ya. Actually, no. Not anymore than usual. They seem to get the bug to shoot when the sun shines. Sunny days are good for business."

As Larry prepared his rack on the table for target practice, Jeff watched from the side. He saw that Larry was as meticulous about his setup as he was with his rifle. When he was finished...

"How far is your farthest target?"

Jeff had seen a lot of shooters who thought they were good enough to punch the bull's eye at five hundred or even a thousand yards. They were also guilty of over inflated egos! "The one you'll want to use is set at 500 yards. The green circle. We use'ta have one at thousand..."

Bang! Under the canopy that was attached to the shed, it was ear splitting loud.

"You might want'ta tell me when you're going to shoot." Jeff reached for his ear muffs that were sitting on the table next to him. "By the way..."

Bang! Jeff was left speechless and near deaf. This was no ordinary rifle but before he could ask…

"Would you mind spotting me?" Larry never raised his head from his position of looking down the rifle scope.

"No! Sure thing. Let me run in the shed and get my range finder." Jeff was back within seconds.

"Ready? On the five hundred marker?"

"Ready." Jeff put on his muffs, putting his right eye on the range finder.

Bang. The sound was muffled but Jeff could see that Larry had hit the green circle. "You're quite a shot!" Jeff was impressed. He watched in amazement as Larry quickly wiped down his rifle and packed it in its case. After placing the sand bags in their original position on the table, he stood and proceeded walking to his truck.

"You only takin' three shots?" Jeff was perplexed. He had removed his ear muffs. He wanted to ask Larry what he did for a living.

Larry turned around slowly and without so much as a twitch, said, "If you look real close, you'll see that I hit the green all three times." He smiled, turned and continued to walk.

Jeff quickly fumbled for the range finder around his neck, raised it and put the sight on the green circle. There were only two holes; one of them was extra wide. "You got two in the same hole!" Absorbed as Jeff was, he still expected to hear Larry confirm his shots. But when he turned around, Larry, or whoever he was, had already left the range. "Wonder where you learned to shoot like that? What do you do…for work? What's your real name?" He was left standing, wondering, talking to himself.

# 58

"Della went home today." Shirley, an RN, joined Jacki and Kassie for lunch. "Funny thing. She was taken to a private home. Real nice people. You know, the hospital has to report any abuse they see in a child...or anyone, I guess. But they're always shipped back home to the same unscrupulous...immoral...place from where they came or they're put into some kind of child custody home. Today was different. I was happy for Della."

Jacki said, "Did you meet the people that were taking her home?"

"I did. In fact I was there when they were told about her history. The mother got tears in her eyes. And well she should. Poor kid! I hope for Della's sake she has a fine home..."

"Della went home?" Cindy had just walked into the break room when she caught the last part of Shirley's sentence. "They sent her home to the same...!"

Kassie said, "No! No! An older couple is taking her into their home. We were just saying all of us hope for Della's sake, she now has a safe environment in which to grow up."

"She wasn't released into child custody then." Cindy kept her head lowered so that the girls wouldn't suspect anything. She was tickled pink that her one telephone call had made a difference in Della's life, a conversation that would forever remain anonymous. Maybe there is some justice in this world, she thought.

"I'm just glad she wasn't given over to the police. Who knows where she would've ended up? Those police are always out for themselves!" Jacki was miffed about something.

"In a private home Della will have a real good chance at life. She's a smart kid; maybe she'll be fortunate to go to college. Become a therapist or something." Cindy smiled.

"Cindy, you got too close to that girl. You know better," Jacki said.

"Suppose I did? I have a heart and a soul and so does she. We connected." Cindy took a sip of her ever present Coke. "Anyway..."

"I know you loved her, Cindy, and I'm happy for you both," Kassie said, softly, as she laid a hand on Cindy's wrist and smiled. "We all have scars of some sort or the other. Some show and some don't. Let's hope she heals well."

Cindy looked up at Kassie and smiled. One day she would have to entrust Kassie with her story. Kassie, she knew, would understand when no one else could.

"Lunch break's over, ladies!" Jacki had heard enough.

# 59

The commander rose and walked to the window. Without turning around, he continued. "I'm not sure that he's missing. I believe he's around. We just have to find him. Rule him out." He turned and, deliberately, walked back to his desk and sat. He opened a drawer on the left hand side of his desk, pulled out two sheets of paper and placed them in front of him. The papers looked as if they had been mangled; someone must have throw them away and then decided to retrieve them. The commander folded his hands and placed them on his desk. He leaned forward and spoke in hushed tones.

"This is classified. Between you and me. Got it?"

"Got it!"

"Two days ago I received this letter from one of the SEALs in his former group." Thrusting the papers across the desk, he continued. "I didn't take it seriously then and trashed it. I have since been informed that two former Navy SEALs were killed in a freak accident. Read what it says and then will talk." The commander sat back in his chair and waited.

The letter itself had no specifics except to say that the author was afraid that a Corporal that washed out of BUDS several years before was very disgruntled and was determined to punish those he thought was responsible for pushing him to ring the bell. The writer was sure that the Corporal had very bad intentions toward someone. After he washed out, the writer of the letter pointed out that, after separation from the service, he went on to college, in medicine.

Personally, the writer thought the situation should be looked into and at least determined if the Corporal was going to act on his hatred. The only physical description of the man the writer offered was that the man had auburn hair.

The author felt compelled to pass on the vague information… what little there was…because he felt apprehensive about what might happen.

As Brad evaluated the contents of the letter, some questions came to mind. He laid the papers on the Commanders desk.

"Where were they killed."

"Texas."

"What kind of accident?"

"Their car was stalled on the railroad track out of view of the oncoming train. Evidently, it happened quickly since neither man exited the vehicle. I was just informed of their demise this morning. Police chief out of Houston."

"Do you have their names?"

"Not yet."

"Had they been drugged?"

"Don't know."

"Were firearms involved?"

"Not that I'm aware of…but I didn't ask." There was a period of silence between the two men. Each had thoughts of their own. Finally Brad spoke.

"What exactly is it that you want me to do?"

# 60

Summers always passed quickly in Colorado; there were so many opportunities to occupy one's time. Any normal year, summer could last well into November. The mountains, if they were lucky, would have a base of snow by early October.

Occasionally, Brad would fill in for a surgeon in ER. It was a rare occurrence though, since the surgical units were kept busy every day. Mercy hospital, with all the latest in technology, was a popular place; it was also known for the expertise of its surgeons.

Kassie divided her time off between oil painting, hiking with Brad, knitting and when she had the chance…she would go to the range. Housekeeping was shared between herself and Jacki; their apartment always appeared immaculate.

Jacki's interests mainly involved men, what they did for a living, where they lived, what kind of transportation they had and where they dined. Howard Harriman was never heard to complain. He was content to know that Jacki dated him and him only. It was a good arrangement for Jacki and a satisfying one for Dr. Harriman.

Dr. Stephen Selway and Cindy Rawlings had become quite an item. As roses appeared on their vines, as birds traveled north from their winter habitats in the south, their relationship blossomed as well. Theirs became a love affair of respect and understanding for each other, which if Kassie were asked, would say that it was due to the demeanor and 'ladylikeness' of Cindy.

Kassie had located Caroline Statler by going through the court records she was allowed to see. Ms. Statler now lived in Pueblo, Colorado, with a listed telephone number and a published address. All she had to do was to give her a call but Kassie hesitated, weighing the ramifications of her doing so. She was sure Ms. Statler wanted her privacy; she probably didn't want to discuss anything about her daughter. It may only cause her pain. But Kassie was inquisitive and because of that she had placed a call to her and asked if she could drive to Pueblo on a weekend to speak with her.

When she arrived she parked her car in front of the house next to Ms. Statler's address. Waiting in the car, she started to have butterflies and misgivings about their meeting. Over the telephone, Ms. Statler was extremely polite. Still, Kassie had no idea what to expect when she asked Ms. Statler about her late daughter.

She rang the doorbell, twice. Whoever came to the door, Kassie determined, she was now committed to learning about Carolyn Selway. When the handle of the door turned, she took a deep breath.

"Hello. Ms. Statler? I'm Kassie Colbert. We spoke on the phone?" Black hair the color of coal with dark eyes, the lady, finely dressed, motioned for her to come in and have a seat in the living room. "About your daughter?" Kassie was forgetting her manners while exhibiting the shakes. "Thank you."

"It's nice to meet you. Come in." With a wave of her hand, she said. "If you'll excuse me one minute, I just arrived home myself. I'll be in the powder room for a moment." She turned and left.

'Exquisite' hardly touched the effects of the place. From the Karastan floor covering to the high ceiling, graced with three gorgeous multi-layered chandeliers, from the white leather covered furniture to the fresh flowers on the mantle over the fireplace, everything spelled money. Yet, it had a peaceful sensitivity within its walls, a place where Kassie could imagine herself knitting or reading a favorite book or just listening to music, which is what she heard playing softly in the background. An Architectural Digest magazine lay open next to the chair in which she was sitting. She was startled when Ms. Statler returned from...

Gone was the black hair; in its place was long gray and white streaked hair that had no curl. The false eyelashes were gone as well as the eye shadow, lipstick and...she had changed into her bathrobe.

"I didn't mean to startle you. Forgive me, but this is the way I prefer to be when I'm at home. May I get you some coffee...or perhaps some tea?"

"I'm fine. I just finished my soda before I came."

"Oh. Alright, then. What is it that you wanted to speak to me about...oh...yes, my daughter." Ms. Statler took the seat opposite Kassie. The room was not highly lit but Kassie was sure she had seen the woman before. But first. "What is it that you do, Ms. Colbert?"

"At present, I'm an OR nurse at Mercy Hospital east of Denver."

"Yes. You mentioned that. How nice. Do you enjoy it? One should always enjoy the profession they choose."

"Thank you. Yes. I love what I do."

"Well. I don't mean to pry." I wonder what you'll think I'll be doing to you, Ms. Statler? Kassie thought.

"Your daughter, Carolyn...I mean..."

"How did you find me?"

"Actually, I looked up the records on 333 Beacon Avenue and..."

"Of course. At the courthouse I suppose." She didn't wait for a reply. "I moved several times before I bought this house, fully furnished. I fell in love with its antiquity."

"It is lovely." Kassie was nervous. She really wanted to hear about her daughter. "I imagine that your daughter came here often."

"Oh, no." Ms. Statler played with a portion of her bathrobe; she appeared to be shaking. "I moved here shortly after Carolyn died. That is, if you believe the press."

"The press?"

"Yes. Carolyn supposedly died in a skiing accident outside of Zurich. I have never believed that, however." The memories appeared to come back to her as she recalled her daughter. "She had several young men court her. Gentlemen. Educated. Well-mannered. But you know what they say? You can raise your daughter but you can't decide for them whom they are to marry?" She appeared to relax. Kassie wasn't at all sure what she should ask next. She wondered if she should change the subject for the moment. But! The worst thing Ms. Statler could do is ask her to leave.

"Can you describe some of the young men she dated?"

"There were several, all different, of course. Let's see. There was Lance Kelly who had his own orchestra. He was so delightful, fun to be around. Carolyn didn't think he was stable enough...he traveled a lot.

"Rudy Spegel was another handsome man. He owned a clothing store in Denver. Always immaculately dressed! I'm not sure why she neglected him. They had only a few dates...then it was over.

"Her first husband was Roger. He was an attorney who came to Denver from Indiana. He was such an attentive guy but he died. Complications, you know, from skiing." Kass wished she could say that she *didn't know* but that would've been a lie. "Am I going too fast for you?"

"No, Ms. Statler. You're just fine." Please. Keep going, Kassie thought.

"Before she met and married Stephen Selway, she dated a different kind of guy, aloof and not very friendly. They did a lot of traveling, overseas. Never did learn what he did but he promised her the moon. You know what I mean!" Ms. Statler straightened herself erect in the chair and without missing a beat, she continued. "I'll never forget the evening Carolyn broke off their relationship. He was very upset; so was she. They had sharp words for each other, words *I never* taught my daughter! I was in the library so I only heard the sharp words. Personally, I was glad when he was gone. He was too nosey as far as I was concerned." She paused while Kassie sucked the air out of the room. "Can't remember his name!" Ms. Statler looked at the ceiling and rolled her eyes. "Of course, she met Stephen, the surgeon. Seems to me I remember him being from Indiana also. I could be wrong; it's been a while." She lost herself in her own memories. "Seems to me he went back to Indiana…some kind of promotion."

"You intimated that you thought your daughter was killed. Why do you think that?"

"Carolyn was an extremely skilled skier. She skied for the fun of it, the exhilaration she got from being in the snow. In the mountains she was always aware the terrain. It was something she always checked before going out on the slopes. Oh, how proud her father was of her! He would get tears in his eyes as he watched her maneuver the moguls. He delighted in her skills, not just on the ski slopes but how she handled herself in life." She grew quiet, reticent. "Her father was killed in an accident. That was a shock to us both."

She began to wonder. How could she inform Ms. Statler that she was also listed as having died according to the Denver Clarion? Kassie couldn't! She just couldn't bring herself to admit…

"You know, Ms. Colbert, everything the press prints is not always accurate. I'm sure they think Carolyn died because of her own mistake. I just don't believe it! I never will! In fact, Dr. Selway was under suspicion for some time. But to be perfectly honest with you, I don't know to this day who she was with or how long Carolyn had been over there. Perhaps someday, someone will be able to tell me exactly what happened to my daughter." She sat back in the chair, almost exhausted.

"I've taken up enough of your time but I'm also profoundly happy that you agreed to see me. If the topic of our conversation could've been lighter..."

"Oh, you mustn't stress yourself. Her life was cut short. Too short!" Yes. But why and how? They both rose and started for the front door. "May you have a long, fulfilling life? Just be careful who you marry, my dear."

As they approached the door, Kassie spotted a cane, sitting by the door jam, almost out of sight. Ms. Statler saw the surprise on her face.

"Oh, that. I use it when I'm tired. Just in case."

As she stepped outside, she turned and smiled. "It has been a pleasure meeting you." *Again*, Kassie thought.

"Perhaps, we'll meet again." Ms. Statler started to close the door. As Kassie walked back to her car, she turned to look at the house. Ms. Statler waved to her and then, disappeared as she closed her front door.

Kassie sat in the car, her hands shaking. After starting the engine, she took in a deep breath, the first and only breath she took since she rang the doorbell! She couldn't tell if it was to keep her alive or to keep her from screaming.

# 61

Ms. Caroline Statler didn't believe in illusions. No one could've surprised her more than the day she received a call from a Ms. Kassie Colbert. She should've been upset with this woman from nowhere who had the gall to call and want to discuss her daughter. In her mind, Ms. Kassie Colbert would probably never have called again if she had just said she didn't wish to reminisce about Carolyn.

Someone had killed her daughter! That was not an illusion or some fairy tale. For several weeks before Carolyn left for overseas, she wasn't herself. Fretful, tired and jumpy, Ms. Statler had never seen Carolyn in such a state. At the time, Ms. Statler occupied a small condo in Denver. She had asked Carolyn if she wanted to come to her place for a couple days. Since there had never been a need for secrets between them, she thought Carolyn would share her thoughts about what she happened to be feeling. Without being asked! It didn't happen. Carolyn came for a week, laid around the condo as though she had no energy, didn't eat enough to spit nor did she venture out of the condo any of the time. Not once did Caroline take the liberty to ask her daughter what was bothering her. Clearly, something was. Since Carolyn was deceased, there were many days she wished she would've asked questions only her daughter could've answered.

After she went back to Stephen and 333 Beacon Avenue, Caroline never heard one word of apprehension in the voice of her daughter. So when she told her mother that she was going to Europe, Caroline figured that all of the tension that Carolyn harbored just a couple weeks before had dissipated. She assumed that she would be accompanied by her husband, Stephen Selway. She wasn't privy to any details of her planned trip, but then, she never queried her either.

After her death, Dr. Selway denied vehemently that he was with her on that fateful day. He was also traumatized by her death.

As Caroline Statler thought back about those last few days she had with Carolyn, she felt a twinge of guilt. If only she would've inquired of her daughter what was bothering her, perhaps she would be alive today. But she wasn't. Now she had had an encounter with someone who wanted to know more about her daughter than she was willing to share.

That street went both ways. At the time of Carolyn's death, Caroline retreated to a safe place…a place where she could mourn her daughter in private. Now she had just been asked to remember aspects of Carolyn's life and death after the fact, maybe…maybe…if she helped Ms. Kassie Colbert with more details…

She decided should Ms. Colbert call again and should they have another meeting, she would happily volunteer other pertinent information she could bring forth that might help Kassie find out more about the incident on the ski slopes outside of Zurich. She determined that Kassie was the curious type, interested in her daughter and her death. Why she had no idea, and she wasn't about to ask. If Kassie wanted more information that was fine with her. What Ms. Statler needed was for someone to tell her the truth about happened with those involved. Being an outside inquisitor, maybe Kassie was the one person who could unexpectedly uncover the truth.

Ms. Statler was a patient woman, not prone to theatrics. She would simply wait for the next telephone call from Ms. Colbert.

# 62

er car seemed to float over I-25 as she hurriedly drove back to Denver. The last thing she needed at the moment was a speeding ticket! With the legal driving limit set at seventy-five MPH, she set the cruise control at seventy-nine miles per hour.

Armed with more details, with the names of men that Carolyn dated prior to marrying Dr. Selway, Kassie was elated at having met with Ms. Statler. And yes, she was the woman in the airport. Funny how life can turn on a dime.

Kassie was modestly happy she had made that one telephone call to Ms. Statler, elated that she took the time to speak with Ms. Statler. Kassie had never questioned her insatiable appetite for knowledge through her own examination of any matter. Ms. Statler was indeed alive; she was the lady she'd encountered at the airport, cane and all. She still believed her daughter had been murdered. Kassie wanted to know more about Stephen Selway than ever before. Admittedly, she had no way of knowing whether he was involved with Carolyn's death, at least not yet. Just because Ms. Statler 'hinted' that he had accompanied Carolyn overseas meant nothing.

Returning to her apartment, Kassie had a few moments to think, to clear her mind. Before she forgot who they were, she wrote the names of Carolyn's former beau's on a slip of paper borrowed from the pad they used for their grocery list. Placing it in her coin purse, she went to her room and flopped on her bed.

So many thoughts, good, bad and difficult, circled within her brain. Restless, anxious, she knew she wouldn't sleep. After changing into more casual clothes, she gently knocked on Jacki's door. When there wasn't an answer, she opened the door to see if she was sleeping. The room was empty. Closing the door, going back in her room, she removed the revolver from the bottom drawer and quickly tucked it in her belt, covering it with her shirt. What better way to remove the cobwebs from her life than to target practice at the rifle range!

# 63

Sunday morning found her in her adopted church, First Baptist on Quail Street, praying earnestly for the week ahead, her work, Brad and his work, her friends and family, thanking God through Jesus Christ for the wonderful life He had given her. She was a sinner like every other individual she knew. Unlike most sinners, Kassie knew the value of repentance. It was with that repentant heart that she earnestly believed she could shed some light on Carolyn Selway and the circumstances surrounding her death. On faith alone, she would continue to seek the truth, knowing that whatever she found would at least answer some of the nagging questions that plagued her day and night.

Sitting in front of the computer, Kassie decided to probe deeper into Carolyn's past. She began by typing in 'Lance Kelly' in the space bar. Several 'Lance Kelly's' came upon the screen. Narrowing it down to Denver, there were only two. The first one turned out to be a Registered Dietitian. She clicked on the second and after signing her life away she found what she was looking for. The screen was filled with all the news about Mr. Kelly and his orchestra that it could possibly hold and then some. At present, Mr. Kelly was a world renowned figure, a true Hollywood celebrity, who, according to the tabloids, had the reputation of having any beauty he pleased to entertain on his arm. A retired Air Force Captain, never married, no children, and an orchestra made to order, Mr. Kelly lived the life of a select minority: a man with lots of money and a paternity suit hanging over his head. Finding the sordid details rather boring, she quickly deleted the screen, leaving behind the thought that Carolyn was correct in not getting messed up with him. Sometimes the frosting looks so good, but the actual cake could consist of cardboard!

Mr. Rudy Spegel was different as far as his occupation was concerned. At the time he dated Carolyn, he owned a very exclusive clothing store, patterned after Neiman Marcus. The clothing was exquisite, the accessories were timeless and the prices were exorbitant. Located in Peach Creek Shopping Center, it was the perfect shopping location for Denverites and out-of-towners, as well. Retired from the Army, he was still active in the Army reserves.

Soon after his maiden store became a favorite, he opened two others, one in Richmond, Virginia and the other in Atlanta, Georgia. Kassie thought it made sense to go south since he had been born in Charleston, South Carolina. He was married and had two children. Rich and stable.

Roger Stiles was educated in law. He had practiced in Indianapolis, Indiana for several years before moving to Denver. It appeared as soon as he set up his law practice, he started dating Carolyn. At least the time frame was about right according to Mrs. Statler. That is, if she relayed her knowledge of Carolyn's men friends in chronological order. Kassie had no way of knowing. His photo showed him to be a handsome fellow, blue eyes, blond hair and a moustache. Looking at his photo, Kassie could understand how Carolyn was taken with him. Photographed in Navy whites, he appeared to be a true gentleman. However, illusions are dangerous! Often times, they lie!

She couldn't help thinking it would've been helpful is Ms. Statler had given her the name of the beau that 'appeared and disappeared.'

How could she remember him so vividly but not remember his name? Were her reflections so abhorrent that they erased any memory of her daughter's liaison with the man? Kassie wondered if there was more to the story than what she was told.

Of course, enter the prestigious Dr. Stephen Selway. Kassie thought she knew enough about him to last her a lifetime! She understood the discipline he showed in surgery started long before he became a surgeon. She knew he was educated in medicine in Indiana and Carolyn was his first and only wife. At least as far as the internet was concerned! Amazing what was available to the general public over a wireless, coaxial cable shot through space retrieving the information and returning it to the exact computer which was requiring the information.

Not being too fond of surfing the web, she was about to shut down the computer when she heard Jackie enter the apartment.

"Hey! What's for dinner?"

"I'll be right out!" It was Sunday evening. It was also Kassie's turn to fix one of her favorite dishes, orange marmalade chicken breasts. Give her thirty minutes and it'd be chow time. Now, she was hungry!

# 64

The surgical suites had been scheduled tightly all week. By Friday evening, Brad was too tired to think, much less attend an outing at Selway's on Saturday. It crossed his mind that he may be getting the flu or maybe just a bad cold. Normally, the harder he worked the more energy he had. However, it was a night out; spending it with Kassie should alleviate any stress.

This particular evening, the men were discussing some of the hilarious feats of nonsense they accomplished when they were teenagers. Turning outdoor toilets over at Halloween, short sheeting their buddies' beds, using tadpoles for fishing bait, piling as many kids in their car as would fit to see if the tires would blow…just to mention a few. Between the stories and the wine, their laughter became contagious, each man feeding off the other.

Kassie excused herself to use the bathroom. In the hallway she passed by Selway's study, or more appropriately, his library. After drying her hands she approached the study and being curious, she entered. It could've substituted for a room at the downtown library; books, books and more books. Running her fingers across some of the bindings, she noticed that in addition to all things medical, he enjoyed reading fiction novels. Passing his desk, she started to walk around the back side. Dark cherry without a speck of dust, with a photo of his late deceased ex-wife sitting on a corner, it had a small reading light with a green lampshade and a leather bound writing pad that took up a good deal of the desk top.

She leaned forward against the desk and picked up the photo. Carolyn Selway was truly a beautiful woman, Kassie thought. Returning it as she had found it, she backed away from the desk. The writing pad had slipped. Trying to straighten it, she noticed a piece of cardstock like paper protruding from the edge. Looking up to see if she was still alone, she raised the pad and picked up two ticket receipts, airplane tickets. From Zurich. One was for a round trip. The other was a one-way. Stephen Selway was the owner of the round trip; Carolyn Selway was the passenger noted on the one-way form.

Kassie looked around as if she thought she might be video-taped. If she was, she was too frightened to see any cameras. Quickly, she replaced the pad as it was on the desk. Never once did she doubt she would be taking the tickets with her. With no pockets in which to hide them, she folded the tickets in half. Turning so her back was to the door, she stuffed them down the front of her dress.

When she again faced the door, Brad stood smiling at her. Perspiration on her forehead was the first thing she noticed. Her arms felt heavy and her feet didn't want to move. Caught in a theft, she wanted to ask Brad how long he had been standing there, but she didn't dare. She couldn't mobilize her tongue.

"Do you suppose we'll have a library like this in our home? Or should we settle for a small desk in the kitchen?" He ambled over to her as she moved to the corner of the desk. "Pretty spiffy, eh!"

"Yes. I was just thinking about that myself."

"A library...or a small kitchen desk?"

"Aaaahhhhh......what?"

"Kass. Are you alright? You're burning up…and you're perspiring." He had his arms around her, holding her tight. Kassie was positive she could hear the crunching of airplane tickets buried in her bosom!

"Don't you think it's warm in here? I'm hot!" Kassie said as she gently pushed herself away from Brad.

"Oh, you're hot alright!" A flushed face before, now she hoped he wouldn't see her blush. Brad smiled, knowing he had embarrassed her. "Come with me. Let's get you some fresh air." Gently placing his hand on the smallest recess of her back, he led her out of the library… or whatever Selway called it.

# 65

"I'm at the Sugarloaf. Meet me there in 10 minutes?"

"Who is this?" Brad wasn't familiar with telephone calls when no one announced who was calling. The voice sounded familiar but he couldn't instantly place it. Besides, he had very few calls on his land line. If it were the hospital calling, he would've taken the call on his beeper. Only Kassie and his fellow surgeons had the number to his cell.

"Perhaps you can...?"

"I'll be right there." Now he remembered. It had been awhile since they had talked. Before leaving the apartment, he grabbed the key to his safe, and upon opening it, withdrew three sheets of paper, stapled. Folding them as a letter, he placed them inside his coat pocket.

Brad parked his truck, 'jalopy' would've fit better, in back of the Sugarloaf Café. Before he could step out, a black sedan drove up and parked itself in such a way Brad had nowhere to go had he wanted to leave. The right front door of the sedan opened as if to tell Brad, come right in.

"Lieutenant! How's work?"

Thinking back over the last year, Brad remembered in detail what had been said between his Commander and himself. "How'd you know I've been waiting to hear from you?"

"Intuition! Someone with an IQ of hundred forty-five should've have known I was in Denver!" Brad was not especially impressed with his Commander's assessment. In actuality, he wanted to share what information he had and if possible, get back to his apartment, sooner rather than later.

"You want a printed copy of what I have?" Brad reached into his inside pocket and pulled out the information.

"What have you got?" The lieutenant took the ramp entrance to I-70 and continued west toward the mountains.

"As you know, I started with the names of those who rang out and went from there. I've listed their names, about twenty-two. Only two have natural red or auburn hair. One of them is Lance Smith. The other is Laurie Samuel."

"You lost me. One of them is a woman?"

"No. Evidently Laurie is short for Lawrence. The records had him listed as Lawrence with 'Laurie' in parenthesis."

"Okay. You're already in territory we've not covered before."

"I found that Lance Smith is a Registered Nurse working in Atlanta. He's married with a family, three kids, and a wife and appears to be quite settled. So I've crossed him off; put him on the back burner. As far as Lawrence Samuel goes, I've not been able to find him. Believe it or not, not even his family knows where he's at!"

"You checked with his family?"

"I'm his former employer from Texas and have a check for him which he never picked up."

"I declare. Who'd ever thought that Brad Phillips would lie?"

"Sir! You asked me to find a SEAL that may or may not have committed a crime. Did you not?" Brad was serious.

"Yes, Sir! What else?"

Brad continued. "His family authenticated the fact he was in medicine, but when I asked if he was still practicing as a nurse, the line went dead."

"What made you ask if he was still practicing...?"

"Just a hunch. If nothing else, it helped me to narrow the field of what he might be doing. I also addressed him as that 'good-looking employee with brilliant red hair' and got an answer that sounded iffy. He answered with 'aahhh...yup.' Made me think he may have changed his hair color." Brad paused. "Assuming I had the right family, I wanted to get as much information as I could. So I casually mentioned that the discipline he showed us at the research facility in Texas must have come from his being a SEAL to which the gentleman on the other end of the line said 'huh?' There was a lot of skepticism in his voice! Anyway, I have it written out for you to read later." He laid the sheets on the console between them.

"Are you thinking what I'm thinking?"

"I have no idea what you're thinking!"

"If you presented...invented...facts about this guy...Laurie, what's-his-name, and his family reacted as though it was news to them, then perhaps this guy has something to hide." They rode in silence, until the Commander pulled off the highway into one of those ready-made rest stops constructed for the weary drivers who couldn't keep their eyes open or for those out-of-towners who'd never seen the snow covered Rockies before.

"Where do we go from here? Do you actually have anytime at all to do more digging? I don't want this to interfere...!"

"I do...and it won't." Now he sounded like Kassie.

"Good. As much as I hate to say it, this guy seems to have something to hide. By the way, a select committee in the Department of Defense is putting together a plan to make use of the SEALs after they retire from active duty. Personally I can hardly wait. Those who participate will be put on an active payroll roster. Of course, they don't know about you! The committee overseeing this plan hasn't got a clue under heaven that we've already enlisted your services. We.....I would still be waiting for Washington to see the light! Three years.

Ouch! They just know 'someone' is getting a small stipend for doing some research for the department."

"Thanks for that 'stipend.' It's enough to give me a little extra when necessary."

"Oh, by the way. Don't know if you heard. There's a training camp for wannabe SEALs in Texas. Just outside of Dallas. Basically teaches fifteen to eighteen year olds the rudiments of basic training. It's operated by two former SEALs, Ken Station and Barry Knott. Station went missing. Thought you better know. Barry, the one with the golden arm, remember? He was in your unit. Anyway, Barry reported it to the police and the police notified us."

"How long has he been missing?"

"According to Barry, let's see, about a year."

"Anything else you can tell me about him?"

"Not at the present. I guess he's quite a family man, good husband, has a couple kids. If I hear anything else I'll let you know."

"A friend of mine is getting married in Dallas, within the month. Maybe I'll attend the wedding."

"Does he happen to be a SEAL?"

"Jake Porter. Steelnose. I'll believe it once the marriage license is signed!"

"Old Jake is getting married! Gees. For some guys it's never too late!" They both enjoyed laughing at the prospect of old Jake settling down. Old Jake was sixty-four, never been married, never wanted to be married. But like most men, Jake reached an age where he acknowledged to himself he didn't want to grow old alone.

"Guess not! I'll let you know what she looks like!"

"You'd do that for me!" The lieutenant gave a hearty laugh. Now, his mind turned to more important matters. "How'd you like some lunch? Evergreen is just over the hill." Without waiting for an answer, he put the vehicle in motion.

"Sounds excellent."

# 66

After getting his pickup, he went back to his apartment. Over the phone, he explained to Kassie why he wasn't coming over; he was on call the next day. Kassie took a deep breath and said she understood perfectly. It was what she didn't say that would've curled the hairs on Brad Phillips chest.

Jackie had another date with Harriman. After speaking to Brad, she turned off all the lights in the apartment. After closing the front door, she walked to her bedroom and locked the door.

Opening the bottom drawer of her dresser she removed the personal property she took from Selway's house. Looking closer at the two duplicate tickets, she realized she had committed a crime! These tickets didn't belong to her, not in the least. They belonged to Stephen Selway! They were his duplicates; they were an asset she wished she weren't holding at the moment. She had no right to confiscate them even though they appeared to be condemning.

The closer she looked at the itinerary, the guiltier Selway appeared, involved in something Kassie didn't want to acknowledge. Murder! She'd never known anyone who would or *could* exhibit such despicable and corrupt behavior! But! The names were printed in carbon ink. In plain English lettering. Stephen planned on returning to the States. He had other plans for his wife.

The more she stared at them the more she became upset. Not just that she, Kassie Colbert, had committed a crime but she held proof that Stephen Selway did! A malicious evil act of intentional murder! She let the duplicates flop on the bed, beside her arm. As light as they were, somehow their miniscule weight became extremely heavy. What could she do with them that wouldn't reveal her part as a thief? What would her parents think if they knew? What could she tell them that would explain why she took something that didn't belong to her? This wouldn't reflect the way she was raised! All the searching she had done! Had it become so compelling it brought her to a place where those tickets became so valuable as to steal them? What about Brad? She couldn't tell him what she did! He'd never trust her again. Ever!

Maybe, she thought, I'm being delusional. Brad wouldn't have to know and as for her parents, if she just put them back, no one would be the wiser. Wrong! Kassie realized what she had in her possession was so offensive, so immoral that to ignore it may put someone else in jeopardy.

As she lay on her bed, staring at the ceiling, she realized what she did was no better than...than what Selway did. *A sin is a sin.* That's what she'd been taught. Two commandments broken, two sins committed. *Thou shalt not commit murder! Thou shalt not steal!* The sixth and eighth commandments! Surely murder was less convicting than stealing! Who was she trying to kid? Admittedly, each commandment was moral, deliberate and equal to all the others. God didn't rank them as we humans have, she thought. There's no difference between a *little* sin and a *big* sin. Let's face it, she enumerated, we're all sinners! Somehow, knowing, without any doubts, Kassie knew what she must do. In spite of holding proof positive in her hands that a great wrong had been done, she'd have to find another way to expose the truth about Stephen and Carolyn Selway and what happened on the ski slopes in Switzerland.

"I'll just put them back. And then, I could pretend to find them for the first time when Brad and Selway are present," she whispered to herself. But how? When? Where? If she put them anywhere other than under the writing pad on his desk, surely he'd know they'd been seen…by someone, at sometime.

Body temperature, being what it is, subjected to stress and guilt, causes perspiration, stickiness and even a foul odor, especially when you know it's not the room temperature that's too high. She was perspiring to the point where she felt the need to take a bath. Wash away the guilt! Oh, if it were that easy. Amazing how a person's conscience works to deceive. *I can do a little stealing but certainly not murder.* Stealing can be rectified; *murder is permanent.* 'That doesn't make stealing any more correct,' she thought.

Somehow, someway, Kassie was going to put those tickets back where she found them. Then she'd ask God to forgive her for having taken them in the first place. What was left would simply be to live out the consequences of her misdeed. Kassie hoped it wouldn't be too painful!

# 67

"Mr. Mantoux, need I ask what you've been up to? The nurses tell me you have a tremendous amount of pain." It was early on a Monday when Brad Phillips learned of the predicament that plagued his former surgical patient. After entering his room, Dr. Phillips took the sheet covering his patient and gently lowered it. "The MRI says you tore the mesh we inserted. I'm not even going to ask how that happened."

"Doc, my bottom is so sore, like a festering boil, ready to burst. What am I going to do?"

"Looks like you already did something!"

"Doc! I'm serious!"

"So am I!" came the quick response.

"Well! Can you fix it?"

"Fix it? We'll have to remove it!"

"Remove it?" Mr. Mantoux tried to sit up in bed, but it was extremely painful, awkward.

"Yes. I told you when you left the hospital you had to let the whole area heal before you had any sexual activity. Obviously, you didn't listen! So, in surgery tomorrow, we'll have to remove what's ailing you." Brad didn't know if all the moaning Mr. Mantoux did was because of the necessity of more surgery or if he was trying to imagine living without certain body parts. In either case, Brad would let him stew about it until scalpel time the next morning.

Meanwhile, Cindy was helping Rhonda with a patient admitted Sunday night with what looked like a case of kidney stones.

"I can't use the bathroom, you know. Help me! Nurse, please... please give me something for the pain."

"We can't give you anything until your physician makes rounds. Then, we'll ask him for something. Are you allergic to any medicine?"

"Dilaudid! It...I...can't take it." The two women helped to make him more comfortable by straightening his bedding and fluffing his pillow. "I'm so thirsty. But I'm afraid to drink anything."

"Try to relax. Being upset will only exaggerate your pain." Cindy knew Rhonda was only trying to make the best of the situation until the physician came in, but in her heart, she knew Rhonda didn't have a clue how physical pain could be so overwhelming.

Later in the morning when Jacki was recording Mrs. Latel's latest symtoms,' all manner of decorum was shelved when Mr. Simpson walked up to the desk on third floor in his birthday suit.

"Mr. Simpson! You're...stark...*naked*! Where's your gown?" Jacki was up and taking him by the arm, trying to turn him around to face the direction of his room. "Have you had anything for your pain?" Jacki sincerely thought he might be suffering disorientation, a side effect some patients experienced after having been given a narcotic.

"Can't remember. Those gowns, miss, get all twisted on me...in bed. Besides, I figure you're not seeing anything God didn't make! Right!"

"Mr. Simpson. Decorum is something we try to have in our hospital. Especially when ladies are present."

"Ma'am! I'm always naked at home. It's more comfortable." Jacki, who never blushed, blushed! Gently leading him into his room, Jacki continued.

"This is not your home! This is your room, in this hospital and here, you're to wear a gown. All the time, except in the shower." After getting Mr. Simpson safely in his gown and into his bed, she continued. "If for some unknown reason you feel as though you must exercise your body by walking and *feel* as though you are at home, then I'll be glad to take you to therapy. '*Lord knows, that's where you belong!*' Until then, stay dressed…in your gown. And it doesn't open in the front!"

"But miss…"

"Mr. Simpson, *what is it?*"

"This gown…it itches something fierce!"

Jacki, in spite of herself, knowing as a nurse political correctness was something desired and expected when working with patients, couldn't help herself. It's just who she was.

"Well! That depends on what's itching?" Jacki didn't wait around for any response from her patient. On the way back to the desk, she murmured, "I'll be happy to give you a cup of coffee, laced with Benadryl. That'll take care of your itch!" Good thing there was no one at the desk to overhear her. She really didn't want to lose her job over somebody's skin irritation!

Things weren't much better in the OR. Kassie, being totally paranoid about the stolen goods, had them in her pocket, sealed in a plastic baggie with a zipper. Lost as to where to put them, carrying them with her seemed to be the safest place at the moment. On her lunch break she would have to go to the bank and rent a safety deposit box. Once out of sight, knowing they were confined in a black box under lock and key, she could relax and wait for the right moment in which she could return them.

Somehow, that thought didn't alleviate her fear of getting caught for what she had done. Soon, very soon, perhaps sooner, she would have to find a way to replace them.

Brad Phillips wasn't faring much better. He was called upon to replace Dr. Martinez in surgery as the latter was in a hurriedly called meeting with the Director of the hospital. It was just an appendectomy, ruptured but contained, but now Dr. Phillips was behind in his schedule.

Priscilla, an RN with an attitude, who worked third floor, had just received a patient from recovery. He'd been in recovery overnight since his procedure was one of the last ones performed the night before. He was wide awake and ornery as a mule.

With the details of his surgery and his proposed recuperation plan along with his profile already transmitted by computer, Priscilla knew what she must do. She took one last look in the half bath mirror located off the nurses' station. Her hair in place, with just the right amount of lipstick, not too much rouge, but with eyes made up like she was related to the raccoon family, she stepped out and decided she had best get Mr. Tally to walk.

"Good day, Mr. Tally." As she entered the room, she realized that Mr. Tally, at thirty-four, was not all that good looking. Anything but being impressed by the bearded, slightly overweight man now lounging in bed, she decided she'd do what was expected of her and entice him out of bed to walk on his repaired foot. One more bunion removed, she thought. "How about a little walk, just you and me?" She proceeded in removing the blanket and sheet from his torso, only to find that she had to replace his gown.

"Wait a minute! *Now*! But my foot…" he said, with disdain.

"I know, Mr. Tally. You don't have to put much weight on it today but you do need to get up and walk. Good for the bowels, you know."

"It's not my bowels that need help! Can I have something for the pain…before we walk?" As he lowered his legs over the side of the bed, the throbbing in his right foot made him wince. "Nurse! Get me something for this pain! I don't think I'm walking anywhere today!"

"Oh, yes, Mr. Tally. You were given a pain shot before recovery brought you here. You're good to go." Priscilla couldn't help but think some unkind thoughts. 'If you weren't overweight, if you were good

looking, if you were someone I would want to impress, well, maybe…
I'd cut you some slack. Not today, buddy!'

It's difficult to watch a grown man cry! It's even worse when in
the process of him having to use a walker, he had to stop to blow his
nose. And, of course, he had to cheat!

"Mr. Tally, don't skip! Put some of your weight on that right foot!
You want to be able to walk out of here on both feet." Or maybe not!

"Nurse, you're killing me!" His tears kept forming and rolling
down his cheeks, disappearing into his beard.

"We don't have to go far, but we do have to get out of this room.
My goodness! You're young and healthy…"

"*I have bunions*! If I'm so healthy, where did they come from?"

"That's something you should ask your doctor. Me! I'm just here
to help you. Now, let's do this right. Take a step on that foot and ease
some weight on it. Okay?"

"Oooohhhh." His whole body went limp. Between Priscilla and
the walker, they made it to the hallway and Mr. Tally recovered
enough to take one more step. This time his body and mind became
like Jell-O. "Take me back. Please, let me go back to my bed."

"In a minute, Mr. Tally, in a minute."

Trying to deal with an individual who was instructed by the
surgeon to get out of bed and walk the same day after having had
bunion surgery, was hard enough; dealing with them under a full
moon was like helping someone with Alzheimer's on Lorazepam!

"After our little walk, you'll feel so much better. Trust me!"

"Nurse! That's it! No more! Just shut up and take me back to
my bed!"

"I beg your pardon! Mr. Tally. Really! I'm only trying to help you!"

"What is it with these patients today? I swear I never signed up
for this; not while I was awake!" Shirley was fuming over the little
matter of one of her patients spilling his urine sample all over himself

with Shirley catching the splatter. *"Today,* I should've called in sick!" Shirley had, unlike Priscilla, a patient that was confined to bed; they could make unspeakable messes. Most times all the bedding had to be changed. More than once in a day. It was a never ending battle.

"I've got a patient that would gladly entertain…"

"Jacki!"

"Well! Things could always get worse. At least you can wash your uniform! Now, you'll have to force fluids on Mr. Lowery, just so he can pee again. Don't you dare leave something like that for night shift?" Jacki was right, of course. She had seen much worse! But then, she was thankful Mr. Lowery wasn't her patient.

That evening, as they left work, they were covered in rain gear before stepping outside. Colorado needed the rain, the moisture, but did it have to rain buckets? Only in Colorado!

A full moon always brought out strangest, most disturbing features of a human's unpredictable side, especially if they were in pain. With pain, patients became a different human being. Even for the ordinary healthy working individual, who possessed a remarkable civil character, full moons could have a most confusing deleterious effect on their personalities. It was a phenomenon of the ill and the industrious that no one could explain.

# 68

After the full moon passed, all things seemed to settle down a bit. Brad and Kassie had even found more time to spend with each other.

He was taken aback when his cell phone startled him. He had dozed off while reading, with Kassie's head on his lap. It was late; who would call at this hour? The two of them had spent a restful evening at Kassie's since Jacki was on another date.

"Lieutenant?" Only his commander called him by his rank.

"Yes, Sir," he whispered. Kassie, curled up on the couch, repositioning herself as Brad moved her head to a pillow. "Just a moment, Sir." Brad hoped she wouldn't wake up. He stepped into the kitchen, quietly opened the door, and stepped into the hall. "What's up?"

"They found Ken Station. They're calling it a suicide."

"What are you calling it?"

"Haven't seen the full report yet. But since he's a SEAL…I'll ask to see it soon. Just wanted to let you know. From what little I know, the body has deteriorated. Probably no fingerprints. I'll call you as soon as I know more."

"I guess I won't have to attend the wedding…"

"If I were you…please go. Never know who might turn up. Catch you later."

"I have to work away from the hospital this weekend. Research. Something I've been asked to do."

"As long as you do the research for Martinez's published papers, why don't you include your name as a contributor?" Kassie was slightly annoyed by the fact some physicians and surgeons did all the leg work on a particular subject when in fact they never seemed to get any of the credit.

"If I wasn't good at it, or enjoy it, I wouldn't do it. Besides, it pays well."

"But…you're a surgeon in your own right. I don't understand why you think it's so important…"

"Kass. Someday, perhaps I'll have another surgeon do my research. At least, I'll know what to expect of him…or her." What Brad couldn't tell her was that the research being done wouldn't be for another physician or surgeon. He didn't want to lie to her; he'd said enough. He was going away for the weekend. He was doing research, of sorts. Although a wedding was going on…well, he didn't lie. "I'll only be gone overnight. When I get back, let's spend a day in Estes. I think the old pickup can still make it!"

There was always so much left unsaid. Brad never told her where he went; she could've asked. But she never did. What he did on those few weekends away from her and the hospital didn't affect their relationship, or so it seemed. Brad never gave her any indication he'd be doing something illegal or clandestine. So she never worried about him being gone, without her. She did fret, however, over the fact he wasn't getting the recognition that he was making possible for his superiors.

# 69

She couldn't leave well enough alone. After she entered the bank, she felt foolish thinking someone had done anything to the ticket stubs in the vault. But she had to prove to herself they were safe.

After the teller left her alone with the safety deposit box, she opened it. The ticket stubs were still there. For reasons known only to Kassie, she picked them up, placed them in her bag, closed the box and left the private cubicle.

She acknowledged the receptionist as she hurriedly left the bank, but she'd decided to keep the safety box. Just in case of an emergency, she thought.

September can be a cool month in Colorado, in the way of weather and activities. Hunting season is well under way, the ski slopes are usually getting some snow, the temperature isn't suffocating and the tourists have been retreating toward home, in lieu of their cookie crunchers returning to school.

It had been in the nineties for over 30 days consecutively; everyone was tired of the heat. On September first, the temperature dropped considerably. On September tenth, it began to rain, seriously, in the mountains, on the Front Range, from the Wyoming border to the southern border of Colorado. Once it got started, it just kept coming. It didn't take long before the Little Thompson and St. Vrain Rivers were overflowing their banks. A disaster of a flood occurred. Churches were being used at capacity; for sleeping, food, counseling, and toiletries. Some of the people were showing up at emergency rooms with nausea, depression and just plain mental fatigue. Over a hundred homes washed away, along with vehicles, trees and anything not nailed down. Bridges all over the area just disappeared; roads were closed to the point going somewhere, anywhere, took triple the normal time to get there. Under the circumstances, Kassie was glad she didn't have a house to worry about.

After work, Kassie did some errands and finished by going to the library. Returning to the apartment she found Jacki had made Burritos Supreme, without beans. Neither of them relished the beans!

"Just dish up whatever you want after you heat the burrito in the microwave. The pork sauce is *re-lee-y* good."

As she sat at the table, she opened her bag to find the sticky letters she had bought at the hobby store. Since it was raining and Brad was still at the hospital, she had decided to scrapbook for a while. "What're you doing this evening? Anything?"

"Howie's coming over. We'll probably try to see a movie. Nothing special. Just being together is great. Hope there's a theatre that's open where we don't have to navigate a river of water!"

"It's nice to have company on a rainy evening." What Kassie didn't say was more important to her than anything she could verbalize. She had put her bag on the floor, by her feet, and continued eating. She had to admit that Jacki's meals were always delicious, *when* she decided to cook. The doorbell rang. "I'm so glad we're not affected by this flood. What a mess!"

"Gotta go. When you're done, throw your dishes in the sink. I'll do'em when we get back." Jacki was gone and Kassie felt somewhat relieved. She got up, walked to their front door and made sure it was locked. From her bag on the floor she pulled out the tickets that were burning a hole in her mental stability. Glad to be alone, she put them under her sweater in her bottom dresser drawer next to her revolver. Satisfied they were safer with her, she got out her scrapbook and began to lay out her supplies; paper, scissors, glue tape, some embellishments and photos. Covering their entire table, she determined she would have to cut down on supplies or get a larger table. Since she kept buying a few supplies here and there, the larger table seemed to be the better idea.

It was getting close to midnight when, in placing some of the letters on her fifteenth scrapbooked page, she placed a capital 'S' in place to say 'Stunning' in describing Vanity. She looked at the 'S' as if it were misshapen. Realizing that the alphabet letters came in all shapes and sizes and colors, she wondered why on this particular sheet of letters, the 'S' had been formed so differently. Viewing it on the page, she wasn't quite sure she liked it enough to leave it. Getting tired, she decided, after some contemplation, she'd leave it; it matched the rest of that particular letter design.

Before closing the album, she took one last look at the letter. Something in the back of mind bothered her about that letter! But being sleepy, she decided to think about it later.

Back in her bedroom, she checked the bottom drawer of her dresser. The revolver and the ticket stubs were still there. She thought it was truly amazing how those tickets played on her mind. Kassie wished she had a vault or safe in her bedroom where she could put them. She would have to look for one the next time she went shopping.

# 70

It continued to rain. Tempers began to flare and traffic was at times backed up for a mile anywhere one chose to drive. Kassie was thankful she could walk to work and avoid the texting and make-up frenzied females along with the drunk and insane drivers on the roads. Driving had become extremely hazardous to ones' health!

Although she had a latent temper, there were times that it rose to the surface. One of those times came upon her in an incredibly unexpected way. Kassie had decided to walk the stairs instead of using the elevator. Between second and third floor, she ran into Dr. Selway sitting on the steps.

"Oh! I didn't mean to intrude on your space..."

"You didn't. Just grabbing a snack. Haven't seen much of you lately?" Dr. Selway kept eating. She thought she'd walk past him and continue on her way. But as circumstances would have it...here at the hospital she wasn't afraid of him.

"No. No. I've kept quite busy, actually. I've been thinking. I was wondering about your wife...that is...when I saw you here...she came to mind. She was such a beautiful woman. Did the two of you do much traveling...together?" Kassie wanted to blurt out 'did you kill her, because that's what the tickets say!'

"Actually," Selway answered with a mouth full of sandwich, "we did some. Both of us had done a lot of traveling before we met, so I kind'a lost interest. Better things to do, you know?"

"I've had my share as well. And not particularly places I wanted to see." Trying to sound aloof, she started up the steps. As she passed him, she asked, "Did you accompany your wife to Switzerland...to go skiing?" She was glad that Selway didn't see her shaking like a leaf in the wind. Even her legs felt rubbery.

"No, I didn't. Wish I had though." '*I'll bet you did!*' Kassie thought. 'She would be alive today.' Too inquisitive for her own good, she continued.

"Who did she go with? Or...I mean...did she go alone or with someone...you know...like her friend...or her mother?"

"As far as I know, she went by herself. Good for me 'cause she wanted to stop in Paris for one of the style shows...I detest those things...if you've been to one you've seen them all. Come to think of it, I think she said she was meeting someone over there. It's been a while...I've kind'a forgotten." Kassie reached the top of the stairs and was ready to pull the handle on the door when Selway spoke. Turning to look up at her, he asked, "Funny you should mention my wife. I was just thinking about her myself. Well. Have a good day. See ya later." He continued working on his sandwich.

Kassie. The calm one. The one who never got flustered. The one who kept her mind focused on what she was doing. Upon leaving the stairwell, she pondered why she took the stairs instead of the elevator. The reason escaped her, but it must have been important.

For the rest of the afternoon, Kassie mulled over what Selway had said about his wife. He didn't appear a bit upset about the circumstances surrounding her departure from this earth. "I'll bet you were thinking about her! How can you lie like that? The tickets say it pretty well. Proof positive, I'd say."

"Are you okay?" It was Shirley. "I think I heard you talking to yourself. Are you exhausted...or ill?" Kassie was caught off guard.

"Oh! No. I'm fine. I didn't mean to speak out loud. What did I say... did you hear?" Kassie had a moment of regret. Stymied, bewildered for just a moment, she tried to regain some composure. For reasons known only to her, Kassie had lost control of her self control!

"Just some mumbling, Kass, nothing pertinent."

"Okay. I'll try to keep my thoughts to myself from now on." But in her mind, she knew that soon someone...everyone...would know about Dr. Selway. And her theft!

That evening she found herself alone, again, scrapbooking. It wasn't as though she didn't want to be alone. Quite the opposite. Whatever she was doing, she invariably accomplished more alone than when Jacki or Brad were present.

But she was restless. After turning on the fireplace, she grabbed her latest book and curled up in front of the fireplace, wrapped up in her fleece blanket. She tried to read. But as she did, her eyelids became heavy and the warmth under her blanket was too much to overcome. Within minutes she was asleep.

# *71*

The following evening, after dinner, she went back to her scrapbooking. The album was turning into a very sweet, enlightening revelation, about a colt that turned into a ravishingly beautiful stallion. The album would surely impress her mother. She'd have to show it to her the next time she traveled to Wyoming. Then her cell rang. It was Cindy.

"He wants me to go on vacation with him when he takes leave." Kassie was instantly alert.

"You're not planning on going with him...are you? I mean...that kind of arrangement doesn't sound like you at all."

"Kass. I know how you feel about Stephen. But he kind of grows on you. Actually, on me."

"Cindy. Wherever you would go, whenever...I'd worry about you. Just because Priscilla or Jacki would go in a heartbeat, doesn't make it right for you." Kassie couldn't get her arms around the idea of Cindy and Stephen going on vacation together. Not after having found the tickets! "Perhaps, after giving it a little more thought, you'll see that taking a vacation with your beau isn't the right or correct thing to do at this time. Maybe...maybe later...after you've gone together a while." Even to Kassie that seemed like a lame excuse.

"Oh, maybe you're right. You just have a way of setting me straight. Thanks, Kass. By the way, what're you doing this evening?"

"Scrapbooking. I want to finish my album on Vanity. I want it finished the next time I see Mom."

"I'll let you go then. Thanks, Kass, for being such a good friend. Good night."

"Good night." Kassie breathed a deep sigh. After she cut the connection, she accepted the premise those tickets were becoming even more important than at first. They had to be exposed ...or... she'd have to tell Cindy what she surmised. The second option was not a viable alternative!

# 72

rad had taken a circuitous route. In his favor, the ticket was cheaper even though the trip was longer. Premier Airlines proved themselves worthy of his time spent. Arriving in Dallas, he deboarded and walked into a sweltering, humid heat. He'd momentarily forgotten how hot and uncomfortable it could get in the Deep South. Instantly, he was thankful for the mild temperatures in Colorado. The heat around the Fourth of July could be a little stifling but as a whole, no where he'd ever been could beat Colorado; it's scenery, its weather, its people.

Jake had set aside several motel rooms at the Joule Hotel for attendees from out of town. The guests would be in a lap of luxury for three days because Jake was only getting married 'once,' or so he said. Since this opulence would be the finest most of his friends would ever experience, he had secured the best rooms with enhanced individual service, costing him a pretty penny which, in all honesty, he felt privileged to give. After all, it was just 'his money.'

After his shower, Brad dressed for dinner. His parents lived in Dallas making him quite familiar with the restaurants that catered to the 'in' crowd. To say the least, no outsider he ever knew became a part of or was allowed to become part of the crowd to which his parents belonged. One had to be born and raised, schooled and married in Dallas and had to be wealthy beyond reasonable means to be a part of their particular community. It was a facade of sorts. Some of his families' friends were part of the group because they grew up on the same street as they did; Brad knew they were not considered 'rich.' For every rule, there was an equal but opposite rule that broke it. Life.

After renting a vehicle, he drove toward northwest Dallas where he had made reservations at Pappas Bros. Steakhouse. Even though the prices were way above what he could comfortably afford on his current salary, Pappas was considered to be the place to dine; their steaks were second to none. Honestly! He didn't eat out that often, he thought, so why shouldn't he splurge!

It was a good two hours later when he left the restaurant. On his drive back to the hotel he tried to imagine ways to ferret out other SEALs who may or may not know anything about the tragedies that had taken place. It was something he had to tackle without letting anyone know the reason behind his inquiries. At the wedding, more SEALs than he knew personally would be in attendance. SEALS were bright, astute, clever and knowing, besides their physical prowess; getting information of a clandestine sort would be challenging.

The wedding was scheduled for two o'clock the following day. Brad drove by St. Patrick's Cathedral on Ferndale, off the 625 loop, thinking he may catch some of the wedding party still practicing. The church was closed, however. He drove through the neighborhood for a while, reminiscing, then returned to the hotel.

"There's a message for you, Mr. Phillips." The receptionist at the desk had stopped Brad as he came in through the doors. Handing him the note, it read "Call me, brother. Jake." The telephone number he gave was short. Room 516.

Back in his room, he dialed Jake's room number.

"Glad to see you made it. Since I hadn't heard from you, I didn't know if you even got the invitation. How ya' been, Brains?" Brains was the pseudonym the SEALs had given Brad and in every respect, it fit.

"So you're finally going to do it. How does it feel to be almost married?" Jake brushed off his initial question. "Sure thought you'd take the plunge before now. She must be pretty special to put up with the likes of you!"

"Watch out, Brains, those are fightin' words. But, yes. She's very special. You'll like her. What I'd really like to know...if you're not busy at the moment...can I come up to your room? I'd like to see ya' before the wedding."

"Sure. I'm not going anywhere."

They hadn't seen each other since Brad retired from the Navy. A lot of history had been made from then till now. In each other's eyes, neither had changed all that much. Jake had put on some weight and Brad had a light summer tan but essentially, they would've known each other had they met on the street. They swapped stories for a while, laughed a bunch and relayed to each other basically what was happening in their lives and their country since they left the service. Then, their conversation turned serious.

"Gees, Brains, I'm in the company of a real surgeon! Is it everything you thought you'd like to do...I mean, after seeing some of our buddies die...it was like, surreal...like Karl. Remember him? Gees, what I wouldn't do..."

"Karl was special and truthfully...I don't want to discuss him right now." Thinking ahead to tomorrow, being in the company of SEALS that had made it home, the memory of Karl was as fresh in Brad's mind as though he'd lost his friend yesterday. There was something about Karl...Brad couldn't name it...perhaps with time he'd recall what bothered him about his friends death.

"You know, I'm watching my country change for the worse right before my eyes. I know it sounds defeatist..." Jake just shook his head as though the act would purge him of any cobwebs being spun in his brain. "Anyway, I wish Karl could've been here for my wedding."

When the subject came to the infiltration of migrant illegal's, Jake said, "They should enforce the border, period. Put some Ex-Navy SEALS down there. I'd be first in line! Governor Perry is doing what he can but it's not enough. Not near enough!"

"Jake."

"Who ever said this president was smart? He's doing nothing to enforce legal entry into the U.S.! In fact…"

"Jake!"

"You and I! We fought to keep this country free from the culprits… criminals, might as well call them for what they are…gees, Brains, even my wife, who is Hispanic, says she wishes they'd control the border and keep all illegal's out!" Jake shook his head as though the problem was unsolvable.

"Jake?"

"Whaaaat?" Jake was agitated vociferously.

"In my personal opinion…" Brad hesitated, not knowing how much Jake actually understood about the latest news or if he'd paid attention to it lately.

"Yeh. I'm listening."

"In my opinion, the President doesn't care about illegals or open borders or people dying without health care or whatever. He wants the people to rise up against the government in Washington so he can declare Marshall Law thus prolonging his second term as president."

"What? You have got to be bull…"

"Jake! I said, in my opinion!" Brad had given a great deal of thought to the state of the country and had watched as people across the nation were becoming more agitated against those policies Obama was enforcing and ignoring, especially when it came to the Affordable Care Act, or as he and his fellow surgeons were calling it 'the murderous rampage of unbridled neglect with no accountability.'

Everything he had read thus far enlightened his consciousness to the fact the President and his 'enlightened few advisors' along with some in Congress wanted nothing less than total control of the people of his country. Brad *being Brad* made no excuses for the assumption that with this president, his life as a practicing surgeon would alterably change. It would be up to him to use his expertise in the most expeditiously and innovative ways he could afford in order to practice medicine according to the Hippocratic Oath in which he believed.

Jake, on the other hand, knew nothing of the medical field or 'socialized medicine' as it was being currently executed. Perhaps, Brad thought, he would learn firsthand if he ever had to go to a VA.

"I'm just saying, Jake, it wouldn't surprise me…"

"Brains! Gees!" Jake got up and started pacing in the room. He'd heard the rumors, saw illegal's coming across the border, heard of the deaths and the corruption accompanying those trespassing on American soil…lawlessness in the extreme. He didn't want to think about those contrary actions today. After all, he was getting married! *"I'm just sayin'* Brains, that's an incredible leap you've made. From… from freedom…to Marshall Law?" Jake decided he'd have to think about Brains reasoning another day. Besides… "I have to pee. May I use your bathroom?" Jake was done listening.

"Of course." Even with people who should know better, Brad was always conflicted with what they didn't know or what they *chose not to know.* Unfortunately, he knew, Jake fell into that group.

After returning from using the bathroom, Jake had the opening he had wanted since he knew Brad had arrived. And since they were already discussing grotesque matters…

"Brad. These guys, SEALs that have been killed…ya' know anything about them. I can't believe Station is gone. I understand he's not the only one that's been killed. Ya' hear about the two…?"

"What makes you think they were killed?" Brad interrupted.

"Then you do know about them!"

"I suspect you know about as much about them as I do." Brad did his best to appear relaxed when the subject of the SEALs deaths was raised.

"Come on, Brad. Is there something you're not telling me?"

"'Fraid not, Jake. I'm just here to attend your wedding. To see the old man get married."

Jake wanted to pursue the topic of the SEALs but he exhibited a nervous twitch that he hoped Brad wouldn't notice. "I wish I could light a cigarette in here. Everything has become so screwy, smoke free zones in a hotel. I thought government control was bad when I was a SEAL; now it's breathing down our necks, as you so expeditiously volunteered."

"So! You're no longer a SEAL?"

Jake shot Brad a glance of profound irritation. "Of course, I am. I'll always be a SEAL. And doctor, so will you! Just in case ya' forgot." Their laughter had quieted, leaving them both thinking seriously about their dead buddies...and the state of their nation. "Look! I didn't mean that like...ya' know...but I can't help remembering Station and the others. They were *some* brothers...go through what we did and come home and be mauled down by those we fought to protect." Nothing was said for a dead moment. "Sometimes, I'd still like to go back. I've never found anything in civilian life that comes even close to the camaraderie that we had in our unit, ya' know. Some days are just hard."

Brad got up, went to the small refrigerator and pulled out a Jack Daniels whiskey bottle and a soda, hotel size, from the cooler. Pouring them into two ice filled glasses, he handed one to Jake. "Will the missus mind you sharing a drink with an old buddy?" Jake took the glass and smiled. They both sipped after they raised their glasses to each other.

"Seriously, Brad, if ya' know something...or if ya' find out something...about what's been going on...keep me in the loop. We've got a little house we bought together closer to Galveston…I'll get the number for ya.' Keep me informed, Brains. I mean it." Again, he stood, ready to leave, hesitating long enough to voice his real concern. "All three were from our unit." He and Brad exchanged looks that made it plain that both were concerned. "Don't drink too much. See ya' at the wedding." By the door, he turned and added, "I never figured you for one to be interested in politics."

Brad smiled. Funny you should call it politics, he thought. It's real life, Jake. It rains on you just like it rains on me.

After Jake left, Brad put what was left of his drink in the sink, pouring it out. He knew Jake was bothered by the deaths of their fellow SEALs, but so was he. He started to turn on the TV but changed his mind. *Three guys from one unit meeting an untimely death. Their unit.* It wouldn't have been a stretch for Brad to articulate what was beginning to hit too close to home.

Not a cloud in the sky, warm and low humidity, Saturday turned out to be a perfect wedding day. The wedding lasted longer than he knew his and Kassie's would last. High mass was like that. Afterwards, they enjoyed a feast at the reception held in the building bordering the church. It was there Brad greeted some old friends.

"Henry Stans, how are you? How's the old Hawk?" Brad couldn't get over how Hawk had changed; a little overweight and more than just a few gray hairs. His personality was the same. Henry had got his pseudo name because he was the only one in the unit who knew if something, anything, was out of place, at any time. It served him well in the field; Hawk was highly respected among the others.

"Jamie Maxwell. Good to see you, Spud. I just was speaking to Hawk…" And so it went all afternoon. For Brad, the wedding was a reuniting of old friends, his buddies. After his third drink, he decided to leave before his vision and attentiveness went berserk. Upon giving his best wishes to the newly married couple, he exited the banquet hall.

As he was walking to the rental he was driving, he heard a noise to his left. It was a blond haired attendee talking to some gal about three cars away. He stood and watched them for what seemed like a minute and realized the gentleman was someone he'd seen before... and not that long ago. Dressed in a tux, he escorted the gal into the hotel, never looking toward Brad. Once he was out of sight, Brad got in the car and left.

When he arrived back at the hotel, he took a shower and tried to relax. Too many hands to shake, his smile lines had been overworked. But relaxation didn't follow. The nagging truth hung in the air like cigarette smoke in a telephone booth with the door closed. Pushing all other thoughts from his mind, he was dead certain that he'd seen the man in the tuxedo before. But where? Why did it bother him? Getting no answers, he decided to sleep. Maybe in the morning...

It was late in the evening on Sunday when he arrived back in Denver. He had taken the afternoon to visit his parents; nothing new with them. For whatever reason, Brad was glad that his visit with them didn't last very long. His life was so different from theirs. Perhaps he could've made a greater effort to understand what they were doing and why, but their lives seemed to be so artificial, so mundane. They didn't understand why he chose to attend church while in town for such a short period of time. Perhaps if they knew the grace that comes from knowing Christ personally, they would attend as well. On that thought, he wasn't going to hold his breath!

"Hi, Kass. How's my favorite friend? I'd come over but got back late so I'll see you tomorrow at work. Love you. Miss you." The message was short and sweet. He figured Kassie was already in bed. The way he felt that's where he was headed. Tomorrow would come soon enough.

# 73

Kassie wasn't at all sure why she checked the tickets every day, as though she was checking to see they hadn't got up and walked off. She knew it was ridiculous; she needed to know they were still where she had put them.

After seeing Brad earlier in the evening, she couldn't sleep. As much as she trusted him, she couldn't bring herself to tell him what she'd found. Besides, she thought, what would he be able to do about it? Tell her that what she did was wrong? Tell her to place them back where she found them? She doubted very much if he would've told her to do that. The tickets clearly pointed to Selway as the murderer of his own wife! The words stuck in her mind like super glue on fingers. Would Brad insist she go to the police? Who else would he suggest she tell? What would he have her say? As she lay quietly, thinking, her mind wandered to the one person that she would have to trust in order to iron this wrinkle, this sin in her life that crept in so innocently. Words from Scripture came to her: *But those who wait upon the Lord, shall renew their strength; they shall mount up with wings as eagles; they shall run, and not be weary; and they shall walk, and not faint.* Isaiah 40:31. She remembered it as though it was just yesterday she'd memorized this powerful verse. As though someone turned on a light, she knew in an instant her prayers, and all the questions that would surely come up, would be answered. And yes, she would be able to face all of it. *Thank you, Lord, for your unending grace.*

She fell asleep before she finished turning over.

The morning came too early; the alarm was too loud. Jacki had worked the night shift so Kassie assumed she'd still be asleep. After using the bathroom, she locked her bedroom door and checked her bottom dresser drawer, again. They were still there but she picked them up and read them again. Stephen Selway. Stephen Selway. Carolyn Selway. There wasn't a thing she could do or say that would change the names on the tickets. Frustrated and disappointed, at this point she wished that she had never concerned herself over what happened to Carolyn Selway. Obviously, in her mind, there was a substantial reason to inquire about her since Stephen Selway was such a 'ladies man.' Something wasn't right. She felt it in her bones!

She wasn't looking for any errors. It just happened. Being bathed in the glow of a Colorado morning, her room was still in shadows. She looked closer at Stephen's ticket. She couldn't be sure...maybe if she looked at it under the light. She walked over to her bedside and turned on the light. Holding the ticket up to the light...oh my... the 'S.' The 'S' on Selway was different than the 'S' on Stephen. She examined it closer, turning the ticket different ways to make sure she wasn't just imagining things that weren't there.

It became eye-popping clear, like the moment you know you're going to crash and your foot won't reach the brake pedal in time to stop it from happening. Why? How did he do it? Or who did it? Why would he try to cover another name with his own? What if he covered a different name with his own in order to protect someone? There are episodes of clarity in life that make you wonder if what you're seeing is really authentic. Perhaps the change was done at the ticket counter at the airport. Did they really recycle tickets? Kassie, taking into account her level of aggravation and curiosity, decided that now she had more reason than ever to discover exactly what had happened to Carolyn Selway.

# 74

After breakfast, Kassie walked to the corral, looking for her father. Waiting by the gate, she whistled for Vanity, even though she couldn't see where he was. From somewhere beneath the slope that was some distance from the barn, Vanity appeared galloping full bore to reach the corral. Reaching for the saddle, she realized that a ride would do more good to clear her mind than anything else she would endeavor.

"Where you going?" It was Kassie's father.

"Dad? You surprised me. But! You're just the one I was waiting for. I was hoping you'd take a ride with me down to the river."

"How much are you paying?" Mark asked as he reached for a saddle. Emitting a low whistle, one of the Arabs in the stall began to whinny. "Francisco just said he doesn't come cheap!"

"Dad! Really?"

With an impish grin that revealed his indented laugh lines, he said, "It was worth a try!"

The river at this time of year was running slow and narrow, with just enough water to make fording it possible. It was a beautiful, meandering flow with sporadic trees and brush on its banks kept green by the moisture provided to their roots. The horses had been exposed to the river many times and found it to be refreshing rather than an impediment.

After they had crossed to an open space of lush grass and high ground, Mark commented that he preferred to ford the river when it was as low.

"No sense in getting wet on such a beautiful day."

They rode in silence, taking in the vistas of Wyoming and the mountainous terrain Kassie suspected could only be found on her father and mother's ranch. Under the sun, it was a never ending sea of beauty and serenity, something she coveted for her mind at the moment.

Riding alongside her father, she asked, "Could we stop for a moment? There's something I'd like to talk to you about, something heavy on my mind?"

"Sure." Dismounting and throwing the reins over a tree branch, he continued. "Since you arrived you've had something pressing on your mind." He picked up a pebble and threw it lazily into the river below. "Are you ready to share it?"

"Father." Kassie sucked in a deep breath of Wyoming fresh air, the memory of which stays with you forever and can be recalled at a moment's notice. Kassie dismounted as well. She wondered exactly what to say and how she should say it. It had bothered her for so many days she hoped whatever came out of her mouth her father would understand. "Have I ever disappointed you...beyond repair, I mean? Or maybe I should ask if there was anything I could do you couldn't forgive?" She stood next to him, wondering how he would answer. It was important to her as to how he would answer. For all her worry and angst, perhaps she should keep her little secret to herself.

"Kass, darling, if ever there was a person who couldn't disappoint me, I'm afraid it would be you. Remember, you're just human with the same frailties' that I or your mother or anyone else possesses. So don't be so hard on yourself...at least not until I hear what you have to say."

"That's the problem, Dad. This is something I've never done before. At least that I can remember." There was a long silence as they walked, each with their own thoughts. "I took something that wasn't mine to have." She quickly added, "But I intend to return it! It's just that it looks like someone may have been murdered." They both stopped, Kassie taking the opportunity to sit down in the grass, on the earth, where surprisingly she felt safer, more secure. As her father listened, Kassie told him about her suspicions regarding Stephen Selway and the events which brought her to this point. Mark listened intently, allowing no outward sign of emotion as to what he was thinking. When Kassie stopped for a breath, he spoke.

"Hummm. Do you have with you...what you took?"

Kassie reached inside her coat and pulled out the two ticket stubs, handing them to her father. "These. I found them sticking out from under his pad on his desk. Selway was having a party and..."

"You think he killed his wife? Why? *Because of these*?" He held the stubs, reluctantly, looking at them as though they might bite. Bringing them up to his eyes closer than normal, he started to say something but Kassie interrupted. "Kass, these..."

"Dad, look at the printed letters in their names. I think someone ..."

But her father had already noticed. "Kass. Someone has imprinted Dr. Selways' name over another name. The "S" in Selway is different. That's quite obvious, at least to me. Is that what you're upset about?"

"I needed to hear your opinion, Dad. I don't trust anyone else as I do you. Actually, I wanted to be wrong. It would make things a lot easier." The silence between them was deafening. "I haven't showed them to anyone else, even Brad. He doesn't need to know what I've done."

"What you've done? Hardly think that matters in light of what these tickets tell me. What do you plan on doing about this?"

"I'm not sure. It doesn't matter to whom or where I take them. They're going to want to know why I have them in my possession. For that, I have no excuse. Least, not an honest one."

Mark eventually sat down on one of the many boulders that bordered the river. Continuing to chew on the raw end of a straw, he too, wondered who would want to do such a despicable thing. Kassie played with the grass in front of her eventually finding just the right length of straw on which to chew and vent her thoughts. As though Mark was praying, he looked up toward the sky and let out a deep sigh. "Don't take them to the police. I have a friend..."

"*Dad*! I can't show them to anyone, not mother, not Brad nor Jackie...not anyone. That's part of my problem." Mark got up and handed the stubs back to Kassie. She replaced them in her jacket.

"How long are you staying?" Kassie didn't have to ponder it at all. "As long as it takes...maybe...if you can help me?" She knew better than to extend her stay without a valid excuse, at least one her supervisor would understand. She'd have to tell another lie! That wasn't going to happen. "Actually, I have to be back by Monday afternoon."

Mark grabbed the reins and led his horse as though they were going for a walk. He said, "I have a friend that might help...he *can* help...but not until Monday. He's fishing this weekend." Kassie, leading Vanity, walked quietly beside her father, hoping that something good would come out of her misdeed. Each was lost in their individual thoughts; a beautiful day for riding, being in each other's company, with a problem they now shared.

When Mark stopped, Kassie did also. The horses went back to grazing. As they mounted their horses, Mark had one last comment. "Someone had a pernicious intent to do what he...or she...did. Pure evil, I'd say." The horses were ready to run, jittery as they were. "What d'ya say, we ride to Carmel Ridge and just enjoy the ride." Without another word, they took off, both pushing their hats down snug on their heads, while the horses fed their spirits with the need to run, their tails sailing on the wind.

# 75

Monday morning, Mark was the first one up. Not bothering to eat his normal breakfast of a couple eggs and toast, he was out the door and in his truck before Kassie realized he was gone.

She hadn't wanted to sleep late, but the fresh air on a breeze through her open window, gently pushing the curtains aside, with the melody of hearing the horses whinny and the birds chirping out her windows, made resting on her old bed more inviting.

She wondered if her father left without the ticket stubs. Checking her jacket pocket, she found them missing. Good, she thought. After dressing, she went downstairs, quietly, to wait on Mark to get home. When his truck appeared at the bend in the road just prior to entering the ranch, she went outside.

Mark motioned with his hand for her to come to the truck. Approaching her father, she asked, "Any good news?"

"Get in the truck. Let's take a ride." He casually placed the ticket stubs on the seat between them.

"My friend is ex-FBI." He paused, collecting his thoughts. "You could be in more trouble...not for exposing a murderer...but for illegally confiscating property that might lead someone to the pen or worse."

"You think for a minute that I haven't thought about that! Father! Really? Now that I have them, what should be my next step? Did he think they were forged?"

"Someone has clearly typed or overlaid someone else's name with the name that's presently on the tickets. Don't be concerned about Mr. Selway. It's the name underneath that is going to be your problem. I've been thinking."

"How to get me off the hook, I hope…I hope."

"How well do you know Mr. Selway?"

"Well enough, for what?"

"Can you trust him?"

"He's sort of sleazy, Dad. I told you about him!"

"That has nothing to do with you being able to trust him!" Mark spoke so softly that it was difficult for Kassie to be suitably upset with him. She couldn't remember a time…ever…that Mark spoke any other way. It was an attribute of his that made him so appealing to all who knew him.

Kassie, in spite of what she thought of him, believed if she asked Selway in a private and considerate manner, *perhaps plausibly*…he would understand how critical it was to find who altered the ticket stubs…with his name! After all, it was his name he should be worried about, lest the tickets fall into someone else's hands. At present the tickets were being held tightly, by her hand in her pocket.

Her mind was full of knots, the kind that lingers and produces conflict with oneself. How did she ever get in this mess anyway? Why did she ever concern herself with Carolyn Selway or how she died? The library. Why did she even enter his library? Who was she to question Dr. Selway? How many hoops would she have to go through to achieve some semblance of sanity concerning her own peace of mind? She was a responsible woman who stuck her nose where it had no business going…and for that there undoubtedly would be consequences.

"Don't be so hard on yourself. You found something validating what you thought a certain man could possibly have done. Now, it's different. However, Kass, it appears that a murder may well have occurred."

"I know. Therein lays my problem." Mark knew a thousand thoughts were imploding in his daughter's mind. Knowing his daughter, at some point she would adopt a precise strategy she couldn't alter, an outcome that would produce a murderer or a fickle, meddling opportunist. "At some point, Dad, I will tell Stephen what I've done, and possibly what someone is trying to do to him and prayerfully, he'll forgive me and help me. That's all I can hope for. But I must do this in my own way. I may be guilty of many things, but I won't be a party to condemning a man for something he may not have done."

"You'll be in my prayers...and no, I won't tell your mother. But please, for your father's peace of mind, keep me informed. Okay?"

"Got it." Kassie let out a huge sigh of relief. "Thanks, Dad."

# 76

Working with her fellow nurses, making sure the surgical patients were prepped properly, helped her to cope. It kept her mind from wandering while she planned for her encounter with Dr. Selway. He'd been in surgery all week just as Brad and Drs. Harriman and Reynolds had been.

Her mother had taught her the Lord always answers prayer. That was beautiful to remember 'cause now she was trying to figure out how to approach Dr. Selway. And she was praying!

Truth be told, Kassie prayed every night for as long as she could remember. Hers wasn't a habit formed over many days spent in an airplane or working as a nurse; her habit of praying started as a young girl. In fact, she would've never characterized it as a 'habit.' Praying was a way of communicating with her Lord; at night, during the day, at work or play, in serene times or times of stress. Anytime she wanted a quiet conversation with her Lord, she prayed.

The whole day she contemplated what her attitude should be when she crossed paths with Dr. Selway. What if the shoe was on the other foot? Her foot! What if someone had found tickets with her name forged over another name? Would she want to know? Of course! What would she say if confronted with that possibility? What if she was told they were taken from her home? Illegally! Purposefully! Would she be the kind of person to forgive such an atrocity, a crime against her person? By whom? By someone she loved? By a stranger? Would she be upset by the confession of such a person bringing her that kind of news? *'You took the tickets because...you think I killed someone?'* The questions never stopped, that is, until she realized the same type of questions may come from Dr. Selway of her, questions when answered may not prove to be the answers he was willing to swallow.

"Lord, please help me. I don't know why I took the tickets? I know it was wrong, deliberately wrong. If I was presented with the same scenario again, I wouldn't take them. Or. Yes, I'd probably do the same thing again. My curiosity gets the best of me...all the time! So. Please forgive me...again. Show me find the path you wish me to take. Help me to be humble and not accusatory when I show him the tickets. Help me to understand Dr. Selway in a way that had never presented itself before. Help me to approach him as I would want someone to approach me under the same circumstances. I can't do this alone and only you, Lord, can give me the strength and courage to do what I must. If it be thy will, in Christ's name I ask it, amen."

When she got off work, she slipped into the chapel. She was glad no one else was present; the silence soothed her nerves. As she sat in one of the front pews, she fingered the bracelet that Brad had given her. She wasn't nervous or distraught but thankful she had made the decision to show Dr. Selway what she had found...and taken. *'God's timing has always been perfect,'* she heard her mother say. *'When you seek and acknowledge him in His sovereignty, he knows exactly what to do with your problem.'* That's who Kassie would cling to, her faith in the Lord who never fails, until she received an answer.

# 77

"Kass, can I stop over at your place after work? I'd like to speak to you about something…rather personal."

Kassie had just finished the dishes and was getting ready to sit down, relax and knit. Jackie had gone to a movie with Howie. Theatre food was definitely not better than what Kassie prepared; apples, cottage cheese, onions and some canned chicken. When mixed and served together, Kassie thought, it was delicious; much more nourishing than popcorn!

Thinking about Cindy's arrival had Kassie thinking something was terribly wrong; the hesitancy in her voice was a telltale sign of something not being quite right. When she knocked at the door, Kassie was quick to answer.

"Hey, girl! Come on in. I'm glad you could stop for awhile. Did you drive…or walk?" To Kassie, Cindy didn't appear to be distracted or depressed. So what was the problem…she knew there was a problem.

"Hi. I'm glad you were at home. Oh, my. Your apartment is so beautiful. Nothing like mine. I have the bare necessities."

"Jackie and I decided…or Jackie decided…that we should fix it up as soon as we began working as nurses. Jackie has a thing for…"

"Being acceptable? I know. But I like her anyway. Her family must be wealthy." Cindy walked to the couch and took a seat. "Your place is so homey and yet, so elegant. I can see why you don't want to leave it on your days off."

"I'm getting better, though, at going out. You're just not around to see it."

"Perhaps." Cindy fell silent. Kassie went back into the kitchen to get some cookies for Cindy. One always needed a little pickup after work.

"Do you prefer water or milk. Or Pepsi."

"I'd like a martini laced with Zoloft, if you don't mind."

"What? An antidepressant...with liquor?" Kassie scoffed.

"Sounds good to me!" Cindy walked over to the windows and viewed the landscape.

"Sorry! But a glass of water with a lemon squeeze will have to do." She walked up to Cindy who was still standing by the picture windows and handed her the drink. "I baked some cookies yesterday. Want some?" She took a drink of her own water.

"Maybe later. I thought I would tell you what Stephen is up to, since you work with him and know him fairly well." Kassie held her breath for a moment, knowing that somehow she was involved with what Cindy was about to reveal. "He's decided to install motion detectors in his study and throughout his house." Kassie coughed, more like choked, as she held back a gasp. "He claims someone has been in his house when he wasn't there. How would you know that sort of thing? I asked him what made him think so and he just grunted." Kassie wasn't sure what to say, if anything. So she acted surprised.

"Really! I'm wondering why he didn't have them installed before now. It's a pretty big house...and he is a surgeon. Maybe...maybe someone thought he kept money at the house."

"I don't think so." Cindy reached for a cookie. "Anyway, I forgot my favorite hairbrush over there the other night and I'd like to go it. Want to ride along?"

"You have a way to get in?"

"I have a key. Let's go." She grabbed another cookie, sticking it in her pocket. Kassie excused herself, used the bathroom and then went to her room. She grabbed the ticket stubs, stuck them inside her blouse, covered by her sweater, and left with Cindy.

Kassie fully intended to return the tickets and place them under the pad on Stephen's desk. However, on the ride over to Beacon Avenue, she began to think of questions that may be asked and opinions ventured. What if Stephen knew the tickets were missing? What if he hadn't had anyone in the house but himself? Should he find them again, what if he surmised the only people inside the house had been Cindy and herself? What if he asks Cindy if she had been in his study when he wasn't there? How would she answer? What if? What if? What if? Kassie thought she would die from fear for being found out. She couldn't tell Cindy what she wanted to do, or what she had already done, since Stephen was obviously suspicious about someone being in his house that didn't belong there...what was she to do? Whichever question influenced her decision, she wasn't about to return the tickets at this time.

After entering the house, Cindy started to walk off in search of her hairbrush.

"I'll just wait here, by the door."

"Don't be silly. You can help me look and then I want to show you the study."

"Like I haven't seen it before!" Kassie mumbled under her breath.

"I found it." As she approached Kassie, she said, "It was on the kitchen counter. I'm surprised Stephen didn't through it away. He's such a neatness freak. Come on. Here's the study. Isn't it just gorgeous! All those books! I wonder if he's read all of them."

"There is not a speck of dust anywhere. Does he have a cleaning lady?" As Kassie and Cindy walked around the study, as Cindy called it, the library appeared to be immaculately clean. There was an aroma in the air of fresh lilac and the flowers on his desk were real roses. "I wonder how much time he spends in here."

"Evidently a lot but no…he doesn't have a cleaning lady that I'm aware of…but that doesn't mean anything. I'm not always here." Cindy kept looking up towards the ceiling, looking for something that was as yet unseen. "Can you see where he put the motion detectors?"

Kassie was in her own realm of disquieting thought. She didn't accept Cindy's explanation for the motion detectors as being what she stated: had Stephen thought there was an intruder in his house, he would have notified the authorities. She looked at Cindy presently scanning the upper book shelves and realized she had been asked a question.

"No, I don't see any but have you looked in the air ducts?"

"That's a good idea. Whatever made you think of that, Kass?"

"The 'Godfather!'"

"The who?"

"Nothing. Let's look in that one," she said as she pointed to a duct above an alcove, "maybe that's where he put it." Of all the things she needed at the moment, which was very little, she could easily live without finding anything obtrusive among Stephen's books.

Cindy climbed up on the desk, after removing her shoes, stretched and looked in the vent above the alcove behind Stephen's desk. "I don't believe it! There's a thingamajig behind the vent!" She stepped down, got in her shoes and went to look at the vent on the outer wall.

"Cindy, I don't think I'd do that. It's probably recording our movements as we speak." Of all the things she could've been doing, she found herself snooping in someone's house! Another thought hit her. "What if he's recording our conversation…not that we said anything wrong or detrimental."

"Oh, my. What if he is? Guess I'll say 'Hi.'" She waved at the vent.

"Let's get out of here. I've seen everything and yes, it is gorgeous." Approaching the double doors leading into the library, a tiny green light flickered and caught her eye. It was placed on the outside binding of a fake book, about eye height, and had meant to be viewed as the dot on the 'i' in the title of "A Married Woman." Without fanfare, Kassie knew it was time to leave, and quickly. The last thing she wanted was having to contend with Stephen should he come back to the house before they had a chance to escape. She said nothing to Cindy, walking directly to the front door. "Time to leave."

"Hey! What's the hurry?" Cindy followed her out the door. There was an almost soundless clink of the door lock being slid into place as Cindy pulled the door shut.

Kassie tried to recall if she said anything in the library that would lead Stephen to think twice about them being there. Off hand, she felt like both of them were in the clear. But! A shower would feel great about now, she thought. On the ride back to the apartment, Kassie asked a legitimate question of Cindy.

"What was so important about you stopping to see me this afternoon? Or did I miss something?"

Cindy hesitated. "I wondered what you thought of him putting cameras all over his house. Don't you think that's a bit paranoid?"

"It's his house! He can do anything he likes."

"Oh! Perhaps." But Cindy didn't sound convincing, not even to herself.

"Just how well do you think you know Stephen? That is, other than the obvious things all of us know about him. For instance, have the two of you ever discussed his deceased wife? Have you been to his house when his company was someone other than the surgical staff?" Very aware of the ticket stubs stuck in her blouse, they now made themselves known.

"Why?"

"Just asking? I know it's none of my business but I don't want you to get in too deep and then find out something that you really don't like about him." Kassie was afraid she had said too much. "I mean, breaking up with someone is difficult, especially at our age. Neither one of us is getting any younger and…"

"Do you think we're really that serious? I'm surprised, Kass, coming from you. I've got a question for *you*. Does Brad have any skeletons in his closet? Maybe something he's done or…or…you know what I mean?"

Kassie now knew she had pursued the conversation too long: she certainly didn't like the way it was going. After all, she thought, it wasn't Brad's name on those ticket stubs!

"You're right, Cindy. Please accept my apology for being so intrusive. I had no right."

Neither said anything until they got back to Kassie's apartment.

Once inside the apartment, the tickets went back into the bottom drawer. She couldn't help feeling confused about Cindy and her relationship with Stephen. She no longer harbored any doubts; someone wanted to get Stephen Selway into deep trouble!

# 78

During the last month, Brad had decided to stay on at Mercy until an opportunity presented itself in Wyoming. He knew Kassie wanted to return to her home state and while the possibilities of a surgical position opening up in Laramie or Sheridan were slim, he could always hope. Besides, he rather liked Wyoming with its open spaces, warm people and the freedoms all those he had met so far espoused. Wyoming had all the makings of a state to which he had been exposed but never lived. Finally, with the liberties, economical, social and political they all seemed to enjoy, it would be a wonderful place to raise children.

Even the practice he envisioned of setting up would be more practical for him in the state. Brad was tired of living the city life. He'd been born and raised in a big city; his former life had taken him to cities, where you had to lock your car and house every time you left them, pick up your pets' poop when taking them for a walk, buy a house that was an expected assumption for a highly educated man and have season tickets to a major athletic team.

He'd had a wonderful life thus far, one to envy, one for which he was thankful but it was time for a change: a place where he could find solitude and peace, and practice his profession without the interference of the government, as he viewed the Hippocratic Oath. If the Affordable Care Act was ever going to be implemented, Brad Phillips wanted to put as much space between him and the bureaucracy of the Federal government as he could, for as long as he could.

He had finished his shift in surgery and was headed to check on his patients, when upon reaching third floor he was approached by one of the nurses who again looked familiar. 'It is him,' Brad thought, 'the same face that was in Dallas.' But the hair. The hair was different. 'In Dallas he was a blonde; now he was a redhead. Oh, well, men can change their hair color as well as women, I suppose.'

"Anything I can help you with? On my way to catch a snack."

Brad thought for an instant, the redhead was taken aback when he first laid eyes on him. 'Maybe it's just my imagination run wild.'

"No, thanks." For Brad to say to him, 'I thought you were a blonde the last time I saw you' would have only raised some uncomfortable flags. Especially for the redhead. He reminded himself before he left the floor, he'd have to find out the man's name.

"Mr. Longren. How's the leg?" Brad should've never asked!

"Doc. Why am I back in the hospital? I really don't want to be here."

"When you find someone that does, you let me know."

"That's not what I mean! My leg isn't healing and I want to know why!" Mr. Longren had a set of lungs that could rival the Broncos quarterback.

"Did you change the dressings like I asked you to do?"

"The missus did. Poured peroxide over it and then, alcohol. Added ten years to my short life! Anything else you'd like to know?"

"Mr. Longren. Not quite so loud. Have you had your hearing checked lately?" Brad wrote in the chart a request for a hearing test. "How much alcohol have you had lately?"

"What's my drinking got to do with anything? My liver's fine."

"Why did you say your liver is fine? Have you had it checked or are you guessing? Or maybe you don't have any pain in your abdomen...yet?"

"Doc! What's my drinking got to do with my sore leg?"

"Everything. I asked you to change the dressings aseptically and not to drink until your leg was healed. You shouldn't be drinking, period! Obviously, you chose to ignore my orders."

"My missus changed those cloths and she's right good at it, even though she about killed me."

"And your drinking?"

"That's my business!"

Brad knew the poor man wouldn't quit drinking until Boulder became something other than twenty square miles surrounded by reality.

Brad flipped the chart closed, laid it on the bed and proceeded to remove the sheet that covered Mr. Longren's leg. What he saw was an open wound, raw, bloody and full of pus; it reminded him of some of the wounds his fellow SEALs had suffered. The memory of such fleshly intrusions was best left on the battlefield. He covered the leg with the sheet, grabbed the chart and said, "Mr. Longren, your leg is infected and smells. Probably gangrene. I'll have the nurses come and remove the affected tissue and treat it. You probably won't appreciate the pain so we'll give you something to help you cope." Brad thought for a moment. "On the other hand, maybe not!"

"Doc! When can I get out of here?" Brad was already out of the room. Back at the desk, he requested a full body MRI and blood work on Mr. Longren.

"What's the name of the new fellow on the floor?"

Without looking up, one of the nurses at the desk simply said, "Samuel. Goes by Sam."

"Is he a...?"

"Nurse. Don't know his last name. Don't know where he's from. Not married. No kids. Likes to flirt. Rather spooky, if you ask me. Which you did. A redhead without freckles. Anything else?" All that said without looking up or taking a breath.

Brad couldn't blame her. At her age she'd seen many a nurse, and surgeon, come and go. She'd probably been married, divorced, married again, unhappy in her current marriage and looking forward to retirement. "Wonder what I'll be like at your age," Brad mumbled under his breath.

"You say something?"

"Not really." Brad smiled to himself. 'Probably hard of hearing and severely constipated.' It was best to keep those thoughts to himself.

"See you tomorrow." She didn't bother to look up.

# 79

As he left the chapel, his cell phone rang.

"Are you off duty or just taking a break?"

"Off duty." Brad could see his black sedan with darkened windows parked across the street. 'Someday,' he thought, 'maybe I'll get myself a black car, spotless and shiny. But with children, maybe not!' He crossed the street and slid into the seat where the door had been opened for him. The car began to move.

"How ya' been? We have to have a quick conversation since I'm due to be at DIA in forty-five minutes. Have you got anything for me?"

"I think I know who our mystery man is. I have yet to find out if he's a SEAL."

"What makes you think it's a SEAL?"

"The guy was in Dallas at the wedding."

"So?"

"Most of our team attended the wedding. The wedding was extremely nice, thank you very much for asking."

"I was there!"

"Where?"

"Around. We're SEALs, you know. We're supposed to be invisible."

"You could've said hello…or something."

"I was just doing my job."

"You have a number where I can reach you…a secure line, perhaps? Something local?" The Commander reached in his jacket and pulled out a folded piece of paper.

"Here. You'll also find some information there that I picked up in Dallas. We may be thinking about the same man. But he's not a SEAL. Good luck. Gotta go."

The sedan had already stopped. Brad pulled the handle and was out on the sidewalk before he could say 'one Mississippi.'

Since he was back in front of the emergency entrance of Mercy, Brad walked home. As he did, he read what was typed on the piece of paper. The commander was correct, as usual. They were thinking about the same individual. One thought bothered him. 'Why would a civilian bother to kill SEALs?' Unless. 'Unless he washed out or rang the bell. That might make him bitter.'

Once at the apartment, he called his mother. Of all the times he thought of making such a call, this time he fervently hoped she would answer.

"Hello."

"Mother. How are you…and father?"

"Wonders never cease. Brad, I thought you may have…oh, never mind. It's been a long time since you called."

"Been busy. Mother, I have a favor to ask of you. In your cedar chest there is a list of my team members…SEALs…that you wanted to keep for me. Do you still have it?" Brad felt as though he should cross his fingers.

"Which one, dear?"

"Which one what?"

"Which cedar chest? The one in the basement or the one in the attic?"

"Mother! I haven't got the faintest idea which one you would've put it in. But can you look?"

"Sure, dear. I'll have your father help me. When do you need it?"

"As soon as possible."

"Oh, dear. We're giving a dinner party tonight as a Democratic benefit. You caught me at a very busy time."

"Mother. I wouldn't ask…"

"I know, dear. I'll try to make time to look."

"Thanks, Mother. Say hi to father."

One thing stuck in his mind that was unwittingly put there from the time he was a child. The household staff did the house cleaning and cooking, setting the table with his mother's exquisite china and anything else that needed to be done for a dinner party. The only work his mother accomplished was to give the orders and get herself ready! A second item was a bit more disturbing. Was his mother absentminded or…was she getting forgetful? Probably neither but the last thought was a bit disquieting.

Brad could only wait and hope that his mother would come up with the list of names faster than if he himself flew to Dallas and retrieved it!

# 80

He learned Dr. Selway would be at the hospital working since he was called in on an emergency. The patient would be transferred to the floor as soon as the surgery was completed and he was sufficiently awake to leave recovery. The patients' information would've already been transmitted to third floor and since Stephen was on call, he would be the one to perform for the patient what was necessary.

It was black as India ink as he approached the garage; no moon in an overcast, gloomy sky. The key he had left by the access door was still there. The thought did present itself that perhaps he should make more than one key. It wasn't important at the moment.

Inside the garage, he had to find his way around the convertible Porsche that Selway drove only on sunny, warm weekend days. It was just a reminder that he too could've owned the same vehicle, in a different color, of course. Presently, the Porsche could've been any color and it still would've looked black.

Inside the house through the door leading from the garage, he made his way through the hallway, separating the laundry room from the kitchen. Above the cabinets he noticed a tiny green light that flickered on and off. He stopped cold, knowing he was still in the shadows. He backed up into the garage and began looking for the control box that would hold the switch to turn off the security cameras. 'Why did he install cameras,' he thought. 'Did I mess up and leave some tell tale sign that I had been here before? Surely not!'

Feeling along the wall, his eyesight grew accustomed to the dark; he tried to find the fuse box. On the other two walls were stacked bicycles and tools, including a Harley Davidson motorcycle. To maintain a house as large as his a riding lawnmower and assortment of other items were present. To his dismay, he couldn't locate any sign of a security control box. "It must be inside," he said, although his whispering seemed to penetrate the very walls of the garage. "Well, *Dr. Selway*, I'll just have to stay in the shadows."

He maneuvered himself as quickly as he could from room to room until he reached the library. Before entering he surveyed the room, at least that part which he could see. "Where would you put the sensors?" From where he stood, there didn't appear to be any cameras in place. Cautiously moving into the room, moving to his left, he kept his back to the wall and continued until he was almost to his desk. He waited. He was good at what he did and he knew it but this was a personal quest he was on and of all people, he didn't want to make any unnecessary mistakes before Dr. Stephen Selway was aware of what he had done. Once at the desk, he stepped forward and carefully lifted the pad on the desk. He stared in disbelief! The ticket stubs were gone! "*So, Dr. Selway.* You have seen them and probably threw them away. But I'm not finished with you yet!" He replaced the pad and began to walk toward the door. Completely at ease now he surveyed the room as if he had never seen it before. "Must be nice to be so comfortable."

A bolt of lightning couldn't have done more damage to his brain as what the little green light did. There, beside the door, was a blinking light, almost imperceptible, on the cover of a book. Now he was angry! Disgusted with himself about being so stupid, he couldn't make the intentional leap to understand why Selway would put a sensor facing toward the desk as opposed to being in a corner of the ceiling! He was glad he was in a darkened room. Somehow he felt safer. It crossed his mind to take the book and destroy it but what if… and it was. The false book when removed was connected by wires and a switch on its backside. Giving it a tug he knew to remove it would alert Selway, proving someone had been in his office, uninvited.

After carefully putting it back on the shelf, he left the room. But he had what he wanted. The green light stayed on while he removed the tape from the small cassette. Placing the tape in his pocket, he again moved in the shadows and retreated to the back door. Opening the door, letting his eyes adjust to the complete blackness of the garage, he listened. Everything was still. He put the key back where he'd planted it before and then, very deliberately decided to take it with him.

He walked the block or so to his waiting vehicle, completely confident in his mind Stephen Selway must be sweating bullets by now, knowing his name was on the ticket copies. The camera sensors were another indication to him that Selway felt entirely exposed to someone wanting to do irreparable harm to him and 'his precious reputation.' Sitting in his car, feeling convinced that he was making Dr. Selway very anxious about his precarious position, destroyed stubs or not, he smiled, started the vehicle and drove away.

"I've only just begun to make your life miserable, *Mister Selway*… if you only knew."

# 81

'Kass left her mailbox open. Wonder if she remembered…nope, there's a letter in the box.' Kassie and Jackie had separate mailboxes just inside their apartment complex from which they would retrieve their mail. Brad always took a moment to check the box since Kassie had had him check for her mail on a day when she wasn't feeling well. Taking the letter, Brad closed the box and proceeded to the stairs.

After ringing her doorbell three times, he knocked. No answer. He wondered where she was. He was to pick her up for dinner but remembered she had said something about 'shopping' and knowing women and their habitual state of window shopping, he wasn't surprised she hadn't returned home, yet.

As he stood waiting he glanced at the letter. It was addressed to Kassie with a return address of a simple name: Caroline. No post office box number, no street number and no city or state. The postmark was stamped as having been mailed from Colorado Springs, Colorado. What a curious notion to identify yourself by a first name only, he thought. He knew some of Kassie's friends but except for Carolyn Selway, he wasn't aware of anyone named Caroline.

After sitting on the steps for fifteen minutes, he decided to leave the letter stuck in her door beside the handle. On the outside of the envelope, he wrote: I was here. Please call me. B.

He jogged back to his apartment, grabbed a soda from the refrigerator and flopped down in his only easy chair. His mother hadn't called back yet and that frustrated him, to a point. It had been less than twenty-four hours and to his mother, a day wasn't considered a long time. Just the same he thought he would give her another call. If only he could share with her how much could be, and actually was, accomplished in one day but it would take an immense amount of understanding on her part. Brad doubted whether she could comprehend any life without all the pleasures and comforts her life had provided for her.

"Oh, you should have been here last night! We had a delightful time and I must say, your father worked the table like the pro he is. A considerable amount of money was raised; the Democratic establishment will be pleased."

"Who paid for all the food...or was it donated?" Brad doubted anyone offered to donate any food and since his father...well...pride would make him pick up the tab for food!

"No, my dear. Your father always picks up the bill. Have you forgotten his quiet sense of pride? Anyway, you called for something... what was it?"

"Names, mother, names. On a sheet of paper that you professed to keep safe for me...for whatever reason. Maybe I asked you to save it...I can't remember...but I had you look for it."

"Just a moment dear, I...I found it but...I must get it from my desk." Brad could hear the receiver hit the countertop in the kitchen; marble makes its own sound. A bit of paper shuffling and then... "Okay. I have it. Now what was it...?"

"On that list is there a fellow with the first name of Samuel?"

"Let's see. John Carpenter...Barry Knott...Manuel Rodriguez... Hank Robinson...I'm so sorry for what happened to him...Joseph Porter. Oh, how is Jake doing, dear? We heard he got married. I really liked that fellow, you know..."

"Mother! The list. Keep reading."

"Yes, of course, dear. You have always been right to the point..."

"Mother. Please stop! Just look at the list and tell me if there is someone whose first name is Samuel?"

"You mustn't be so short with your mother. I'm trying to help!"

Poor Brad! He began to wonder if all middle age men had to deal with a mother such as he had. It wasn't like he was ungrateful! Quite the opposite! He was born into opulence which he alone decided to shed. As a young boy he was a slow reluctant follower who somehow managed to become a richly self sufficient man, much as a worm builds for itself a cocoon and through a process of brilliant transformation known only to God, becomes a butterfly. As his mother had patience with him when he was young, always teaching him, subtlety, the mannerisms of what it took to be successful, he decided he too could have patience with his mother as she grew older. But it was a chore!

"Okay. I'm sorry. Forgive me, mother."

"There. That's more like my son."

"I just have one question to ask. Is there anyone on that list whose first name is Samuel?"

"Let me look. Hummmmmm..."

What was it that Hank had always said? 'Patience is a virtue. A God given spiritual gift.' Hank. The memories of Hank were all too real. He was not only a great SEAL team member, but he was Brad's special friend. It wasn't until he died Brad realized Hank had been a great friend to everyone he met.

His funeral brought out people from every race, creed and color; and because Hank was who he was, a Christian who lived his life as though it belonged to everyone else, all the mourners were instant friends with each other as though they'd known each other all their lives. For Brad, it was a remarkable scene, one of love, and hope and peace. Although there wasn't an arrogant bone in his body, Brad thought Hank would've been pleased at his funeral. Not only was it a time to bring together all those people he loved, it also united everyone he loved that believed in Christ. With tears turning to smiles, everyone's life was richer because they all knew and loved Hank.

Hank was the most patient of any man Brad had ever known. He was the example that Brad wanted to follow now...

"There's a name on here...but his last name is Samuel. Lawrence Samuel. Does that help?"

"Yes, it does. Anything written beside his name?"

"Yes. Looks like someone scribbled an asterisk beside his name. Any help?"

"Mother. I don't care what stuffy, self indulged people may say about you! I love you. I only have one mother and I'm so glad it was you."

"What? Surely that's not what my friends say...!"

"Mother! It was a joke."

"Oh. Sure. I get it...I think."

"Thanks a bunch, mother." A click on the phone told her that Brad was gone...again. Gladys Phillips wondered when she would hear from her son again. In the meantime, she would worry about what her friends might be saying behind her back.

# 82

It had been a busy day; four surgeries, one of which would undoubtedly be accompanied by unwanted side effects. Stephen Selway would never become accustomed to the marvels of modern day surgery. With all the innovations that medical technology had put at his disposal, he still couldn't alter some of the after effects that manifested themselves without warning. Every human body is different and the effects of the same identical surgery in two or more individuals can have entirely unexplained contrasting modalities.

The removal of any portion of the body also altered the mind of the patient. Mr. Marcus Lincoln wasn't a 'spring chicken'; at seventy two years old and an ex-Marine, he had experienced pain in all forms. The loss of a Marine buddy, the breakup of his marriage, the estrangement of his children, the doubts he had about being a career Marine, the ugly effects of war on those who came home who had left a portion of their soul on the battlefield. Yet, he wouldn't have traded his life for any other. He was a soldier and proud of it. As with everything else in his world, he would weather this storm as well.

As tough and craggy as he was, the removal of his pancreas would present problems that would initially frustrate him and in time, would alter the rest of his life. Foods he couldn't eat, alcohol he could no longer consume, constipation or diarrhea, eating several small meals throughout the day, pain that may result in his abdomen because of enzymes and insulin that were no longer there. He would have to supplement those to compensate for the organ that would no longer be present. And yet, depending on his acceptance, the removal of his pancreas shouldn't prevent him from living a wonderful life.

But something else was on his mind. Obamacare! Yes, he was seventy two years old; perhaps he didn't have many years left. In the mind of Mr. Marcus Lincoln, his surgery was necessary. After serving his country for so many years, he expected to keep his private health insurance. They *said* they would pay for the surgery regardless of his age. So why was his government intent on him signing up for Obamacare?

Mr. Lincoln had discussed his dilemma with Dr. Selway prior to the surgery. Cancer waits for no man; the surgery had to be done, the sooner the better. In spite of overwhelming odds that the surgeon and hospital wouldn't be reimbursed, the surgery was scheduled.

It wasn't that Dr. Selway thought of himself as an angel in disguise. He simply decided that his professional ethics told him it was the right thing to do. Besides, he thought, 'they can't put me in jail for doing the right thing…or,…they could take my money.' Money, in his mind, was only good for one thing: separation for a good cause.

# *83*

She couldn't help but wonder what Dr. Selway would do when he opened the letter. Something sparked her imagination when Brad had retrieved her mail for her. Kassie hadn't thought much about it at the time but now she had some hot material she would've been happy not to have in her possession, the mail route might be the way for her to get out of her own way.

She couldn't tell anyone that she had made copies of the tickets; the copies were insurance that someone had tampered with airline tickets and Dr. Selway's name. Figuring they could come in handy she placed them in the bottom drawer of her dresser. Along with the copies she placed the registered mail receipt in the drawer, as well.

She wondered what her father would say when he heard what she had done. He never suggested that she mail them back or that she return them at all.

Surely, Dr. Selway must have known the tickets were placed under the pad on his desk in his house. She had to go on that assumption unless, of course, she found them before he saw them. In her mind it meant someone who was at Selway's parties was responsible for placing them there. Kassie couldn't resolve the thought when thinking of the attendees. She couldn't get her mind around the fact she might very well know the person who was the actual murderer. Now the tickets had been mailed; she was determined to forget about them. Ironically, even Kassie thought that was an impossibility!

When Kassie arrived at work the next morning around seven, she was met by Brad, already in surgical scrubs.

"Hey. I thought we were supposed to have dinner together last night? Mind if I ask what happened?"

"Oh, I'm sorry." Kassie was more apprehensive than upset. How was she going to explain to Brad where she had been? "I went window shopping and completely forgot about it. Let's do it tonight."

"Sounds good."

# 84

Sometimes life can be so pathetically corrupted by the minutiae of living that little time is left to think: working, watching the tube and all the gore, listening to the radio with mental images coming to mind, dinners with friends, housekeeping, cooking, walking the dog, bathing the cat, washing the car, sending appropriate cards at the appropriate time, marking the calendar, paying bills. It reminded Kassie of eating crabs: so much work for so little to eat!

Alone in her apartment, she made time to takes notes on all that she had learned. Aware everything put into her computer could be retrieved by anyone scared the living daylights out of her. Kassie actually disliked the computers she had to deal with at work. In her case, being a detailed person didn't include machinery! She was, for all practical purposes, technologically impaired!

With each new development, it found a place in the bottom drawer of her dresser.

She had just finished the few dishes that were crusted over with mashed potatoes and gravy when her cell sounded.

"Hey! Stephen is planning another party, inviting the unscrupulous detached surgical team and the third floor…"

"Unscrupulous?"

"Hey! Lighten up, Kass. You know I'm kidding."

"Brad. Words mean something. Even when you're kidding, words still mean something."

"Wow! So serious. What's going on?"

"What do you mean…what's going on?"

"Kass, how about if I drop over tonight after work? We can discuss the party then."

"Fine. I'll fix you a snack."

Brad was getting concerned for Kassie and the seriousness with which she was taking everything lately. She'd always been serious about her work and all the regulations that were being forced on the surgical staff due to political correctness. Now that it was law, with all the new regulations coming due to the Affordable Care Act, both she and Brad had critical thoughts about the outcome. The consequences were unthinkable. Political hacks along with graduates with no experience making decisions concerning every enrolled individual and their health insurance coverage was becoming a threat not only to patients but to their own livelihood.

Perhaps he was reading too much into her attitude, the distance he heard in her voice. Conceivably he could be wrong. Brad had been trained to read another's emotions or lack thereof and in the case of Kassie, he knew only too well where there was smoke, there was fire.

Maybe, just maybe, he thought, he was reading too much into what she *wasn't* saying. Tonight he would lay all those thoughts to rest.

It had already been a long Monday.

# *85*

After eating leftovers and a rich dessert, Brad sat relaxed in front of the fireplace. Brad's tummy was full and Kassie's was tied in knots.

"Mind if I use the bathroom?" Kassie shook her head negatively. Brad had barely closed the door, when his cell phone rang. Kassie nonchalantly reached over and picked it up. The voice at the other end responded to her touch.

"Tomorrow at the front entrance. 7 PM. Don't be late." Silence followed. Sensing it was something she shouldn't have heard, she replaced Brad's cell phone back immediately. The unknowing didn't stop her from thinking. Front entrance to what? How did the caller know Brad would be available at seven? Don't be late? Who could be calling? A man with a deep bass voice, she was sure she had heard it before. What was it all about? Maybe Cindy was correct. Perhaps there were things about Brad Phillips that she would prefer not knowing.

"I think I'll make some coffee. Maybe a coffee latte. Care for some?" Brad said as he returned to the living room. It wasn't the first time that Brad had made his own strong brew. So black and thick that it supported a fork standing on its tines, Kassie declined with a smile. "Suit yourself."

"You had a phone call. I let it ring." Another lie! She wondered how long it would take before someone would challenge her memory.

Truth was always the truth but lies…well; you had to remember the details of the lie that was told. Brad walked over and checked his cell.

"Oh." Wanting to show no emotion when he recognized the number, he offered, "Must be a wrong number."

After discussing the party to be held at Selway's, their attention took a different course. "Do you ever wonder about Stephen…and what really brought him to Denver?" Kassie asked.

"You make it sound as though there's a mystery about his working here. Do you know something you're not telling me?" Brad's curiosity was peaked! "Did Cindy mention anything to you about Stephen?"

"Only good stuff. She really likes him…but I'm not sure she really knows him that well. Anyway, he asked Cindy to spend a weekend with him and…"

"He told me," Brad interrupted. "He thinks he's in love." Brad slid off his chair and made himself comfortable in front of the fireplace. "Course he also thinks someone has been visiting his home without an invitation. I really didn't want to get mixed up in his paranoia; it's better to leave sleeping dogs lie." Brad grabbed a pillow and placing it under his head, laid down on the area rug. Meanwhile, Kassie was hoping that he'd quit speaking and prayerfully, fall asleep. That would alleviate her from asking if Stephen had told him anything about the missing plane tickets. Surely Stephen should have them by this evening. Tomorrow, perhaps, Brad would hear Stephen explain how his mail had become corrupted!

Kassie felt somewhat sleepy herself. Casually throwing the other pillow to the floor, she carefully laid down beside Brad. Realizing it was a bit chilly, she reached for Brad's sweater that he'd placed on the chair. Hearing a crunch of paper as she tried to cover herself, she searched his pockets and came up with a scrap of paper, paper that had been folded, then scrunched. She was in the process of throwing it up in the chair when something stopped her. She carefully pealed back the layers until it was flat. On it was a drawing, resembling a star. In the center was a question mark. On one tip the letters of K.S. was printed. On another tip was printed 'unknown,' on the third tip, C.S. appeared. Another had the initials B.P. The fifth tip had S.S.in parenthesis.

Kassie stared at the paper for an indeterminate amount of time. As she studied the letters, she realized that B.P. could be Brad. She caught her breath when she concluded that C.S. could be Carolyn Selway. But why? Why would Brad use their initials on this star? She was beginning to doubt herself. She had no idea who or what K.S. stood for and quite frankly she convinced herself that 'these initials could stand for a clean syringe, or…a…bed pan, or…a…specimen sample…or a kinky spine!' Not wanting to get caught in an act of snooping, she carefully rolled the paper into a ball and placed it back in Brad's sweater pocket. Whereas she was sleepy before, sleep now seemed to be the last thing on her mind.

She awakened about ten thirty and realized Brad better leave before Jacki came home. She didn't know if her light touch on his back would even wake him. Before she finished her thought, Brad had rolled over, flinging his arm to the outside of his body, smacking Kassie in the mouth.

"Ouch! What did I do?" Her lips stung from the blow.

"Oh, geez, I'm so sorry. I forgot where I was. Wow, I must have been dreaming…not something pleasant." Brad helped her to her feet and lovingly led her to the bathroom. "Let me clean off your lip…you should probably put some ice on it. I'm so sorry." After drying her lips, he asked, "What time is it?"

"You're not even going to ask me if I'm hurting…or whether I even want to marry a man who dreams so vividly that he accidently smacks his wife?" She started to grin but her lip began to burn. Brad looked serious. Immediately sorry for what she had said, she put her arm around him, laying her head on his chest and continued. "It's okay. I'm kidding."

Brad felt foolish about what he had done. Not only did he hit her unknowingly but now Kassie knew he had difficult dreams and sometimes, they could be dangerous.

# *86*

Kassie had just walked out of the chapel when Selway approached her, taking her by the elbow and compelled her to go with him. Once they were in the stairwell, he spoke.

"What were you doing in my study? With Cindy?"

"How...how did you know...that...?" Bewildered, yet not surprised, she knew she must feign disbelief.

"Cindy told me...when she wanted to find her brush. Why did you go into my study?"

"Cindy...she...Cindy...wanted me to see how beautiful it was...how many books you had." 'Watch out, Kassie. Knowing you looked at books could mean real trouble.' Her mind was racing; she was beginning to perspire profusely. Selway appeared to relax.

"She could've waited until I got home...but that's so like her. However, it was only a hairbrush." He rubbed Kassie's arm where he had grabbed it. But Kassie waved him off. "I gave Cindy a key for emergencies in case I lost my key or...in the event I was away she could have access to my home. It's okay. Relax." Selway started up the stairs. Kassie followed. "So! How do you like my study?"

After reaching the surgical unit, Kassie heaved a sigh of relief. Selway didn't say a word about receiving the tickets; since she had just survived a near collapse she wasn't about to bring the subject up. Perhaps after she collected herself she would pull Selway aside by yanking on his super clean, starched and unwrinkled uniform and give the man more gray hair.

The OR was in an uproar. A call had been taken by one of the surgical staff from Admitting that frightened and dismayed the staff. A young girl was coming to surgery that needed immediate attention. Like yesterday would've been more appropriate. Since only one surgical suite was open, she was wheeled in and appropriately placed on the operating table. Having been sedated in ER, the anesthetist started an IV. Brad Phillips was on break. Responding immediately to his pager while having a quick bite to eat, he appeared chewing a mouthful of food.

"What have we got?" Upon looking at the admittance sheet, all he could bring himself to say was "Dear God." He looked for Kassie but she was assisting Howard Harriman in another suite. "Carla, prep with me. Now!"

For scheduled surgeries, the operating surgeons always prepared themselves beforehand, even considering events that might go awry. Those instances were far and few between but they were contemplated as not to be a surprise if they occurred.

Brad was not prepared to see the present problem lying on his surgical table. The young girl, 'she can't be more than ten,' was bleeding. Brad also noticed her frail arms and ankles were black and blue against her lightly tanned skin. There were tape marks on her face which made Brad wince with disgust.

While cleaning the area he became angry to the point where he couldn't speak. Someone had taken this young girl, obviously against her wishes, and they, whoever *they* was, had carelessly, without emotion, had maimed the God given life of this little girl.

If ever there was a time that Brad felt the need to pray, it was now. 'How could this happen? Who would do such a thing of this magnitude to anyone, much less a precious young child? I know you're listening, Lord, but where were you when this was happening? Everything known has been put under your feet, yet this travesty was allowed? Why?'

"Dr. Phillips?" It was Carla but she wasn't getting his attention. A little louder, she repeated, "Dr. Phillips!"

"Okay. For a moment..." Brad looked at Carla. "Let's get to work." The staff moved with precision, moving from anger and the unimaginable to empathy and empowerment.

"I've done all I can, surgically. I'd like to know her name. Also, her home circumstances." As he stripped off his gloves and removed his mask, he continued. "Find out if her parents..."

"I was just told that she was living with her adopted family. I'll try to get more details when she's removed from recovery." Carla was elated that she could even speak after being traumatized with the event she had just witnessed. There were occasions that being a professional just wasn't enough; at times like these, Carla understood with enhanced clarity, that she couldn't park her humanity at the door. Likewise, with Dr. Brad Phillips. It was comforting to know that in addition to becoming a prodigious surgeon, he carried his compassion as a human being with him. 'I do believe he was praying during surgery...as were the rest of us,' she thought. After Carla finished cleaning up she set about finding the information that Dr. Phillips requested.

"That's Della!" Cindy was just this side of becoming hysterical, knowing that she had helped place Della with a foster family. "How did this happen? What have I done?"

"As far as I know, you didn't do anything but try to help her." Jacki was helping place Della on her bed, removing her from the gurney that brought her from recovery. "Don't go getting your britches in a twist! Dr. Phillips did the surgery. She'll recover."

Cindy knew better. There were some traumatic events from which one never recovered. Until recently, she always felt as though she was one of those victims. With her father safely but isolated in prison and the understanding she received from friends like Kassie and Dr. Selway, life was becoming a new adventure for her, one in which her self esteem was beginning to blossom. Now was not the time to think only of herself. At the moment, Della, the little girl with the wounded body, was uppermost in her mind.

Between Cindy and Jacki, Della was more comfortable than she had been in sometime, knowing she could trust Cindy. But pain was pain! Nothing could erase the memory of it or the pain she was feeling now. "I have to use the bathroom, but I'm afraid to move."

"Let me see what the doctor ordered for pain medication. I'll be right back."

Jacki checked the IV that was running; the injection site on her arm showed no infiltration. "Cindy and I can carry you to the bathroom, if you'd like. Walking might be tough…"

"Thank you."

When Cindy returned, she had a morphine injection in her hand. As she administered the shot, she said, "Let's give this shot a little time to work and then…can you hold it for a bit?"

"I think so." Della's voice was weak.

"Honey. Let me tell you something! If you can't hold it, let it discharge. We can always remake your bed. Got it?" Jacki never did mince words. It was what it was. Had she been in the same circumstances, she'd already drenched the sheets.

After carefully lifting her from the bed, with the IV pole as a companion, they sat her on the stool. "We'll be right outside the door if you need anything. When you're finished, let us clean your bottom.

Don't do it yourself. You might pull out some stitches. Okay?" For the first time since they had started working together, Cindy decided in spite of Jacki's worldly ways and quick wit, buried beneath the surface was a compassionate woman, especially where children were concerned.

The screaming could be heard in the hall, the nurse's desk and by every patient on third floor. It could've peeled the paint off the walls! The fury seemed endless.

"Della...Della..." Once they were in the bathroom, it was evident that she had urinated, by the amount of blood in the commode. Afraid of having any more pain, Della didn't want to be touched. As Cindy picked her up, her screaming became shrill.

"It hurts...it hurts." Once in bed, the screams turned to crying. While Jacki retrieved a pan of warm water, Cindy laid out some gauze and a couple clean towels.

"I'll be as careful as I can. The warm water will feel soothing and I'll just pat the area dry. Then I'll place a soft pad between your legs and by that time, the morphine should be working really well."

Della tried to be a valiant patient. Jacki made sure that the IV line didn't get caught by the sheet or somehow wind up under her fragile body. "You okay?" Della shook her head affirmatively. She was feeling lightheaded and somewhat sleepy. But as gentle as Cindy and Jacki cleaned her wounds, Della couldn't stop crying.

That evening when Cindy's shift was over she stopped in Della's room. Awake for the second time that day, Della smiled weakly at Cindy when she entered.

"Hey. You're awake. How you doing?" Cindy checked the IV and unobtrusively checked her pulse. "Do you need another shot for pain before I leave?" Della moved her head as if to say yes. "Your foster parents want to know how you're doing...but..."

"My father did this to me, him and a friend. They picked me up after school. My foster parents…I really like my foster parents. They make me feel like I'm wanted…" Della responded between sobs.

"That's good…good." Cindy gently patted her arm. "I'll let the nurse know you need a shot. And I'll see you tomorrow."

Cindy had to leave the room. She stood in the darkened hallway while the tears rolled down her face, falling on her uniform. 'What kind of person would do this to a young girl? What more would Della have to experience before she could leave home?' After wiping her tears she informed the night shift about the morphine shot needed for Della and then prepared to go home. But first, she would stop in the chapel.

# 87

Kassie found Dr. Selway at his desk in the hospital. It was just off the surgical wing. She didn't know exactly what she was going to say. But she felt, after being in the chapel, praying, that God would give her the words at the right time.

"Dr. Selway. May I bother you for a moment?"

"Kassie. Of course. Come in." He stood as he motioned for her to have a seat. Sitting down didn't make her any more comfortable than had she remained standing. "What's on your mind?"

"I need to share something with you…something that I'm not comfortable saying…confessing. So I'm just…"

"Going to tell me you took something from my office and returned it through the mail?" It was said as though he was telling his housekeeper to sweep the floor. Kassie exhaled a sigh of relief only to hear that Dr. Selway had more to say. "Am I correct in my assumptions? I think so. But I must tell you something. The tickets had been on my desk for some time. I, too, was shocked by seeing my name on one of them. However. That ticket was never used by me."

"I know, I know. I had it checked…"

"So did I. Quite frankly, it's obvious that the name has been altered. So I put them under the desk pad, evidently *not* hidden out of sight. So! Now that you and I and at least two other people have seen them as they now exist, what do *you and I* plan on doing about it?" Pointing his finger at Kassie and himself, he settled back in his chair.

"I thought you'd be angry with me..."

"For why? I know I'm not guilty of any wrongdoing concerning my ex-wife."

"Your deceased ex-wife."

"Yes. Yes. That's what I have always said. Because it's true. Our divorce was to legally take place...Carolyn wanted the divorce. But in her will she was most gracious to me." He got up and walked to the window and became lost in thought. Kassie refrained from saying another word; the memories he harbored were painful. "She always said it didn't have anything to do with me. Oh, we were happy for a few years, supremely so. But when her personality began to change, she became another person, a person I didn't know. I was in the way...of something...or...someone. I never asked. I didn't want to know." After sipping on a can of pop, he addressed Kassie. "What do you intend to do with this information? May I ask as to others you may have told?"

"No one. I haven't told..." Another lie! 'At least it's not anyone you know.'

"Good. Perhaps between the two of us we can figure out who is trying to implicate me in a murder! After seeing the one way ticket for Carolyn, that's the only conclusion I could infer."

"Dr. Selway, I want to apologize for taking them in the first place. It wasn't right and...I'm sorry. I'm truly sorry."

"Kass. Kass. Kass! I know you. I accept your apology. Actually, I'm glad someone else knows about them besides me and the...I'm glad you're the one...perhaps...look, I'm giving a dinner party on Saturday. For now, let's say nothing and let's see who shows up at the party."

"Fair enough. And thank you for being so kind. I didn't know..."

"What is it they say: courage is fear that has said its prayers? I'm sure you've said yours...and I know I've said mine."

# 88

It was early Wednesday morning when Kassie woke up to her cell phone ringing. She had planned on sleeping in after having had an exhausting Tuesday between working and her admission to Selway. The headache she had was the result of her 'photo image' dreams: she was glad to be awake.

"Hello."

"Kass. Hi, it's Dad. You okay?"

"Hi Dad. You woke me up," as she tried sitting up in bed, "and I haven't cleared my throat yet. What's up?" Coughing, she cleared her throat.

"If your mother comes in I may have to change the subject. Have you decided what you're going to do with the tickets?"

Kassie hesitated but since the act had been completed and discussed with Selway, she said, "Dad, I sent them back to him...after I made copies." There was dead silence on the other end of the phone.

"Dad! Dad! You there?"

"Why did you do that?" Her father was always composed in speaking regardless of the situation.

"It's okay. Dr. Selway and I had a conversation about what I had done and in his own way he told me he's glad someone else knows about the tickets. I'm confident he didn't have anything to do with the death of his wife. But neither one of us knows who might have done this. Don't be upset with me, Dad, I just had to give them back."

"Have you heard of Grey Cloud?"

"Who? Grey…what…Grey…?"

"Grey Cloud?"

"Dad, that sounds like a name for a horse! Grey Cloud? Is that what you said?"

"Evidently not. I thought you might have heard of it." Now her father knew Brad had yet to tell Kassie anything about his background. He had to cover his tracks; what should he say. "I heard of them from a friend of mine who was in the service." This really wasn't the whole truth. How could he inform Kassie of how she might be entangled with an entity completely unknown to her that by any means of one's imagination could be dangerous to her existence? "My friend told me about them in some great detail. They're an independent security company, supposedly nonpolitical, that engages in warfare and protection with our military; totally politically incorrect and discreetly *indefensible*." He paused to let Kassie get in a word. Nothing. He continued. "Since they're independent…made up of retired military and retired SEALs…they can say and do almost anything in any war zone without repercussions."

"Dad. They're mercenaries!" Kassie was shocked!

"Call them what you want. They're a necessary evil if nothing else. They protect a lot of our people overseas…but…"

"Are you saying…do you mean Selway could be mixed up with these men? How could that be? He's a surgeon!"

"Do you know if he's been in the military?"

"Of course not! Perhaps he has…"

"They employ medical personnel as well, and attorneys…and the like. What I'm trying to say is…there's more to this story than you know."

"What aren't you telling me? Dad?"

"They employ women, as well." It was Kassie's turn to be silent. Her mind was on a perpetual spin, trying to fit together all the little pieces she knew.

"Dad."

"Hey, Kass."

"I'm going to hang up now. Got a headache. Love you, Dad." No good bye this morning. It was just the impetus she needed to go to the range.

Approaching the range, Kassie decided to park on the far side of the buildings, out of sight of the entrance. One building held supplies and clothing for purchase by anyone who came to practice. The second building was more open with a lean-to roof running the length of the building. It was under the lean-to where the shooters stood, spaced apart from each other, firing their weapons. After paying for the privilege of using the range, she set about, moving the bean bags on her stand, getting her revolver out of duffle bag and making herself comfortable. Two men were shooting their rifles at targets down range; they appeared oblivious to her presence.

"Hi, Jeff. Looks like you're keeping busy."

"Shooting the little one today, eh?"

Kassie smiled, knowing Jeff remembered her from before. "You weren't here the last time I was out here. Were you ill?"

"Naw. Went hunting in Alaska. Got me a caribou! Big one! I'll show ya the pictures. They sure are pretty animals. And fast!"

"I'll bet. They run in herds, I hear."

"Ya. That they do. If you ever hunt them ya better be ready to shoot as soon as ya hear their clatter. They'll be right on top of ya."

"Well, Jeff. I don't know if I'll ever hunt caribou. Moose, maybe. Elk, for sure. And maybe deer."

"It's a shame not to put all your abilities with your firearms to work. I have to say, I've never seen anybody shoot any better, straighter or more relaxed than you do." He started to leave. "I better get back to work. Have fun."

She did as she spent two boxes of shells, target practicing. Never know when I might be grateful that I took the time to remain effective with this firearm, she thought. She decided to leave before anyone came to practice she might know or that knew her.

It was her secret passion to be honorable and proficient in the way she handled her firearms. She'd learned from her father and Jake that along with knowing how to use a firearm there came a tremendous personal responsibility. The same responsibility was also applied when it came to her license to open carry. Kassie Colbert took their advice seriously; they were men she trusted. Perhaps someday, she thought, Brad would also get his own license to open carry. She liked that idea.

# 89

That afternoon, Cindy sat with Kassie and Jacki on break, one of those rare times when all three of the nurses could get together and unwind.

"Jacki, how do you like working with Samuel?" Kassie didn't look up from what she had on her plate: a croissant with chocolate. She wondered why Cindy was interested in Jacki's opinion. "You have worked with him...no?"

"He's okay. Pretty good nurse. He's different though. Can't put my finger on why...he's just...aloof. Why? Did he try to hit on you."

"He's real friendly toward me. Too friendly. He asked if I was going with anybody. When I told him I was dating Dr. Selway I thought he was going to upchuck...he got white as a sheet. Needless to say, I kept busy and he disappeared."

"Go figure." Jacki rolled her eyes.

"Disappeared? To where?" Kassie was curious.

Jacki said, "Probably the bathroom, duh, since he was going to vomit!"

"He probably returned to fourth." Cindy was entirely too serious.

After they finished their break, all three returned to work, their individual personalities intact.

Leaving the chapel after work, Kassie drove to the library. Sitting in a secluded alcove, she pulled up information that she had seen before. If nothing else, she wanted to make certain what she found was solid information, that it wasn't a mistake. In her mind, before going to the party on Saturday, she wanted all her ducks in a row. For the rest of the week, she would be careful what she said, especially to Brad. Her constitution had been shaken badly with the telephone call from her father; the knowledge she had was just enough to authorize her to worry. She didn't have all the pieces but she was real close.

Brad sat looking at the diagram of a star he had drawn, trying to place the appropriate names on each tip. He had met with the Lieutenant but that encounter left more questions unanswered, questions that begged for an answer, than he'd had before.

"Have you come up with anymore on the blond?"

Brad said, "You mean the redhead…or blond. No, nothing substantial. He's a good nurse. No problems there."

"But he was in those cities where the murders took place, was he not?"

Brad sat thinking. If he had placed Samuel in those cities at the times the Lieutenant referred to, then why would it have been impossible for the Lieutenant to also know that information? Why was he asking him something he could've known for himself? After all, he'd said he was in Houston during the wedding. Was he or wasn't he? Brad couldn't bring himself to think it was just a flippant remark. If the Lieutenant had been in Houston, sight unseen, perhaps he was in the other cities, sight unseen, where the murders took place. But why? Why wouldn't he share that bit of information with Brad?

It bothered Brad in a way that he couldn't verbalize. But…he *could* lightheartedly bring it up in another context. "Hey! Didn't you tell me 'once a SEAL, always a SEAL?' If you were in Houston, sight unseen, you could show up anywhere unseen!" Brad laughed as though it was the funniest line he had delivered since he decided, almost choking himself to death, that chickens surely existed before eggs. What he didn't see was the lieutenant turn red; his eyes bulging like those of frogs before they jump. Before Brad turned back to him, sitting in the drivers' seat, the Lieutenant had regained his composure.

"Yes. I suppose I could. But I never told you 'once a SEAL, always a SEAL.'" The Lieutenant let the statement hang in the air. "But it sounded good, I'll give you that." He started the ignition which was Brad's invitation to leave. "I'll call you next time I want to be unseen!"

Brad was considerably bothered by the sarcasm in the Lieutenant's last statement. But hadn't he been facetious himself?

As a rule, upon leaving work, Kassie bought a newspaper. Sometimes it was the Denver Clarion; occasionally she purchased the Sentinel.

It had been another regular day but she felt unusually hungry. While the pizza was in the oven, she picked up the Sentinel and began scanning the pages. I didn't take her long to find an article that perked her interest. Buried on page seven was a piece concerning the military and their use of private contractors. She read it but it didn't touch a nerve until she saw the adjoining article titled:

US General: CHRISTIANS ARE BEING PERSECUTED

A family of four was taken from their home when a team of armed military personnel appeared at their door with the excuse that a hijacker had been traced to the house next door....

The disgust that Kassie exhibited couldn't come close to what she knew to be true. The author of the article went on to explain the family were indeed practicing Christians and although they allowed the entry they felt their Fourth Amendment rights had been violated. 'This took place in the United States, in my country!'

Kassie wondered what she would do had the same thing happened to her. With what she knew, she couldn't help but assume her rights as a legal, voting citizen; she would've felt violated as well. When did the military get the privilege of walking into a person's home and without as much as a 'please' and ask the homeowners to leave? If the military could accomplish that task without firing a shot, then how long would it take before the police could do the same thing?

Kassie knew that the information she had tucked in her drawer would have to see the light of day before she could put any of it to rest. She put the paper aside, ate her two pieces of pizza and decided she'd ask her father about it in the morning. Had she not been so tired perhaps…no!…definitely not!…no one should have to put up with anyone simply taking control of your home! And then there was Brad. What if she told him what she had learned from all her snooping, something that he probably would frown upon. No! She'd wait and speak to her father about her anxieties.

During the night, her dreams returned. Only this night, a clear image of Carolyn Selway appeared in a brilliant picture frame, set on a grand piano. Standing beside her in the photo was an unmistakable gentleman in full military gear, smiling, as though he had a secret he couldn't wait to share. As much as she wanted to walk away from the piano she couldn't move. Her eyes were fixed on the image. Startled and only half awake, she realized it had only been a dream. Again, she was soaked with perspiration. Rolling over, she went back to sleep.

# *90*

Upon waking in the morning, her body ached from not having rested. As soon as she shared what she knew...maybe speaking to her father...maybe just taking a hot shower would revive her senses! Whether she acted like a zombie, looked like a zombie or spoke like one, Kassie had determined she was going to work. After her shower, she'd give her father a call. In her mind, her father could always put her at ease; his advice was always sound.

"You're calling early. I was just about to feed the heifers in the corral. What's been happening?"

"Depends on your point of view. I guess. Dad, did your friend elaborate on what he called the Grey Cloud, something you could share with me?"

"Like what, for instance?"

"What exactly do they do?"

"He filled in some of the gaps in my...our story...I didn't get everything I wanted. These private military type groups...enforcers for protection...they hold their information close to their chests." Mark wasn't sure how much he should pass on to Kassie in spite of the fact that knowing his daughter, she wouldn't quit asking questions until she was satisfied with the answers, answers he probably didn't have. "They do a lot of protection detail for the actual United States military, a job they obviously love. Their individual pay is extremely high, which in itself is enough incentive for them to belong to these groups. Grey Cloud is just one of several that have cropped up in the last ten years." What Mark did not divulge was that Brad, as a SEAL, was probably approached by Grey Cloud or another group to work as an agent. Brad was retired Navy, a SEAL, intelligent and therefore a potential candidate for hire. Had Brad told Kassie about his SEAL days, Mark was sure she would've brought the subject up. And how much did she know about Grey Cloud? Since he couldn't be sure on either point, it was best to avoid saying too much.

"Dad. What if I told you Grey Cloud might be doing domestic surveillance? You know, mercenaries acting as police."

Mark remained silent for a moment, realizing that his daughter knew more than she was telling. It was conceivable she knew more than he did; it wasn't easy for him to admit. Without having to lie, but skirting the truth, after ruminating over what knowledge he had, he said, "Kassie, what exactly are you getting at?"

Not being known for her gullibility, Kassie decided what she knew was authentic and absolutely terrifying, something she knew her father was holding back. Would her father 'lie' to her 'by omission,' by not revealing the whole truth? She wondered why.

"There have been articles in the papers here in Denver about these paramilitary groups…and how they've operated."

"Are you speaking of the tanks and helicopters that are being purchased…by police departments?"

"You know what Dad? I forgot about the time. I've got to get ready for work. How about if I call you tomorrow?"

Mark, fearing for his daughter and what she had planned, said, "Kass. Whatever you do, wherever you go…carry your firearm. Okay?

Remember the rule. Don't pull it out if you don't intentionally need to use it. I'll wait for your call tomorrow."

"Thanks, Dad."

She was afraid her father knew much more than what he cared to share with her. On the other hand, he had no way of knowing all the information she had. Thoughts of her bottom dresser drawer came to mind. She was glad she had her work. She remembered her mother saying 'sometimes you have to live moment to moment;' thinking too far ahead could have dangerous consequences. Just before leaving the apartment, she checked her bottom dresser drawer; she let out a sigh of relief. Grabbing a sweater, including a Pepsi from the fridge, she was out the door.

"Good morning, Brad." He had just left one of the operating suites and was passing through the patient pre-op room where those who were waiting for surgery were being prepped. Being the quintessential professional, he graciously responded.

"Hi, Kass. Working only four hours today! Got anything planned for the afternoon?"

"Thought I'd clean my apartment, probably wash some clothes, iron...the usual. What time do you get off?"

"At four...providing there aren't any emergencies." He continued to write in the current patient's chart while Kassie folded a few linens. "I thought I'd stop by and have some pizza. Okay with you?"

"How'd you know I have pizza at home?"

As he reached for the chart belonging to his next patient, he leaned over and whispered. "You have the unmistakable aroma of fresh pizza." He grinned.

"Well! As long as it's pleasant. It could've been floor polish or ceiling wax or cabbages of kings!" Kassie rolled her eyes accompanied by such a provocative smile that Brad would've rather given her a hug and kiss than attend to business.

"Della is going to go with her adoptive parents. They were given a restraining order by the court against all of her immediate family."

"Cindy! How do they know that her father won't break the law? Or her mother? Or for anyone else, for that matter. They live by Sharia law, not our laws! Don't you get it?"

"Perhaps they have made other plans…" Cindy wanted to share with Jacki in the worst way Della and her adoptive parents had made plans, plans that would remove Della from the immediate vicinity of her actual parents. The respect Cindy had for Della's adoptive family was shadowed only by her realization that they had an intense love for an abused little girl of ten.

"Let's hope so. When they find out that they can't legally… at least U. S. legally…can't see their daughter, there's going to be reprecussions." Remembering her manners, she continued. "Oops! Sorry I said it that way. Here I am a woman of the world…ignorant of what some men are capable of…dating men as though they're God's gift to women, never thinking that…"

"Yes." Cindy waited.

"Of all the men I've dated, seriously…"

"All of two weeks, huh?" Again, Cindy waited.

"Maybe one or two of them turned out to be a…that's a terrible thought! Imagine. What if all men were like that? That's just not right, you know. Della's been through a lot but prayerfully, she'll be fine. Did I just say 'prayerfully?' Jacki scoffed at herself. "Kassie's beliefs are beginning to penetrate and alter my brain. If only she could do something constructive about my attitude!"

As soon as he finished in surgery, he went to swap his scrubs for street clothes. In putting on his sweater, he felt the paper in his pocket. He sat down on the twin bed located in the changing room, the bed where residents could nap when doing their twenty-four and thirty-six hour shifts. Removing the paper and looking at the star points, there was one vacant. He knew a SEAL had been killed with a shot to his head. Someone where in the south. His name was Lincoln Smith. Tentatively, he put LS on the fourth point. Barry Knott, a friend to Ken Station, had yet to be found. He'd put different names to the points before but erased them because of new information he'd found.

"Somehow these names are all connected to one person. But who?" The one thing they had in common was their brotherhood as Navy SEALs. As he pondered his own question, he wondered whose initials he should put in the center of the star. Reluctantly, he put the paper back in his pocket. He'd had a good day in surgery; now he was hungry.

As he walked to his apartment to freshen up before going to Kassie's apartment, with his photographic memory he put his own initials in the middle of the star. It hit him between the eyes as he was crossing the street. He stopped walking, not mindful of oncoming traffic. "Why didn't I think of this before? How could I not see it? It's so obvious!" Several horns were honking and cars swerving in order not to hit him. Oblivious to the mayhem he had caused, he ran to his apartment and drew a new star.

# *91*

hey kissed as Brad entered the apartment, embracing for an extended period of time. Kassie had made another pizza with everything on it except anchovies. Between lima beans and anchovies, she didn't know which Brad hated more. Having worked a whole day herself, pizza seemed to be the easiest meal she could think of to make.

Making himself comfortable on a chair, she served him two pieces of pizza accompanied by a napkin.

"This looks so good. Smells good, too. How about you, Kass? Aren't you going to have some?"

"I'm coming. One of these large pieces is enough for me." After taking a bite, she continued. "Oh, this is good. No anchovies but with three meats, three kinds of cheese…"

"Loaded with calories. But hunger takes precedence. Hummmm, good."

After they were finished eating, Kassie took their plates and placed them in the sink. "Would you like a Pepsi?"

"I would. Thank you. Thanks for the pizza." Brad had a full tummy; it felt good. But he had other things on his mind. The call he had placed to the Lieutenant went unanswered. That bothered him. He was sure he had the correct cell number; it was the one the Lieutenant had given him. Brad suspected he'd eventually get a return call; he just hoped it wasn't while he was at Kassie's.

"In the paper it says that the Speaker of the House feels that we have too large a population. Too many people on this planet! Now with that little tad bit of heresy hitting the news, abortion may never be overturned! And the State Department still hasn't revealed how out Ambassador got himself killed?" Pensive, she looked at her hands. "And Obamacare. It's a mess. Did Selway tell you about the surgery he did before he found out if it was going to covered? I'll say this. The man has a heart."

"I'm sure he has the money to cover…"

"I'm sure he does. He didn't have to do it, you know." Kassie was thinking. "You think you would ever do something similar, help somebody who had served our country, who was an older individual without insurance?"

"Kass, I hadn't thought about it. In truth, there's going to be a lot of really sick people who will lose their insurance. I'm not sure I… we…as physicians and surgeons…could help all of them."

Kassie smiled, knowing that should Brad be asked to do the impossible, somehow…someway…he would get it done as a surgeon. With the thought passed, it again turned to the inadequacies of people in government, people who were supposed to be looking out for all the people young or old, rich or poor, well or ill. She felt a disgust for the current system in government she couldn't quantify; was it possible to repair by one person? Perhaps someday…

"I will always vote but I really have to wonder if our votes are actually counted." She sighed. "We put men and women into office based on what they say before getting elected and then…"

"…they do their own thing. Is that what you're trying to say?"

"I'm not going to buy the paper anymore. It's depressing. By the way, have you ever heard of Grey Cloud?" Kassie thought by discussing the abhorrent evils of the government, she could ease Brad into a conversation about the matter of Grey Cloud without raising his curiosity to the extreme. She didn't anticipate portraying her own deep, negative beliefs on the matter.

"Grey Cloud?"

"Yup. Grey Cloud. It's in the paper…somewhere."

"Isn't that the private security company that aids our military?"

"Is that all they do?"

"Kass! That's a lot. It means our military can do their job without having to protect big wigs when they travel to foreign countries… among other things. Where's the article. I'd like to read what it says."

After grabbing the paper, Kassie feigned looking for the 'article' that *wasn't* in the paper. 'There is no article in the paper,' she wanted to say. Another lie! "I can't seem to find it." Laying the paper aside, she moved toward her bedroom. Brad's cell went off. 'Thank you, Lord. Saved by the bell!'

"Hello." Listening attentively Brad didn't say a word. Kassie watched from the hallway, wondering if it was the same man that she had heard another time. Brad closed his cell and getting up from the chair, he said, "Kass. I think I'll be going. By the way, I did want to know if you were planning on attending Selway's party with me. I'm not scheduled on Saturday but I know you have to work."

"I get off at three." She should've just let it go but curiosity wasn't limited to cats. "Short phone call? Emergency at the hospital?" She walked over to him.

"Wrong number. I'll see you tomorrow. Friday's can be disastrous and complicated." Brad leaned over giving her a warm, loving kiss and then, he was gone.

Kassie ran some water and proceeded to do the few dishes that were in the sink. "Brad, if you're lying…'and what do you think you were doing, bringing up Grey Cloud, searching for information'… perhaps I better wait until Selway and I get to the bottom of his problem." Speaking her thoughts out loud wasn't her typical form of entertainment.

On the way back to his apartment his thoughts were all over the place except where they should be. 'Why did Kassie ask about Grey Cloud? What did she know? And the Lieutenant's call. How did he get an invitation to Selway's party? What difference was it to him if I attended? From where did he know Selway?' The Lieutenant had been so secretive about talking to Brad, all those clandestine meetings. Grey Cloud? The lieutenant. Kassie. Selway. As much as he hoped that their connection was casual, something told him that the 'initials I scribbled on a crumpled sheet of paper' were correct. Accepting that was one thing. The other thing that bothered him was...did Kassie know he was a Navy SEAL...had Mark told her about him... if he did, did she think he was a part of Grey Cloud? Grey Cloud. The words made his brain hurt...he had heard those words before, just not as clearly. They were as viable in his head as if he had heard them yesterday...but from where? Maybe he had read about it in a newspaper or periodical. He realized that Kassie hadn't given him the newspaper. He wondered why.

# 92

Jacki was working late, Brad had just left, so Kassie decided to retire early. But first. She found a piece of paper and a pencil in the kitchen. Sitting at the table, she tried her best to draw star. If she remembered correctly, she put the initials of SS, CS, KS and BP on four of the tips. What did it mean? As she tried to remember what the center looked like, she realized the letters that had been written there at one time had been erased. Trying too hard, she thought, drawing the star for the umpteenth time, something would trigger her memory and the initials would mean something, stand for something. Her eye lids became heavy and with the apartment cozy and warm, it was just a matter of time before she would lay her head down on her left arm, draped on top of the table, and fall asleep.

Back at his apartment, he pulled one of his check stubs out and read it under the bright light emanating from his bedside lamp. There it was. Why hadn't he seen it before? When held to the light, a faint watermark, the initials of 'GC' appeared in the background, undetectable unless someone was deliberately looking for it.

Brad placed a call to his mother.

"Hello, son. How are you?"

"Hi, mother. Any more parties?"

"Not at the moment. Actually it's fairly late. Everything all right?"

"Mother. Do you still have that list handy, you know, the one I asked you to get..."

"Yes, Brad, I do. I haven't had a chance to put it away...for safe keeping. It's right here. Anything you want..."

"Look at the list and find Anderson, Richard, please."

"Just a moment. I think I hear your father stirring. To trouble him about anything this late at night will only keep him awake for hours. We sleep in different bedrooms now so..."

"Mother. You were sleeping in different bedrooms when I left home."

"Really. It must've slipped my mind." Brad could hear her close a bedroom door, supposedly that of his father. "He's sound asleep." The paper she was holding made for a disgusting background noise. Brad could only guess what she was doing with it. "Is his name Anderson Richard or Richard Anderson? Anderson Richard doesn't sound right."

"His name is actually Richard Anderson, mother."

"Ah, yes. It's actually the first name on the list. Now what was it you wanted...?"

"Are there any notations or words written by his name, either before or after?"

"Only that he's retired. Is that what you mean?" Brad was not shocked. Somehow, in his training, he had overlooked the man who... "Brad. There's an LC by his name also. Does that mean anything to you?"

"Mother. You've been just what I needed. As always. Thank you and I don't care if father does think..."

"Brad! Stop! I don't need to know what your father thinks..."

"Mother. I'm kidding. Love you." Brad closed his cell phone.

"Brad? Brad?" Altogether too loud, clearly his mother wondered what her husband was thinking...about her...about what?

"Darling. Is something wrong with Brad?" The question came from her adjoining bedroom. She opened her bedroom door.

"No, dear. Go back to sleep." Since he was awake, maybe...on second thought, it could wait until morning.

In the morning, Brad would place a call to Mark Phillips.

# *93*

olorado sunrises were made in heaven; this morning wasn't any different. It was Friday and that was good, especially when one didn't have to work the weekend. The weather report revealed the high could reach seventy-five degrees with no precipitation. Saturday's forecast was even higher.

As Brad entered the hospital, he passed through the lobby on his way to the elevators. Coming off the elevators were Cindy and Della. Brad had released Della the day before but the circumstances under which she was leaving prevented her from leaving until this morning. Off to the side, he noticed Della's foster parents. Walking over to them he said, "Good morning. It appears everything is going as planned. I just want to wish all three of you good luck. Della will come out of this a stronger person and I know she'll have your love and support. She's healing well and her spirits are up. That's more than I expected." The foster mom put her arms around Brad and thanked him profusely. The father shook Brad's hand, with tears in his eyes, clearly not finding his voice to say anything. "With all you've done to give her a good home, she'll do well. I wish you the best."

Brad stepped over to the wheelchair where Della was sitting. Smiling at Della, he continued. "Okay, little girl. Get good grades, ignore all the boys, love and respect your new parents and live well. I want you to have a full life." He smiled at Cindy. "Go on, now. And behave!" Cindy began pushing the wheelchair toward the enormous front doors at the entry to the hospital, when Brad stopped them. Looking at Della's parents, he said, "Bring your car around to the back. The first service entrance door. We'll take Della with us. Let's not load here. Okay?" Cindy swung the wheelchair around and headed down the hall. Cindy knew what he was doing and she was only too happy to comply.

"Thanks, Brad," Cindy whispered.

"Anytime." Brad took the first exit door they came to on his right. "I'm not good at good-byes," he mouthed to Cindy.

"I love you, Dr. Phillips. Thank you." Della had the sweetest smile, a smile so sincere and lovely that it melted Brad's heart. Knowing in his heart, in spite of what she had already weathered, Brad *and Dr. Phillips* knew she had the instinctive energy of a child to survive overwhelming odds.

Starting on third floor, the nurse making rounds with him handed Brad his first chart.

"Mr. Mantoux! What brings you back so soon? Oh, you missed us. That's good to know."

"Doc. It's my plumbing! It doesn't work without pain! An' now, I'm bleedin' like Niagara Falls!"

"When did this all start," Brad asked, as he read the chart.

"Bout ten days ago. A week, maybe. I don' know! Gees, it burns when I pee."

"Have you been doing any heavy lifting? Weights? Working out? Anything like that?" Brad looked up from the chart. "Get the blood work, x-ray ordered and the pain killer I've noted." The nurse left with the chart. "You realize of course a lot of things changed after you had prostate surgery. But of course…you know that." Brad tried hard to sound serious.

"I know, Doc. This kind' a thing worries me. And my missus, too. She wonders if I'll ever be normal again, you know wha' I mean?"

"Mr. Mantoux, I've ordered some blood work and an x-ray. Until I see them I won't know exactly what your problem is. By the end of the day, I should have the results. In the meantime, I'm going to give you something for pain…just a small dose…and a muscle relaxer. It'll help you to use the bathroom but after the shot, don't try to get out of bed by yourself. Okay? Turn your light on and one of the staff will help you." Brad took the man's hand and gave it a squeeze. "You'll feel better in a while."

"Thanks, Doc. Apprech'ate it."

The nurse returned with a shot for pain before Brad walked out the door. Walking to the next patient, Brad looked at the nurse and said, "Mr. Mantoux is in *pain!* Otherwise, he'd be razing the whole floor."

"Amen." The nurse smiled.

When Kassie clocked in, Sissy, an RN who worked on fifth floor, was right behind her.

"Another day, another dollar." Sissy looked like she could've used more rest but Kassie didn't say anything. Instead, she managed a weak smile.

The OR was a beehive of activity. The curtains were all pulled for privacy meaning ten patients were being prepped for surgery. Kassie was scheduled to help Dr. Guiterrez, his case being a liver transplant. A new liver on ice was not a thing to waste.

"Kass! Suite three, pronto. Guiterrez is scrubbing!"

Kassie put on scrubs, tied her hair up with a blue net over the top, put a face mask around her neck, stepped out of her shoes and into blue coverlets and almost ran to suite three. Outside the suite, she placed her face mask on. Stepping over to the sink in the anteroom, she washed her hands and arms, putting on gloves that reached to her elbows. By the time she reached the side of Guiterrez, she was winded, but ready.

About two o'clock she went to the break room, poured herself a cup of coffee, grabbed a couple cookies that someone had the forethought to make and sat, allowing her feet to rest.

"I was hoping to find you here. I brought Cindy with me. And Priscilla." Jacki must have some good gossip, she thought, as she ruminated about what it might be. All three got some coffee and proceeded to sit at the table.

"Forgive me, Kass, but I haven't seen much of you this week. We are housemates, you know. And of all things, I didn't know you took up drawing stars."

Had she put her brain on pause, the remark would've never registered. "What are you talking about?" As if Kass didn't know.

"Darling, I saw the paper by your hand when I came in. You were dead to the world, so I just left you there, sleeping on the table."

"Oh, yah…I went to bed a little later, I guess."

"What were you drawing…looked like a star with some…"

"It was nothing really, I was just doodling." Drop it, Jacki, I really don't want to discuss it any further.

"Hey, Cindy, that black kid…on third, you know the one that…" Priscilla never did say much but when she spoke, it was always said as though she had just migrated to Mercy from the street.

"You mean Della? Just so you know, she has a name. Priscilla, everyone has a name so the next time you speak to me or anyone else, use their name. Okay?" Any respect Cindy had for Priscilla wasn't present at the moment. "I really don't appreciate it when people I care about are referred to as black or white…or yellow…or whatever. They're people…people with names…like you…or me." Cindy paused to catch her breath. "Yes, Della went home. Enough said."

"Gees, settle down you two. Everybody get up on the wrong side of the bed this morning…excluding yours truly?" Jacki looked at Cindy and said, "I think she got your point dear." When she turned her gaze at Priscilla, she said, "Just so you know. We…Kassie, Cindy and I don't look at people in terms of color. Everyone one is human, with a heart, and a soul and a few other attributes. Words are important; they mean things. I'm just sayin'."

"I'll be glad when this shift is over. One more critical surgery left for me to attend and I'm going home." Kassie was looking droopy.

"Aren't you going to the party tomorrow night? Kass, you gotta go. We're all going, even Priscilla. Prissy is going with Samuel, aren't you dear?" Jacki couldn't keep a secret if her life depended on it.

"Who told you?"

"You did, when you asked me what to wear with a guy that's blond! I told you any color would do as long as it's not your birthday suit. Remember?"

"Okay, guys. I have to get back. If I don't see you tonight, Jacki, just in case, I plan on attending the party. See you guys later." Kassie had had enough conversation to last the rest of the day. Women!

# *94*

Exhausted, she walked home. She'd been to the chapel early in the morning; her prayers for relief kept her going the whole day.

After a brief respite with a cookie and a glass of milk, she had to lay out what she was going to wear on Saturday. Since she had to work…on fourth…at present, she forgot who she was subbing for… her mind preoccupied with the information she'd collected in her bottom drawer. Tomorrow evening would give her some relief even though both she and Dr. Selway thought the culprit who forged the tickets would be in attendance. After hanging her dress on the back of her bedroom door, along with her high heels and hose beside her dresser, she went to the fridge, grabbed a piece of cold pizza and ate it while walking to the bathroom.

After her shower, her cell phone rang as she was climbing into bed. From the number she knew it was her father.

"Hi, Dad."

"You sound tired. You alright?"

"I'm fine. Tired, but fine. And you?" Mark ignored the question.

"Brad called."

"When?"

"This morning, early. Got me out of bed."

"Wasn't that nice! Has he called you before?"

"Once, I think. Kass? He's concerned about you. Said you asked him about Grey Cloud. I played dumb. Said I didn't know how you would come by that name. But I'm not sure he bought it."

"Dad!" She paused, wondering how to word what she wanted to say. "Something very strange is going on down here. Three helicopters and three tanks were delivered to the Denver Police Department. Why would they need tanks...they're big and bulky and noisy? I saw them when I went to the library. Anyone who takes the time to look can't miss them."

"Kass. Look!" How much should he reveal to her, his one and only child, his daughter. Suddenly, he was afraid for her. He was in Wyoming and she, in Denver. "Brad told me you were going to a party tomorrow evening, at Dr. Selway's home. He's the same man that supposedly has his name on a suspicious airline ticket, no?"

"That's correct. But I told you that I didn't..."

"How do you know for sure that it's not really him? He could've had his name purposefully imprinted over his own name to throw people off? Maybe, he wanted someone to find those tickets. Do you understand?"

Kassie wondered about what she had just heard. In her head she knew that Dr. Selway hadn't done what her father suspected. She had proof on paper; he was innocent. "Dad, don't worry about me. Remember, you taught me very well. And...I'll be packin'."

"Kass. I didn't tell Brad you own a firearm. I just told him you know how to handle yourself. Knowing Brad, he'll put two and two together and realize..."

"I'll talk to Brad tomorrow. It won't be my secret anymore but as long as it's only Brad that knows...besides you and Jake...my family...I can live with that."

"Let me know how the party goes. And if you can, have a good time."

"Thanks, Dad. Love you."

# 95

The clock said four thirty and she was ready to go home. But first, she had to get Jacki's uniforms, of all things, since Jacki forgot to take them with her on Friday. On her way down from fourth to third, she decided the next time she volunteered to work for someone she'd be more discerning. It always seemed to be an easy fit until the day came you had to do it. If only she'd remember *that* the next time someone asked her to work for them.

The lady sitting behind the main desk was an older lady, one that never looked up when she spoke. Kassie wondered how she knew to whom she was talking. Somehow, she accomplished the feat with grace and a monotone timbre. "Jacki's uniforms are in the coffee room."

"Got it." When Kassie emerged from the recesses of the nurse's conclave, the older lady spoke again without looking up.

"There's a man here to see you. He's around the corner. I put him in room 301A. Nice looking chap. Nice deep voice."

"How did he know...*how did you know*..."

"I don't know!...I didn't know!...I'm just the messenger."

As she opened the door to 301A, she really expected to see Brad. To her surprise, there was no one in the room. Then, she heard the toilet flush. She turned around just in time to see a tall, rather good looking gentlemen come out of the bathroom. Immediately, she knew his face from a time past. But where? When? Think!

Without a word, he walked by her and took the only chair in the room. "Hi, Kassie. How nice to see you again!" Kassie stood where her feet were planted.

"Do I know you?" It was a rhetorical question but at the same time, it bought her some time. "When did we ever meet?" Think, Kassie, think! His voice. It was his voice that was more familiar to her then his actual looks.

"You don't remember, do you? I'm not surprised. But I'll say you look as good in a nurse's uniform as you did in a flight attendants' suit."

'Of course, on the plane! The grandpa and his grandson! The man was insulted, mortified that somehow, someone had taken his first class seats! Seats! He had had a woman with him! At the time, she hadn't paid any attention to the lady. He had grabbed the tickets before she could hand them to him. But she saw their destination. But that was an age ago! I have to get out of here! Now!'

Trying not to show her panic, she started to say something but she couldn't engage her mouth. It was so dry her tongue stuck to her palette, her dry lips clinging to her front teeth. Forcing herself to move, she backed up to the door, making a vague attempt to smile.

"Why, Kassie. You look enervated...pallid actually. You remember now, don't you?" The smirk on his face actually frightened her.

"Excuse me a minute. I'll be right back."

Out the door, she grabbed Jacki's uniforms off the counter where she had left it and ran to the stair well. Two flights of stairs, three blocks to run and she'd be home. It couldn't happen fast enough. She wouldn't look back to see if he was following her until she reached the door to her apartment building. She'd been followed once before; it wasn't a figment of her imagination. Even though she couldn't see him behind her, she felt his presence as though she was caught in an envelope of malicious intent. Who was this man? Why did he confront her as though they had been friends? How did he find her? Why did he seek her out? Did he expect...know...she would remember their little confrontation? What difference did it make? Was there a truth she had uncovered that alarmed him? How would he know? She knew their destination was Zurich. He scared her, to her very core. But why? The woman with him! Of course! Now it all made sense. Maybe if she knew ...a zillion questions with no answers. Of all the information she had collected, of one thing she was positive. Dr. Stephen Selway was not a murderer.

"Brad, honey, I have to talk to you. It's important so please listen. I'll talk..."

"**Please leave your name and number**." It was the message machine.

"Not now, please, Lord, let him answer." All Kassie heard was a follow-up beep. She checked to see if her door was locked. 'Why am I so apprehensive, like I think he's going to break down my door? This is crazy!' Looking at the clock she wondered when Brad would pick her up. He'd never said and she never asked. Standing somewhat back from the living room windows she tried to reach Brad again. No answer; just the message and a beep. After her heart rate had slowed and her blood pressure returned to normal, she decided to take a shower.

Out of the shower and drying off, she heard noises in Jacki's bedroom. Quickly throwing on her robe, she cautiously listened by her door. Upon opening it she saw the uniforms she had brought with her from the hospital were missing from the chair by the table.

"Hey! You done with your shower?" It was Jacki. Kassie sighed and met her in the living room.

"Where have you been? I know you didn't work today."

"I went to Dillard's and bought a new dress. Pristine red! Howie's going to love it. You want to see it?"

"I'll see it later. Do you know if Brad called?"

"Now, *why* would *he* call *me*?"

"I was just wondering." She picked up her cell; there were no messages. "I wonder what time he's coming over."

"You don't know! Huh! That's not like Brad. Maybe he drove over to Selway's early. You know, for some man gossip! Like they never see each other at work!"

"Oh well. He'll call before he comes over. I've got to do my hair," Kassie lamented as she walked toward her bedroom.

"Hey! You can ride with us, you know. Howie will be here in an hour. Just saying."

"I'd best be getting dressed, then."

Jacki looked gorgeous in her new dress and Howie looked sharp, as well. Both women were ready when Dr. Howard Harriman came to their door. Kassie still had not heard from Brad although she had called him several times. In fact, she had her phone set to call him every two minutes.

"Are you sure you don't want to ride with us? Brad is probably busy...or maybe he's there already. Doesn't make any sense to me, even though I said it," said Dr. Harriman.

"I'm sure he'll call. Patience is not one of my virtues, sad to say. At least, not lately. You guys go ahead and I'll wait until he calls." Kassie was worried sick but decided to smile. Pretending to 'push' the two of them out the door, she said, "Go on now. Spread your wings, fly low and watch for cops!" She absolutely refused to let her present emotional state ruin Howie and Jacki's evening.

"Okay. We'll see you soon." The two of them left, laughing.

# 96

"There is something terribly wrong. Brad, where are you?" Asking questions of oneself was never comforting. The same one who asked the questions had to come up with the answers! "Dad! I wish you were here. But in lieu of that, I'm going to take precautions." She opened the bottom drawer of her dresser, removed her firearm, checked the safety and placed it in the small of her back, tucked in her skirt. Looking in the long mirror she had hanging on the wall, she checked to see if it was visible under her jacket. "Great! No lump." She fiddled with her earrings, making sure the backs were on tight, checked her hose for runs, flattened her skirt, fluffed her hair and ran a finger in the side crevasses of her lips. She checked to make sure the lock on the bracelet that Brad had given her was set. "This will have to do."

She wasn't going to wait any longer. Grabbing her keys and a sweater, just in case it got chilly, she left the apartment and walked to her car. Since Brad didn't answer his phone she figured he'd had an emergency surgery or was in some kind of meeting. He'd have to come alone.

On the drive over to Selway's she thought over all the things she had written down concerning those blasted tickets. Why she did what she did, she'd never understand. Presently, one thing did bother her. Why, when her life was so hectic, had she not taken more time to pray? Are we only supposed to pray when our lives are going well? Or when we're deliriously happy? Or do we only pray when we're hurting and beyond any relief? She didn't think so. Lately, she had gone to the chapel and prayed fervently about her sin, those blasted tickets and Selway. She hoped tonight, there may be some resolution to his…their…problem. Hope. Hope was for things unknown, unseen. Well. She prayed and was thankful when things…her life…was going smoothly. But tonight…she had faced adversity before but nothing like this. "Lord, please take care of this situation. I'm truly sorry for what I did. But…that's water over the bridge. Tonight, lead me according to Your will and I'll behave much better. In Jesus' precious name I ask it. Amen." Now she was ready to party.

The circular driveway was full of cars; they had begun parking off to the side on the manicured lawn. Turning off the ignition, she recognized Brad's pickup parked in the circle. In a way she couldn't reconcile, it troubled her. He was already here but not answering his phone. Why?

Looking around the parking lot for anyone else attending late but seeing no one, she locked her car and proceeded to walk to the front door. What she saw looking in the side light startled her. All the guests, standing or seated, were located on one side of the living room facing Laurie, who had a firearm pointed at Selway to his right. She turned around and stood sideways by the center door jam. Not wanting to be seen, she stepped lightly off the steps and moved quickly around to the side of the house. The door under the portico would put her near the kitchen. It was unlocked. She decided to enter, silently. But first, she needed to make a phone call.

Once inside, she let the door ease smoothly, quietly shut, avoiding the sound of any click it may make when fully closed. She waited.

Nothing. If anyone was in the kitchen, they weren't making any noise. Past the laundry room, she slipped quietly past the breach to the kitchen, seeing no one. Looking into the dining room she saw that it was elegantly decorated with a centerpiece that 'must've cost Selway a small fortune' or so she thought. She didn't bother counting the number of chairs for the guests; she had a difficult enough time straining to hear the conversation coming from the living room, standing in the shadows of the hallway. She let her jacket slip to the floor and retrieved her firearm. What possible good it would do, having a pistol in her hand, she had no idea. Her breathing was shallow; she began to perspire. Not a good time for a headache...or an anxiety attack.

As she edged closer, still in the shadows of the hallway, she heard the familiar voice from an hour ago. 'Why did he come from the hospital to Selway's? What was he doing *here*?' The arguing between the parties involved was controlled in volume but the words spoken were sharp and nasty. Then...

Kassie heard Brad address Selway: "Stephen! I know you're innocent of any wrongdoing. Do you trust me?" Selway said nothing. "Stephen, *do you trust me*?" Selway must have nodded his head affirmatively since nothing was audible. After a discreet pause...

"Do I trust you? Hey, I'm innocent of...if you don't know me by now?"

Then, Laurie spoke: "Hey, man. I'm also innocent! Just because I worked in those cities doesn't mean..."

Kassie decided this conversation started long before she arrived. Details she alone thought she knew were being said.

"You were not only in those cities at the time of their demise...," from the man with the deep baritone voice.

"How would you know that? You were following me?" Laurie sounded terrible, angry, frustrated. "What are you trying to say?" As though a light came on in a dark room, Laurie got it. Moving away from Selway, he pointed his firearm at the baritone voice. With his left hand he motioned for the Lieutenant to stand up. The fury that Laurie was beginning to feel was real; his hands beginning to shake.

"When the first SEAL was killed, I was shocked. We'd trained together. But when the second one was shot...I decided to move, changing jobs. Dyed my hair, grew a beard and ran."

"Laurie. Laurie, look at me! Don't be doing anything rash. Let's discuss this for a moment." From where Brad was standing, Kassie was afraid he would see her. Slowly she moved farther back into the shadows of the hall.

"Again, a SEAL was killed in the same city where I was working. I get it! There's nothing to discuss, Brad. Don't you see...I'm being framed for murder!" screamed Laurie.

"Being framed? No, just caught red handed." The Lieutenant continued. "You came in here unannounced, brandishing a gun at Selway because you had to cover up..."

"You're right. I thought I was on a death list...Selway's list..."

"Laurie. Let's talk." The last thing Brad wanted to be involved in was a shooting. In spite of the tension in the room Brad didn't see the necessity for any more drama. It wasn't something he wanted on his resume'. "Stephen. You're a SEAL? How come you never mentioned..."

"There's nothing to talk about. It was before your time. Brad, I really think you ought to call the police. You've done a magnificent job! I owe you a huge thank you. You've cornered a killer!" It was as though the Lieutenant hadn't heard a word of innocence spoken.

Selway and the others stayed in place, not moving, not whispering and not breathing. Basically a dozen people with nothing to say and everything to fear.

"You know, it took me a while to figure you out. But after you told me you were in Dallas...then the pieces fell into place. Laurie was there as well. In fact, Laurie was in every city...working... where each of the murders took place." The Commander started to clap, accompanied by a smirk that spread across his face. "Tell me something, Lieutenant. Do you belong to Grey Cloud?" Brad could hardly believe what he was saying.

"No! Definitely not! Grey Cloud? I don't even know what that is!" It was Laurie.

"I'm not talking to you, Laurie."

Kassie didn't know how long she could hold out before she would choose to enter the fray. All the information she had accumulated was now on the tip of her tongue. More than that, this was the very house that at one time had a mistress that was married to Stephen Selway, a happy entrepreneur who tried to use her money, which was ample, for good, a woman with a mother who had raised her, loved her and now missed her, a woman whose life had gone terribly awry. Kassie had to ask herself. 'Why did this woman spark such intense scrutiny as to raise more questions than could be answered? Why couldn't Kassie have just left it at that? Carolyn Selway, a beautiful woman, young, vibrant, wanting for nothing became someone in a beautiful frame on a grand piano, someone to admire, someone with a past that had to be buried. In truth, Kassie wasn't interested in her or any of the photos on the baby grand or in her dreams until she'd heard Stephen Selway refer to Carolyn as his 'deceased ex-wife.'

"Laurie, I'm so sorry you're in such a state of denial. But you know that…" It was the same voice as Kassie had heard in the hospital. Now she'd heard enough. Coming into the living room, pointing her pistol at the tall, rather good looking man she had met earlier in the evening, she spoke.

"Every place I've worked…I can't believe it! How many have you killed?" Poor Laurie.

"That's quite enough." Kassie left the safety of the darkened hallway.

"Kass!" Brad was shocked to see her there, much less holding a firearm. He started toward her. The Lieutenant turned to the voice.

"Brad, would you check and see if the gentleman across from you has any firearm on his person?" She motioned to the Lieutenant with her revolver.

"Yes…NO!…That's Lieutenant Commander Richard Anderson and you want me to *frisk him*? On second thought, *why not!*" Brad's voice became a squeak, as if he was asked to commit a crime. "Kass? What do you think you're…" Brad was finding it difficult believing Kassie was holding a firearm pointing at…

"Brad! Just do it. Please." Brad stepped toward the Lieutenant. "Laurie, put your gun down. Please?"

"Kass. You've got a gun…*in your hand!*" Jacki was catching on.

"No way!" Selway appeared somewhat anxious.

"You know how to use a weapon? You look so relaxed. I will say that." Jacki exercised her nervous laugh.

"Jacki, please. This is not the time."

"Really!"

"Laurie, you can put your firearm away." Kassie appeared a bit impatient. No time for nerves!

"Not yet. Why are you pointing your pistol at that guy?" Laurie nodded toward the Lieutenant. Brad gave him a cursory once over.

"He's clean." Brad stepped away, toward Kassie. Out of the corner of her eye she saw Laurie relax, holding his firearm by his side.

"Because over the last two years he's been raising mayhem, killing off SEALs that disagreed with him, including a certain Carolyn Selway."

"What? Who?" Selway started to move toward Kassie.

"Oh, this ought to be interesting!" Jacki was just being herself.

"Stop! I'm not sure where to start." Kassie held up her left hand, palm out. "But just for kicks, let's start with the little mix-up we had on the flight to Zurich. You grabbed the tickets out of my hand so I wouldn't see that you had a round trip ticket and your lady friend, a certain Carolyn Selway only had a one-way."

"Why you..." It was beginning to dawn on Selway what was happening. He made a further attempt to walk toward the Lieutenant. "You were the one...the tickets...trying to frame *me*..."

"Don't Stephen!" Brad put his arm out in front of Selway to block him from moving any closer to the Lieutenant. "Let her finish. But please put your gun down, Kass." And then... "How *do you know* how to use a gun?" Kassie ignored him.

"You never intended for Carolyn to return to the States." Kassie stepped closer to the Lieutenant. "Laurie was working in those cities all right, where the murders took place, but you were there as well. And since Laurie had washed out of the BUDS program, you picked him as a perfect patsy. However, when he moved to Denver, you decided to dispose of another SEAL. Or blackmail, maybe? But you needed someone to run interference for you. Thus, enter Brad Phillips."

"*You read my notes?*" Brad's voice was getting higher.

"Afraid not. I had notes of my own. You see, Carolyn Selway was the money bag for your little set up. To the tune of four million. She never asked for anything in return but then, she never expected you to turn on your own countrymen. Grey Cloud? That's your own private security company, the one and only company so far that was supplying tanks and helicopters to anyone who wanted to buy them, namely, police departments." Kassie took in a deep breath and exhaled slowly. "I had to ask myself, why would any individual take money from a woman to set up a security company in his own country against his own people? But before I get to that!

"After Carolyn had lost her husband you dated her for a spell. But you didn't catch on with her mother. So, you left her. However, Carolyn kept in touch with you because she liked the idea of security personnel taking care of overt crime instead of the police. After all, police were so *inefficient* and *lazy* and *incompetent!* Her opinion, all. Considering the red tape they had to process only to be told they had to allow a murderer or drug runner go free, free from persecution by the law. So…she gave you the money."

"Carolyn!!! My wife? My Carolyn?" It may have been the first time in Stephen's mind he wasn't the problem in their marriage.

"In addition to the tanks and choppers, you enlisted drones over her sovereign country! She wrote a request for you to relinquish the drones. You wouldn't hear of it. She evidently couldn't abide by that so she told you she wasn't going to support your endeavor anymore. Now you needed outside sources to continue your enterprise. You had to procure and fulfill private contracts to feed your ambition. That wasn't bad enough. You were told in no uncertain terms by Carolyn she would go to the Feds if you launched any more drones *whatsoever*."

"You think you know so much, you twit!" The Lieutenant was scornful.

"But getting rid of Carolyn was only the tip of your problems. Now several of the SEALs in your employ didn't want to eliminate individuals in the U.S. by means of drones because they were…shall we call them true patriots? You enlisted ex-SEALs that were not only courageous, and excellent at their craft, SEALs you had known in the service. What you never expected from your ex-SEALs was that they treated each other like family, at least those who loved their country and each other. They belonged to a brotherhood, brothers with a bond so strong they decided to quit as a unit. So! Your ambitious self said, I have to do what I have to do. Eventually, in addition to Carolyn, you got rid of Hank Robinson, Marcus Lincoln, Ken Station, and Barry Knott. The ex-military you still employ prefer to take your money. But there was one left you had to eliminate. I'll bet he didn't even know he was part of Grey Cloud."

"Wait, wait…wait! Hank was part of Grey Cloud?" asked Brad. He was shocked into silence. It had happened so many years ago. Lieutenant Anderson had followed Hank to the chopper. "Why? Why did you kill Hank?"

'Hank came running to the chopper, dressed in black clothes. At the time I thought he was dressed simply for camouflage purposes. Shot in the back, I pulled on his body until I got him aboard. All the while Hank kept talking. "You're the only brother I ever had. Grey Cloud brother." Between the noise of the chopper and the whispered words of my buddy, I never understood the last thing Hank had uttered. It makes sense now. The clothes, the mumbled words. If only I had heard them clearly...'

"Gees, Kass. Anything else you know that I don't know? Crip! Why don't you just cuff him now?"

"Jacki, it's going to be all right."

"You think you can make any of this stick?" questioned the Lieutenant. "It's only supposition by a flight attendant...oh, excuse me, a nurse. Your word against mine."

"Oh. I know I can," she said with some disdain. "The tickets were just the beginning. But now, you have to confront the last SEAL that could put you out of business. You'll probably want to speak to Brad Phillips about that."

"You have no idea what you're up against!" The Lieutenant was infuriated. "Satellites in the skies can tell when you light a cigarette! Vehicles have sensors on them that tell us where you're going and where you've been..."

"Oh! I know where you're going. The government controls too much already, like our health coverage. Next they'll regulate our cell phone communications, our food consumption, our fuel usage and possibly, even our children. In fact, I read where taking children from their parents was on their to-do list. We already know the children are being indoctrinated in school to be good 'socialists!' Tax forms won't be necessary. The powers that be will just take whatever amount they want..." Kassie knew more than what she was willing to accept.

"You're catching on. I didn't give you that much credit."

"Credit? I think not! With individuals like you running around the country, policing our citizens…what makes you crave the insatiable power you strive for…trying to control the people of the…?"

"Because I can! I'm a United States citizen! I have the freedom…"

"Kass? What are you saying?" It was Brad.

"I'm saying this. One of the men on a flight back to Russia pulled me aside and we had quite a talk. He was well educated, had started his own business in Moscow and was doing well. But he couldn't forget the days of his youth in Russia when his parents suffered under Communist rule. At the time, I didn't think too much about it but he said something I'll never forget. "As a country, you're going where we've been." You could've heard a pin drop in the Selway home! "Now, I understand," she said, speaking in a voice barely audible.

"She's not going to stop ranting…" The lieutenant was flushed.

"Where…when did you learn how to use a gun…firearm?" It was difficult for Brad to comprehend that his fiancé was holding a firearm on someone, ready to use it if necessary.

"Laurie, I asked you to put your firearm away. You don't need it anymore. Please?" Kassie asked politely.

The front door of Selway's home was blown off its hinges, making a terrible noise of metal scrapping on boards, glass hitting the floor. Three swat team members, dressed in black, were in the house within a couple seconds. Without thinking, Laurie turned, with his gun facing them.

"Don't shoot! Don't shoot!" hollered Kassie. Three shots were fired. Selway dove for the setee. Brad dropped to his knees. The other guests let out all forms of cries and shrieks.

"Put the gun down, now. *Hands above your head, now!*"

"Would you please disarm this woman with a pistol pointing at me," asked the Lieutenant, smiling like a Cheshire cat. "I'm afraid she's under the illusion…"

"What's your name, ma'am?" the officer asked, keeping his firearm pointing at the Lieutenant.

"I'm Kassie Colbert. I'm the one who called you. And that gentleman is the one you'll want to interrogate," she said, leveling her firearm at the Lieutenant.

"Okay, okay. Please put your firearm down. You do have a license to carry...a Concealed Weapons Permit?"

"Yes, Sir, I do."

While one of the officers put cuffs on the Lieutenant, the second one read him his Miranda Rights. As Kassie tried to put her firearm in her skirt belt, she noticed the Lieutenant's knees buckle.

"Watch out, officer. He's falling." As he fell his body turned toward Kassie. His brown silk shirt was stained with blood on his shoulder and his abdomen. The officer lowered him to the floor and barked some orders. "Call 911, now!" Kassie went over to him and with one hand placed his head on the pillow she grabbed from the settee. Taking his hand, she whispered, "The ambulance will be here soon. You'll be fine, just fine."

Brad watched as his future bride tried to make the Lieutenant as comfortable as she could, under the circumstances. At this point, everyone at the party was in shock, except for one.

"*Now...isn't...that...sweet!*" Jacki and her mouth, sarcasm dripping from every letter. "Kass! He's a killer! What are you doing, giving him last rites?"

Kassie looked up at Jacki with a calmness she hadn't had for several months. "I *hate* what he did, Jacki, it's *horrible*. Disgusting! I can only imagine the effect that his misdeeds have had on the slain SEALs families. But I can't *hate* the man." When she looked at Lieutenant Commander Richard Anderson again, he had passed out.

"Kass. Come with me." Brad took her arm and took her over by the dining room table. Lawrence Samuel had been hit in his jaw with one of the shots fired by the officers. He was bleeding from that portion of the jaw which was still intact, but he was alive. Kassie knelt down beside him, raised his head and put it on her lap.

"Don't try to speak, Laurie. The ambulance is on the way. They'll give you something for pain. Anything you want to say will just have to wait. Okay?" Kassie stroked his hair, praying he would be alright.

Brad and Selway stood and responded to the police as they asked questions about what had happened. Selway gave them the names of his guests, what he had planned, how the evening played out, all with input from Brad. The guests themselves sat wherever they could find something flat and remained deathly quiet. Even Jacki.

The ambulances arrived and took both men to the hospital. Soon after, the police left as well. The guests kind of mulled around a bit with no one really being hungry, still in shock as to what had happened. Sooner than they could've imagined, each would be questioned by the police as to what they saw and what they heard. Brad and Kassie sat on the chaise longue, each drinking a soda. Both were quiet, each with their own thoughts.

"You really think he would've done any harm to me, Kass?"

"I have no doubt in my mind."

"I did find out I was working for Grey Cloud and didn't even know it. It should've been a given when he asked me to find a killer. That thought seems ludicrous to me now." He took Kassie's hand in his. "You feel all right?"

"I'm fine. I have to use the ladies room." Kassie got up, turned to Brad and said, "I think I'm going to faint." Before Brad could register what she had said, she simply fell lethargically to the floor, her Pepsi spilling over the carpet and hard wood floor.

"My fair lady. You've had all you can take for one evening." He carefully picked her up, cradled her in his arms and walked out the ruined front door.

# 97

When she woke up, she found herself in her own bed, warm and cozy, with a slight headache. After using the bathroom, she moved to the living room. Brad was asleep on the sofa, unaware that Kassie had stepped into the room.

"Where's my gun?"

Brad sat up with a start. "What did you say...ask?"

"Never mind. I see it." She walked into the kitchen and retrieved her firearm from the counter. Checking to make sure it was unloaded she walked back to her bedroom as if she was on autopilot, and placed the firearm in her bottom dresser drawer. Grabbing the paperwork that she had accumulated, she walked into the dining room, placing the papers on the table.

"When did you plan on telling me you were a US Navy SEAL? Or a member of Grey Cloud?"

"Kass?"

"Before the wedding or after?"

"Kass?"

"They had named you 'brains.' I wonder what they would've named me?"

"Kass?" Brad started to get up.

"You know, you can find the most unlikely things on the Internet. Like your family, for instance. Why didn't you tell me you came from a wealthy background? You think my feelings would've been hurt?" At this point, Brad figured it was best to let Kassie talk. "Money has never been my motive for doing anything in my life. Not that it's nice to have. All things considered…"

"Kass. I can explain."

Kassie had walked to the windows, the morning light beginning to creep across the foothills. "Oh, I'm sure you can." She was too tired yet to be fully functional, just inquisitive. "Perhaps we should exchange notes." She walked over to Brad encircling her arms around him. "Don't worry. We're still engaged!"

"For a moment…" Brad held her tightly, wishing last night had never happened.

"I know." She released him and walked over to the table. "You may want to look at these." She walked back to the windows and looked over a city that was still half asleep. "I really don't want to discuss them…ever. It's over. At least until there is a trial. Do you have any information about what the police…?"

"At present, Anderson is in the hospital. ICU unit. He's in bad shape. Dr. Reynolds patched him back together, removed a couple slugs. How about you?"

"I'll be fine but right now I'm still sleepy…bone tired. Good morning, Brad. Glad you're okay." She stepped over to Brad and kissed him on his forehead. "I'm going back to bed."

Once in bed, she recalled a scripture she'd learned a long time ago. I Timothy 6:10. 'For the love of money is a root of all kinds of evil.' "That goes for power, as well, Lieutenant."

Jacki woke her up about two the same afternoon. "You going to sleep all day? Come on. I made us a chicken sandwich." Kassie rolled out of bed. In the bathroom, she washed her face and put on her bathrobe, joining Jacki at the table.

"Smells good. Coffee and all. Thanks."

"Hey, that's the least I could do for my roomie. Where did you get that gun? You really know how to use it?"

"I don't want to talk about it. Where's Brad?"

"He went home...or to the hospital. Somewhere. He brought you home last night. I think your car is still parked on Selway's grass. After everything that's happened, he wasn't too cool about anyone messing with his lawn." After taking a swig of coffee, she continued. "He'll get over it."

"I'm glad it's over. At least for now. Perhaps later we can talk about it. Heard anything about Laurie?"

"Howie said he looks like a mummy, but other than that..."

"What's his prognosis? Did he lose all his teeth?"

"He lost half his face! Does that count?" Kassie made a face that indicated an 'unbelievable ouch.' Jacki had a way with words that Kassie would never understand.

After finishing their sandwiches, Kassie again thanked Jacki. After taking her cup and dish to the kitchen sink, she said, "I have to make a telephone call. I'll be in my room. Thanks for lunch. It was good. If Brad calls...or my Dad...tell them I'll call them back. Appreciate it."

After getting dressed, she found her cell and punched in the numbers.

The morning was beautiful; the mountains were bathed in a blue-gray glow that completely obliterated any white snow that was still present in the mountains. It was a good day for driving. Traffic was light on I-25; normally, it would consist of stop and go vehicles for miles, stretching from the outer limits of Denver to Colorado Springs. In looking around, Kassie decided if they took all the pickups, trucks, and vans off the road, Colorado would have a negligible amount of gridlock, bottlenecks or congestion with which to contend. So much for the government taking away anything larger than a four passenger vehicle on the highways; Coloradoans were born to own a truck!

She pulled into the driveway and waited. But not for long. Caroline came out the front door, walked over to meet Kassie as she exited the car, giving her a warm, generous hug. Smiling at Kassie, with her arm around her shoulder, she spoke.

"I knew I'd see you again."

# Intersection

A NOVEL

Kathryn

# 1

t all started so innocently. He had wanted to try a different restaurant for some time. Being tired by the time his day of work was over, he'd go home, fix himself dinner or heat up leftovers from the previous day. On his shorter work days he'd go to a restaurant or fix himself an elaborate meal at home. So when the opportunity presented itself, at a time when he didn't want to cook for himself, he wasn't at all sure he wanted to dine alone *in an unfamiliar setting* at a restaurant, again.

He had heard *Pepe's Restaurant* served fantastic meals with a diversified menu. It wasn't a long drive from the hospital; he'd bypassd it once on a Sunday because it was closed.

*Pepe's Restaurant* was owned by a man with the name of Peter Gallagher. Peter was actually Italian, from his mother's side, but he looked Spanish, from his father's side and his English was perfect. Soft spoken, tan skinned with eyes that missed nothing in his kitchen, he was not only amiable but could be quite funny. He wasn't short in stature but he wasn't tall either. His physique was slight and his movements measured. As the chef of a high end restaurant, he decided 'Pepe' sounded less aloof than Peter; thus, *Pepe's Restaurant.*

Once an individual ate at Peter's restaurant, they came back again and again. His clientele had been growing steadily since he opened his eatery seven years prior. Besides himself, he employed one other chef, Craig, two chef interns, Bud and Cliff, a receptionist and three hostesses. His hours of operation were limited, from 3 PM to 11PM. However, he was in the kitchen by ten every morning.

Because he was Catholic, he was always closed on Easter, Thanksgiving, Christmas and New Years and every Sunday and Monday. Monday's were *just because*. From the first day he opened his clientele accepted the reality of his schedule and never complained. Occasionally on Monday's, Peter would prepare food that could be made ahead of time so that on Tuesday there wasn't a rush to prepare the exquisite meals for which the restaurant was known.

In seven years, Peter still had the same waiters and chef that he employed when he had the name of the restaurant emblazoned on the front of the building. Peter Gallagher was highly respected, a formidable friend, a loving and faithful husband and father and a presence to be reckoned with; his insight into people was phenomenal. He could expound for a minimum of a half hour on the disposition of any individual that he saw walking into his restaurant just by reading their body language. His clientele was extremely diversified: construction workers, blue collar personnel, nurses, doctors, mothers, housewives, old folks, white collar upper crust managers, farmers, but no children. The menu was too pricey for what children normally left on their plates.

People of different nationalities and backgrounds, color and religion ate at Pepe's and Peter made it a point to meet each one over the course of time, especially a new partaker of his excellent cuisine. It was obvious to anyone paying attention that Peter loved people and frequently, when time permitted, he would sit and talk with them. He was an excellent listener, imparting advice on a need to know basis.

When he walked in the door, through the one-way mirror that fronted the kitchen, Peter spotted him immediately as a new patron.

He had never seen a man so tall, so well built with not a pinch of fat on his body. Peter tried to identify the image before him. He was too tall to be Italian. He could've been Irish with the cleft chin and dimples that he wore. And yet. His complexion reminded him of another fellow, who occasionally frequented the restaurant, whose lineage was Peruvian. This gentleman was more handsome than most, very sure of himself and yet, unpretentious. He moved with the agility of a skater, only slower.

When he removed his sunglasses, Peter surmised his eyes may well be blue. He wasn't sure why he had such a thought; perhaps he'd have a chance to clarify it later.

Peter watched him as he asked the receptionist for a place to be seated by a window...on the far side of the restaurant. He was gracious to her, giving pause before he seated himself. This was definitely a man Peter wanted to meet and get too know. Peter himself was a cultivated and honorable man; it was those men who exhibited the same qualities he chose to befriend. It would be interesting, to say the least, if this gentleman would return. Entirely too busy to think about it at the moment, he let it pass. He'd pay attention to what he ordered; sometimes Peter could tell more about the person from what they chose to eat than how they were dressed.

Back in the kitchen, Peter ruminated over his persona. His dress was casual, wearing a summer weight sweater and a pair of pleated slacks. The belt he wore was shiny black as were his shoes, highly polished but comfortable kilties, and his mane of black hair.

After he ate his dinner, having paid the hostess, he started to leave as quietly as he walked in, stopping only to say something to the receptionist at the front door.

At closing time, Peter walked up to the receptionist before she removed the cash drawer, which was subtlety positioned behind a wall.

"Macy. That guy…the friendly giant, the one who'd never been here before, did you get his name?"

"No, but Peter, was he good looking or what! And the tip he gave the hostess, wow! He even stopped to tell me he was very pleased with the service and the *cuisine*. I didn't think people knew how to use the word anymore. *Cuisine*! " she said as she waved her open hand in the air, like a propeller on a windmill.

"Really! Did you get his name?"

"Are you kidding? I had all I could do just to say 'thank you.' I could hear my own false teeth rattle, I was so nervous!" Macy went ahead with the chores she had every night at closing time. But Peter was still intrigued by the man.

"I wonder what he does…for a living, I mean."

"Well, I'll tell you this. He had the most beautifully manicured hands I've ever seen. Large hands! Nails! Clean as a whistle! Trimmed and everything. Wanted to scratch them, in case they were polished!" As she walked away with the tray and the receipts, she said, "Wonder if he cleans his nails with Clorox?"

"You'd of been able to smell him if he did." Peter laughed. Cleaning hands with Clorox was something even he didn't do. Looking at his hands and nails, he wondered out loud. "Wonder what he does for a living?"